An Extraordinary Boy

Vernon Hewitt

Clink
Street

London | New York

Published by Clink Street Publishing 2015

ISBN: 978-1-910782-59-0

Nicola Manders
1980-1994

Acknowledgements

Many people helped me with his enterprise. I would like to thank Jeannine Osborne and the 'Roswell' brigade, especially Patricia and the Italian lobby for encouraging me over the years. I would like to thank Firuza, Fiona, Beth and Adrian for being dutiful in reading it through at various stages and encouraging me to press on. Various serious scientists whizzed over the genetics to keep it on the right side of plausibility. They know who they are! Thanks also to Steven Gibson for not reading it but knowing where it was set.

VMH
Bristol 2015

Prologue

June 25th, 2006

The connection to the datasets at the Institute of Molecular Science had been lost, timed out by the server. The image frozen in front of me was the schematic diagram of human chromosome 22, mapped by the Human Genome project and presented to the world in 1999. At the bottom of the screen I could still make out several photographs from the Institute's home page; the dome of DeMarr's head, polished and disturbingly egg-like and behind him, the top shelf of his office bookcase, a line of multi-coloured spines with their titles unreadable. Another photograph appeared to show trees, a blush of cloud, a backdrop of buildings and a row of eminent scientists beaming shyly into the camera. Feeling better, more centred, I looked around my study with a sort of mock resolution. It was 2.36 a.m. and the beginning of the last week of my son's life.

I pushed the chair away from me and, with curious stealth, thrust my fists into my dressing gown pockets. What was I to do? What was the great and eminent Professor Grey to do? Collaborate with my enemies? Finally and shamelessly concede defeat? In truth it was too late even for that. It was too late to hand Max over and expect to profit by it or save him. I walked out onto the landing and caught my reflection in an ornate mirror above the staircase: I saw an old, scared man who had literally run out of time, a monster with a conscience, the very worst sort of compromise. The house was incredibly silent; the summer heat thick and accusative. Had anyone else seen what I had just seen? Davies and the American team must know by now, surely? I kept breathing through my nose, counting to ten. I crept to the foot of the stairs and looked down towards Max's bedroom on the floor below, the door half opened and lined with shadow.

It couldn't be.

What I had seen had to be an illusion, a mistake? Even now I threaded out the same old formulas: denial, silence, *complicity*. Even now part of me was determined to pretend that my son was normal and safe, and that I could protect him.

Deftly I avoided the third and fifth stairs, an old habit of stealth, and with my heart racing again I pushed myself into Max's room, careful not to let the door bang or to trip over his discarded clothes cast randomly about the floor. Max had not moved since I had last examined him. He was on his side facing away from me, one arm thrown over his head in an arc of shoulder like a swimmer doing the crawl. The other was wedged under a pillow. The duvet had hitched down to the small of his back and I could see, illuminated by the night light, the broad quilted muscles of his upper back and the rune of his spine curling down away from his neck like a brush stroke. At nearly eighteen, Max was still afraid of the dark, and he still managed to discard most of his bedding, kicking it away mysteriously in the night. I half smiled, recalling a small silent boy with wide, calculating eyes who never slept. Now, over twelve years later, the same boy was spread out before me, like an allegorical nude in a Titian or a Poussin, an inscrutable code – a promise or a warning? I wondered how he could sleep so deeply so close to the end of all things. His smell was all about me, of moss and cold open spaces like trees in winter.

I put a hand to my mouth to hold it still, to stop the lips curling down and shaking, afraid that in my despair I would shout his name. I looked at the walls of his bedroom, at the posters of rock bands blue-tacked to the wall; at a set of cheap shelves stuffed with books and folders. On a nearby desk Max's computer towered over a wide debris field of pens and dirty mugs. Stuck on the top of the monitor was a webcam while behind it on the window he had taped a cartoon of a woman with enormous breasts squeezed into an absurdly small swimsuit. Her nipples showed through the material, erect and firm. Beneath her was written *Foxy Babe*. She was standing – somewhat improbably – on a skateboard. I looked down to the bed, listening intently and then from my back pocket I removed a small thin torch and screwed the top down to engage with the battery. It gave out a bright but narrowly focused beam of white-blue light. Moving forward slightly I directed the torch at Max's shoulder, careful to avoid casting shadows on the wall behind him. Max's head was well down into the crook of his arm; his thick chaotic hair pooled like ink across a cheekbone. Standing there I felt both absurd and vaguely perverse but Max was either genuinely oblivious to me or gently indulging my guilt for one last time. His breathing came in slow, even sighs. He was incredibly still and showed no inclination to move.

Within a few seconds I had found what I was looking for. Between the curve of the neck and the top of the back deltoid, and then in an intricate lattice between the shoulder blades and the upper back, Max had developed a series of bumps or nodules. They were particularly pronounced on the top of the shoulder appearing to emerge from the bone itself or through the well-defined traps of muscles. The nodules were symmetrical, rather like crenulations on a medieval castle and they ran out into the soft tissue at the back of his neck and then disappeared. I had every reason to suppose that these same features were present on the other shoulder as well. I glanced down his spine towards the top of his buttocks. The vertebrae seemed normal but very distinct, incised and separated almost like the links on a bicycle chain. The skin around them was translucent and smooth but oddly mottled now as if he had been intricately tattooed. I thought about prodding Max gently, insinuating the idea that he should turn on his front, but it was too risky. I stood for a while, my hands on my mouth again. Eventually I switched the torch off, my eyes blinking in the sudden dimness until the night lamp asserted itself and then carefully, like a man walking from the scene of a disaster, I turned towards the door and returned to my study.

I walked up and down for a time, disorientated, utterly helpless, and then with sudden resolve I searched through a jacket pocket for my mobile. I scanned the small screen urgently but there were still no messages. None from Margaret Relph. She had been in the US for the last week, desperately trying to find Max's missing device and her silence was ominous, a premonition of further, inevitable failure. There were no messages from Jonathan either, an absence that I felt keenly. He had vanished recently, taken off on some mysterious, urgent errand of his own. My stomach tensed with panic and longing. I had to do something! Should I ring Sally and demand that we talk about our son? Tell her it was finally *happening*? Should I try - as I had been trying for months – to ferret out fat old DeMarr from some secret bunker and beg for his help, all my pretence of arrogant calm abandoned?

Suddenly and with incredible virulence the phone vibrated in my hand like an electric shock, stopped, and vibrated again. I looked blankly at the caller's number even as I snapped it open and said 'Hello!' loudly and breathlessly. I thought I sounded vaguely senile. There was a pause, a hiss and whirl of static and then a voice stammered, 'Professor Grey? Is that Julian?' It was a young man's voice, deep and well-spoken but edgy and although I knew instinctively who he was I could not immediately put a name to him.

'Yes, yes, speaking.' Another odd silence and then the voice said, 'Julian, I mean, Professor Grey – it's Jamie, Jamie Relph.'

I gasped with relief, 'Jamie! Oh good God, is this about your mother?'

'Sorry? Hello?'

'Are you calling me about your mother? Has she contacted you?' I sounded manic and Jamie fell silent again. Clearly it was not about Margaret.

'No! No, it's about Max, Julian.' Jamie's voice suddenly broke as if he was sobbing and he said something incoherent, an apology perhaps.

'Jamie, what is it? What about Max?' It was a pointless question for me to ask, utterly rhetorical, profoundly insincere, but I asked it all the same. I had placed my right hand tightly across my head.

'There's something wrong with him, Julian! There is something seriously wrong with him and he won't tell me what it is!' Jamie's voice poured out over the phone, wavering and dipping as he tried to control himself. That Jamie knew something ought not to have surprised me, but it did. Jamie was Max's oldest and possibly closest friend. He had loved Max with a solitary hard purpose since he was about ten and he would feel this exclusion deeply and not understand what it was about. I stood trying to think of something to say, some fake mantra of reassurance but Jamie suddenly demanded a meeting.

'Jamie, it's nearly 3 a.m.!'

'Then meet me tomorrow! Please!'

'Jamie –' but how could I refuse? My affection for Jamie, for his sheer loyalty to my doomed son overcame my now instinctive dishonesty. I felt his despair almost like a blow. 'Ok, look let's meet tomorrow, say late afternoon? After school? How about *Browns*? Is that good, Jamie?'

'I'll be there.'

I went to ask about his mother but he promptly disconnected the call.

Part One
1993 - 2005

Chapter 1

The road ran flat for a mile or so with neat indifferent housing to either side of it, and then suddenly without warning it swung down and away; past a cemetery incised into a hillside and then out and onward with great purpose towards the village of Newbold Verdon. Trees and hedgerows crowded in around the car choking the view and then suddenly drew back again, revealing a patchwork of wide expansive fields, clay-red and wet with spring frost. Tired and disorientated from a long and indirect journey, I had no clear sense of where I was. All I knew was that the last two children had been found here in this curiously anonymous landscape. I slowed down to check my directions, recalling the brutality of a 4 a.m. telephone conversation, DeMarr's voice constrained but excited: 'You must come immediately – the last two are here, in a wood, Riley thinks they have literally just arrived!' I had been dreaming of something vaguely nostalgic, satisfying, long ago. And afterwards, as I struggled to wake myself and dress I had noticed –

almost casually – that Sally's side of the bed was empty.

Ahead of me outliers of the village started to appear: 1930s bungalows set back in wide open gardens, a footpath, a small post box, brilliant red, and then a turning on the left, conspicuously closed off now by two police patrol cars and an army jeep. A group of men stood around the vehicles stamping their feet in the morning chill, talking and smoking as if gathering for a shoot. I wound my window down and as I pulled up a young soldier, his face red-blue with cold, walked towards me, a hand raised as if in greeting. I succeeded in stalling the usual 'move along' routine or the invidious implication that I was a reporter. When I said my name he frowned and then produced a radio from his tunic to announce that 'Professor Julian Grey' had arrived with a sort of authoritative indifference. He pronounced the term Professor rather like I would pronounce vicar, a sort of joke word. Amid crackle and jargon he was reassured that I was expected. He leaned into the window and gave me brief instructions as to how to proceed, slowly and precisely, as if I was a foreigner. He kept eye contact throughout, perhaps curious to actually meet a Professor. He filled the car with a strong aftershave that smelled not unlike formaldehyde. I smiled weakly, not wishing to appear rude. Perhaps he recognised me from the recent news, the endless TV coverage of the abductions and my own increasing association with them. He could not have been much older than 19, the same age as one of my undergraduates. As I drove away I caught sight of him in the centre mirror, a cloud of steam on his lips, laughing with his colleagues and no doubt at my expense.

About a quarter of a mile from the junction the road turned slightly to the right and I saw a group of vehicles drawn up and abandoned on the verge; a yellow and green ambulance from the Leicestershire service, two police cars, DeMarr's distinctively bottle green Rover, and two more of the ubiquitous army jeeps. On the opposite side of the road a five-barred gate stood open and a rutted track led over a ploughed field towards a line of trees; bars of shade drawn up against the steel grey horizon. Several people were standing close to the hedge: more soldiers, one paramedic in brilliant apple green waterproofs, the leggings marked with florescent strips. There was the hiss and babble of radios, and overhead, I thought I heard the heavy, ponderous clapping of a helicopter.

'Professor Grey! Good to see you again, and so soon!' A middle-aged man in a white mackintosh stepped towards me, a man I had last seen in Brighton just under three days ago. Detective Inspector Mark Riley looked as well-groomed and as affable as ever, a friendly face inclined to smile without warning and, seemingly, at the wrong things. He was heading up the police investigation and was trying, with all his considerable charm, to cooperate with and contain the growing number of agencies – and agents – ballooning around the case and claiming jurisdiction.

'Hello Mark!' We exchanged a firm handshake, a sort of tribal code. I looked up towards the now luminous sky and then glanced again at the wood. The trees were papery white lines bleeding into the wet morning, a hasty sketch of silver birches. It was bitterly cold. Mark turned and followed my gaze.

'The last two were found over there, on some sort of mound. We were called this morning about 3.25 a.m. by the landowner, a Daniel Lockwood, who thought he saw something in the trees and then a fire. He lives quite close by –' Mark turned and pointed vaguely behind me and to my left, across the road and seemingly behind the parked ambulance.

'A fire?'

'Lights, red lights, you know, lights in the sky.' Mark shrugged, like a man who had described something he could not quite agree with. 'He seems a sensible enough fellow. He's over in the trees with our good friend DeMarr.'

'Are the children still here?'

'Good God, no. After a rather unseemly scrap with the local ambulance crew, the children were flown to the John Radcliffe in Oxford around 5 a.m. to join the others.'

I nodded. I was glad to have missed the scrap. There had been several in the last few days. I was too middle-aged and English to enjoy the sight of DeMarr asserting himself.

'And they're definitely Max and Jonathan?'

'Yes, without a doubt. One Max Lennox, aged five, taken just over a week ago from Great Ormond Street Children's Hospital, and one Jonathan Prince, aged eight, abducted from Bristol Children's Hospital last Wednesday. So, there we have it, Julian! All 24 children now accounted for!' He patted my shoulder as if I had found them all by myself. I nodded again slowly, sucking in my cheeks.

'It's not like the other locations,' I said, a bizarre understatement. In my head I was thinking why here and how? I dug my hands into my coat pockets, making them into tight, impatient fists. It had started to rain, a soft grey sleet angling in over the fields and stinging my face. 'And they're medically ok?'

Riley smiled again, revealing deep friendly crease-lines on the side of each eye and about the mouth. 'Apparently they're fine, I mean from the ordeal that is. No immediate sign of trauma but with the usual amnesia. They left with the child psychologist and the doctor. It was quite a crowd!'

'Who's in the wood with DeMarr now?' My mind seemed fuzzy, exhausted. I vaguely resented having bothered to come at all.

'You tell me! At the last count there were about ten different organisational outfits, the majority of which I have never heard of. There is a group of people from the environmental agency and some *spooks*, naturally.' He winked at me. 'But no Americans yet, thank God. Anyway let's get you over to the party and you can perhaps persuade your Belgian friend that we can all go home now?'

I smiled stoically and then looked uneasily at the thick curls of ploughed earth in front of me.

'He's Italian actually, well, half Italian.' In fact DeMarr was in some senses more English than I was.

'Really? It doesn't sound like a very Italian name, does it? Actually it sounds like an American plastics manufacturer!'

We had had this conversation several times already, travelling up and down the UK collecting children in pairs.

The bridle path cut straight across the middle of a wide, dark morass of thick mud littered with pebbles. At the bottom of each plough line stood narrow frozen puddles, marbled into fantastic shapes, blank and empty as the sky. Looking to either side of me as we walked forward I had the curious and disconcerting illusion that we were moving out over emptiness. Several times I slipped and stumbled, caking mud over my shoes and up the inside leg of my corduroys. Mark walked ahead, bear-like; his feet set forward as if he were blindfolded. Eventually, breathless and with my calves aching, we reached a sty in a low hedge. Climbing over it we found ourselves suddenly under the trees. I saw DeMarr immediately. He was wearing a fine dog-tooth tweed coat and hat and was standing with a female paramedic on a sort of green mound with blue and white tape sealing the wood off behind him. The bridle path continued on past the mound and across the next field into the village itself. Standing some way apart from DeMarr was a big curly-haired man, bearded and coatless, wearing a thick blue jumper over black cotton jeans. He stood watching without any trace of impatience, contained; rather meditative. Through the slender trees I could see several people moving about, scouring the ground collecting things or standing about talking into radios.

DeMarr, seeing us approach, terminated his conversation and came over. He rather fastidiously removed his hat when I reintroduced him to Mark.

'Julian! A good drive down I trust? And we have them safe and sound! Thank God it's all over for now.'

I glanced behind me. 'Who *are* these people?'

DeMarr half turned to look.

'Forensics, and several people from the radiation inspectorate –'

'The *what?*'

'Quite!' interrupted Mark, and smiling again walked away towards the paramedic. DeMarr watched him go and then turned into me confidentially.

'Strange groups of experts have been turning up all morning, Julian. But this is the first time that any of the children have been found in a non-urban location, so we're all having a good look!'

'Where were the boys found exactly?'

'They were sitting here on this mound, on the top.'

'Are there any markings on the ground?' I recalled the field, frozen in places but soggy, the water table not far below the surface. A thaw must have set in about dawn although the air was still raw.

'None that we can find. They've been sniffing about since first light. Lockwood came through the wood from the other end and left his triple trail, here, back and here again, but the children's appear only on the mound as if they were literally dropped from the air. Astounding isn't it!'

DeMarr still seemed genuinely excited, as if this was some personal adventure. He had been like this all week, muttering and clapping his plump hands together in general approval. I rather envied him even though I found his superlatives tedious.

'It is Louis, every bit of it.' I was not sure that astounding was exactly the word, though. I would have used the word un-nerving, surreal perhaps, or better still: *un-believable*. A young woman had approached Mark and the paramedic and after several emphatic head movements in my direction, turned and looked at me. I saw Mark nod.

I looked at DeMarr and asked, 'So how does the government wish to proceed, Louis? Have you spoken with the Prime Minister?'

The woman, a security tag flapping down in front of her coat, was slipping towards me. DeMarr puffed out his cheeks like a blowfish.

'There is a meeting taking place between the Home Secretary, the Defence Minister and the PM as we speak, they'll contact us sometime this afternoon. I said we'd be at the Radcliffe later if they need us. I think they'll want to set up a complete investigation and quickly.'

'Just us?' but before DeMarr could answer the woman had pulled up alongside and was offering her hand out towards me.

'Professor Judith MacMillan from the radiation inspectorate.'

I introduced myself and then turned to include DeMarr. Judging from DeMarr's body language he knew her already. She started to speak, looking at me directly as if she wanted to consciously exclude Louis completely.

'Well we've finished for now, Professor Grey. I'm afraid it was far less promising than we at first imagined.' She signed and shook her head sadly.

'Damn – nothing at all?' I sounded more outraged than I had intended.

'Almost nothing. The children were clearly dropped from overhead – there's no other explanation. There does appear to be a lot of debris from the birch trees thrown about on the grass and it looks quite new. We'll need to check the recent weather but it could have blown down last night. It seems spread in a radius from the middle of the wood. Lockwood has given us a statement saying he saw a long arrow shaped vessel low over the wood at about 3.35 a.m. and then a red light. And we have some reports from the nearby village that seem to confirm the time and the general shape of the UFO.'

'And radiation?' DeMarr asked, rather curtly. 'Anything unusual?'

The woman made a sort of equivocal gesture with her mouth and looked hard at DeMarr for the first time. I tried to hide a smile. I knew immediately that she did not like the government's principal scientific advisor. Not many people did. I found myself wincing on behalf of my former student.

'Not an easy question, Louis. The background radiation has spiked a little, but there are granite intrusions nearby and possible radon traces so it could be quite – what is the word – terrestrial in origin? We've taken samples and will get the results to you as soon as we can. We'll have the local tracking and radar report from East Midlands International Airport and some additional satellite data. Several flight paths go right over the area. Two pilots made formal UFO reports last night around 11.20 p.m. and then 2 a.m.' There was a slight pause.

'What's this mound made of?' I asked suddenly, looking immediately behind us back towards the path. It was not high, about three feet at the top.

'Spoila,' said DeMarr rather pompously, 'the remains of some ancient cattle shed or brick work, at least

15

according to our robust yeoman farmer over there!' He smiled emphatically towards the man in the blue jumper who was still standing on his own under the dripping trees. The mound seemed very even and elongated for the remains of a square structure. It was reminiscent of a tumulus. I breathed in and turned to Judith. We seemed to have reached the end of our chat.

'Thank you, Judith. I wouldn't mind seeing the report when it's complete?' I shook her hand again, and she nodded appreciatively.

'*DeMarr,*' she added assertively, and then turned back towards the road. DeMarr pulled a rather childish face as she walked away. Mark Riley caught my eye and then rather self-consciously looked at his watch. I wondered why the paramedic was still here with the crew of the ambulance waiting in the lane. Still arguing over jurisdiction? A bar of sunlight suddenly illuminated the trees, picking out the black attentive markings on their bark, like eyes. I wondered fancifully what they had witnessed in the early hours of the morning.

'Well I think we've done as much as we can here for now –' sighed DeMarr. He made a sort of wave with his hand and Riley beamed with relief. I ducked under the tape and wandered off into the trees, my hands pressed together in the small of my back. I found myself standing next to Lockwood who towered above me. There seemed something vaguely nautical about his clothes. I sensed him watching me intently.

'Is this a plantation?' I asked, offhand. The trees made up a long, narrow spinney with little or no undergrowth, and with the exception of a few holly trees, were all silver birch. In the pale, winter grass I made out the remains of what looked like bracken and stands of cow parsley, black and dripping in the chill, but the place was airy and pleasant.

'No – it isn't, actually.' Lockwood's eyes glinted blue in a weathered, darkened face. His complexion was healthy, freckled, sandy red with streaks of ginger in his blond beard. His blue jumper was beaded silver from the intermittent drizzle. I tried to guess his age: probably just younger than me, mid-forties, perhaps younger still? I found myself thinking that his ancestors were probably Danes.

'Birch trees often form stands like this, especially on recently cleared ground. They're a coloniser, first in before the others, both native and migrant at the same time!' He smiled, almost winking, as if he had read my thoughts. I heard DeMarr bark an officious laugh some way off, no doubt at one of his own jokes.

'Have you owned this land for long?'

'Three generations – far less now than we used to. Cereals mostly and rape seed. What's left I hire out to local dairy farmers who graze here and in the wood. Recently I sold some acres for more houses.'

'And nothing unusual in the history of this place? I mean –' Somehow I still could not get myself to use the word 'sightings' without some initial hesitation, the cautionary stammer of the self-conscious sceptic.

Sensing my dilemma, Lockwood laughed.

'Well!' he said, exaggerating his voice in mock drama. Despite myself I smiled cautiously. I liked him instinctively.

'Some, oddly enough. A handful of sightings over the years, mostly by villagers coming through the bridle path from Desford, and usually the worse for wear. I've seen unusual things but nothing that was definitive or free from more likely explanations. The place has a curious reputation, especially with the local kids, but I've always put that down to boredom and overactive imaginations. And as for the trees –' Lockwood sucked his gums. 'Birches are not particularly long lasting – and the soil is good here, but heavy. Nothing but Midland clays, the remains of a vast ocean, and later, post-glacial lakes. There's a quarry nearby in Cadeby, filtering up quality shale, and as for archaeology –' Again he looked at me and smiled knowingly, 'It draws pretty blank. A few Roman tile factories and some settlements on the edge of what would have then been wild wood, native limes and oak stretching for miles.' He shrugged, sensing my curiosity, looking somewhat mischievous. 'I wasn't always a farmer!' Getting the better of his mirth he then said cautiously, 'so why here Professor?'

The air was warming slightly and there was the sound of water dripping from the tops of the birches.

'I have no idea.' I ground my teeth. 'In fact I have no real idea about any of this. I find it all rather hard to believe!' I tried to sound ironic, but the tone was too honest. Before he could reply DeMarr appeared next to me and cut in brusquely, a gloved hand on my arm.

'I'm off to the John Radcliffe, Julian – and then I am off to see the *leadership*. Get to the Radcliffe as quickly as you can but if we miss each other I'll call you tonight at home? I am presuming that the Prime Minister will use some of the established contingencies.' He sounded pompous, affected, but oddly he was trying to impress me not Lockwood. He nodded at the farmer like one nodded at a porter at an Oxford College, or perhaps a well-respected umpire.

'Who's the big cheese?' asked Lockwood, watching DeMarr slip and totter away towards the sty. Bemused for a second I laughed quietly. The title would have appealed to DeMarr's vanity.

'He's the current advisor to the government on all things scientific and curious! And most likely will head up the investigation into these events when it's formally announced – a geneticist by training, in fact one of my former students.' I frowned. We were alone now, surrounded by the silent, watchful trees. I felt in no hurry to start the drive back to Oxford.

'Do you have any idea who or what is behind these abductions?' Lockwood asked finally, cautiously, as if he were afraid to pry. 'I mean can you discuss this? Or is it already top secret?' I thought at first he was joking but when he spoke he didn't smile. I wondered if Riley had said something to him or some of the spooks.

'Well, it's been very difficult keeping the lid on this so far,' I said. I recalled the pointless security brief just a few days ago. I looked tentatively into Lockwood's face. He had been watching me all the time.

'Twenty-four terminally ill children are effectively kidnapped in broad daylight from twenty-four entirely separate institutions. There are no signs of any break-in and no one sees or hears anything. They are all taken, more or less at the same time. With the exception of Jonathan, they are all about the same age – five or six. After a week they are returned in pairs, seemingly at random, and dropped across the whole country. A majority of them are found in the middle of cities, some in suburban areas, and one pair here – in open country. Almost in the middle of nowhere! Again, no one sees anything until the children are discovered in our midst. And of course they can't remember anything!' I shrugged. Had I sounded melodramatic? It was hard not to. Who could have masterminded such an operation? What did it mean? *Aliens?* The word was absurd.

'Is it true that a majority of the pairs are boy-girl? And that these events have been confined to the UK?' Lockwood asked.

'Yes. Yes to both.' I was only confirming what the news had been reporting since Wednesday. 'Ten pairs were boy-girl, one pair of girls, and one pair of boys – Max and Jonathan. Who, of course, like all the others, had never met until, well, until they were *taken*.' I ground my teeth together again, causing a pain to flash through my gums. I thought the word *taken* sounded far more ominous and sinister than the word abducted.

'And the sightings?' asked Lockwood. 'Do they coincide with the places where the children were found?'

'Not always, but enough to imply a connection of sorts; Bristol, the outskirts of Norwich, Brighton Beach, here –' Lockwood pulled down the corners of his mouth, nodding sagely, as if he understood my dilemma and my tone of disbelief. We had returned full circle to the question that had struck me immediately on my arrival: why here?

'But I saw something last night, Professor Grey, over the very place where the boys were found.' He had sounded passionate for a moment, almost angry. As he spoke he turned to look at the mound.

'Julian – you must call me Julian.' We stood again in silence. The sun was bright now, framed on either side by low grey clouds but the day seemed set to be fair. Suddenly Lockwood turned to me.

'Listen, I live literally at the top of Kirby Lane, just over the fields. You're welcome to come back and rest up before driving back?'

I was surprisingly tempted by the offer. There was no need for me to be around the buzz and drama of the preliminary medical check-ups on the boys, or witness the sight of DeMarr preparing ostentatiously to meet 'the leadership'.

'That's very kind of you. A powerful stimulant would be much in order, and perhaps a quick nap?' He laughed and we started to walk through the woods, away from the bridle path behind us, away from the houses, and towards a distant five-barred gate set in the middle of a bare, black hedgerow.

Lockwood lived alone in a fine but remote farmhouse, set in the middle of a wide field and connected to the Kirby Lane by a long rather baronial gravel drive. I asked him if he minded living alone and it transpired that he was not long divorced and that solitude still had a sense of novelty about it. Born in north London and used to metropolitan surroundings for much of my life, the isolation of the farm astounded me. Lockwood reassured me that the nearby village had a population of around 3,000 and that Leicester was not far, but the place still struck me as bordering on the reclusive. We passed several large Friesian cows who stared mournfully in our direction like beggars. The main house stood opposite a clutter of outbuildings, random (and seemingly) abandoned vehicles and a curious collection of circular hay bales wrapped in black plastic. The air was thick and sweet with the smell of silage and manure. I felt hopelessly urban.

Once inside Daniel put on some coffee. He had decorated a wide open-plan kitchen with a certain masculine sparseness. The sudden warmth made me feel sleepy. After a few pleasantries we walked through to a low, well-lit room with wooden beams criss-crossing the ceiling. One broad bay window showed the driveway while another looked out in the direction of the spinney. I could vaguely make it out, a brooding dark line now low behind bare winter fields.

'I was sitting there last night,' said Daniel almost casually, pointing to a red leather chair behind me. He cleared several books and newspapers away for me to sit. As he placed them on a coffee table I saw a battered copy of Shakespeare's *The Tempest*, and, intriguingly, John Wyndham's *The Midwich Cuckoos*. They seemed an incongruous pair of authors and the Wyndham uncannily appropriate. He caught me scanning the books and smiled.

'Some slight literary pretensions – sorry!' he sounded apologetic. I made an ambivalent gesture with my hand. I had read both of them.

'Scientists normally don't read, but *The Tempest* is one of my favourite plays. When I was a young man I had pretensions of being Prospero; you know, all those books, the academy, a quiet life!' I said oddly, almost a confession. He laughed, understanding me completely.

'Not to say revenge! I always wanted to be Caliban actually!' he said.

'Really? You mean Ariel, surely?'

Daniel smiled and seemed to colour slightly, as if he had accidentally let something slip. He handed me a large mug of hot, bitter coffee. We sat down opposite each other as if I was going to interrogate him. I felt fuzzy, an odd buzz in my ears and now almost insensible with exhaustion.

'Mark Riley said you thought you saw a fire?'

'I came in about 2 a.m. from a lock-in at the local pub, the Wind Mill, just over the fields –'

'A lock-in?'

'Yeah – you know – the landlord locks the doors and serves after hours, the locals play poker and talk about the good old days!' He smiled at my apparent naivety. 'When I got back I heard the cattle moving and went over to the main sheds to see if they were ok. They were distressed over something, sweating, agitated. I came back to the house to worry over what to do when I saw it.'

Daniel stood up and walked to the window opposite me.

'The fire?' I prompted.

'No – not at first.' He ran his hand over his face and beard rather aggressively. 'I sat down and worried about the cattle. They'd been off their feed for some days and the restlessness bothered me. It was beginning to look like a sickness. So I sat down where you are now and tried to think. The curtains were open and I had left the main light off. The only light came from back there.' He waved in the direction of the kitchen. 'Oddly I'd been looking at it for some time, without seeing it at all if you know what I mean.'

'At what, Daniel?'

'At a huge black shape over the wood.'

Something in the way he said this struck me suddenly cold.

'Would you mind describing it to me, Daniel?'

He smiled rather wearily. No doubt he had already told his story several times.

'No lights, nothing *Close Encounters* like, just a huge black shape, motionless. It was so still. I only saw it because it was a frosty night. It blocked out the stars. I thought for a minute I was seeing things, a shadow, something in the room reflecting on the window. When I stood up and went outside it was still there, and it seemed to be literally over the wood. So I pulled on my coat and set out to investigate. It was *so* strange...' his voice fell away as if he was re-living the sensations of seeing it again. 'I couldn't tell what shape it was – it seemed cigar-like until I crossed the road, and worked out it was side on to me. As I got closer it seemed wedge-shaped, almost like an arrow head, but totally dark –'

'How high was it from the ground?'

'Not far. It was hard to calibrate at first: it might have been very big and far away, or just big and about 10 or 20 meters off the ground – as I got closer I realised it was the latter – aligned with the wood end to end.'

I drank my coffee. Daniel looked briefly out of the window and then, sighing, sat down heavily into his chair again.

'The really disconcerting thing was the silence. It was utterly quiet and dark as if it was watching, waiting. It was like suddenly coming across a damn great predator in your bedroom!'

'But the red light? The fire?'

'I stopped at the first sty that leads off Kirby Lane into the long field. I was just about to continue when, from the far end, the 'point' of the arrow, I saw a red beam – intensely bright – stab down to the ground and I thought I saw a fire start beneath it.'

'Near the mound where the children were found?'

He nodded cautiously. We looked at each other, with the unspoken incredulity of men who had seen what cannot or should not exist. Daniel smiled wistfully. 'Ok I had been drinking, but not a lot – and I was perfectly sensible – but when I saw that, I ran like a madman and called the police. I expected them to patronise me to death but someone from the village had already called 999, so I grabbed a flashlight and went back, but this time into the wood. By now the object was much higher and clearly making an exit.'

'No noise? No sound of any engines?'

'Still absolute silence. It was freezing hard by then and the fields were frosted over but when I got into the wood I saw that something had melted the tops of the trees, they were running wet. I walked towards the far end, shining my light, and as I got towards the Desford path I saw the children.' His voice faltered slightly. He must have realised almost immediately who they were. The news had been full of Max and Jonathan for two whole days.

'You recognised them?' I asked.

'Not at first – I mean –' he laughed nervously, 'for a start I thought they were – well – literally little green men but they were in blankets, wrapped up, sitting quietly, looking at me quite calmly. I recognised Jonathan first. He stood up and *waved* at me.' Daniel lapsed into silence, an incredulous smile on his face. On the mantelpiece a clock started to chime. It was 11 a.m.

'I walked over and asked him if he was alright and he said he was fine but that Max was cold and I should call for help.'

'He said that? He mentioned Max by name?'

'Yes. I mean he seemed very protective of the younger boy. He was completely composed, unusually calm, but it occurred to me later that they might both be in shock. I waited until the police came. I was worried at first that I would be arrested under suspicion of having abducted the kids, I mean you just can't be too sure, but the first people to arrive took my statement and then gave me to Riley.'

'These are no ordinary abductions, Daniel, you can hardly be a suspect!' I looked meaningfully at the clock. 'I had better get back to Oxford and see how things are progressing.' I stood and Daniel stood with me.

'So what do you do exactly, Julian?' He started to help me on with my coat.

'I'm sorry?'

'Your profession, you're a Professor, a scientist of some kind?' he smiled carefully.

'Yes, I'm a geneticist, Daniel. DeMarr and I are currently working on the Human Genome Project – do you know anything about that?'

'A little bit. It sounds complicated!'

'It is. And expensive. The project aims to map the entire human genome – all of the DNA base sequences required to build a human being: that's about 3 billion base pairings of amino acids, coded into about 250,000 to 350,000 genes located on 23 pairs of chromosomes and set into the nucleus of every cell in your body.' I tried not to sound patronising but I had already detected what Sally referred to as my 'Professorial' voice.

'Wow, that's a lot of sort codes!' he joked intelligently.

'It is! I'm working on chromosome 22, along with DeMarr and the British team. National teams on the genome project have been designated the task of mapping specific chromosomes.' We were standing outside by now, the weather oddly warm and suddenly spring like.

'Is chromosome 22 particularly interesting?' Lockwood asked, rocking back and forth on his heels.

'Well it has the advantage of being incredibly small! And we know it's associated with some genetic disorders but its early days.'

He nodded at me politely and we walked on for a

moment. Then he stopped abruptly.

'Do you have any – what's the word you guys use – working hypotheses for what's happened here?' The question, the way he phrased it, surprised me.

'No, not yet.' I felt sufficiently disarmed to think seriously about the question for the first time. 'Except that it isn't the usual list of suspects; Russians, the IRA, the Japanese – nothing terrestrial.'

'Jesus! You really think its alien?'

'Well you saw the ship Daniel! What else do you think it could be? I mean I am the last man alive to use the word alien or flying saucer in a serious scientific debate, but –'

'Some of the papers are saying it's a secret US stealth weapon? Some sort of test?'

'Yes, well, the papers have been full of rubbish all week! I should know. I have had my office and my house surrounded by journalists and TV crews since I became involved in this!' We resumed crunching off down the drive, Daniel again without a coat. I recalled the novel and the play.

'Incidentally, please tell me you were reading Wyndham's *cuckoos* before any of this happened!'

He got the joke and smiled ruefully.

'No, sorry! I confess I got it out of the library as soon as the press started using the term Midwich cuckoos when reporting on the abductions: I was curious about the reference!'

'I bet!' We were on the road now walking back towards the junction.

'Do *you* have a working hypothesis for what is happening?' I asked suddenly. He paused for a while and then shook his head.

'Not really, not yet – and as you say – the papers are mostly full of rubbish. But the answer lies not so much with the ship and the sightings, but with the wood –'

Something in the way he said this made me stop. In

the distance I could see my car – now the only vehicle – drawn up on the verge.

'Really?' It seemed an oddly prescient point to make. This location was unusual but surely just as random as the others. We continued on in silence. As I climbed in to my car Daniel stood solidly by the open window.

'Well it was a pleasure meeting you Julian, and I hope you get to the bottom of all this and soon. If I can be of any help just let me know - Lockwood Farm, Kirby Mallory, Leicestershire – very straightforward!'

'The pleasure was all mine, Daniel. And if I don't get to the bottom of it, I am sure DeMarr will.' I started the engine. Then, spontaneously, I turned it off.

'Actually it would be rather good to keep in touch with you, Daniel, if you don't mind.' I fished inside my wallet for a card, aware that I was acting slightly out of character. 'Informally I mean – contact me at College? If you see anything else or if anything else occurs.' I had looked vaguely in the direction of the wood. He took the card from me and held it in his giant hand.

'Well of course, thank you.' The card – *Professor Julian Grey, Green College, Oxford DPhil FRCP FRA* – struck me as suddenly pretentious but after scrutinising it for a moment Daniel quickly squirreled it away into his jeans without a second thought.

'Well goodbye, *Professor!*' he said with slight irony as if again he had read my thoughts. I smiled, oddly intrigued by him.

Chapter 2

When I finally arrived at the John Radcliffe it was after 4 o'clock in the afternoon. Max and Jonathan had been evaluated by the child psychologist and were both in the process of being reunited with their parents, or in the case of Jonathan, his foster parents. DeMarr was still ingratiating himself at Chequers and no doubt pressing his agenda and Sally had arrived back from London. She was waiting for me in the reception to ward seven and when I saw her I knew immediately that she had been there for some time. She mimed a gesture of helplessness as I appeared.

'Please don't tell me you took the scenic route home!' She leaned forward and kissed me briskly as if I was a stranger. 'Where in God's name have you been?'

I momentarily recalled the empty bed and considered asking her the same question.

'I have been crossing and re-crossing the wide open spaces of the East Midlands, after talking to the man who found the boys –'

'Lockwood?' She mused correctly. She slipped her arm into mine and walked me towards what had become, since last Monday and the discovery of the first two children, DeMarr's makeshift office. Two security men in black suits looked us up and down and then nodded us through. These were a relatively new addition, a belated response to the mayhem of the first few days wherein reporters and camera crews had walked about with ease helping themselves to patient records and impersonating long lost relatives.

'How are they?' I asked, sitting down heavily amid DeMarr's mess of coffee mugs and half-eaten pastries. For a man who was so fastidious in his personal appearance his eating habits were as mysterious as the food itself. Sally was standing at the other end of the desk casually reading something.

'The boys? Oh, they look astoundingly well given the circumstances and their underlying condition. Just like all the others. No memories of who took them, no memories of being found, except perhaps Jonathan. He's interesting: older and more vocal.' She frowned. 'But it really is bizarre, all of it, from start to finish. Assuming it has finished of course. And now with the bloody government all over us! Louis thinks –' There was the sound of some sort of disturbance outside, somewhere near the far end of the ward. Sally, always easily distracted when talking to me, craned her neck forward while looping a string of blond hair back behind her ear. She screwed her eyes up, trying to focus, still self-conscious about wearing her glasses.

'What is it?' I asked. I thought I heard a buzzer.

'It's Mrs Lennox. She doesn't appear to be as happy on seeing Max as I would have anticipated – hold it, darling –' Sally turned and walked off towards the sound of a woman crying.

By coincidence Max had been Sally's patient at Great

Ormond Street and she had been treating him prior to his abduction. As a result Sally knew Max's mother. There did not appear to be a father. I sat, my eyes closed, thinking over my earlier conversation with Daniel Lockwood. He was not what I had expected of a farmer, but then I did not know any. I thought of the wood again, the mound, the police tape casually tied from tree to tree and twisting in the cold. Questions crowded painfully inside my head, and behind them for the first time I was aware of a slight tension, almost nervousness, like nausea. Could it really involve aliens? Was there not a more obvious, earthly explanation? When I opened my eyes, I saw Sally approaching with a woman and a police officer. The woman was distraught, her face marked red with tears and her eyes puffy and lined. Sally was speaking to her in a low, confident voice. I saw my wife gesture authoritatively as Mrs Lennox was led away. There was something distasteful about the woman's subservience as if something inside her was broken.

'Is everything alright?'

Sally looked up at me, puzzled.

'Apparently not. Mrs Lennox doesn't believe that the boy is Max!' Sally seemed to scoff at the idea and started looking for a clean cup. For a moment I thought I had misheard her. She poured herself a coffee as I repeated her statement as a question.

'Yes – she says it – IT – looks like Max but it isn't! Jesus! I suspected that the burden of the last few days would be worse on the parents than on the children, and with the press printing B Movie Sci-fi scripts instead of news it's little wonder! She probably thinks that Max is a pod creature –'

'She didn't say that, did she?'

Sally laughed spontaneously. 'Oh course she didn't darling! Lighten up, Jules! She's distraught! Max has been hospitalised almost continuously for the last few years on and off, with no hope of any effective treatment, and then this.' Sally pointed the silver thermos pot at me. Her ability to consume coffee exceeded even mine. I declined.

'Have any other parents reacted in this way?' I was still disconcerted, genuinely surprised by Mrs Lennox's reaction. The idea that we had retrieved facsimiles of the abducted children actually shocked me.

'No! Not that I know of. But Mrs Lennox is particularly dysfunctional – and Max is, well, very sweet but a little odd.' Judging by her expression the coffee was either cold or very strong.

'Odd?'

'He's small for his age and very, very quiet. When I first met him I thought he was autistic, but I think he is just very shy or very observant! He comes from a large brood of ill-assorted and illegitimate children and has probably learned to be self-reliant. Mrs Lennox is not what you would call a high achiever, nor is she very monogamous.' It was a risky word for my wife to use. She seemed to sense it, frowning to herself. I politely changed the subject.

'Bone cancer?' I asked, my curiosity about Max aroused. Sally looked up, frowning still.

'Max? Yes – *Ewing's Sarcoma* – like a majority of the other children, more or less –' she walked over to me and ruffled my hair. 'Darling, you look exhausted. You should have flown back with DeMarr! Sorry, I promise I won't make any more comments about pod people, the whole sci-fi theme is a bit tasteless.'

I smiled, trying to understand my growing sense of anxiety. It felt new somehow, unlooked for.

'You're forgiven. When I went to see Lockwood he was reading through the *Midwich Cuckoos* as well, alongside some Shakespeare.'

'You went to his house? God how very populist! If anyone mentions that particular novel again I swear I will scream!' The title had been everywhere: it had already become an implicit code name for the whole drama, a joke amongst the literati and the technicians.

Sally started working her way over DeMarr's papers again, scrutinising documents regardless as to whether they were private or not. It was one of her most irritating habits.

'It's a good story actually,' I said rather pointlessly. Sally glanced up as if she'd forgotten I was there.

'I've never read it – it's the story about the mysterious alien pregnancies? Didn't they make a film starring George Sanders?'

'God yes, but that was years ago. Have you seen it?'

'No, darling.'

'Well it's about a mysterious force that overcomes a small village, making all the good citizens faint and when they regain consciousness all the women are pregnant.' I smiled weakly. I was sure I had told her this already.

Sally, feigning interest, smiled slowly. 'Only the women? How dull, now if the men had been pregnant that would have been interesting!' and then she added as an after-thought: 'Parthenogenesis?'

'Sally it's a story about aliens, it's not a doctoral thesis.'

'And the children are born green I suppose?'

'*No*, they are born with special powers, grow very quickly, and try to take over the planet!' I made a semi-serious expression on my face, as if we ought to consider the possibility.

She didn't laugh. Instead she snaked her hair back again and said, 'I really don't get the connection, darling. And I can't believe we're having this conversation! But then we've been having these sorts of conversations all week!'

'We have indeed,' I agreed, quietly. 'Well some of us have. DeMarr's useless because he doesn't read any fiction at all!' I grimaced. I thought rather spitefully that even *The Tempest* would be lost on him.

'You should stop teasing him, Julian. He thinks you are implying he's stupid, you know!' Sally looked at me rather pointedly and raised an eyebrow. Suitably rebuked we chatted for a while but said nothing of consequence. The finding of the children safe and sound was a relief but somehow I sensed Sally's disappointment and through hers my own. I suggested we go back home and wait for DeMarr to call, but Sally clearly wanted to stay for a while. I stood up and walked towards the door but she looked up at me and suddenly held out her hand.

'Come and see Max!'

To my surprise, I did not object. I had seen some of the other children, but not many, and then only to stand by their bedside, remote and rather austere, observing how they were questioned, examined, reassured. I had hardly spoken to any of them directly. We walked down a modern ward with bays to either side, each one containing six beds. Most of the children were dressed and playing, indifferent to their experiences and the drama of the last week. At the far end we came across a bay containing only two patients. It was quiet and warm and the children wore matching blue pyjamas. A fair haired boy, freckle faced and quite thin – obviously Jonathan given his age – was lying on the bed leafing studiously through a large book containing photographs. He was being watched by a smaller boy perched on the end of the bed opposite, hugging his knees. This was evidently Max.

'Hello Max!' said Sally with sudden charm.

Max looked up with clear, unblinking eyes of a rather striking intensity. They were grey-green, and then, from a different angle, oddly blue. He was an attractive child; a sharp, angular face, exotically boned and with a great thick cloud of black hair pushed back from a high forehead. He had a rather feral quality about him as if he was not entirely tame. Rather self-consciously I tried to arrange a child friendly face. It felt like a mask, a grimace.

'How are you feeling Max?' Sally asked this as if she really wanted to know. Max smiled at her, an elfish look, almost cynical, and then held out his hand.

'He's well, thank you. He's already been asked lots and lots of questions today,' Jonathan answered for him. The older boy had a slight accent, north-eastern perhaps and when he spoke he didn't look up.

'Is that right, Max?' Sally said glaring at the top of Jonathan's head with a slight trace of irritation. I noticed that Jonathan's book was about astronomy. He was staring at what appeared to be photos of Mars.

'Why was Norma upset?' asked Max suddenly.

'Oh I think she was just tired – coming all this way to see you from Scotland,' Sally stroked Max's hair back and away from his face and oddly tactile, he pushed his head into the strokes like a cat.

'Norma?' I asked, to no one in particular.

'Norma Anne Lennox,' said Max, quietly, and with intense concentration, as if his mother's name was a formula. Sally laughed.

'That's right, and she was so pleased to see you safe and sound that she got upset and started crying!' Max looked up at my wife and nodded but his expression was equivocal, as if he suspected she was being tactful or lying in that odd and unnecessary way that adults often did. Suddenly Jonathan closed the book firmly with a deep clap of pages. 'I think Max needs to rest, now,' he said quite simply.

'Sorry Jonathan, I'm sure he does – I just wanted to see if he was alright.' Sally pulled a mock cross face at me and I pressed my lips together to stop myself smiling. It was always difficult seeing Sally with children. Her ease and patience with them still shocked me. For a woman who despised maternal instincts and derided them in others they seemed to come naturally to her and without affectation. I stood watching, gaunt with the realisation that we were childless and that she was to blame. The revelation seemed to come from nowhere.

'Goodbye Sally,' said Max. He waved his left hand carefully and precisely. Sally slipped to her feet and said goodbye to Jonathan as well but he ignored her. Instead he was looking at me intently, a curious adult look as if he half recognised me from somewhere or had sensed my secret reproach against Sally. I waved at Max, self-consciously and then looked at Jonathan and nodded. He nodded back with the self-effacing presence of a really good butler. I felt myself blushing slightly. Sally and I turned and walked away.

'Isn't he cute!' she said eventually. 'He always calls his mother by her first name – it's so sweet.'

I looked back to see that Jonathan had gone to sit next to his new friend. He had his arm around Max.

'Jonathan seems very protective. Is he always so bloody rude?'

'Yes, I'm afraid so. His behaviour towards Max is typical of all the other pairings in which one child watches over the other. I think it's just more obvious here given the age difference.'

'I wonder why Jonathan is so much older than the other children.'

Sally laughed as if this question was the very least of our concerns. 'Well that's *one* of the things we need to find out!' Then she said quietly, 'And Jonathan is interesting in another respect: he is the only child whose tumour is not malignant.'

I stopped, surprised 'Really? I didn't know that.'

'Yes. He was misdiagnosed and referred two weeks ago, but a day before he was abducted it was confirmed that he had a series of non-malignant tumours in his left knee and femur. It might cast some light on how the abductors identified the patients: his records were in the process of being re-evaluated when he was taken –'

'Curious – or perhaps he was a control of some kind?' We had reached the entrance to DeMarr's office.

'Control? I suppose so,' Sally fell silent for a moment and then said with curious intensity, 'but why experiment on children!'

I shrugged and left her sitting in DeMarr's office quietly and unashamedly reading his mail.

I drove home to North Oxford preoccupied, anxious, keen to play a part in whatever investigatory team the government felt fit to appoint and yet already annoyed that DeMarr would probably end up chairing it. I then found myself irritated by my annoyance. As for the children themselves, the abductions were still so bizarre and unintelligible an event that I couldn't really see them properly: in the right context or on the right scale. Did it mark the beginning of something? Alien contact? An invasion? Despite the fact that the children were all now safely in our hands and carefully watched over, would there be more abductions? I wondered how Riley was progressing with the criminal investigation, bemused as to how and where he would start and how co-operative the secret service would be. The evening traffic was light, the air chilling again toward another frost. I stopped off at Green College to check my mail and sort out some administration. The usual crowd of reporters waved at me like a celebrity and asked for a few words on Max and Jonathan as I parked. I caught sight of several of my doctoral students grinning at me from the library windows, enjoying my embarrassment, and probably my fame. Eventually I got home and, after a frugal meal, read into the early hours. Sally did not join me but stayed away, probably having gone back to London, and there was no call from Louis.

For a married man, I spent – and had spent – a not inconsiderable amount of time on my own. And yet my natural inclination to solitude could not by itself disguise the fact that my marriage had been a failure. Sally and I had been together for twelve years following a sudden and incautious courtship marked in turn by an equally sudden if not obscure decline. Yet like Rome in the 3rd century AD, we lingered long amidst the ruins of domestic prosperity. We lived on Farndon Road in the spacious ranks of the *haute* bourgeoisie, occupying a large detached mid-Victorian house bought cheaply (and with gratitude) from one of the poorer colleges. The place was picturesque and well preserved, definitively original in that it retained a tiled hall, ornate cornicing, wooden shutters, and the later vandalism of single room conversions which gave us a useable basement, an attic and a curiously large number of bathrooms. Vault like reception rooms faced east and west, and there was a garden with the remnants of an Anderson shelter and a fruit plantation. I could walk to work and Sally could – and often did – cycle to the train station to commute to London. Such advantages were the envy of my friends and colleagues, but, like the marriage itself, such appearances were deceptive. The house was large and stubbornly cold even in summer, prone to damp and infested with dark unfriendly corners despite numerous attempts to modernise. The rooms seemed to watch our Spartan celibate lives with an air of malignancy as if brooding nostalgically on the memory of student house parties and the odd orgy. The cellar boasted a large and unusually noisy rodent population, predominantly grey squirrels, which invariably chewed the wiring before Sally gassed them. And the house grew larger and bleaker with each passing year.

By the late 1980s we had blunted the conveniences it offered us and the joy of experiencing them. When we had first bought it Sally and I had joked about having a floor each with two to spare but the joke quickly wore thin, and the house slowly lent itself to a sort of marital apartheid. In principle we still shared a bedroom but by 1990 Sally had started staying down in London where she owned a small, distressingly organised apartment in Pimlico and I increasingly slept in a long narrow bedroom at the back of the house just off from my study. It was a dispiriting room filled with dark Germanic furniture inherited from Sally's mother and it gave the room the look and feel of an Edwardian railway carriage. More recently still, indeed just before the abductions took place, we had finally started to talk openly about selling and moving on, her to London and me into a smaller property, but I had baulked over such an overt acknowledgment of our separation. Like so many failed couples, we remained locked together through habit and routine and the desire to be seen to have succeeded. The deception of love was deep and convincing and the truth would be shocking to our friends and even, in its own way, to both of us. And the cause of this profound failure? To Sally the explanation was complex. To me it was shockingly simple: we had never had children.

A single child myself, I had longed for a large family, beginning, perhaps imprudently (or selfishly), not long after we were married. Sally had never openly dissented from this plan but then typically I had never really discussed it with her. And initially there had been 'complications', not with Sally but oddly – distressingly – with me. Nothing insurmountable but by the time the problem had been identified (and after Sally had laboured under the blame for almost a year) she suddenly set her mind against a family. In the arguments that followed I often found myself sounding like some 18th century patriarch and Sally like a martyred first generation feminist. I resented her conceit and my infertility and the sheer posturing of the arguments, but nothing would move her. And my consequent failure to be a father brought with it a bitterness I found hard to understand and impossible to analyse. There was, of course, a profound irony in a geneticist being sterile, or put more generously, hard pressed to breed, but why did it make me feel so diminished? Many people chose not to have children. Did they consciously lack something? Why did it matter so much to me? I pressed on with my professional life as a form of consolation, the joy of my students, the fun of sharing vicariously in other people's children but despite myself, Sally's veto became a source of unspoken ill will; a soft, insidious cancer at the heart of our relationship. And then there were Sally's men of course, the technicians, the young porters; the odd junior doctor. Nothing serious enough to risk divorce or too qualified to compromise Sally's self-esteem, but enough to corrode away at what was left of our relationship. Each time I uncovered her latest affair I felt not so much anger as a growing indifference, a sort of exhausted humiliation like an actor in a West End production who knows that if he quits there is no other play to go to, no other companion, nothing but solitude and faded reviews.

On the morning of March 20th DeMarr appeared on the doorstep of Farndon road booted and coated and wearing an elegant silk scarf rather pointlessly on the outside of his collar. It was much colder than the day before and overnight the pavements had caked up white with frost. It was foggy too, a chilling haze that smudged the morning darkness outside the doorway and cut itself into the house and into my legs. DeMarr was not alone either. He was accompanied by two plain clothes police officers linked mysteriously to Downing Street. Louis mentioned this matter so many times that for one moment of acute distress I thought he had the Prime Minister outside waiting in a car or behind the porch. I led the trio to the back of the house into the nearest thing we had achieved to a comfortable pleasant room but DeMarr followed me into the kitchen next door where I made fresh coffee and to my irritation, the police followed him. They hung about with the indifferent air of estate agents trying to reassure but not intrude on a prospective buyer. We all then trooped back into the garden room. I felt strangely embarrassed by all this.

Finally DeMarr got down to business. 'The PM wants to start immediately. He wants a small committee, no more than six, and he wants you to chair it.' The news shocked me although I tried not to show it. I thought DeMarr sounded disappointed but before I could say anything he added carefully that it made sense to keep his role as the principle scientific advisor to the government separate. I nodded.

'But the most obvious choice is Sally?' I queried, 'she's a leading paediatric oncologist, I mean – this has her name written all over it!'

DeMarr looked down and away, a look I recognised from his student days denoting either a lie or an omission. Sensing some tangible disagreement the policemen rattled their cups and stood up, 'We'll take a look outside Prof, if that's alright?'

'Outside?'

'Routine, sir, nothing to worry about.' They clattered out into the hall. It had started to snow.

'She turned it down,' said DeMarr quietly as we heard the front door close.

'Oh –' I was both relieved and dismayed to find I was second choice to my wife.

'And besides –' DeMarr hesitated, holding the white cup in his still gloved hands, 'they don't appear to have cancer anymore.' There was a silence. I heard a clock ticking from the hallway, a car alarm, the gritty soft whisper of snow on the windows.

'I'm afraid I don't understand, Louis.'

'The children are all in remission – that's one of the

reasons I didn't call you last night. We wanted to check on Max to confirm what we had already found in the other 22. Presumably you know about Jonathan?'

I sat down. The room still felt cold. 'Yes I did, although not from you.'

DeMarr narrowed his eyes slightly at the rebuke but said nothing.

'So when did you find out that the children's condition had changed?'

'A few days ago my dear. I'd been meaning to tell you but – well – we have been rather busy!'

DeMarr sat down carefully and removed his gloves as if he had concluded some form of surgical procedure, pulling at each finger in turn.

'I mean, my dear Julian, it was so extraordinary that we needed to check for instrument failure or some cock-up in the tests: especially since the same team performed the initial screenings. It was only re-confirmed early this morning.'

'In remission?' I echoed. I thought of Mrs Lennox, and then of Max, sitting on the end of the bed. Following his move to Great Ormond Street in February he had been given six months to live at best. 'Good God,' I whispered.

Louis made an odd facial expression as if he thought God had little to do with. He turned to me and spoke quietly despite the fact that we were alone.

'Whoever did this clearly and deliberately chose children suffering from *Ewings Sarcoma*, and in the case of five of them, pretty well advanced. In all cases now the cancer is in remission and the children's blood chemistry is completely normal.' DeMarr looked at me as if he expected me to say something. 'Do you accept the offer of chairing this committee? We would need to relieve you of your academic responsibilities for a time. I've already spoken to the warden at College.'

'Are you saying they've been – *cured*?' It seemed an imprecise word to use. DeMarr scowled again.

'I'd rather use the word remission, Julian. What has happened here is unprecedented. This is an astounding opportunity for us, just think of it!' I could only think of Max for a while, his life seemingly spared. A miracle? I felt a rush of excitement, close to panic.

'I *will* chair the committee – but,' my voice hardened, 'I will want to be involved in all data collection and in all clinical and surgical aspects of the investigation. Is that clear? Has Sally agreed to work on the committee with us?'

'Yes,' said DeMarr, feigning ignorance to my tone. Then he smirked rather knowingly, 'Professor and Professor Grey! Like the old days! I would recommend we have a virologist and some competent biochemists other than our good selves, that is. Unfortunately the Americans are insisting that they have two people on it as well – some sort of psychologist, and a 'first contact' specialist who appears to be an etymologist! She's linked to SETI and the usual alien brigade who will somehow be involved as well.' He pulled another face. DeMarr's expressive nature was one of the many characteristics that led people to believe he was foreign.

'The Americans?' I asked, blankly.

'Yes, you know, *the special relationship* and all that. They've been rather nasty about the whole British response apparently.' DeMarr tapped the side of his nose.

'But I thought all the abductions had taken place in the United Kingdom?'

'They have my dear, but there might be more, and remember Julian, the Americans run the planet, fingers in every pie and the British can never say no to them.'

I looked at him with a sudden trace of affection.

'Well we can manage two Americans, Louis.'

'Quite!' DeMarr seemed genuinely pleased. As we stood up I spotted the two policemen walking rather listlessly about the garden.

DeMarr walked into the hall talking excitedly. 'I do have an idea about the virologist, incidentally.'

'Really? Who do you have in mind?'

'DeSilva. James DeSilva?'

It was an obvious choice and I was happy to agree but then mildly annoyed to find that DeMarr had already offered him the post. It also transpired that the two Americans were on their way and would be at some US airbase that evening. Near the front door the conversation turned to facilities and funding. Again DeMarr seemed to have sorted this out. The local health trust had agreed to allow us to stay in the John Radcliffe, and the government had already made arrangements to use labs in Oxford and London, and then in the US and Japan if necessary. It was only as DeMarr went to let himself out that he seemed to consider the need to ask my opinion on these various arrangements. 'If you agree to all this of course?'

I tried to be generous. 'Of course, but Louis I will need to be involved from now on, even though you remain the principle advisor to the government.'

He nodded tactfully. Through the door I could see the drive already covered in snow.

'The cancers might be irrelevant,' I said, almost to myself. DeMarr pulled up his collar and looked at me, his face pale. 'I mean whoever took the children might have used the cancers to indicate a specific genetic sequence. Perhaps that is what they wanted? We know that childhood cancers are linked to autosomal recessive disorders – a specific genetic inheritance?' DeMarr made no immediate response but looked at me and smiled knowingly. As I closed the door I realised he had already thought much the same.

On the evening of March 20th the committee met for the very first time. We ere from the beginning a curious assortment of the over qualified, capable but socially challenged. Joseph Braedabarker was a leading child psychologist and behavioural therapist with an established practice in Boston. He was a genial, austere man who conformed neither to my prejudices about psychologists or indeed Americans. The second American was the language specialist and cryptographer, Dena Small, the youngest of the team and, as far as Sally and DeMarr were concerned, the least qualified. Indeed DeMarr treated her as a quack from the moment she arrived despite a raft of qualifications from a number of Ivy League universities. She was a small, intense woman of afro-Caribbean descent, incapable (thankfully) of offending; highly motivated, and profoundly observant. The sixth member was James DeSilva, a tall, beaked nose man with powerful, hooded eyes. Painfully thin and confined to a wardrobe of grey nylon suits, he had the bearing of an undertaker, of a man skilled in telling other people bad news. He was entirely humourless, and although graceful, cold and inclined to be offensive. He had worked with DeMarr before but I sensed they did not get on. I had read a great deal of his work on HIV in the mid-1980s and knew his formidable reputation from the journals.

Chapter 3

The revelation that the children had been cured was a clue, a tantalising hint that something startling and inexplicable had been done to them. And it took us only three days to discover the extent to which the children had been modified – *altered* – by their abductors. On the evening of the 22nd, a series of MRI scans revealed that all the children had received some sort of 'tag' or marker placed at the base of their pituitary gland. DeMarr wanted to use the word implant, but I refused since it was too loaded a term and the actual material seemed very slight. The small shadowy squares were rather more like barcodes, as if each child had been ringed with a serial number like something caught, labelled, and re-released – a chilling image perhaps, but more accurate in both its description and implication. There was no evidence of any surgical procedure behind their insertion and our best guess was that they had been placed through the nose, or up through the back of the mouth. Attempts to analyse the actual composition of the tag proved inconclusive. Thankfully it wasn't metal otherwise the scan would have ripped it out, and close observation showed that it seemed to be disintegrating quite quickly. It was likely that the tag was organic and was either being destroyed by a normal immune response from the children or had been deliberately designed to break down.

On the 23rd March we produced a simple genetic summary for each child's genome with all the chromosomal pairings placed next to each other on a conventional slide or karyograph, a stock in trade image known to student and scientist alike. Given both my and DeMarr's expertise much of this work was familiar and routine, even tedious, but in this case the results were not. A typical human karyograph reveals 46 chromosomes arranged into 23 pairs with each pair having a familiar shape and size: from the long gangly lines of chromosomes 1 to 2 through to the very small stubs of chromosomes 18 through to 22. In all but one of the children, what we revealed was truly shocking. With the exception of Jonathan each child now contained entirely *new sets* of chromosomes – five pairs to be precise – inserted during their abduction and placed into every cell of their bodies. The chromosomal count of a somatic cell taken from the children was now a staggering 56 chromosomes consisting of 28 pairs, the same number as an elephant.

In each child the additional chromosomal pairs appeared identical, smoother than their human counterparts, uniform in length and crammed with DNA. Yet in each cell nucleus the alien visitors stood apart from the human coding in some strange genetic stand-off, a stable pattern that was reproduced and maintained after countless replication and cell divisions. Was this related to the cancer cure or was it, as both I and DeMarr had speculated, largely incidental and linked to some other purpose? And clearly Jonathan's case was revealing: although he had a tag, his genome was entirely normal, and the fact that he turned out not to have cancer implied that the presence of the extra chromosomes was related to the condition of Ewings Sarcoma. The scale and intricacy of what we were looking at shocked even DeSilva, and once informed of these provisional findings the government racked up security around the hospital and clamped down on the number of staff and technicians who had access to the data. Confounded, the committee sat down to establish a research agenda and to answer a set of very specific questions. What were the functions of the additional chromosomes and why had they been added? What was the significance of the tags? Who could have done this and with what sort of technology? What were the consequences for the children and for the rest of us?

Finding the right questions to ask was the easy part; answering them with any certainty was almost impossible. In the early 1990s mapping DNA was literally rocket science. Relating chromosomes to genes and then genes to functional sequences of DNA was difficult and contentious, and understanding what the children's karyographs signified was then at the very limit of our ability. The obvious first step was to analyse the DNA from the alien chromosomes and compare it to a known section removed from the human genome. Yet even with the best labs in the world close to hand, I wasn't sure we could do it at the speed required to stem the sense of panic overcoming the government, and indeed to ensure that we kept the whole committee under my control. Microbiology should not be rushed, but in this case rushed it was. Rumours quickly leaked to the press of 'spectacular' findings, the cure for cancer, an 'Alien First Contact' – and although we quickly obtained a briefing officer to lie to and manage the media, the damage was done. Despite being forbidden to talk to anybody so much as resembling a journalist and compelled, down to the last porter and mail handler, to sign the Official Secrets Act, it proved simply impossible to avoid the more ambitious (and indeed imaginative) members of the press. They crowded the perimeter fence of the hospital like a resentful football crowd excluded from a match, remaining from dawn until dusk despite a continuous cold snap and unseasonable, heavy snow falls. Nowhere was safe. I was awoken one morning by a member of CNN in my bathroom at Farndon Road, a plucky intern who had scaled the drainpipe, and then two days later an intrepid ITN reporter broke his leg on University property when he fell through a sky light trying to spy on my secretary. Frankly I found the attention terrifying. Driving from North Oxford to the John Radcliffe each morning was a surreal and disconcerting experience, and I frequently slept in my office at the hospital to avoid it. Sally, in her own ironic way, appeared to be oblivious of the fuss and the scuffles as if somehow she was not involved at all while, not surprisingly, DeMarr thrived on the attention and had, towards the end of the second week, bought several new and expensive looking suits in which to confront the media. He had started the unusual act of waving rather coyly to people as he drove himself home, nudging through a glittering cascade of flashlights and cameras as if he was the President of a minor republic.

The ubiquity and sensationalism of the press fed into what quickly became a much bigger problem however; the political pressure from the US and some of our apparent European partners, primarily the French. Washington tried to bus in a whole team of experts and remove the investigation to the US, not just once, but on three separate occasions, while the French argued continuously that we were hiding things; data, technology, even a space ship of some sort. Since the children were British there was no issue over extradition despite US interference and an insidious whispering campaign in the UN that we were not cooperating with the 'international community' of nations. DeMarr repeatedly pointed out that the committee was already international and that two of the experts were Americans. He even succeeded in making DeSilva a Sri Lankan national, who despite his ethnicity had in fact been born in Bracknell. Each day brought some fresh onslaught. A real crisis occurred on the 24th of March when it was obvious – even to Louis – that we lacked the resources to analyse the alien samples and would require outside – foreign – assistance. Only two facilities had the technology and the perquisite expertise: The University of Maryland, and the Institute of Molecular Studies in Tokyo.

'We'll have to bring in the Japanese, there's no other option. If we involve Maryland now we're finished. The Americans will take it off us and share nothing.'

DeMarr and I had been sitting around his office having a coffee break, exhausted, plaintive, and surrounded now with soldiers clearly armed with live ammunition. I thought the case was hopeless and said so. To so openly acknowledge our need for help would question our competence no matter where we turned. I had been a week without proper sleep and, as a strange side effect, was suffering from acute tinnitus. I felt I was hallucinating, and that everything about me lacked substance.

'What does DeSilva think, Louis?'

I had asked the question innocently enough. James was, after all, leading the investigation into the alien DNA. DeMarr had wrinkled his nose up to great dramatic effect, oddly holding his breath.

'He's fine with the Japanese,' he snorted after a pause.

I had sensed nothing amiss, nothing in addition to DeMarr's usual possessive efficiency, and on the morning of the 26th we sent blood samples off to Tokyo in a chartered plane under a discreet military escort. The press actually missed it.

The children were themselves model patients, still oddly and tenaciously bound in their original pairings but willing to read and play quietly without fuss and without demanding to go home. They re-adapted to hospital life after the trauma of their abductions as if it were a game or a holiday. Visited each morning by Braedabarker and his support staff, the children revealed no repressed memories or recollections of any of the events surrounding their abduction. Hypnosis revealed nothing of their ordeal, and skilfully designed art projects on the theme of Martians failed to give us a clue as to what the children had seen or experienced. They cooperated with every possible test and interview the psychologist and security officer could devise. Most confirmed their normality, but gradually a series of results seemed to imply that the pairings of the children were significant and initial attempts to separate them resulted in tantrums and panic attacks. Despite the obvious cynicism of DeMarr, it became increasingly obvious that the pairings seemed able to empathise with particular accuracy, and indeed even communicate with each other when physically apart. The cognitive and behavioural tests grew more elaborate and the results more bizarre, implying that the children had been placed together almost as a unit, to cooperate together, and for one in particular to protect the other. Everyone studiously avoided using the word telepathy, except DeMarr of course, who made it into an elaborate rather cruel joke aimed mostly at Dena Small. He would sometimes even put his hand to his forehead and wave his fingers about, tentacle like, in her general direction, until Sally told him to stop it. Yet the findings were pretty conclusive – a function of the tag? But if so why had the tags all but gone?

And there were the parents, of course. Throughout these time consuming and difficult observations they grew more and more impatient and demanding. By the 30th of March the 'grown ups' (as Louis called them; himself a bachelor and contemptuous of children as constituting expensive if not necessary genetic add-ons) were beginning to call for the immediate release of their children. Quickly organised into some sort of action committee, they made frequent complaints about the level of security around the ward and the complete lack of any real information over what was being done to their children. If they were cured of cancer why could they not come home? Conspiracy theories on experiments and alien technology dominated the press. For the most part they were absurd but in the light of our continuing discoveries some were chillingly *accurate*. And as the evidence of the children's exceptional nature continued to mount, the government grew increasingly indifferent to parental pressure, restricting access until the committee came up with something definitive, an attitude that, around April 2nd, culminated in a legal challenge over custody. The pressure was acute and unrelenting. I had never experienced anything like it. And on the day the writ was issued we still had no news from Japan about the additional chromosomes. The prospect of having to release the children early became less disturbing than the likelihood that the government would simply detain them indefinitely and generate almost intolerable levels of international and domestic criticism.

By the 3rd of April I had a blunt ultimatum from the government to act. In the circumstances I decided that the committee should meet immediately to summarise our provisional findings and draw up some recommendations: enough to keep the Prime Minister off my desk, and enough for him to keep the US State Department out of Whitehall. Yet it was hardly an ideal solution. On the face of it the continuous monitoring of the children revealed that their karyographs had remained the same since the discovery of the alien chromosomes, the tags had gone except for Jonathan's, and all of the patients remained free of any signs of illness or infection, but by itself this information was too general and rather meaningless. DeMarr was typically to the point: 'We have nothing to discuss, Julian, until we get the Tokyo report!' but I had gathered us together for a meeting anyway, a forced march through the unprecedented nature of the children and how best to respond to it. The committee sat for twelve hours.

Two quite separate scenarios emerged on the basis of the chromosomal evidence and the psychological and behavioural findings from the children. The first, tentatively proposed by DeMarr, argued that the abductions were an attempt to hybridise two different but possibly distantly related species. The theory was supported by the dominant boy-girl pairings. DeMarr hypothesised that the additional chromosomes had been implanted into the children to enhance the human genome. He speculated that on reaching puberty the children would re-associate into their original pairings to mate and produce a new humanoid species. As a possible line of investigation he proposed that we modified somatic cells from the pairings and fertilised them in the laboratory, a crude (and indeed illegal) means to evaluate whether sex cells from the children (their future sperm and eggs) could successfully recombine without mutation. Such a process would allow us to investigate what a 56 chromosomal foetus would look like, and whether it would survive at all. DeMarr ended rather theatrically on the implications of all this: it was obvious that such offspring would pose unknown security risks as well as unprecedented opportunities. He suggested that the children would have to be carefully monitored even before they reached puberty but he was convinced that the experiment was, in rather crude terms, a breeding program. He ended on an aside about the importance of these findings for cancer research and correcting recessive genetic disorders generally. DeMarr urged us not to overlook the fact that, although possibly incidental to the outcome of the experiment, whoever was behind this had demonstrated that gene manipulation had seemingly 'cured' cancer even in terminal cases.

It was an interesting proposal, and the clinical work aimed to investigate the physiology and survival chances of a new humanoid species was correct if ethically problematic. But I was not persuaded by the practicalities of such an experiment and thought DeMarr wrong from the start. Why was it done at all? Why abduct children, alert us to the existence of some massive experiment, and then wait for about twelve years for the first results, with all the evident risks of failure? Anyone capable of the sort of advanced genetic manipulation we had seen could surely have used some form of artificial insemination and gene therapy as DeMarr himself had suggested, a safer and quicker route to achieve and evaluate the hazards associated with hybridised offspring and one that would not have revealed the experiment so soon? The time frame of DeMarr's proposal just didn't make sense, unless whoever was behind the abductions wanted to be discovered and wanted to reveal the extent of their technologies.

It was at this stage that a second hypothesis began to emerge; an elaborate First Contact procedure disguising in part a different kind of experiment altogether. It did not help that the suggestion came from Dena Small, the least *medically* qualified person on the committee. Indeed throughout her entire delivery DeMarr composed a series of po-faced, roller-coaster looks of sheer disbelief and incredulity that I had seen him use at conferences and in seminars, childish and irritating. Dena studiously ignored him, aided by tactful asides from Braedabarker who sensed some urgent need for American solidarity. Dena argued that this was not a breeding program but rather an attempt to communicate. She began by suggesting that we should think of the children's genetic summaries rather like characters in a script. She then made the intriguing proposal that we treated the pairings of the children as fundamental to the meaning of the message as a whole. When Sally tried to undermine her by commenting that this was not a MENSA test, the joke backfired when Dena laughed and said it was exactly the analogy she was looking for – the children were, in effect, a puzzle that we had to complete, a sort of IQ test. But where was the text of the message? On the alien chromosomes; in conjunction with the human genome; in some imminent change to the children we had yet to observe; or in their future offspring? How long had we to wait for the message to emerge?

Indulging her for a moment I steered the committee through the mass of evidence and tried to see patterns, between children in a pair, between pairs, between chromosomes, between the newly added genetic material in each child, between their earlier cancers, even about the tags in their heads and the locations in which they were found. Braedabarker reminded us that the basis of the DNA code itself was a pair of amino acids, combined together in determined patterns and then coded en mass in bewildering complexity. Were the children echoing this basic pairing? More coffee; more arguments; more distractions. The DNA code was both the most complex and yet the simplest piece of bio-chemistry in the world. Using it as a metaphor was not necessarily obvious or accurate. We thought about the children for hours and any patterns eluded me. DeSilva doubted why such an elaborate first contact procedure should be adopted when it was surely much more direct and potentially useful to appear with the data!

'If you want to set someone a puzzle, you don't steel their offspring and then drop them off, seemingly at random, all over the country. It was bound to be misunderstood – even if the children were not harmed or even seemingly distressed by the ordeal. It is in itself a hostile act.'

'But why cure them?' Braedabarker had asked, in his quiet, soft voice. 'Isn't that a sign of something, a gesture? A gift?'

'I think the cure is irrelevant –' said Sally rather brutally although she was in fact echoing my own thoughts. 'I think it was an indicator that these children had the necessary genetic makeup most suitable for inserting the additional material, and if DeMarr is right, then the cancer is somehow part of what they were looking for. Anything else is pure sentiment, Joseph.'

I had gone to mention *Occam's razor* but a look from Sally cautioned me against doing so.

We sat and debated the two scenarios back and forth, proposing variants of each, but after 7 p.m. we were exhausted and tetchy and no nearer an agreement. Sally had glowered at me several times and pointedly looked at her watch, a mute accusation that I was wantonly detaining her. Her hostility was rather shocking. We had not been getting on for the last week or so. She spent what free time she had in

London, and when I occasionally came across her at home, she was like a stranger, distant, critical, and often contemptuous of my chairing and handling of the committee. Although I was willing to excuse this sudden outbreak of hostilities to the stress and pace of work, I also wondered whether she was now regretting her refusal to chair the committee herself.

'We should break for tonight and get our bearings,' I said after a rather heavy, gaunt silence. 'I suggest we reconvene tomorrow at eight o'clock in the morning.'

DeMarr was pawing through his notes. He seemed distracted by something. He was looking at the latest photographic plates of the children's chromosomes which were circulated each day to the committee.

Braedabarker coughed softly.

'Could we not reconvene later this evening, perhaps, Julian? I need to report back to the US state department –'

I saw DeMarr shake his head at me just outside Braedabarker's field of vision.

'I think we're just too close to this now, Joseph. I think we need to clear our heads. Perhaps the Japanese report will be here tomorrow.'

'Or the court verdict!' snapped DeSilva. 'If the children are released our work here will become almost impossible!'

Sally yawned and then smirked at the virologist. 'We'll appeal James, or we'll find some obscure Elizabethan statute through which to avoid Parliament completely.'

Dena Small suggested we offered the government the two scenarios together or that we should just sit all night until we got an answer. Neither suggestion appealed.

'Dena my instructions are very clear. The committee must make unanimous recommendations, or slog it out until an agreement emerges but I am completely exhausted! We need to discuss this with great care.'

Sally looked at me and then gathered her papers

together.

'I agree with the chair.' I felt pitifully grateful for her support, nodded at no one in particular, saw the official stenographer switch off the recorders and tried, unsuccessfully, to smile at Sally but she was staring down at the desk and then promptly stood up and left behind DeSilva. After a tactful pause to give her a head start Dena followed. The rest of us remained sitting and then, slowly, DeMarr and Braedabarker peeled themselves away from the table and left as well. When I was sure I was alone, I wedged my hands into my face and started to rub my eyes awake. I was finding it increasingly difficult to concentrate. I felt about 1,000 years old and although we now had an enormous amount of information about the children, we were still no nearer any answers: indeed typical of inductive research we knew too much. What did any of this data *mean*?

I stopped rubbing my eyes and leaned back into my chair sighing. I started doodling something on a note pad, my brain a morass of useless information, soggy, churned up by my anger over Sally and her behaviour towards me. I saw a sudden movement behind me in the doorway, something furtive, and DeSilva stepped suddenly into the room. I could tell immediately from his face that something had happened or was very wrong. He hovered in the background for a while, a folder up close to his chest like someone rehearsing a line and then after a curious pause, he walked towards me. I saw he was perspiring.

'It's here – it's just arrived – the Japanese analysis of the five chromosomal pairings. It confirms that they contain alien DNA. I mean *non-terrestrial*,' he added un-necessarily. He sounded short of breath. I looked at him but said nothing.

'It arrived just now?'

'Yes – by courier –'

'Oh.'

Was I irritated that I had not seen the report first? That it had arrived so unexpectedly and at such an odd hour? DeSilva was speaking, repeating himself, telling me about the DNA as if I had not heard him or had not comprehended the significance of what he had already said.

'There are three entirely new bases in the DNA coding, three completely new amino acids!'

'I heard you the first time, James. Perhaps you'll give me the report?' I breathed in deeply. Suddenly I felt completely awake, highly focused, but strangely uneasy. James put the report down in front of me as if it would explode. The plastic cover reflected and glared in the low angled light. It hurt my eyes. I thought of something to say but all I could think of were pointless exclamations or some petulant remark. James was still muttering but I was not listening. Instead I was watching his hands move through the pages of the report like a nervous pair of large fish, twitching and flapping.

'Julian? Did you hear what I said? And there is some interesting blood chemistry that we might have missed.'

I concentrated on his hands and the turning pages, catching sight of fleeting summaries of the children's medical history, white cell counts, and blood enzymes. There was no way that DeSilva could have read these summaries so quickly unless he had been in possession of the report for some time. Yet the committee had sat for most of the day with him literally in front of me.

'I think there is something here that suggests an alternative explanation for the experiment, a more disturbing variation on DeMarr's hybridisation theory. I think we should look for evidence of retroviral activity.'

He emphasised the word retroviral, making it sound savage. None of the evidence we had accumulated from the children so far had implied anything like an infection. Did the Japanese report suggest this? I looked at him with sudden contempt.

'Perhaps it would help, James, if we all had time to read the report properly and not jump to any immediate conclusions.'

James ignored me, clearly and distressingly agitated.

'I think it very likely that the children have been *infected* by the additional chromosomes in order to immediately compromise their human identity.'

It wasn't a question. He seemed to have made a statement about some bizarre fact that only he had spotted. I thought the use of the word 'infected' entirely emotional.

'Does the report suggest this at all?'

'No, not *exactly*.'

'James call the others back and we may as well *all* read this now, however late it is.' DeSilva glared at me as if he had finally worked out I was angry.

'*Very* well, I was only trying to be helpful.' He had no need to move, of course, or call out to anyone. My colleagues had not wandered far and having sensed that something was afoot were drifting back into the room. I beckoned them to their chairs.

'What's going on Julian?' DeMarr asked sitting down slowly, some monstrous pastry in his hand.

'The Japanese report has just arrived, somewhat unexpectedly,' I said quietly.

'I am having copies made for us,' said DeSilva almost apologetically, avoiding my gaze.

'How very thoughtful.' I tried to sound indifferent to DeSilva's impertinence. 'James informs me that the document reveals the alien DNA molecules to be quite different to the human ones and he was just speculating that there MIGHT be evidence that the children are infected – is that right, James?'

Louis and Sally, people who knew me well, had picked up my tone and were looking at me curiously and then at James. Dena Small looked genuinely alarmed.

'Infected?'

DeMarr laughed quite loudly. 'He's a virologist my dear, he is bound to say that! That's what virologists always say!' A young man came in with a stack of reports and placed them on the table.

It took about half an hour for us to read the document carefully. Throughout, DeSilva's legs twitched under the desk as he waited impatiently for us to finish. DeMarr concluded first, a curious, anonymous look on his face. He started to take a series of notes in a long thin leather-bound pad he kept in his inside jacket pocket, a habit he had retained from graduate days. Sally read her copy briskly, as if it was a travel brochure or a menu, spending most of the time on the summary sheets. The last to finish was Dena. Sally asked her contemptuously if she had understood it all. I read quickly, briskly, anxious to find DeSilva's source of anxiety. Apart from a bewildering array of unknown proteins and enzymes – all of which we had already noted – nothing seemed unduly suspicious or sinister about the children's blood. The base sequences on the alien DNA were without a doubt startlingly new but they were confined to the additional five chromosomal pairings. There was no evidence that they had substituted themselves into the human genome: something the Japanese report reiterated several times. As soon as the discussion started DeMarr made immediate reference to this and started poking fun at DeSilva but as DeMarr paused to consume another pastry, the virologist snapped back with focused outrage.

'We're missing something I tell you! There is something else here.'

Sally looked at him and then at me, quizzically. He was working through the summaries of the children's blood chemistry.

'Look at the immune response in the children from

the 19th to the 21st March? A spiked white cell count, elevated temperature, and look at these peptides and protein chains: the bio-chemistry of the children seems radically different!'

'James none of the children have been ill. We test for an infection on a daily basis. Moreover, a karyograph of each child is prepared every day from a cheek swab or a blood sample. We have seen no change to the chromosomal pattern at all and the report from Japan confirms that. What could we have possibly missed?'

Then suddenly James lost his temper, exploding into some sort of incandescent rage. I had never actually seen anything like it.

'Don't you understand that the children are probably being used as *hosts!*'

He had raised his voice and all but Sally jumped slightly. Then he fell silent, his lips moving rapidly.

'I'm really uncomfortable with this discussion, Professor Grey,' said Dena. She indeed looked far from happy and had half turned on her seat as if she were contemplating a rapid exit. I tried to appease her while turning to face the virologist.

'James I don't have the slightest idea what you are talking about.' I tried to sound reasonable, even affable. 'You are implying that the additional chromosomes have been added in order to invade the children's genome and recode it, over-writing it *like* a virus, but unless you are reading a different report to the rest of us there is no evidence for this at all, and I resent you being so deliberately inaccurate in your language!'

'Fanciful even!' added Louis, smirking. He had a ring of white sugar around his lips. The room fell silent except for James who seemed to be holding some form of inner debate with himself. He seemed quite mad.

'Perhaps we should hear what James is proposing in some more detail?' Braedabarker suggested carefully and not unreasonably. I curtly offered DeSilva the floor.

He looked astoundingly nervous.

'I am merely suggesting that the purpose of the experiment is to modify the human genome, not through sexual reproduction but by directly infiltrating entire DNA sequences and recoding the organism, I mean, the *child*, to create an entirely new organism – *in situ* as it were?' DeSilva faltered, as if what he was suggesting was too astounding even for him.

Sally scowled spectacularly. 'James what on Earth is wrong with you this evening!'

'I am hypothesising –' he replied tartly.

Sally caught my eye and tried to draw me into the discussion. 'These are children, James, they're not single cell organisms or fruit flies! Even if it were possible to change the genotype of an organism and through it, the way it looked – its actual physiology – it would kill something as complex as a human being! Think of the energy required! Remember the principle of conservation, and as Julian keeps saying there is no evidence of retroviral activity, or that the alien DNA has migrated onto any of the human chromosomes! If it was happening we would see evidence of it!'

'I am merely suggesting you consider the possibility that this is the purpose behind these experiments!' repeated DeSilva belligerently.

'We would if you could present some evidence!' said DeMarr, not unkindly, as if he was speaking to a rather obtuse undergraduate.

DeSilva acknowledged the rebuke with a downward gesture of the mouth, an inverted smile as if he was about to have a stroke but said nothing.

I was surprised to see DeSilva so distressed. The way in which he had arrived with the report, the way he had anticipated its contents and then, oddly, misrepresented them, left me disconcerted and deeply puzzled. I leaned back and attempted to be conciliatory.

'Ok, James. Look. The recoding process might be dormant for now, it might require some sort of trigger which we haven't found yet, it might be related to the tags but the tags have all gone except for Jonathan Price who doesn't have any alien chromosomes! I hope you will forgive me if I say that your whole argument is surprisingly undocumented?'

'The recoding might relate to the original cancer, the trigger may lie in the children's own metabolism, puberty, whatever! These children could be genetic weapons with a very long time fuse!'

Dena made a strange gasping noise.

'Oh James, for God's sake!' DeMarr waved his hands impatiently. More silence. Then James had one last push. He sounded tired but also afraid and astoundingly determined.

'In plain, simple English, what I am suggesting is that someone – something – is attempting to physically transform the children into actual aliens or carriers of some sort of biological entity, possibly benign most likely lethal and that either the experiment has failed, or that it is taking place over an as yet undisclosed time period.'

'Good God!' Dena said again. To my surprise Sally actually laughed, as if James had made some sort of elaborate joke.

'James, have you been drinking!' He ignored her, being a well-known and rather passionate teetotaller and looked at me with such ferocity that I was almost winded.

'At the very least, we should use this report to put aside legal niceties and quarantine the children!'

'For how long?' asked my wife.

'For as long as necessary!'

'They're children, for God's sake, not animals!' stammered Dena. DeSilva looked at her blankly as if the distinction momentarily struck him as academic.

'Ok, alright everyone, let's try and stay calm.' I pinched the bridge of my nose. It was getting late – almost 10 p.m. 'The confirmation that the additional chromosomes are alien is significant, but not conclusive enough to support some outlandish body snatching scenario that the children are being used as hosts or weapons! What we have here could, as DeMarr suggested, support the theory that this is a hybridization program, it doesn't even necessarily rule out Dena's theory that this is some form of first contact procedure. It could,' I raised my voice slightly, anticipating that DeSilva would interrupt, 'it *could* suggest a third and alarming aspect to the experiment, that alien DNA may, at some stage alter and re-sequence the genetic makeup of the children but we cannot proceed on the basis that this is self-evident or that it is actually happening!'

I stopped, sensing that the atmosphere of the meeting had improved slightly. Why did I feel that we were still wrong about all of this? The wide table in front of me was littered with prints and data, trays of cups, dirty plates and endless memos. I thought of Dena and her interests in patterns and James with his brooding preoccupations. Yet despite his mysterious anxiety when I looked at the data as a scientist, I saw something rushed, something done in a hurry, and then almost abandoned. Whatever this experiment was, whatever its purpose, it struck me as oddly desperate, a *failure*.

It was Sally who eventually broke the silence. 'Surely we can proceed as if all three explanations are likely. To deal with the alarming implications of Professor DeSilva's novel interpretation of this report, we can keep the children for another 28 days regardless of a legal challenge and if, at the end of that period, they show no genetic or physical change, they can be released at the end of May. But we should continue monitoring them until they reach puberty and, as Louis has suggested, observe whether they try to reconstitute in their original pairings and breed. I'm sure we have a contingency plan that we can adapt for such a purpose, or in case of any sudden illness in the children before they reach 18? And in the meantime we should analyse the data we have for any indication of communication or patterns that support Dena's suggestion?' It was an eminently sensible intervention. It cut through the indecision with one swift, confident stroke. Everyone looked at DeSilva who was shaking his head slowly in disbelief.

'Professor Grey,' he whispered, meaning my wife actually. 'I am not sure you have grasped the implications of my suggestion – if I am right, not only are the children at risk, but so is everyone else!'

'James!' Sally said with iron precision and he stopped dead in his tracks. We voted on her proposal and seeing he was outvoted DeSilva abstained. We agreed to see a draft of the recommendation in the morning before we sent it to the government. We finally broke up at about 10.35 p.m.

But despite his tacit consent, DeSilva was not happy. He came into my office just as I was preparing to drive home; sweaty, bullish.

'Julian, I don't want to be difficult or indeed demanding about all this. I know how hard you have worked for this consensus, but I do not believe that we are adequately prepared for some sort of nightmare scenario in which the children are being *used* –' He looked about him. We were in the annex, outside the main ward. 'Used as some sort of incubator to create a new organism, or indeed designed as a weapon –'

I was by now so tired that the whole encounter seemed unreal, dream-like, slowed down and thick as if it were taking place under water or in zero gravity.

'James – look – calm yourself. I do understand the implications of the report, and I believe that we have adequate safeguards to monitor them –'

'But how frequently and for how long? We have no idea what we're looking for – we're trying to guess someone else's project – the children should be detained – there is also a risk of common opportunistic infections interacting with the alien chromosomes and producing more virulent forms of known pathogens!'

'James! They *are* being detained!' I said firmly and with some effort to avoid raising my voice. 'We have detected no changes to their physical condition since we found them, and we have not seen any changes in their genetic makeup other than that observed on the 23rd of March. We are going to keep them here for another 28 days and test them exhaustively. If we come up with anything by then we'll deal with the consequences!'

DeSilva sighed and ran his hand across his forehead. Why was he so agitated? He made a visible attempt to pull himself together.

'Ok, ok – I'm sorry – but Dena talked of patterns of contact and communication – what if they want to find a way to destroy us slowly, by putting us off our guard, tricking us?'

'Why must we assume that this is about conquest?' I was taken aback by his tone.

'Why must we assume it isn't! If we draw on our own histories, conquest and war is about strategy and cunning – using blankets infected with smallpox and giving them out as gifts to enemies, fake tokens of friendship, building a wooden horse and leaving it on the shore as a trick, a lie –'

I caught his eyes. He looked wild, still frightened. The use of the wooden horse as a metaphor for the children chilled me. For a moment I felt again a deep sense of unease, the fear that I was missing something or that DeSilva knew more than he was letting on.

'We will check and check again, James, but what is he alternative? You cannot seriously be considering removing the children, I mean,' my voice trailed away. His blank, cold stare revealed that he had indeed already contemplated every possibility. I was hard pressed to hide my shock. I was almost physically disgusted.

'I will ensure that your concerns are expressed fully in the report and you can attach a qualifying comment if you wish. The report will be ready by tomorrow.' James hesitated and then half turned, his hands locked together as if in prayer. He was still preoccupied with something. I turned and walked away from him.

'We've done it ourselves, already,' he said suddenly, with extraordinary venom. With my back to him, I stabbed the lift call button and clenched my teeth.

'Done what, James?'

'Used viral RNA to over-write genomes to enhance or degrade an organism, to increase the virulence of known pathogens – we do it all the time!'

'I know. To my shame as a geneticist, I know that!' I heard the lift approaching. 'But not on this scale – and we have not even started to unpick the bio-chemistry involved or required to design something from the genetic level up!' The lift pinged and I walked in quickly, almost knocking over DeMarr. I apologised and DeMarr raised an eyebrow as the doors sealed behind me.

'James seems unduly rattled by the findings – you can almost smell his fear!' he snorted straightening his jacket and fluffing up his pocket handkerchief. He was obviously about to drive home himself and wave at his supporters. I wondered if Sally was still in the building.

'He thinks the children are weapons, left behind to be taken in by a hapless, trusting race – little wooden horses on the beach! Can you believe it?'

'Well, it's possible – I mean *'beware aliens bearing gifts!'* does have a pleasant ring about it!' his eyes beamed. I was not in the mood for DeMarr's indestructibly high spirits. He sensed it and relented. 'He'll be alright, Jules, relax old thing. James gets very uptight very easily and it's probably guilt –' then he paused.

'Guilt?' It seemed an odd word to use. 'I don't understand, Louis?'

DeMarr frowned and looked guarded, unsure of something. Then he shrugged, an expansive but strangely ambiguous gesture. 'I meant guilty about sounding off like that in front of his peers without any evidence: most unprofessional! But forget it, Julian: we have a plan now, and a good one, relax my dear!'

'But will the government buy it though?' Inviting DeSilva to write what was, in effect, a minority report, now seemed a particularly bad idea. But DeMarr laughed at my doubt, profoundly amused and said in all seriousness, 'My dear Julian we ARE the government on this!'

Chapter 4

Of course DeMarr was right: the committee had come up with an eminently sensible solution or rather my wife had. And yet DeSilva's behaviour had profoundly un-nerved me. He had a formidable reputation in the profession but the nature of his outburst – especially his fear – had struck me as profoundly out of character. DeMarr, who knew him better and was more attuned to his manner, seemed far less concerned. But, in truth, I was beginning to have my doubts about Louis as well; vague, insubstantial suspicions that both embarrassed and irritated me. Discreetly, and with the air of a petty man put out by bad etiquette I checked how and when the Japanese report had arrived and how it was that DeSilva had seen it first. It seemed to make sense, more or less. We were all in the meeting when it arrived and so it was placed ready to come in to the conference room as soon as we took a break. But how had he found the time to scrutinise it so quickly? More bizarrely – why was he so obsessed with a retro virus when there was no evidence that any existed? Perhaps he *hadn't* read it – perhaps that was the whole point – and merely jumped to a conclusion he wanted to find? But there was something oddly precise and definitive about his conclusion that left me cold; as if it was a sort of premonition.

A few days after the 'DeSilva Incident' the legal appeal to release the children was denied but the government moved to reassure the parents and the public that they would be at liberty very soon. To ease the growing pressure they relaxed rules on visitors and allowed the press freer access to the hospital, and later that same day the Prime Minister informed me that although there would be international disquiet with the committee's recommendations, the cabinet was prepared to accept them. It was now quite impossible, in the current political circumstances, to hold them any longer. The committee was, however, granted a final 28 days to finish up the examinations and to make various follow up arrangements for monitoring the children once they had been returned to their parents. I agreed, relieved that DeSilva's long memo appended to my report had carried so little weight, although I remained anxious how he would react to the news. Luckily circumstances intervened to assist me in this potentially hazardous task: not long after the committee had been ambushed by DeSilva's sinister theory, the alien chromosomes within the children began to atrophy and disintegrate. The change in the genome was sudden and entirely unexpected. Close molecular analysis revealed that they were no longer capable of replication and division, and within hours they were quickly reduced to small rinds of debris cluttering the cell nucleus. Between the 15th and 19th of April they vanished completely.

Initially the discovery caused heightened anxiety that this might be a prequel to the contamination of the human chromosomes, a dispersal of the alien chromatin itself, but close scrutiny showed this not to be the case. The alien chromosomes had been destroyed, most likely the result, as with the tags earlier, of some delayed autoimmune response from the host cell itself. There remained some concern that, freed of their microscopic alien visitors, the children's cancer might resume but there was no immediate sign of this and the cure, however it had been engineered or administered, seemed to be permanent. There remained the stubborn exception of Jonathan Price, whose tag persisted despite the fact he had never been modified. There was throughout the committee a palpable sense of relief, but also – I have to confess – one of bewilderment and disappointment. For my part the final collapse of the five chromosomal pairings confirmed what I had always suspected: that whatever the experiment's purpose it had simply not worked. Certainly something had been attempted; something literally out of this world, but it had not succeeded. I mentioned this to DeMarr, around the 22nd of April as we prepared the children for their release. We had been musing over the latest set of images produced by the labs and had found ourselves between things; at a loss, speculative. Dena and Joseph were sitting outside in bright spring sunshine, while James DeSilva was stalking the labs, a habit he had developed of late to the irritation of the staff. Louis was much taken with the point about failure.

'Curious to think that someone or something so much more advanced than we are can still make a mistake.' In the fine warm weather DeMarr had switched from scarves to wearing rather bizarre, floral cravats. 'But does this mean they will try again, Julian?'

'God knows. Whoever they are, they probably 'do' science in much the same way that we do.' I had yawned deeply, dog like, my ears popping. It was an intriguing thought. 'I mean: thought experiments, hypotheses, hope, even luck. Initially geneticists ignored DNA before they finally realised that the molecule had exactly the properties they were looking for. And were not antibiotics discovered by accident and poor experimental hygiene?'

DeMarr pursed up his lips, fleshy and expressive.

'Then perhaps DeSilva was right, this was indeed an attempt to build a wooden horse but it fell apart? Or perhaps they miscalculated the reaction and tenacity of the human genome?' he said thoughtfully.

'Perhaps, Louis. In H. G. Wells' version of an invasion, the Martians die from being accidentally exposed to micro-organisms once they reach Earth. As a child I used to think it implausible that the Martians would go to all that trouble, scrutinise our planet, build all those ships, and plan for genocide before testing for something as obvious as microbes! Now I realise it's exactly the sort of mistake you make if you are in a hurry.'

DeMarr frowned. 'More literature I haven't read, Julian – really – if I didn't have such a robust view of my own abilities, my dear, you might well give me an inferiority complex!'

'It's *War of the Worlds* for God's sake, you must have read that!' I was joking, but DeMarr had looked suddenly quite put out. He collected his copies of prints and papers together petulantly and walked out without saying anything. He had seemed touchy recently, curiously prone to sulking.

I put his sensitivity down to boredom. We had been hanging about for some time now, winding down the investigation, anxious to resume our lives. All that remained to be done was for us to draw up the procedures wherein the children would be scrutinised on and off until they were 18. Naturally agreeing on the extent of the monitoring proved controversial. DeSilva, subdued after the collapse of the chromosomes wanted each child assigned a team of doctors and an electronic tag to prevent them leaving a designated area. The rest of us were quite content to start off with weekly drop-ins to local clinics and then scale the undertakings up or down as proved necessary. Braedabarker, for his part, believed that even this would be too difficult and might have long term effects on the children and their families. In the end, we agreed on weekly drop-ins but only for a month, and then to revert to an examination every six months, gradually working down towards yearly check-ups. I had expected more trouble from James but he had nodded savagely in agreement and then left the room. All now seemed finally set for a return to normality. There had been no more confirmed sightings, and no fresh abductions. Even the press started to become preoccupied by other things; rumours of an election, a war in the Balkans, the flotsam and jetsam of everyday existence, leaving the hospital precincts strangely deserted. Then, unexpectedly, around the 29th of April, something happened concerning Max and Jonathan, minor at first and seemingly coincidental but then by slow degrees blowing up about me without warning.

I had formed the habit of accompanying Braedabarker on his evening visits to see the children before driving home, partly to spend some time with him, partly to try and get to know the children better and more personably. As their principal contact Braedabarker had quickly earned their trust and was in many senses an ideal parental figure to them all. Friendly, patient and incredibly calm, he spent time which each child before they went to bed and liaised effortlessly with their parents. I had grown to admire the man a great deal. On this particular evening we ended our round as we always did with Max and Jonathan who still occupied the last bay at the end of the ward. It was getting dark and the long dim corridor around us was quiet and almost deserted. Jonathan was reading something to Max from the large astronomy book that had become something of a fixture with him. They were sitting side by side, a curious reverse image of each other – Jonathan, fair headed, pale, and Max with his mass of black hair and his sharp long face.

They both looked up as we approached; eyeing us with the cautious but curious attention I associated with Lockwood's cattle. I stood by the window, self-consciously playing with the blinds, while Braedabarker asked them a few routine questions about their day and then suggested it was time to go to sleep. All the time I was conscious of Max looking at me with an odd unsettling gaze. Suddenly I asked him how he felt about going home to Norma. He didn't answer but looked at Jonathan who, after a pause, stated it was now impossible for Max to go home at all. Braedabarker looked up from his notes, evidently surprised, but then asked in a matter of fact voice,

'Why do you say that, Jonathan?'

'Because Max's mother doesn't want him back, Professor.'

Braedabarker made no outward show of surprise and looked back down at his paperwork.

'That's not true at all, Jonathan – Max's mother has not been well but she's now looking forward to getting him back home, safe and sound!'

Braedabarker glanced briefly at me, his eyes obscured behind thin reading glasses. They seemed expressionless. I pursed my lips and looked blankly at the psychologist. At this, Max stirred himself.

'My mother doesn't like me anymore. It isn't safe for me to be with her.' As he spoke he looked firstly at Jonathan and then at me again.

Jonathan nodded gravely. The use of the word safe struck me as curiously adult.

'In what way unsafe, Max?' I asked suddenly, intrigued, worried.

'My mother thinks I'm a monster.'

I tried to look indifferent to this strange news but I felt a flash of physical shock. I recalled Mrs Lennox's strange outburst on the afternoon she had been reunited with Max, although nothing seemed to have come from it. I could not actually recall her visiting Max again. Braedabarker and I exchanged coded glances until Jonathan closed his book and said with an air of authority,

'You see Max is an orphan now, like me. My mother doesn't want me back either!'

Braedabarker was tapping his thin lips with a pencil.

'She thinks you're a monster now as well?' he said calmly, ironically, as if he was playing some sort of game.

'Yes she does.' There was a brief almost imperceptible pause and then Braedabarker said 'Ok, now let's get you both into bed and we can talk about this in the morning if you want! What sort of monsters, incidentally?'

'Lizards,' said Max after a pause. Braedabarker laughed softly.

'Really? Come on – under the sheets with you!' He dimmed the main lights and said goodnight. It was only as we walked away that I realised how disturbed the American was. Later as I prepared to drive home I heard him on the phone to Jonathan's foster parents, his voice measured but strained. It was about 8.30 p.m.

With some effort I put the matter out of my mind and stopped by at College to collect some mail. My pigeonhole was crammed with letters and a small overflow box had been placed on a nearby table. This, too, was full of envelopes addressed to me. Since the abductions, and despite help from the committee's secretariat, I had been receiving on average about 300 *personal* letters a day, a vast majority from cranks accusing me of carrying out unethical experiments on children and of being involved in an international cover up. Evading the committee's shredder, I had initially binned everything in my pigeonhole on a daily basis but this risked losing some genuine correspondence from students and indeed the odd batch of essays. Following the embarrassing loss of three exam scripts I had devised a hasty selection process. As I started skimming through piles, absentmindedly, I noticed almost immediately a letter postmarked Newbold Verdon, Leicestershire. My name was written out in a flowing, rather classical hand, and on the back Daniel Lockwood had, sensible as ever, put on his own name and return address. I sequestered the letter into my inside pocket and disposed of the rest.

When I reached Farndon Road, Sally was on the phone trying very hard not to raise her voice. I went through into the kitchen and started getting something to eat. For the past few weeks I had lived on a whole array of microwaved meals and was now beginning to suspect I was addicted to them. As I stabbed the cellophane covering with a fork I heard Sally put down the phone quietly. She walked in to greet me but still looking agitated and angry.

'Who was that?' I had lost my glasses and was holding the carton with the cooking instructions away from my face, squinting.

'Hello darling. Just put it in for six minutes.'

Sally kissed the side of my face randomly. '*That* was Mrs Lennox. She is refusing to make the arrangements to receive Max. In fact she doesn't want Max at all.' Sally started putting things away from the draining board absentmindedly,

'Really?' I froze; the microwave door half closed. 'How strange.'

'She's *very* strange. I think she got used to the idea of Max being ill, and the fact that he's now better is too much for her. I don't think it has anything to do with the abductions at all. I think she has been mentally unwell for many years.'

'No, I didn't mean she's strange, I mean it's strange you say this now. I saw Max and Jonathan earlier this evening with Joe and just before I left, Jonathan announced that Max's mother didn't want him anymore.'

Sally was turned away from me, but I saw her stiffen slightly.

'And odder still, Jonathan concluded by saying that his mother didn't want him back either!' The microwave pinged. I added a few more minutes for good measure. Sally turned to look at me, her face carefully arranged.

'Jonathan *said* that? This evening? How did Braedabarker respond?'

'Well, he's a bit inscrutable but I think he was as surprised as I was.' I tried again to decode Braedabarker's look as he had glanced up from his clipboard. 'Or perhaps he's quite used to the possessive nature of Jonathan!' The room was full of the hot, ripe smell of curry. My wife was frowning.

'But Jonathan *has* devoted foster parents, Julian, they've been to see him several times, although come to think about it, *not* recently.' Her curiosity was engaged. She sat down opposite me and watched me eat, distracted, looking at my plate. I moved scalding hot rice from one part of my mouth to the other.

'Curious how those two have bonded,' she added quietly. 'Wait a minute,' Sally stood up and walked into the hall with purpose. I heard her phoning someone.

'It's probably nothing, darling –' I shouted, my eyes watering. My tongue was sore, either from the heat or the spice. I felt tired and almost comatose and simply wanted to go to bed. Sally was speaking to someone, slowly and precisely in a way that usually froze the recipient into a sort of stupor. I'd witnessed this technique many times. Eventually I heard her use

Braedabarker's first name. After a rather prolonged monosyllabic exchange she came back into the kitchen evidently more concerned than ever. I recognised the look immediately. It did not bode well.

'What now?' It was nearly midnight.

'You're right, how *very weird*! Braedabarker called Jonathan's foster parents this evening and after a few painful asides the father confessed that they'd decided – this evening – that they didn't want Jonathan back and were *just about to call.*'

I looked at Sally with my eyes narrowing slightly. My food sat uncomfortably at the top of my stomach.

'You're saying that Jonathan knew this before the parents had told anyone?'

'I guess I am, yes. Jonathan's father told Joe that they had decided that they couldn't provide him with the care he needed in the circumstances, that they have two children of their own, and that Jonathan is a difficult and demanding child –'

'Difficult?'

'Well, yes, but wait darling – it's all rubbish – because eventually Braedabarker got the real reason off the father: Jonathan's foster mother doesn't think the child *is* Jonathan, just as Mrs Lennox doesn't think that Max is Max!' Sally sat down again and we stared at each other in silence.

'Perhaps Mrs Price had called Jonathan herself earlier in the day and told him privately?' I suggested doubtfully. I knew full well that one of the things that had most irritated the parents was their inability to contact their children without having to go through Braedabarker first, despite numerous attempts to circumvent the psychologist and his team.

'That's next to impossible and well you know it!' said Sally now deeply preoccupied with the matter. I felt both anxious and irritated.

'Bugger! This is all we need! And we're sending them

all home soon! We'd better meet Braedabarker, Sally, and have a chat –' I stood up, frustrated, feeling vaguely nauseous and then suddenly I found the whole thing ominous. Sally, as always, was ahead of me.

'It's already taken care of, darling. I've asked him just now to meet with us first thing tomorrow.' She was watching me closely for some reason, attentively, like a patient who is about to be told bad news. 'It's probably nothing Julian, and there are no signs that the other parents are getting distressed about their offspring! It's just Max and Jonathan.'

'*Good*!' I said, heavily, sitting down again. 'The last thing I want is James DeSilva going off on some bloody witch hunt! This is exactly the sort of thing he needs to claw his theory of bodysnatching back onto the table!'

'Jules relax about James: he's been sweetness and light recently.'

He had. I found this almost as troubling as when he was foaming at the mouth ranting about alien weapons. I sat thinking of Max and Jonathan.

'He makes no sense to me –' I said quietly, half to myself. 'I mean Jonathan. I think it's the oddest pairing of the lot!' The central heating had long gone off and, outside the kitchen, I sensed the large house cooling, creaking and snapping like an abandoned ship. Sally mulled over the proposition and then added.

'Did you know that Max is actually the youngest child taken? By just a matter of months. And yes, Jonathan is the oldest. Is that significant?'

I thought of Dena Small and her endless discussions on patterns and meanings.

'Possibly, but Jonathan was never ill in the first place, never received the extra chromosomes and yet he is the only child with a tag still in his brain. It's utterly bizarre! Now they've both managed to freak out their parents to the point at which they think they're monsters.'

'Their mothers –' corrected Sally. 'To be precise

they've freaked out their *mothers*! You fancy a drink?'
She went over to a cabinet and retrieved two crystal
tumblers. She didn't wait for me to answer but poured
two shots of brandy. I had a powerful sense of déjà vu
from our courting days, a lost era of hope and intimacy.

'Hmm, ok – that's interesting – yes, alright, their
mothers, although Jonathan's father might have blamed
his wife but secretly agreed with her!'

'He might well have done – it's the sort of thing a
man would do!' Sally put one tumbler down in front of
me. 'So why would they not want their children back?
It doesn't make sense. Max has been seriously ill since
he was a very small child and now he's cured and is
perfectly well and charming? Jonathan's foster parents
are model, *Guardian* reading citizens with a successful
track record of adoptions and fostering along with
two delightful children of their own!' I felt my stomach
tighten slightly but Sally seemed unaware of this tacit
subject violation. I scrambled to change the subject.

'Well, the children *could* be different – they *might* be
pod children after all! Is it possible that the maternal
instincts are correct?' I said, half-jokingly, but to my
dismay, half seriously as well.

'Julian! Don't be ridiculous! It's more likely that the
bloody media and all the attention have really scared
the mothers out of their wits! Mrs Lennox was always
a bit flaky, but Jonathan's foster mother is some sort of
medical professional, a dentist or something!'

I felt light headed, speculative, even argumentative.
'Ok, so let's drop the full on body snatcher scenario. What
if the children feel that their parental arrangements are
not very conducive to the experiment, to the purpose
behind it?' I suggested, smiling. Sally pressed her lips
together tightly, holding a swig of brandy in her mouth
before swallowing it theatrically.

'Conducive, conducive for what? You're suggesting

that the children are changing the attitude of their parents? To reject them? For what purpose?'

'I don't know – I'm thinking along the lines of Dawkin's selfish gene, perhaps now they want to maximise their survival; they want *better* parents to look after them? Perhaps this is how their species procreate.'

'Oh God so we're back to Wyndham and intergalactic cuckoos!' Sally sighed but the thought evidently intrigued her. 'Alright, let's run with this absurd idea just for a moment: I can understand Max doing that. I mean, Mrs Lennox is hardly a model parent, but Jonathan's foster parents are wealthy and caring, and they have evidently looked *after* him. Perhaps it's about Max? Perhaps Jonathan wants to make sure he can stay with Max? Jonathan's foster parents live just north of Newcastle.'

'And Max lived in Perth, Scotland?' I asked.

'Well yes, but not for ages. He's been in London for a year, and before that he was in Inverness and then Edinburgh. He's hardly had a home life at all. In fact prior to his abduction I was about to recommend that we stopped treatment: his case was quite hopeless.' She drained her glass.

'Thank God it didn't come to that!' I felt an odd sense of revelation, a chill across my face. 'You're quite taken with Max, aren't you?' I added suddenly, perhaps tactlessly.

To my surprise she thought about it and then said quite simply, 'Yes. Yes I suppose I am. He is strangely attentive – and astoundingly brave. For example, despite all of his ordeals at Great Ormond Street, I never once saw him cry! I have never heard him complain either. In some really disturbing way I think I have always slightly resented his mother for not realising how special he was – or rather is! He's a very clever boy, incredibly attentive, and very cute! He has astounding eyes! Have you noticed them?'

I had actually. I had noticed Max's eyes immediately, their unknown *remembered* gaze. How could this make any sense? I nodded, feeling so emotional and anxious that if I spoke I would reveal it. We sat in silence for a while and eventually Sally went to bed. I washed and tidied up downstairs and sneaked myself another drink. As I settled down to read I suddenly remembered the letter from Daniel Lockwood. I retrieved it from my jacket, opening it to find a short note written on cheap blue lined paper, accompanied by a series of newspaper clippings.

Dear Julian,

I hope you are well and bearing up with all the work. I catch a glimpse of you all occasionally on the news! As you requested, I am writing to you to report that there have been a few odd goings on here: a series of fresh sightings over the wood, and secondly, some sort of excavation. Forgive me if you know all about these already. There have been three separate sightings since 19th March, and all have been reported in the local press. Two are, I think, just mass hysteria, and the description of bright lights etc is too contrived to be genuine. The third one is genuine. I saw it myself. It was exactly a fortnight after the discovery of the boys. It was also about the same time – just after 3 a.m., and I saw what I thought was the same shadow, but the weather was bad and it was hard to see from the house. By the time I managed to get out and cross the fields, people were already in the woods and I was not allowed through – despite the fact it's my land, incidentally! Anyway, I will keep you briefed as best I can.

Four days ago, a series of tractors turned up and started to remove the mound on which the boys were found. I am quite angry about this, since the vehicles came in from the Kirby Lane and destroyed a lot of standing crop in the long field between the road and the wood. They also dug up parts of the footpath and are refusing any compensation. When I complained to Mark Riley – the officer in charge of the investigation – he seemed as angry as I did. He seemed to think that DeMarr was behind it? Whoever authorised it has left a bloody great hole now full of water! Any reason why this mound was removed? It used to be a cattle shed. I told DeMarr this repeatedly.

Daniel.

The newspaper clippings were from local papers in the county reporting further sightings and the now 'persistent rumour' that some sort of alien artefact had been retrieved from the wood where Jonathan and Max had been found. There was no mention of DeMarr although Riley was mentioned as being in charge of a national investigation. There was a photograph of him looking cautiously into the camera. I folded the letter and the clippings together before placing them in my office desk under lock and key and stood looking at my reflection on the darkened window for some time: why had the aliens *come back to the same place*?

Chapter 5

I cannot recall exactly when the idea of adopting Max first suggested itself, I mean unambiguously; a proper determined plan as opposed to a day dream; a sort of idle fantasy. The rejection of Mrs Lennox made it possible. My conversation with Sally in the kitchen was perhaps a turning point in that it revealed she liked him, and the probability that she would agree to it. But did I really make the decision in the first place? I did not then believe in fate, in the mysterious planned conjunction of my life with Max. Now many years later, I have no doubts that Max and I were set to converge, that he was saved and set down for me to find. On the morning of April 30th Sally and I had met with Braedabarker to discuss Max and Jonathan's bizarre effect on their parents and what it could mean. He related to us at length his conversation with Jonathan's foster father the previous evening. It was a curious example of inverted causality. Mr. Price had literally been about to call Braedabarker himself and pretend that their financial circumstances made it impossible to take Jonathan back. Yet almost immediately he had confessed that, due to the sudden perilous state of his wife's mental health, it was impossible to ensure Jonathan's safety. Braedabarker had then shown us the latest psychological assessments of Mrs Lennox: the detail of her hallucinations and delusions as to Max's 'real' identity were uncannily similar to those of Mrs Price's. Both imagined their children as impostors, fake, not human but rather beasts or animals in disguise. Furthermore, both mothers had experienced dreams in which their children had turned *into* animals; birds or reptiles, Ovidian transformations triggered by darkness and moonlight. Braedabarker was much taken with this, especially the singular lack of any explicit reference to aliens. This seemed to him oddly significant. 'It's all very interesting, and nothing like the stylised conventional images I would expect if this was media induced, green men, probing and experimentation, the usual hysteria of aliens. Shamanism and shape shifting are archetypes of western demonology. It is almost as if this is somehow terrestrial. Astounding!'

Sally smirked rather unkindly, but Braedabarker, oblivious to her contempt, merely confirmed that it was now quite impossible to release them from the hospital until alternative arrangements had been made. He confirmed that none of the other parents had exhibited similar delusions and were all desperate to be reunited with their children, but the situation was bad enough.

'So what will happen to the boys now?' I asked, conscious that we were entering the final phase of detention, anxious too of DeSilva looming over the boys' fate like a cloud. Surely he would make the most of this sudden, bizarre turn of events?

'Well in the case of Jonathan it's relatively straight forward. He will have to go back into the fostering system. And we'll have to change his identity of course,' Braedabarker sighed.

'And Max? What happens to Max?' Sally asked this casually, almost as an aside, although I sensed that the indifference was contrived.

'As he's younger I think we can get him fostered quickly or even adopted – but again there is the matter of his identity. The publicity around this case has been very unfortunate. Both children are well known, and Max is a rather photogenic child and his face has appeared in rather a lot of newspapers despite our best efforts with the media.' Sally made an unusual, rather shocking cooing noise. I stood hands in pockets, troubled, afraid I would suggest we adopted him there and then, calling it out like a man with Tourette Syndrome, but were we not missing the fact that the fears of the parents might be real, that such images were suggestive of something sinister, dangerous?

'But there's something not right here, Joe. Surely it isn't a coincidence that both the mothers have reacted like this? Some of these fantasies are virtually identical. And Jonathan knew of this before he was told, Braedabarker? You were shocked, I saw it.' We had walked out of the cramped office and into the car park.

'Yes, I confess to it, Julian. I was shocked and it does further separate this pair of children from the others, implying that they are different. Yet there may be a series of perfectly rational explanations. We'll have to do further physical examinations to see that this is not the symptom of some physical change in the boys that we've somehow missed or overlooked.' Braedabarker lit up a cigarette with evident hunger. He spat tobacco from his tongue and emitted a single plume of grey-blue smoke.

'At the moment however I am at a loss to explain it. We have compelling evidence of telepathy in the children but only with each other and not with any third party. It is possible that Jonathan has been able to manipulate his parents, especially his mother, to replicate Mrs Lennox's behaviour. Jonathan was there when Max's mother broke down and was led away that first morning. He observed it and had evidently talked to Max about it. His own foster parents visited him frequently for the first few weeks but then they stopped coming –' Braedabarker struggled to analyse the sequence of events. The effort seemed to exhaust him.

'Sally suggested that Jonathan might want to stay with Max after they've been released from hospital,' I suggested after a pause. Braedabarker had obviously thought of this and already dismissed it.

'Yes, but if so then surely the most logical thing would be for Jonathan to insinuate to his parents the idea that they offer to foster Max, why get both mothers to abandon them? It almost guarantees that they will in fact be separated.' He shrugged, defeated. We watched the psychologist enjoying his cigarette in the spring sunshine.

'Perhaps neither parent will do?' I added finally, getting a sharp look from Sally.

She turned to the American. 'My husband is developing an idea that the children are maximising their chances of survival by upgrading their parents!'

To Sally's horror Braedabarker did not smile but instead he turned to me and said, 'Really? The committee should discuss this when we meet this afternoon.'

I felt myself panicking 'It was just an idea, and we can hardly extend their detention, Joe?'

'We might have to! I still think we can explain it, but it might take time, more than we bargained for.'

'But what about James?' I hesitated, anxious not to sound unprofessional; factional. Joe shrugged and threw down the cigarette and left it smouldering on the gravel. As he crunched off towards his office Sally crushed it out under the heel of an expensive, stylish shoe with a certain spite.

Later, and with admirable calm, Braedabarker presented the evidence on Max and Jonathan's parents to the committee. Were the images of the mothers largely coincidental? Or had they been induced by the children or something external, something linked to the original abductions? While there was clear *prima facia* evidence of manipulation, what purpose did it serve in the light of the medical evidence? As I had anticipated, DeSilva was especially unreasonable and alarmist. Although prepared to release the rest of the children, he now demanded that the two boys be detained indefinitely, a sort of personal compensation for his earlier generosity in abstaining on the committee's vote. In an attempt to reassure him I pointed out that Jonathan had never been modified and that Max now had no extra chromosomes. Apart from Jonathan's tag, they were therefore in an identical position to the other children. It seemed unreasonable to treat them differently on the basis of their mothers' behaviour alone. Dena Small expressed confidence in the monitoring system and gradually, thankfully, a consensus emerged to keep to their imminent release date. DeSilva was eventually beaten back by the rest of us, but as always, he left me with the disconcerting impression that he was privy to some secret information, something he had not shared with the rest of us, some deviously planned contingency. He forced us to agree to undertake another set of tests on Max and Jonathan; in Max's case to confirm the status of his genome. He also urged Braedabarker to carry out an in-depth psychological profiling of both boys as a further condition for their release. It was a satisfactory outcome but the mood was turning sour; people were clearly tired, impatient. I was also irritated to see DeMarr and Sally passing notes to each other throughout the entire meeting; messages scrawled on bright yellow post-its, or drawn up on the margins of the committee agenda and angled so that only the other could see. It struck me as childish and disrespectful.

When the meeting ended I cornered DeMarr and asked him if he knew of any 'digs' or excavations going on in the Leicestershire wood and whether anything had been found in the vicinity of the mound itself. I also asked him if he had heard of the additional sightings mentioned in Lockwood's letter to me, although I made no mention of Daniel by name. DeMarr denied any knowledge but in the disconcertingly equivocal way of his that made me suspicious immediately. I then asked him how Riley was getting on and he merely added that the case had been handed over to the intelligence services on the grounds of national security and the need for international co-operation; an odd very un-DeMarrian phrase. I stood in front of his desk ready to push the matter further: Did he know how the wider investigation was progressing? Were there any clues yet? Had the radiology report from Professor Macmillan been submitted? DeMarr reminded me curtly that had anything been found he would know about it, and would therefore *naturally* inform me and the committee. He reassured me with rapid hand movements and an odd swivelling of his eye. As he shuffled off towards the lifts I was surprised by the sudden, intense conviction that Louis was indeed up to something. He had been elusive of late, often away in London at important and evidently private meetings and once to New York for a closed session of the United Nations Security Council. Moreover, on several occasions I had caught him with Sally going over something in detail, not so much arguing as continuing a conversation that was evidently important and of long standing. At first I put it down to the hot house atmosphere of the hospital and the intense pressure of our routine. But slowly, and against my better judgement, I had begun to feel excluded from something, left out. DeMarr vanished behind the lift doors and I stood thinking about the note passing and whisperings with Sally. I let the matter go and returned to my office. Was Louis having an affair with my wife? The idea that he was sleeping with Sally was absurd but plausible and irritatingly insistent.

And yet it wasn't just De Marr who played on my nerves, or indeed DeSilva, it was rather the realisation that I was becoming obsessed with Max. Each day it became stronger and more pronounced, more distracting, and soon it was of such an extraordinary intensity that I began to worry that, like Mrs Lennox, I was the subject of some externally induced hysteria, some malevolent force aimed at changing my behaviour. I was troubled by the idea that *there was* something sinister about Max and Jonathan but that I was being hoodwinked by my growing affection for them and for Max in particular. *Max, Max, Max.* Distressingly, I even dreamed about the boy: a strange allegorical sequence in which he flagged me down on a deserted roadside and asked me for a lift in my car. In the dream he was darkly handsome, almost androgynous, older than his real world self. My dreamed self politely pointed out that he must never get into a stranger's car but he would have none of it: he replied that I was no stranger but his father. Usually I jumped awake at that point, delirious with joy, but sometimes as I swam up into the dull light of consciousness I thought I caught sight of animals, wolves perhaps, sitting around Max and watching me with a sort of pitiful contempt, or did I once glimpse the sharp gimlet gaze of a lizard?

From that first moment the dream unconsciously appealed to my paternal instinct, my obsession knew no bounds. It was like a form of madness. On one occasion I found myself talking about the boys with Braedabarker. I suggested that we tried as much as we could to keep them together, but he thought that this would only cause a long delay and complicate the process further. I had gone to ask him, there and then, what the likelihood was that Sally and I could adopt them both but I had managed to strangle the question before it could prejudice a later and more measured approach to the matter. What was wrong with me? Later I resolved to speak with Sally directly and urgently but backed off because it seemed so strange, so oddly irrational. And yet as we approached the end of the detention period all I could think of was Max. He had taken to haunting dark corners of the house, or appearing in crowds or on the opposite side of the street. However adept at disguise I knew instinctively it was Max. One evening, alone in the house with Sally away on yet another mysterious trip to London, the idea of adopting him insinuated itself so suddenly and sharply into my consciousness that I found myself holding the telephone and tracing out Braedabarker's number on the dial! My nerve failed me and I hung up. Later I tried to imagine Sally's reaction, anticipate her behaviour. *Could it be done?* Was it fair? Could we cope with children? And what about Jonathan? For two days I tried to broach the subject with Braedabarker, with my wife, even DeMarr, but on each occasion I failed. The dilemma consumed me, like an illness, to the extent that Sally actually asked me if I was alright.

'You look feverish, darling, you need to rest!' I had feigned some cold. On May 24th the laboratories in Oxford produced a final detailed genetic summary of Max and a last MRI scan of Jonathan. The rest of the children; normal, tagless, cured, left for home early that morning to avoid the press and to give them some well-earned privacy as they were reunited with their families. To Braedabarker's relief (and perhaps surprise) the breaking up of the pairs caused almost no fuss except a few tears and the exchanging of addresses and phone numbers. The bonds between the children had broken

broken down as mysteriously as the alien chromosomes.

As the other children left, Max and Jonathan remained in a now strangely silent, deserted ward with their faces pressed to the window, watching and chatting as the cars came and went. Meanwhile the committee went over their data which was exactly the same as that of the other children. The continuing presence of Jonathan's tag was confirmed but had ceased to be an issue of concern; it had atrophied slightly, and was barely visible even at high resolution. To my relief it was agreed that the boys should go as soon as adequate arrangements could be made. I had expected DeSilva to throw one last calculated tantrum but to my surprise he seemed now almost indifferent. He said he thought the monitoring was adequate but seemed bored suddenly with the whole adventure and anxious to leave. Dena Small told me later that he was going off to Australia to take up a Chair in Brisbane. The dispersal of the committee was oddly anticlimactic. We finished the session earlier than usual. I felt suddenly depressed and strangely anxious. Sally left promptly and rather secretively and DeMarr went off like a head boy to report directly to the Prime Minister. I did not relish the idea of being alone at home again so I lingered about the now deserted offices thinking about Max and how, and in what way, I could intervene to claim him. I talked to some of the technicians and some of the students who had worked on the preparation of the samples. They had been industrious throughout but somewhat over-awed, of DeMarr, who was generally good with students, but especially of DeSilva who was quite rude and patronising as he prowled about preoccupied with his metaphors of alien trickery. Eventually, as the support staff too drifted away, I found myself hanging about with Max and Jonathan at the end of the empty ward. They seemed cheerful enough. Max gave me a pebble he insisted I should keep. It was white and bean-shaped, quartz; probably picked up from the nearby garden. I said I would use it as a paperweight. Jonathan thought it would not be heavy enough. We then talked about telescopes, a subject that Jonathan seemed to know something about. He seemed a polite but oddly opinionated child.

Eventually, overjoyed by their company but afraid I was boring them, I said I had better go back to College and do some work. I ruffled up Max's hair as if he was a small dog. It was remarkably thick and corded, almost pelt like. He laughed; his grey-blue eyes remarkably bright. They seemed almost luminous. I looked closely; absentmindedly and for a moment I thought they flashed oddly, catching the light in a strange, fluorescent way like a cat. I was startled and Max frowned at my surprise. Puzzled by my attention he rolled his eyes about for me to look as if we were playing a game. I held his small face in my hands and examined them; the pupils, the lenses. There was something almost Native American about Max's face; the cheekbones, the line of the jaw, sleek, streamlined. The eyes appeared to be fine. I held his face gently as if it was something fragile and precious and Max then said 'Julian!' very precisely, as if he has been rehearsing it for a surprise. The name implied a question, a hint that he had sensed my unease.
'Max?'
'What do you see?'
I frowned, surprised by the question.
'Nothing, Max.'

I turned around and started the long walk to the top of the ward, past the nursing station, and towards the nest of offices but half way I heard the soft patter of bare feet and turned to look back, expecting – hoping – to see Max but instead I saw Jonathan.
'Hello! Do you want to come and see my office?' I

reached out my hand towards him.

'No, not really, thanks all the same.' He paused and then said suddenly and quickly in a whisper, 'You must keep Max safe!'

I felt a sudden chill at the nature and intensity of the boy's request. Jonathan took my hand suddenly as if he had proposed a deal. I was not a man then used to children and their sudden, touching immediacy. Taken aback I turned over Max's pebble in my jacket pocket. It was cold and smooth like a small egg.

'Of course we'll keep him safe!' I looked up to see Max watching us both carefully. 'You're very fond of Max, aren't you?'

Jonathan ignored the question. Instead, in a disconcertingly adult voice, he corrected me 'You must keep him safe, Julian.'

'Oh.' I felt something close to panic.

'I might not always be here –' Jonathan added. 'Max is very special. I might not always be able to look after him.'

I glanced about me, hoping to see one of the nurses, or Braedabarker, anyone. For a moment I felt almost incapable of doing or saying anything. Jonathan watched with me an air of mild pity.

'Jonathan, I'm not sure I understand. *Why* is Max special?'

Jonathan shook his head oddly as if I was being dense or missing the point. I then noticed that he was close to tears.

'Jonathan! What's the matter?' I clasped his small hand in mine. I knelt down so our faces were almost level. He looked at me with a sort of anger.

'Nothing is the matter. You have been given a *son*, Julian.'

A flash of very real fear struck my face and neck, a sense of intense danger. To a man who lived anchored to the mundane and rational it was not a sensation I was familiar with at all. Jonathan and I stared at each other. Questions and anxieties started in my head but ran aground or disintegrated before I could articulate them. In the end I nodded with as much authority as I could muster. Jonathan nodded back, rather curtly, let go of my hand gently like someone refusing to be saved, and ran back to his bed.

I went back to my office in a sort of trance and then, determined to act, started to dial Braedabarker's number but as I did so, I heard Dena Small and James DeSilva having an argument. It was coming from the direction of the stairwell as they walked towards my office and then suddenly it seemed to be happening right in front of me.

'Professor Grey! Are you aware of any protocols governing the conduct and dissemination of the committee's findings that I am unaware of?'

Their sudden appearance startled me and as such I only half heard Dena Small's question. I must have looked bewildered, pebble in hand, because she asked it again.

'Protocol?' It seemed an odd word, almost foreign. DeSilva stood in my office doorway putting on a light coat over his angular, narrow shoulders. I tried to look reasonably competent.

'I'm not sure I understand, Dena. We all received clear guidelines at the start of the committee and we all signed the Official Secrets Act. You and Braedabarker signed the American equivalent, of course, but much to the same effect. All the reports we make are classified for the time being. It is for the government to decide when to release them –'

'Or not, as the case may be,' added James. He was angry and glowering at the back of Dena's neck.

'Quite,' I said vaguely, a trace of irritation in my voice. I was still shocked by Jonathan's behavious, by his singular, blinding offer. Dena was looking at me and at the pebble, her dark attractive face animated with barely contained rage.

'What's all this about?' I asked, standing up.

DeSilva made a sort of hopeless shrug. 'Dr. Small has heard some conspiracy theory from one of the technicians that DeMarr is reporting to the government behind our backs, withholding information, and that this whole thing, your entire committee, is a cover up!' DeSilva evidently did not believe it. His voice was heavy with sarcasm and spite. Dena threatened to explode again. I pressed my lips together feeling bizarrely emotional, almost ill.

'Look, Dena there are no doubt *endless* committees working on this event. I mean it has been pretty unprecedented: the implications of what we have found are life changing. But look at the way we have been working together in the last few weeks? It would be almost impossible to exclude anyone from any important or relevant data. And why would anyone want to? We're already a secret committee! Once we reach a consensus, our daily briefings are sent to the British cabinet through its principle scientific advisor, who is of course Louis DeMarr – he reports our recommendations and –'

'I know that! Don't patronise me,' she said quietly, and then turning to glare at DeSilva she said suddenly, 'I know what I know, Julian!' at which she stalked out of the room without any further explanation. DeSilva, who had swung aside to let her past, sighed loudly and then laughed rather bitterly.

'Americans! She thinks DeMarr is running some sort of secret show! I mean, as if DeMarr could ever be discreet!' We watched in silence as the half glass half metal swing doors leading into the stairwell rocked slowly back into place.

'I think we could all do with a break!' I said not wanting to get drawn into a conversation with DeSilva, especially one at Dena's expense. Yet he hung about for a while, talking about the weather, the chances facing the Conservative Government; the *joys* of working with me. I struggled to be polite and finally he got the message and left. I leaned back in my chair and tried to relax but I was too upset.

I did not like DeSilva. Ever since the Japanese report he had been strangely intense and emotional; deliberately argumentative but also distressingly secretive. As for Dena, despite being vaguely off the wall on the subject of puzzles and quests and alien IQ tests, I liked her and admired her courage in the face of DeMarr's ceaseless bullying and my wife's glacial snobbery. And there was something about their argument that alarmed me. Perhaps I was still upset over Jonathan, over Max's odd show of affection, or was it worse than that: did I sense the implicit accuracy of Dena's allegations: that I was a cover to Louis? I leaned back in my chair and looked up at the strip lighting, cased in ugly plastic squares like egg crates. Dena's comments seemed like the final push at an opening door: in some subliminal way I had grown suspicious about DeMarr all by myself. Was Louis working with DeSilva behind my back? I scoffed at the idea and yet in truth I feared it. What was wrong with me! Why was I so insecure? I had heard it said that I was cold, mistrustful and *jealous* of DeMarr's genius. I had heard this a lot recently, especially after Louis was appointed co-chair to the chromosome 22 committee, and had I not in my heart taken this as a sign of my gradual decline, a public recognition that the pupil was soon to replace the tutor? *Was* I jealous? I seemed to sense the enormity of the accusation for the first time. A jealous, miserable man who resented the success of someone who had been his most able student, a friend of sorts?

This was not how I pictured it myself. Ever since he had been awarded his doctorate I had helped DeMarr, I had collaborated with him on a number of projects and I had helped him step up to his first academic Chair at Cambridge. I had even recommended his appointment to the government. In fact long after he had outgrown my patronage I had remained affectionate and courteous to him. I did not resent any of his achievements; although at times I found him slightly ridiculous, especially regarding his affectations, his curious obsession with foreignness, his pretensions about wealth and status, and sometimes I was suspicious where his wealth came from. I moved Max's pebble about in the palm of my hand, like a squeeze ball. What did Louis think of me? Did he value my friendship? Had he not been oddly distant of late, preoccupied, even impatient with me? I recalled again his long absences and his semi-private conversations with my wife, almost like arguments. I thought then of the conversation with Louis in the lift, the evening DeSilva had appeared alone in my office, sweaty and almost incoherent with rage. Louis had been somehow disingenuous, mentioning DeSilva's guilt before closing down the conversation as if he had made a mistake. And hadn't Louis been too quick in the denial of Lockwood's story that something had been found in the wood?

I sat still for a while, disturbed and to some extent angry and then suddenly I did something I had never done in my entire professional or personal life before: I searched through someone else's office. It was a relatively easy thing to do – since mine was next to DeMarr's, and we usually worked cheek by jowl with the whole team anyway. The place was by now completely empty, apart from the security staff who patrolled the rooms, but I knew a majority of them and they recognised me as the undisputed Chair of this infamous, secret committee –

was that what this was about? That Dena Small's comment had touched my conceit? God, was I really that jealous of DeMarr! I moped about the office. I was hesitant at first, distracted; in truth rather nervous. I worked my way across his desk and around the islands of half eaten cakes with a certain disdain. I saw nothing unusual: odd memos from me covered in DeMarr's intricate, rococo doodles, letters and reports side by side with piles of private correspondence, bills from book clubs, reservations for concerts, a credit card statement, a wine glass encrusted with dried claret. I was not even sure what I was looking for – something obviously sinister, a letter from the Prime Minister on M16 letter headed note paper, or the initials of some completely unknown agency. But there was nothing. I looked about the rest of the office. I looked furtively on several bookcases, embarrassed, in part now ashamed, and then, just as I was about to leave, I saw them.

The daily summaries of the children's chromosomes were reproduced by photographing the magnified images of stained and prepared cell nuclei. These were then enlarged and the prints went around to the committee members in yellow, reusable A3 envelopes marked 'internal' and, to my initial amusement, TOP SECRET. We had none of the complex, computer based paraphernalia for cell imaging, molecular modelling or enhancement that would come to dominate genetics from the late 1990s onwards. It was all pretty crude and time consuming to prepare. But it was effective. By the middle of May each child had accumulated a massive portfolio of such photographs along with countless karyographs and other mostly paper-based, hardcopy data. The photographic plates were all dated and numbered, firstly on the print itself, and then again by a blue memo attached to it which summarised the debate of the committee and all the observations and recommendations made. The print also reproduced a serial number on the bottom left corner which I presumed was from the film itself and relatively meaningless.

Since every committee member's office was overflowing with such envelopes and plates there was nothing odd or out of place in seeing such a pile on top of DeMarr's filing cabinet. Perhaps what caught my attention was the fact that, amid the unsorted and random scree of DeMarr's office, they were neatly piled up in chronological order and placed next to a large packing box. I walked over and started thumbing through them. Several had been additionally labelled with yellow stickers, the sort that my students used to deface and damage College library books, and identical to the ones that DeMarr had used to pass notes to Sally that afternoon. My curiosity aroused, I fished out my reading glasses and took a closer look.

DeMarr's stash of photographic plates consisted of Max's summaries only. On the top were the latest plates that had informed our discussion earlier that day. I looked through them and noticed immediately that there were several ones I had not seen. At first I assumed that they were duplicates, but squinting over them in the failing light I saw that the serial number on the print and the dates on the slip did not correspond. Moreover several had no blue memo slip attached to the front at all and some of the plates had been written on. I stood, frowning, and then with care not to cause an avalanche of filing I lifted up the whole lot and took them into my office. Sitting with my back to the door I slowly examined each print starting at the beginning, on the afternoon of March 21st. There were numerous plates that had no memo attached, and whose serial number and date implied that they were from a sequence of prints that had not been circulated to the committee. The ones marked with yellow stickers were of particular interest. They showed Max's genome from mid-April onwards, around the time that the alien chromosomes had started to atrophy. Feeling sick with excitement I stood up and took Max's prints over to a raised desk near the window and, angling a lamp above me, I scrutinised them all again through a block mounted lens.

From the 16th to the 21st of April, Max's karyograph showed the extra chromosomes breaking up and collapsing. On the 22nd however, fragments of alien chromatin appeared to have collided with, and attached themselves to human *chromosome 22*. On the 23rd these fragments were still there, like small dark buds, but increasingly integrated into the structure of 22 itself. By the 24th the absorption was complete with the dark buds just visible as black bandings along the human chromosome's long arm. This was in itself revelatory. The alien chromosomes had contaminated – and merged with – Max's genome. But there was something else equally disturbing. This entire sequence of events would have been almost invisible was it not for a particular staining deployed skilfully on every additional plate secretly produced from March 21st. I looked at photograph after photograph of Max's emerging uniqueness, breathless, my chest tight and airless. On the last plate produced and stained, someone had written in red pen 'replication asymptomatic?' and there was one word – written in a *different* hand – scrawled underneath this – 'incubate?'

I stood up and looked out of the window like a man who has seen a ghost. Who had devised and used the unusual staining without which the karyograph would have looked perfectly normal even to a trained observer? And why use the technique on plates taken *before* the alien chromosomes disintegrated, and before the Japanese report had arrived? With some effort I calmed myself. It was crucial that I understood what I was looking at. I turned around from the desk and took the precaution of locking my office door, and then I re-examined each plate again in turn. I then gathered the sheets and envelopes together, unlocked the door and went outside into the corridor and photocopied all of DeMarr's mysterious data before carefully returning everything to his office. Here I looked briefly through DeMarr's data sets of the other children. Again, numerous plates had been prepared but not circulated and all with the tell tale staining technique, but unlike Max's, the plates merely confirmed what the committee had seen anyway, that by the middle of April the alien chromosomes had gone and the children's human genome was free of contamination.

I rubbed my chin thoughtfully and prowled back to stand in the doorway of DeMarr's office. What did this mean? Firstly that Dena was right and that DeMarr was withholding information from some – most – members of the committee, including its chair. Secondly, and more seriously, that Max was *different* from the other children. Max was, to use Jonathan's word – special. I leaned against the doorframe and closed my eyes. I breathed evenly and deeply and tried to think. Patterns. What were the patterns here? By either accident or design, material from the now defunct alien chromosomes had attached themselves to part of his genome – in this case, chromosome 22. This process itself had been meticulously observed. The evidence showed clearly that genetic information had integrated itself from alien to human in such a way that they did not physically alter or enlarge chromosome 22. And chromosome 22 was of course the one that myself and DeMarr had been working on for the Human Genome Project *before the abductions had taken place*. A strange, astounding coincidence? I recalled my conversation with DeMarr about failure and experimentation.

Twenty-four children taken, 24 attempts to modify a genome. Jonathan appeared to be a mistake, some inexplicable anomaly. Twenty-four attempts and one success?

I contemplated further searches, even accessing his computer, expanding my interests to the rumour that something had been retrieved from the wood, something alien, some artefact or a device that might well be linked to the abductions. It seemed self-evident to me now that it existed and that DeMarr knew about it. Was there a *conspiracy* here? The word was shocking, almost absurd. And how was this linked to Jonathan's simple almost understated offer of fatherhood? Suddenly DeMarr's phone rang in front of me, loud and insistent. I literally jumped back, startled. For a moment I stood looking at it and then on impulse I picked it up. It was Sally.

'There you are!' She didn't sound in the least surprised to find me in someone else's office, or answering someone else's phone.

'I've just called you at home – I've been trying since 6 o'clock! What in God's name are you still doing at work!'

'I was bored –' I said, my heart somewhere in my throat. I was not a convincing liar and thought I sounded breathless and hysterical.

'Are you alright, darling?'

'I'm fine – I was just about to leave – DeMarr isn't here, I think he's with the great and the good again.' I tried to sound nonchalant but all I could hear was my blood surging in my ears.

'That's ok, I didn't want to speak with him. I was worried where you were! I'm in London but I am coming home tomorrow and I thought we could go off for a break somewhere, somewhere exotic?'

'Oh – really – a holiday?'

'*Yes* darling, you know treat ourselves. Go somewhere other than Wales!' and then she hung up.

Why she had not rung my phone struck me as odd but not unusual. Sally had often phoned in at random places to speak with me; restaurants, once at the issue desk of the Bodleian, but tonight her habit merely compounded my panic. With some effort I returned to my office, placed the photocopies into my briefcase and then walked through the Radcliffe preoccupied and oddly frightened.

Back home I was hyperactive and edgy. Once in the hallway I picked up the telephone and dialled an automated service that told me the telephone number of the last person to call the line. It was a recent innovation that I was much taken with and it appeared to be free. A robotic female voice spat out a series of digits. The last call had been just after midday from an Oxford area code. If Sally was indeed in London, she had not tried to contact me here at all. Sally was usually a consummate liar. Her ability to lie (and her memory that she had lied and therefore needed to keep lying) never ceased to astound me. It seemed a stupid error for her to have made. I tried to relax and acquire some sort of rational perspective on the day's events, but every time I closed my eyes I saw a strange collage of Max and Jonathan, of Jonathan especially, close to tears from his prophetic comment, and then piles of Max's karyographs in DeMarr's office, stained and revelatory. Brilliant though he was, DeMarr could not have done this work alone. Someone must have helped him. Dena said she had heard about secret evidence from one of the technicians, presumably the one who had helped prepare the slides? And DeSilva? DeSilva *had* to be involved given the fact that Max's 22 revealed exactly the sort of proof he needed to establish his alien body snatching thesis: but there lay another mystery. Had he seen the evidence of the changes to Max's chromosome, James would surely never have agreed to release Max. He had played up enough about infection and recoding even without hard evidence. Braedabarker was hardly qualified, nor was Dena, and she had been the one to blow DeMarr's cover.

There was, of course, Sally. The thought, the mere suggestion was madness. I went into the kitchen and fussed over a bottle of claret, my mind elsewhere and then meandered back upstairs in a sort of stupor. In my study there was a photo of my wife, dutifully framed and pristinely placed near the telephone. It had been taken after she had been awarded her Chair at the University of London. She was standing up against her office window holding out a photo of me in a sort of parody of the gravedigger in Hamlet, with my portrait as a substitute for a skull. Later Sally had written 'the professors grey!' across the bottom, half a joke, and half a competitive stab at me. I picked it up and looked at it carefully. *Professor and Professor Grey* had become a sort of institutional joke; it had led to endless confusion and misunderstandings at conference dinners and in the press. I had started to smile to myself thinking it impossible that Sally could do something so inexcusably deceitful until I suddenly seemed to recognise the handwriting across the photo in DeMarr's office for the first time. The word 'incubate', written on Max's final plate, had not been written by DeSilva at all but by my wife.

This revelation was far more of a surprise than it should have been but, standing by my desk with an opened bottle of 1979 *Chateau Tassin* in one hand and Sally's photo in the other, I had felt a sense of deep, insensible shock almost like a blow. Only as I sat down slowly and gingerly did the absurd fact make any sense to me: the odd behaviour of my wife, her endless trips to London, and her intimacies with DeMarr. The fact that the secret work had been carried out in front of me, even during the committee sessions itself, merely added a degree of authenticity to the discovery. It was typical of DeMarr's brazen skills at deception and his contempt for my naivety! DeMarr had seen no reason to hide anything! But *why* Sally? Why had Louis not gone to DeSilva, the only other virologist on the committee? Sally was a competent cellular biologist, but not really a geneticist or had Louis been aiming at some deep personal blow? I closed my eyes and tried to reassert some order to what I now knew. Perhaps DeSilva was involved as well and more discreet. His argument with Dena a sham? Surely only he could have devised the staining or understood what it revealed? I poured myself a glass of deep, mellowed claret. Its aroma filled the room. Was I the only other person to not know, besides Dena? I tried to see the irony of a secret committee only notionally under my control but failed rather bleakly. I spread the photocopies of Max's karyographs out across the broad, mock-antique desk top in front of me and listlessly picked up the one with the word 'incubate' written on it: there was no doubt now – it was so obviously Sally's handwriting that I was amazed I had not recognised it immediately. But incubate what?

With sudden decision, and despite the lateness of the hour, I picked up the phone and called Dena Small's hotel. She had been staying in central Oxford not far from Broad Street. A receptionist answered, a strong, angular accent, probably South African. When I asked for Dena he said he thought that she had already left for Heathrow.

'Bugger!'

'Excuse me, sir?'

'I'm sorry –' I left a message asking Dena to call me urgently at home if somehow, miraculously, she was still packing. When I gave my name there was a hint of recognition in the receptionist's voice, a heightened octave. I sighed briefly, put the phone down and looked back at Max spread out in front of me. Everything there was to Max was here, blue prints for his entire bio-chemical, molecular, cellular and physiological existence; the mechanical schematics to build a highly evolved, sentient being. But was there something else here that I couldn't recognise? Something alien, demonic, something insinuated so deep into the boy that it could not yet be observed? Was it possible? On the desk in front of me was Max's pebble. I picked it up almost like a talisman. Was this change to Max something his mother had sensed almost immediately?

The phone rang. It was Dena sounding breathless and with a lot of noise in the background.

'Julian? What's up? I'm just on my way to the airport –'

'Dena, about your argument with DeSilva –'

She went to apologise but I spoke over her, 'Dena I need to see you urgently. Perhaps I could drive you to the airport myself – Heathrow?' I sensed her alarm. There was a pause.

'Sure – but we need to leave right away.' I looked at my half empty glass, frowned, and said I would meet her in fifteen minutes. When I arrived near George Street she was standing on the edge of the pavement with a surprisingly small suitcase and a holdall. It was starting to drizzle, the first rain I could recall in ages. I got out of the car, helped stow her luggage away in the boot, and then opened the door for her. I felt oddly illicit as if I were having an affair.

'I am sorry about earlier, Julian. It was very

unprofessional, I guess I was dog tired.'

'I rather think you were right actually.' A car horn blared behind me as I pulled out myopically without a signal. I made a contrite gesture to the driver in my mirror and then headed towards the ring road. Dena seemed stunned by the news.

'Excuse me?' she said eventually.

'DeMarr and my wife have been carrying out a series of investigations on their own, probably involving DeSilva although I can't be sure.'

Her wide eyes were white in the gloom.

'Shit! What about Braedabarker?'

'No, I don't think so. I suspect that he isn't of much direct use to them.'

'What sort of investigations?' It was raining heavily now, pounding on the windscreen. The wipers squeaked on the down stroke and then juddered slightly back up across the glass.

'One of the children is different.'

'*Different?* Which child?'

'Max. Max Lennox. It would seem that one of his human chromosomal pairs took on and retained some alien DNA. Moreover someone anticipated it happening and spent a great deal of time looking for it. They used a novel staining method quite new to me. Whoever it was had clearly been monitoring all the children as soon as they arrived, but after mid-April they concentrated just on Max.'

'From the beginning? You mean from mid-March?' echoed Dena and then she said with remarkably hostility. 'I *fucking* knew it! DeMarr is one sneaky son of a bitch. Sorry, I know he's a friend of yours, but really!'

'Evidently not as good a friend as I may have thought!' I had never heard Dena swear before. She half smiled. She leaned back and then whispered

'But I wouldn't be too sure about DeSilva's involvement, Julian.'

'Why do you say that? Isn't this data exactly what he would need to prove his "children as hosts" theory?'

'Exactly! But then he lets Max go to swan off to Australia? Come on! Besides, there was something about the way he teased me when I told him about DeMarr running the conspiracy, something that was too genuine! He clearly thinks DeMarr is too stupid to trick him!' Dena then looked across at me. '*Your wife?*'

I made a small affirmative movement with my head and we drove in silence for quite a while. At one stage I did feel a curious urge to tell the long and rather pathetic story of my married life to a relative stranger, or to confess that like James I had always seen DeMarr as a sort of joke, clever but oddly incompetent. In the end I said simply, 'It's complicated.'

'It sure is! So how far do you think this goes?'

'What?'

'The conspiracy? Who is DeMarr reporting this to?'

I had no idea. I was still appalled by it all, almost in a sense of shock.

'He may be submitting this to the government along with the official committee reports – but he might well be keeping the data for himself and Sally, hiding it?' I hadn't even thought about it properly. Dena looked slightly incredulous at my theory.

'Why would Sally and DeMarr want to keep it to themselves?'

We were seeing frequent signs to Heathrow now, large blue panels illuminated by bright up-lighting hazed with heavy rain. Dena asked me about the staining technique. It took rather a long time to explain and the more I said the scarier it all seemed to become; the precision, the clear purposefulness of it. When I'd finished Dena was as alarmed and as excited as I was. I turned off the motorway and drove through the curiously abandoned expanse of Heathrow itself, warehouses, wire fencing, wide empty roads.

'Do you have any idea what the stain was targeting?' Dena asked. It was a perceptive comment for a non-biologist to make.

'I suspect it was designed to identify the three amino acid bases found in the alien DNA molecule. As soon as the alien chromatin hit Max's 22, it would appear that these substituted themselves for their terrestrial base equivalents and the staining revealed it all, step by step.'

We splashed to a halt alongside a row of taxis.

'But wait a minute Jules, if the dates add up you're saying that someone knew about the three unique base sequences on the alien DNA before the committee got the report from Japan? I don't understand?'

'Neither do I but the evidence points to that.'

'Then it has to be DeSilva! I mean, look at his behaviour that night! He clearly *knew* something.'

I nodded, in part relieved to hear Dena confirm my own views, but they made the logic and membership of the conspiracy nonsensical.

'Dena, what was the name of the technician who told you about DeMarr and his secret investigation, the one that led you to have your argument with James? I need to know.'

'Ok, sure, of course but please –' she seemed to hesitate, doubtful. 'Be careful. She told me in confidence. She's a smart cookie, her name is Margaret Relph, a doctoral student of DeMarr's I think, or was. I don't want to get her into trouble!' The name seemed dimly familiar and I vaguely recalled an attractive, rather silent woman in her early to mid-thirties, multi-tasking about the labs.

'I will be very discreet. And Dena, you be careful as well.' Moments later we were standing outside the car assembling her luggage on the wet gleaming tarmac.

'So what are you going to do?' Dena asked me.

'Well I guess I'll keep a close eye on Louis.'

'And Max?'

I closed my eyes tightly, my face wet with rain. I felt her touch my arm.

'Email me and let me know what we should do, Jules? If there is anything I can do just email.'

'Email?'

She looked at me in surprise. 'Yeah? Oh I forgot you guys here aren't wired up yet!' She laughed and turned to make the quick dash towards the covered concourse but then paused.

'Don't you think it's odd that DeMarr left the plates in his office, so casually? I mean – on top of a cabinet?'

'Perhaps – but then I think DeMarr is so contemptuous of me that it never really occurred to him that he would be found out!' I sounded bitter but Dena rolled her eyes in tacit agreement.

'He is a real bastard, Julian, watch your back with that one! You think he's all stupid and funny but he doesn't miss a god damn trick. He always gave me the creeps, much more than DeSilva to be honest. James looks nuts but Louis, he looks all kind and reasonable!' We shook hands again and I watched her vanish in a press of dark, anonymous people at the entrance to Terminal Four.

The realisation that this was probably a widespread conspiracy disturbed me deeply. I felt out of my depth, clueless as to how to proceed and who to tell. Of course the idea itself was not absurd: children had been abducted by aliens and they had been genetically modified - this was exactly the sort of place you would expect to find a conspiracy. But one involving DeMarr, my wife and excluding the only man who seemed to have an account of what was happening and the skill required to detect it? Under what circumstances would DeSilva have allowed Max to be released knowing what I, DeMarr and my wife all knew – that Max was now 'infected' or modified? Driving home alone I could only think of two hypotheses – that he genuinely didn't know what was afoot, or that he knew full well and Max's release was somehow, inexplicably, part of his plan.

When I arrived at Farndon Road there were several messages on the answerphone. Two from Sally who seemed unusually worried as to my whereabouts and one from DeMarr. He was full of himself, thanking me for my hard work and assuring me that I would get a 'gong' from the government for all my assistance. 'A knighthood! Think of it! Sir Julian! A life peerage? *Call me!*' Despite my anger I could not help smiling at the tone of his voice, the sheer size of his character but Dena had been right about that: it was in part a disguise, a mask to hide his abilities and his ruthlessness. I resumed my claret and although tired, I scrutinised the photocopies of Max's genetic summaries again. I put on some music, a Schumann piano sonata and stared morosely at the pictures as if they depicted an abstract crime, which of course in some sense they did. Eventually I swept them all safely into a lockable drawer along with Daniel Lockwood's letter. I sat down and eventually fell asleep, Wyndham's edgy tale of alien pregnancies flat and unopened against my chest and I dreamt of Max in the company of wolf-lizards, their form indistinct and peripheral in the singular presence of my son.

I was awoken by Sally who in the clear light of *late* morning was looking at the empty wine bottle on my desk in a sort of studied outrage. My eyes rapidly came into focus. For a moment I was afraid I had left out other more incriminating material for her to see but the desk top was thankfully clear.

'Is that one of the *Tassin 79s*?' She shook the bottle in front of my face. 'Please don't tell me you drank it with a microwaved meal!'

'I drank it entirely on its own.'

'God, Jules – we have *plonk* for that! You look dreadful.

I hope you haven't been doing this sort of thing often!'

'No, but perhaps I should. I rather enjoyed it and it's probably good for me!' She seemed in a good mood despite her irritation. Without warning, before I could even think it through and freeze myself into indecision, I stood up and said, 'Sally I want to adopt Max, and possibly Jonathan as well.' I felt nervous and sick. At first I wasn't sure she had heard me or that I had actually said it. She stood holding the bottle pretending to read the label. It was only when she looked up that I saw she had registered the question. Her face looked suspicious, tight around the mouth but there was another expression – a sort of sadness – that I had not seen before. She didn't say anything for a while but walked to the window which looked out over the road. When she turned back to talk to me, the light caught her face, the cheek, the curve of hair. She looked astoundingly beautiful but cold, her face utterly devoid of sentiment.

'How long have you been thinking about this?' she asked quietly. Her right hand played with a simple string of pearls around her neck, bunching them and then releasing them, a tell tale sign of contemplation or worry.

'I'm not sure – since Mrs Lennox called you here that night saying she couldn't take Max back? Since I saw you with Max that first day at the John Radcliffe?' I looked down at the desk thinking furiously. Since my dream? Since Jonathan told me I had a son? Sally stared back through the window, inscrutable still, perhaps troubled, but I was staggered to see that she was actually thinking about it.

'Sally I really want this! I have really wanted it for a long, long time!'

She turned to me quickly, her eyes narrowed.

'I know you have, and surprisingly, Julian, so have I but I simply wasn't prepared to pay the disproportionate price for it!' Her voice then softened, 'Now, however, now I'm not so sure – and perhaps, perhaps this is different.' She turned and sat down behind my desk, leaning back, scrutinising the ceiling.

'Would it surprise you to know that I have been thinking about it too – not so much Jonathan, but about Max? Especially since his mother went AWOL, it seemed the obvious thing to do.' She frowned and then looked directly at me. 'But can we cope? Is this the right thing for the boys? I mean, aren't we too old, too taken up in our careers? And aren't the circumstances too unusual?'

'At the moment I can't think of anything better for them. And we can cope now. Max is nearly six, it's not like we've got to get up at 4 a.m. and feed him. And Jonathan –'

'Darling, we couldn't deal with them both! Jonathan is too old. Seriously, I know you want to keep them together – but –' I though the statement oddly prescient and I felt myself tense slightly.

'They do seem to have taken to each other.'

'That's not reason enough to burden ourselves with two children, Jules! Jonathan is nearly nine. It's a difficult age as it is, let alone in the context of a new family and new surroundings!' She sounded adamant. I sat strumming my fingers on the desk, unsure whether to push for Jonathan or simply take what I had with Max. Sally then said 'And I'm not even sure that keeping them together is a good idea anyway. Perhaps we can arrange to keep Jonathan close by? Braedabarker said someone over in Witney was interested.' We paused, both still looking at each other.

'Then you agree to Max's adoption?' I asked eventually. She nodded, slowly at first, and then slightly more definitively.

'Yes. But –' she closed her eyes, 'Isn't this a bit impetuous? Perhaps we should think about it, talk to someone –'

'I think we've both thought about it enough. I'll call

Braedabarker!' My joy was momentarily overwhelming, it flooded through my chest and face with sudden heat. 'I wonder what DeMarr will think?'

Chapter 6

I had imagined, given my position and the circumstances surrounding Max, that the process of adoption would prove easy and straight forward. It did not, and despite Braedabarker's enthusiastic support and my reassurances to the government that we could protect his identity, it was well into July before we finally brought Max home. June was dominated by endless meetings, lengthy familiarisations between Max, Sally and myself, and then exhaustive form filling and lengthy interviews with regiments of social workers. Sally often joked that we were in fact being head hunted for some senior UN position! During this bewildering time I tried to balance my own complex reactions to having a child in our lives while managing the aftermath of the formal investigations and my own furtive attempts to find out what DeMarr and my wife had been up to.

I was not then the specialist in deception that I later became and I was careful not to change my behaviour towards DeMarr, who appeared to have become a fixture in Oxford, in my house, even in my college. Everywhere I turned, Louis was there, usually wearing some absurd outfit and suddenly much taken to wearing hats. Oddly he had not been particularly enthusiastic about Max joining us at Farndon Road and seemed strangely suspicious that Sally had suggested it first. On several occasions he tried quite hard to get me to talk her out of it on the grounds that it was mysteriously inappropriate, as if Max was a dog and she was simply infatuated and not prepared for the hard work once he started growing and damaging the furniture. I thought this very strange but put it down to a sort of double bluff. DeMarr spent a lot of time with Max, playing and remonstrating with the boy and many years later I found out that while Sally and I sought to convince the state that we knew how to look after Max, feed him properly and not leave him in an empty house on a chain, DeMarr had actually trekked off to Glasgow to see Mrs Lennox on some strange mission of his own.

And I continued to watch my wife closely to see how and why she was involved with Louis and the mysterious chromosome. That was by far the hardest part. I resisted the endless temptations to nose about her office at home or go through her files, although once I did take the opportunity of going through her diary. It was a disappointing trawl through a busy, dreary professionalism with no hint of anything out of place. I put it aside conscious that Sally seemingly had little time to devote to raising a child let alone take part in some deep-seated conspiracy. It also occurred to me that, given her commitments, it was no surprise that I saw so little of her. I considered the possibility that she was somehow DeMarr's unwitting accomplice, tricked somehow into aiding and abetting Louis' plans, but Sally was too powerful, too strong for such a foil and she had power over Louis somehow, I had seen it demonstrated often, a sort of implicit authority.

As for the formal investigation over the abductions, once the government accepted the committee's last report, the tissue samples from the children along with the entire data archives produced at the Radcliffe were boxed up under the Official Secrets Act and buried in a series of vaults at the Institute of Molecular Biology, close to Keble College at the front of the University Park. Settling on the location had prompted one of those obscure turf wars so common in government, with Louis pressing for Cambridge and the Americans apparently suggesting somewhere in California. It was therefore no mean victory to get it located in what was effectively my own backyard. Yet a brief foray through the files revealed that all the additional stained plates prepared for Max, and any references to any interest in chromosome 22, had vanished without trace. I also discovered that all copies of the Japanese report on the alien DNA sequences had gone as well although revealingly the transcripts and the minutes of the relevant committee discussion on its findings were still there, a curious oversight. Luckily by sheer coincidence I had managed to lose my own copy of the report before they were shredded and some months later it turned up in the boot of my car under some gardening sacks.

Research continued into the alien material of course, some under my direction, some under DeMarr's but it was not encouraging. We were more generous to foreigners as well at this stage, especially the South Koreans who had recently made some significant breakthroughs in cloning, but nothing came to light and it was clear that the Americans were not fully cooperating even then. We knew that the five chromosomal pairings were part of a bigger genome but there seemed no residual clues as to what or how to find it. The interest in the cancer cure continued for a while, but that, too, appeared to bog down in failure. Gradually and with a certain reluctance Louis and I drifted back into the graft of mapping Chromosome 22 for the Genome Project, and in hassling the government for funding and facilities. Slowly and surely like some sort of collective hallucination the whole strange event of the abductions faded from the public consciousness, growing rapidly into some sort of urban myth, supported and sustained by the sudden explosion of the internet and the infrequent accusation of a cover-up. I often speculated that instead of finding answers, the committee had merely unearthed endless questions, strung out one after the other and then, the crisis seemingly over, the first contact botched, we had turned away and ignored them.

I had more luck with Margaret Relph however, the technician involved in preparing the extra karyographs, the one who had alerted Dena to the odd goings on around Louis DeMarr. While she had been one of his graduate students, Ms Relph had suspended her studies for a year and then, in 1991 withdrawn from research altogether to spend time with her young family; a girl called Katherine and a boy called Jamie. She had impressed DeMarr, starting her doctoral thesis at the relatively advanced age of 28 and he had clearly been put out when she abandoned him for a life of domesticity. DeMarr told me this himself. I had been incautious enough to insinuate her name into a late night conversation not long after Dena's departure, but DeMarr had been quite forthcoming in his cups and seemingly unguarded in his information. By another curious twist, it turned out that her husband worked as a printer at the Clarendon Press building in Oxford and that they now lived on Walton Street, literally just around the corner from Farndon Road.

In the wake of the abductions, and when it was clear that we would have to assemble a team of technicians who were competent and discreet, DeMarr had remembered her immediately and approached her for the job. He had been overjoyed when she had accepted and bitterly disappointed when she had left without question once the work had been completed. Clearly he had hoped to lure her back into his own private research. It later occurred to me that DeMarr might well have been physically attracted to Margaret and that on subsequently overplaying the part of 'caring patron' he had alarmed her to the point of breaking his trust. Or perhaps what she had seen on the secret plates had genuinely alarmed her? It was hard to guess. With some difficulty I persuaded Margaret to meet me in college on the pretence of offering her some part-time work.

I was not surprised to see why DeMarr had been so infatuated. She was an attractive, tall, slightly Nordic looking woman, neatly dressed and with considerable, no nonsense charm. She brought the children with her to college for our interview, something that surprised me at the time, and they sat playing quietly by themselves while we talked about the committee, the abductions, and indeed eventually – as I had not intended – about Max himself. I was deeply impressed by her acumen. It had been evident to her from the onset what the real purpose of the meeting was, and she allowed me to talk about funding and research and her own interests until she finally put a stop to my ramblings over a fictional job.

'Professor Grey, please don't think me rude or tactless, but I presume that this is about Dena Small and her conspiracy theory?'

'*Her* theory?' I had been watching Jamie playing, his blond almost white hair luminous in a patch of sunlight. He seemed to be about the same age as Max, remarkably contemplative, self-contained.

'Well, yes. I'm sorry if she told you what I said about DeMarr – I know you are close to him. But I objected to the way he had evidently lied to me – it was outrageous!' Her eyes flashed and she drained her teacup with particular resolution. I confessed to the real reason why she was here and then I further confessed that I was extremely sketchy on the details of the argument. She seemed sceptical of my ignorance.

'Has someone complained?' she asked, sounding momentarily anxious. When I reassured her that I was merely asking for her assistance in clearing up what had happened she related to me an intriguing story of misunderstanding and chance.

Unaware that DeMarr's instructions to her were not from me, and convinced that her data was going to the committee as a whole, she had approached James and Dena on the afternoon in question curious to see what the general views were on the latest plates, above all the ones that confirmed the unusual nature of Max's 22. Margaret had the advantage of having met DeSilva at several conferences while setting out her initial research. She already knew Dena Small well, and unlike the other technicians was not intimidated by DeSilva's rudeness. She was surprised however to find that DeSilva had no idea what she was talking about and in the awkwardness that followed, Dena had asked a series of questions that revealed the extent to which DeMarr had been working with and directing the technicians on his own. Margaret paused on her story at this stage and poured herself some more tea.

'So you never actually mentioned that DeMarr was working for a secret committee?' I asked eventually.

'No, it was Dr Small who mentioned that. Dena had taken a dislike to both James and Louis DeMarr and to what she believed was a cult of secrecy around the children. She clearly thought they were working together behind her back, but I knew straight away that DeSilva was genuinely clueless. I managed somehow to dig myself out of the hole, saying I'd clearly been mistaken but I was furious with Louis! What had he been playing at! DeSilva let it go but Dena came back to me later on, just as I was leaving and demanded to know what I had been working on for DeMarr. She was extremely angry.'

'What did you tell her?' I recalled Dena's anger vividly.

Margaret winced slightly. 'I said I thought DeMarr was a sneak, evidently up to something, getting extra plates made up and asking us to work overtime, whether the committee knew about it or not.'

'Did you tell her what the plates revealed about Max?'

'No, I didn't. I'm not sure why either, but I did agree with her that DeMarr was probably working for someone against you, I mean –' she hesitated, 'I've heard stories about you two.' She looked down self-consciously at her cup.

'Yes, quite. How did your conversation with Dena end?'

'Well enough. Dena told me to be careful but said I could always speak with her or you if necessary.' She looked at me rather pointedly.

'Did you mention a protocol of some kind to Dr Small?' I asked suddenly. Margaret frowned and seemed seriously puzzled.

'Well, yes. The one we all signed up to.' Her eyes narrowed. 'I'm not sure I understand?'

'What did this protocol say exactly?'

Margaret sat perfectly still but it was clear that she was thinking furiously about something.

'Professor Grey I'm not sure I appreciate being blindsided like this! It was the same protocol we all signed, all the technicians. You must have seen it? It was authorised by you.'

'Indulge me, Ms Relph, just for a moment! Please. This isn't a trick.'

She looked at me doubtfully before answering but then answered all the same.

'It was a protocol about viral research, asking us to be careful and observe the usual safeguards. It stressed the need to be attentive to the possibility of retroviral activity in the cell nuclei and in the human chromosomes of the children. It also contained a schematic of a helic molecule. DeSilva circulated it, although it was signed by you!'

'When was this?'

'When the first pair of children was found, around March 14th? I can't remember exactly.'

I disguised my surprise. Could I have signed something by error, in the rush of business? Yet I had no doubt that the schematic attached to the protocol was a representation of the alien DNA, the three base sequences *yet* to be analysed by the Japanese. I stood up and walked over to the large mullioned windows that looked down over the lower quad. Outside was a peerless summer day, a white blue arch of sky and butter sandstone walls glowing in the heat. Swifts screamed and dived overhead.

'Ms Relph –'

'I prefer being called Margaret.'

'Margaret I am not sure quite how to say this – but it would appear that DeMarr *was* acting on his own and working without *my* knowledge.' I half turned to see her looking at me as if this was some sort of joke. 'And this protocol is quite new to me. The only 'protocol' I signed concerned itself about confidentiality and secrecy over the disclosure of the committee's findings.' There was a prolonged silence. I could see Margaret mentally regrouping, gathering her wits about her. The children, sensing something was amiss, had stopped reading and were looking at their mother for some sign of reassurance.

'So there was – is – a conspiracy?' she suggested eventually.

'It would appear so. Of course DeMarr could not have been acting entirely alone, and I have some evidence that he was consulting someone else on the committee.' I said evasively. There was no need to mention Sally. It was complex enough. I saw her frown questioningly and then she asked 'Is, is this an investigation?' Her voice had changed. It was more cautious now and reserved.

'Well, yes and no. I'm just trying to find out what has been going on. It's not official if that's what you mean and I'd rather we keep this matter between us.'

'Of course,' she seemed relieved. 'Should I get a lawyer?'

I laughed, shaking my head and walked away from the window down a long line of bookcases, my shoes squeaking and eventually sat at my desk. Margaret was attentive but drawn in on herself now, her hands folded neatly on her lap, her steel grey-blue eyes fixed on me.

'No, no. No need for that. Can I ask you about the staining technique? Who devised it?'

'I did.'

I looked startled and she laughed. 'I can cook as well! It wasn't that hard! Once I knew what I was looking for!'

'The DNA?'

'Yes. The specific base sequences.'

Margaret would not have seen the Japanese report and probably, given her level of clearance, still hadn't.

'Didn't they strike you as odd, Margaret, I mean, unusual?'

She looked puzzled, and there was a trace of irritation about her eyes and mouth that I found oddly appealing.

'I was employed as a technician, not a bio-chemist. I just did my job.'

I nodded apologetically. There was no reason why she should have noticed the amino acids as unique or even as alien in the first instance. I leaned away, back into my chair.

'And when did DeMarr first notice Max's anomaly, Margaret? Immediately? Around the 22nd April?'

'He didn't notice anything.' She coloured slightly. 'I'm afraid I did. Around the 16th of April I noticed that there were some peculiarities in the DNA transcription and recombination process of Max's normal human genome, something that suggested that new proteins were being manufactured; that something was changing. Do you have the plates on you?'

'I have photocopies – yes.' I stood up somewhat stiffly, found my briefcase and rummaged through it carefully. 'I'm afraid they're poorly done – I was in rather a hurry.'

'You don't have the original photographs?' Again there was an edge to her voice.

'They've been removed.' I said, spreading the photocopies out across my already cluttered desk. I had not intended to sound dramatic but her face registered a further look of unease.

Margaret walked over and leaning down beside me started to pick up one sheet after another. I caught the scent of a subtle, sophisticated perfume as I watched her scrutinise the papers. She paused on Max's.

'Here – this is Max on the 16th of April. This was the first time that I noticed the protein changes, and here – the 22nd – this is when I discovered that material from the alien chromatin had attached itself to his genome. The stain was designed to pick up the bases in minute traces, and here – look – by the 24th they are already present throughout his 22, especially concentrated on the long arm,' she pointed rather forcibly. 'You see it?'

'Do you know how this process worked?' I was straining my eyes at a grey black smudge.

'No, not really. I'm a technician remember! I suspect that the base sequences DeMarr was looking for somehow 'unzipped' during the collapse of the alien chromatin and migrated to Max's 22. I didn't get time to examine the RNA data.'

I started walking about my desk again. 'A virus?' I used the word cautiously.

'No. No way. Look at the evidence. It's a systematic substitution base for base. There is nothing random here. It's an act of translation.'

'Translation?'

'Yes. A rough equivalence of one code for another but controlled, precise.'

'Quite.' I glanced down at the quad again and watched a clutch of dons talking near the Observatory building. I found the simile distressing. 'A message in a bottle perhaps!'

'Excuse me?'

'Nothing, sorry. But why chromosome 22? Why deliberately target one of the smallest chromosomal pairings in the human genome? Why not the sex chromosomes? Or why not a number of chromosomes? And is this what the experiment was designed to do?' It looked so random, so accidental.

'I have no idea, Julian,' her use of my first name rather startled me. 'I mean presumably that's what DeMarr is finding out? And –' her voice sounded uncertain for a moment, 'and you of course. Aren't you still both involved in mapping 22 for the Genome Project?' The coincidence seemed to strike her for the first time. 'Hmm. That is odd!'

I laughed at the understatement, a disconcertingly contemptuous noise, and then sat down heavily in my chair.

'We seem to be less involved with each other's work than I had previously assumed!' I tried to smile but sounded pompous; upset. Margaret was looking at me intently.

'Have you confronted DeMarr with the fact that you

found the plates, Julian? Does he know you know?'

'No and I don't intend to just yet. I want to see where he goes with it. You see I am not entirely convinced that this is a conspiracy as such, more rather to do with DeMarr's sense of mission and drive, something he might have been working on for some time, something private?'

She frowned, smiling slowly. 'So the rumours are true then, you do hate each other?'

'I wouldn't put it quite like that!'

Margaret looked at me sceptically. 'I wouldn't trust DeMarr, not an inch and I should know! But even if he is trying to startle the world with a breakthrough and win a Nobel Prize he's taking a terrible risk doing it alone and he would need huge resources. I can't believe he would be that ruthless and even he doesn't have that much money. No, I'm afraid I have to favour Dena's conspiracy theory. Surely you must as well! Remember I devised a staining technique for amino acids already identified, not by DeMarr but by James DeSilva.'

I sat with my hands pressed together as if in prayer and then it was obvious to me, a sudden click of perception.

'In fact Margaret there are two conspiracies going on here!'

'I don't understand?'

I felt a sudden intense wave of anger and upset all over again.

'The DNA directive protocol came from DeSilva. Obviously he knew the alien DNA before the Japanese confirmed it. DeMarr didn't. But DeMarr signed the protocol, briefed you and with your genius managed to isolate the alien DNA base sequences on Max's 22 without DeSilva ever finding out or suspecting.'

I glanced up at the young woman expecting her to be incredulous or cynical but I could see that, however shocked, she was already in broad agreement.

'That figures' she said quietly. 'I heard rumours that

DeSilva wanted the kids locked up forever. It did always mystify me as to why, having seen the evidence, the committee agreed so readily to release the children, especially Max: but of course they didn't see it! Especially DeSilva. Do you have any idea how DeSilva was as familiar with the alien DNA as to know the actual base sequences?'

I closed my eyes. 'Not exactly, but I can guess. This is not the first alien experiment he has encountered. Clearly what has been done here has been *tried before*.'

She sighed loudly, clearly overwhelmed by the whole discussion. 'This is just unbelievable! Actually, thank God DeMarr found the evidence first!'

I hadn't thought of it quite in that way and found myself reluctantly agreeing.

'So what are we going to do?' she said and her use of the word we gave me a sudden and unlooked for sense of relief.

At that point my phone rang. I ignored it, preoccupied, but when it cut to the answer phone I heard Braedabarker's sonorous tones announce that Max Lennox was now legally my son. It was a short message but before I could find the contraption to turn down the volume Margaret had heard the whole thing. She looked directly at me clearly surprised, almost angry.

'You've *adopted* Max?'

'Yes. I'd been thinking about it for some time, actually – especially since his mother rejected him. When I discovered that DeMarr was up to something, I decided to go ahead with it. I don't trust the idea of him being away from me and if there is a conspiracy, I might be able to study him and protect him,' I stopped, embarrassed. Was that my prime motive – to keep Max close to me like a lab rat? Or bait? And I did not add that, ironically, my adoption of Max also kept him close to Sally, and through her, to DeMarr.

'Do you think that's wise?' she asked simply.

'Yes. For the time being. I mean Max's genome has been modified by genetic material from another species!' It still sounded absurd. 'Clearly the purpose of the experiments on the children was to carry out a glorified form of gene splicing on a scale that we can scarcely imagine let alone replicate – that much is obvious now – and the abductions are probably part of some ongoing process. Yet Max remains healthy and without any sign of physical or mental change. And as you said earlier, James would probably kill him.' I felt strangely and intensely emotional. Margaret pursed her lips in a strange intimate gesture.

'He's a small child, Julian. I just hope you haven't adopted him in order to *study him*? Or to compete with Louis!'

I was suitably appalled by the candidness of both observations. I thought it pointless to deny either.

'That's part of it. I know it sounds callous, Margaret, but it's more than that. It's complicated.' I stopped. Was it? Should I tell her about the dreams and my sense of being haunted by this boy, about Jonathan's strange comment? Or was I inventing some complex excuse?

'Do you still want to help?' I asked carefully.

'More than ever!'

'Good. Good. You'll need to see the official committee reports and our final recommendations. I don't have copies here. I keep them at home in a safe although they should have been shredded. You'll also need to see the Japanese report as well which confirmed the alien status of the five chromosomal pairings and the bases in some detail. I have that in a safe as well.'

'Yeah, sure,' she seemed breathless. 'Is that legal?'

'Keeping it in a safe?'

'No – showing it to me!'

'Ah. No, I suppose not but I think both Louis and James have already taken us deep into illegal territory. I don't trust DeMarr, and yet he is very close to me and deeply involved in my social life as a former student and a close friend. And as you know we are both working on the same thing, the very thing that sets Max apart from the rest of us. This makes any investigation rather difficult. I could so do with your help.'

Margaret laughed. 'Yeah right. What will Louis think of your sudden adoption? Won't it look odd?'

'He hasn't said much,' I said evasively.

She flashed her eyes appealingly and then, standing up, held out her hands towards her children who had been watching me rather suspiciously. We made arrangements to meet again, joking about the proximity of our addresses. As I opened my office door I was surprised to hear myself ask her the same question she had earlier asked me.

'Do you think this is wise? Do you think Max is safe?'

Margaret paused. She had clearly given the matter much thought. Jamie and Katherine stood around her and waited patiently for her to answer. The girl was probably old enough to have understood some of the conversation. I wondered if it had been sensible speaking so freely in front of them.

'He's safe for now. Or rather, until we find out otherwise. Max's genome has been modified, not infected. Presumably you – we – will need to keep an eye on the status of his 22?'

I nodded in agreement. 'Margaret I can't thank you enough. You have put my mind at rest, to some extent at least.'

She paused, smiling and turned into the corridor. Suddenly I thought of something else. I touched her arm and then drew back my hand as if startled by the intimacy of my own gesture.

'There is one more thing, Margaret. Did DeMarr ever mention alien artefacts – *technology*?'

She frowned beautifully, her eyes flashing again.

Clearly the word artefacts struck us both as vaguely absurd.

'I don't understand?'

'There are persistent stories that something was dug up in the wood, the wood where the boys were found? Something related to the abductions?' I sounded quite mad and felt myself beginning to blush.

'No. Louis never mentioned anything about technology – but then he wouldn't, would he? I do know that he went back there several times.'

'To the Midlands?'

'Yes, *back* to the wood. I thought it was to do with the committee?'

Chapter 7

It is time to talk of Max; and through Max, it is time to talk of Jonathan. On spotting Daniel Lockwood's copy of *The Tempest* in 1993 I had confessed to him that I was once pretentious and arrogant enough to compare myself to Prospero, a deeply learned man, powerful, forgiving and wise. As an aging academic I soon lost such intellectual vanity but in the years that followed Max's adoption I often found myself thinking about Prospero all over again. In my now fanciful, allegorical adaptation I read Max as Ariel and poor Jonathan as Caliban. Like Prospero I was deeply involved with them both, and, for different reasons, I *used* them both for my own complex ends. I make no bones about this now. I used Jonathan especially. Despite his complicity in the decision, I was guilty of having abandoned the older boy quickly and effortlessly as a ruse to gain Max. And although I struggled to stay in touch with Jonathan once he went into fostering, I did not come to love him. It was impossible because there was something in his nature that was broken and angry; something that did not *want* love. Often his reactions to things merely bewildered and angered me and it was only at the very end, the final revelation, that I realised Jonathan had no moral centre, no social code except that offered by the promise of what Max would become. For many years it was this promise alone that sustained Jonathan through his own private hell.

Braedabarker, true to his word, managed to get Jonathan fostered by a family in Whitney, not far from Oxford. They lived in a large, rambling farmhouse full of children and animals in the middle of a wide green country. Most children would have thought it heaven on earth, but Jonathan seemed curiously indifferent, disjointed from domestic life and the small satisfying routines that bound the family together. He was stubbornly solitary, as if his solitude was a form of grief or intense reflection. He was not good in company, both shy and arrogant, and often silent. For the first three years or so I travelled frequently to see him and tried to become his friend. I still have no idea if he enjoyed my visits or saw any purpose to them. We would often end up talking about Max as if Jonathan wanted me to acknowledge that Max was the only thing that bound us together, the only reason I was there. Was it true? Was Jonathan just part of Max's mystery, another route to the answer of what my adopted son was for? I tried to engage with Jonathan, tried to find some glimmer of joy in him. He remained vaguely interested in astronomy and several times we sat out to look at the moon or to check off some seasonal constellation, Orion once, resplendent in the frosty sky and again, early and grumpy with sleep, Venus ascendant in a pre-dawn summer sky. I bought him several books on stars and then a small hand held planetarium ingeniously painted with constellations on the inside of a plastic ball. It glowed at night. He seemed quite taken with it and for a while I felt absurdly optimistic that I had engineered some sort of breakthrough. But the hope did not last.

By his 13th birthday Jonathan was slipping behind at school, struggling to concentrate and prone to strange outbursts of rage. Quickly he began to turn into a stranger, to me, to his foster parents, and to what few friends he had managed to muster. Secure in my convictions that bad schooling was invariably about resources and encouragement, I helped out as much as I could; extra books, some private tuition, but Jonathan resented the attention as if I was consciously trying to make him into someone else. He swallowed affection without a trace and without reciprocation and then, just as he turned fourteen, he suddenly and dramatically gave up everything; school, home, me, as if something inside him had suddenly stopped working. The first manifestations were bullying, both of the children around him at home and then at school. Then came strange acts of wanton destruction, calculated acts of violence aimed to shock. One was particularly alarming. One fine spring day, armed with a bamboo cane fitted at one end with a nail, Jonathan massacred hundreds of frogs in a local nature reserve, slitting their throats and lining them up on the edge of the water. A local teacher had witnessed their end, the shallow waters red with blood with Jonathan squatting down looking at them impassively, surprised perhaps that they no longer moved.

The foster parents were appalled, and in extremis, the mother started to articulate familiar images of Jonathan being evil and dangerous, ghostly traces of Mrs Price's fears. I tried to intervene, psychological support, counselling, walks in the wood but then began to suspect that my presence was not helpful and was indeed rather resented by the foster family itself. And then on his 15th birthday, the night after a disastrously misjudged party, Jonathan ran away and after a few weeks turned up in London on the South Bank in a night shelter. His foster mother went off to try and persuade him to return but it was of no use and Jonathan finally slipped away into the colourful, improvised, sordid underbelly of the capital. My attempts to engineer numerous interventions foundered on his almost bestial cunning and the mood of bureaucratic despair that then pervaded London's provision of social services. My only luck was with the Salvation Army in Whitechapel where I once managed to get Jonathan a room for about a month until he absconded one night with most of the bedding.

I have no clear recollection when the first serious incident with drugs occurred but it quickly overwhelmed him, ketamin of all things, as if Jonathan wanted to anesthetise his very identity. Perhaps it gave him his first sense of peace since he had left Max? There followed detentions and a spell in prison and although this at last opened up the prospect of some clinical rehabilitation, Jonathan was not inclined to take it. I stayed on his trail until 1999 when in a desperately sad meeting in the shadow of the soon to be opened Tate Modern he told me in no uncertain terms that I should leave him alone. He was skeletal, a sort of yellow-grey and appallingly under-nourished. He had a vivid raw look to his mouth and nostrils as if he was actually decaying, somehow incomplete, a sort of un-man. I asked him why he was doing this and he had looked at me with such intense hatred that I was unable to speak. I finally left but as I was approaching the tube station Jonathan came up suddenly from behind me and threw his arms clumsily around my waist. At first I thought he had intended to hit me, but he was sobbing and inarticulate with grief.

We had stood locked in an that awkward embrace for a while, to the bemusement and embarrassment of commuters and drivers, and then we had parted, an absolute separation as if some covenant had been broken and would now never be retrieved.

Max of course was different, shockingly, dazzlingly different. He arrived at Farndon Road on July 23rd 1993 at 12.33 p.m., a quiet and attentive boy, bereft of almost any belongings except a series of boxes sent to him from Scotland; parting gifts from his soon to be incarcerated mother. The image I recall is always the same; a brooding, observant child with a great cloud of black hair and brilliant, curious eyes. He thought the house massive and potentially dangerous, and he quickly acquired a fear of the dark that never entirely left him. Throughout the exhaustive and bewildering adoption process Sally and I had worked hard to re-orientate ourselves to his arrival. We had decorated a room, sorted out the pitfalls and dangers of basement stairs, sharp corners and lose floorboards. We also ensured that for the first two years both of us would be around for him. For me this was relatively easy to do since apart from the supervisory work of the Genome Project (which tended to be either in Cambridge or London) I was based in Oxford. For Sally, Max's arrival involved a massive degree of self-sacrifice, indefinite leave from her consultancy in London and the end to what had been for many years a bewildering variety of public and social events. Yet she withdrew from her professional life without complaint and with apparent enthusiasm. So it was that Max's arrival re-centred us both after many years of a typically peripatetic, competitive academic existence, but more difficult still, at a stage when we had both concluded our marriage was in effect over. Of course Sally and I never discussed this but implicitly and in a spectacularly dishonest way, we negotiated an armistice without ever once mentioning Max's bizarre chromosome or the fact that we no longer loved each other. The details are irrelevant, perhaps even shaming but the result was a commitment to work together for Max's well being and of course, to find out *what Max was*. It was an astounding, audacious piece of dishonesty but for just over a decade it worked remarkably well.

There was of course the complication of Max's identity and how best to protect him from the continuing public interest in the events of March 1993. By July this was already beginning to wane but unless as prospective parents we were prepared to move from Oxford and resume new identities there could be no real guarantee of anonymity for Max, and no real elimination of the risk that someone might link him to the abductions. Neither Sally nor I were prepared to become, in effect, different people, and so we were forced to compromise. We chose a local primary school in North Oxford and the senior staff were briefed selectively on Max, vaguely and rather ominously, to the point at which they probably thought he was the child of a drug baron or a former Soviet dissident. Without doubt Max was helped by the government terrifying the press through the use of the Official Secrets Act long after all the children had been released. As I used to joke to DeMarr, the State is a marvellous thing. Yet Max was also assisted by the fact that the mid-1990s witnessed the insidious securitisation of children generally and a bizarre obsession with their welfare to the point at which he was afforded the protection of coded entrances, caged playing areas, and constant supervision along with the rest of his peers. By the time he was in the fifth grade there was no real indication that Max's adoption was widely known or that anyone had connected him with the story of the events at the John Radcliffe Infirmary. No connection was ever made with *the children*, or with aliens, or with experiments of any kind, until Max's sudden illness in 2005. No one ever interviewed Max or jumped up from behind a hedge with a camera. The only person who ever successfully photographed Max without him knowing it was, ironically enough, Jonathan.

Unwisely perhaps we kept his first name because I simply could not envisage him being called anything else. It was as impossible as imagining him with short hair (and Sally tried that on numerous occasions). Later, in his mid teens Max created the enduring, somewhat intriguing fiction that his middle name was Lennox, by then a surprising gesture that worried me a great deal. It formed my last conversation with Braedabarker, who despite being a dying man, gently reassured me not to worry. Max clearly remembered his mother and sometimes he would talk about her quite openly but he never *asked* about her and never showed any interest in memories of the hospital or his illness. It was as if he had managed to utterly compartmentalise his life. On the day that Sally led him into our house Max closed a door that he never reopened until 2006.

And so it was that freed from illness and the grimness of his former life, Max bloomed into a tall athletic young man, graceful, secretive at times, but above all else *disconcertingly* beautiful. As he approached the shadow lands of adulthood it was impossible to hide or to understate Max's presence. There is no other way of putting it. By the age of 16 Max exerted a powerful gravitational field that disrupted everything; he broke up the physical world and reorganised it into a natural extension of himself. Max *stopped* most people in their tracks, *stunned* them. I observed it countless times, like a new law of the physical universe. He *made* people look at him, often surreptitiously, a backward glance, a double take, and everywhere his passing elicited whispers, spilt drinks, attentive, gaunt silences. People asked me about his looks, about his body, the least likely people, often indeed perfect strangers compelled to engage with some detail of Max's existence. More often than not they asked Max himself who shyly reciprocated their enthusiasm without arrogance or self consciousness like a lesser Greek god doomed to send the world mad. And people wanted to be his friend or to know his favourite colour or what his History scores were or which football team he supported. It was bizarre and never at any stage during our time together did it cease to amaze me. When Max became old enough to drop by my college and fetch and carry for me (a missing exam script, a lost library book, my spectacles) my colleagues would invariably whisper to me 'we saw Max today' and then quite unselfconsciously they would ask about his body: 'does he work out? Is he a model? What weight can he lift?' Endless, endless questions about diet and habit and interests, questions as bewildering to me as those relating to car engines, the specific make and design of fighter aircraft, or how to win a hand at bridge. For a while it was comical but at all times it was also vaguely sinister.

I often mused over Max's physicality. All parents no doubt think their children clever and attractive and part of the deception is often the logic of physical inheritance and resemblance. With Max of course I was freed from that particular conceit, although I took great pride in him and often enjoyed his fitness and his good looks vicariously. He seemed indefatigable. He ran, he swam, played football, rugby; cricket occasionally. By the age of 17 he had become a sort of totem for the local gym, despite Sally's mysterious objections and my own lack of personal body image. Max inhabited these strange worlds completely and effortlessly while at the same time he excelled academically, a head for maths, for abstract theorising, and a tendency to ask difficult and unexpected questions. It all seemed so effortless, just too promising; *too* perfect. Everything he did he did almost too well. As he entered his final year in the sixth form his physics teachers discussed his preparations for University with a sort of hushed reverence as if Max was already a genius. His English teacher noted that Max's grasp of Evelyn Waugh's use of irony was exemplary and that encouraging him to study Shakespeare had been a revelation to the whole class. At parent evenings the praise was excessive and although quite true I often feared there had been some ghastly administrative error and that we were talking about the wrong child. How did Max ever have time to read a novel let alone a play? How could he remember so much as to once, at the age of 14, thoughtfully correct me on an obscure point relating to the quantum movements of hydrogen? One evening – close to the end of all things – Max startled me by suddenly asking what I thought the central message of T. S. Eliot's *The Four Quartets* might be. He had asked it innocently enough; spread-eagled over the sofa with his hair gathered into a sort of impromptu ponytail, his body sleek and wet from a run. I had sat foundering with shock and embarrassment, never having read it, despite having a copy in the library. My prolonged silence had been rewarded by a mischievous wink, as if Max knew my fraudulent literary pretensions but was ready to overlook them.

It is impossible to describe Max, even now, especially now. In an era in which youth and beauty were commodities that fed power and greed Max had enormous influence – it often scared me – and combined with his intelligence he had no rival and yet he remained oblivious to his looks and the advantages they gave him, and modest about his academic achievements to the point I often felt he was embarrassed by them. Indeed towards the end of his late teenage years he grew cautious of his physical presence, almost secretive, as if his beauty and conversation were now a kind of deformity, as if he wanted to protect us from excess, from staring wantonly into the sun. I will always wonder why Max was chosen, why the experiment worked in him and no other, and perhaps his beauty was part of the explanation. Was he beautiful *because* he had been chosen, because it had worked? Were his looks and brilliance merely the outward manifestation of his inner secret? Throughout my long and rather crowded vigil over my son I worked and plotted and sought to translate Max into something I could understand and indeed finally save but in the end he eluded me. Like Ariel, Max was not human or rather he was *half-human*, and through our love he tried to emulate our ways and to regain the secret of our humanity. I now know that, in the final analysis, this was part of the experiment as well.

Retrospect is a poignant gift. Between 1993 and 2005 we lived out a placid, domestic era, a long decade of relative middle class tranquillity. There were dramas and crises, of course, but nothing shocking, life threatening or alien. We were, however, shadowed by various coincidences. Jamie Relph, Margaret's son, became Max's best friend, curiously having run into Max on his first day at primary school and broken his arm! When Margaret and I had met at the hospital to collect our respective offspring we had laughed long and hard over the sheer improbability of the event, much to the puzzlement of the children and the initial anxiety of the staff. And almost immediately Jamie and Max became inseparable. At first Jamie was the sort of fall guy for Max and then a sort of passionate understudy: a permanent addition to the household as Max was to the Relph's. Together they indulged us with the usual dramas of ear piercing, small tattoos, cigarettes in blazer pockets, and panics over drugs and adventurous sports. From the age of fourteen onwards the boys became enthusiastic, suicidal skateboarders. Max excelled, Jamie followed and competed. Following a series of collisions with pavements, people and finally a metal gate Margaret intervened and Jamie was banned and his gear confiscated until I discovered that Max had colluded in re-equipping him from his own money, hiding the evidence in the basement of Farndon Road.

It was a gesture that defined their relationship perfectly, something devotional, unequivocal, a kind of love even then before the word took on the complicated nuances and obligations of Jamie's sexuality. They were a curious, touching pair. Jamie was generous and loyal; inclined to be overly demonstrative in his affection and quite moody. Max was quiet and firm; observant, often in a crisis monosyllabic, yet attentive to the slightest thing. Yet I had quickly noticed that Jamie invariably proved the stronger in getting his way, in bending Max slowly to his will or in getting him to change his mind: the outward appearance of Max's casual dominance was in this regard quite deceptive. Of all the people that crowded into my son's life, Jamie was the one I cared for most. Perhaps it was because in his love for Max there was an imprint of my affection and love for his mother, or perhaps an echo of my first sight of Max with Jonathan, sitting in the hospital ward in their blue pyjamas. If Jonathan had stayed; if I had adopted him, if, if – would he have looked after my son in this way? Would I have discovered the enormity of my mistake sooner?

These years were joyous for the most part, crammed with the elation and frustration of parenthood, but they were also years of anxiety as if we acted out the minutia of our days with an eye to the horizon and the impending threat that Max's intangible secret might break out with sudden violence. In fact this secret actually consumed us, for behind the middle class conventions of the Grey-Relph households lay the combined industry of some of the greatest scientific minds of the century, focused exclusively on Max and his small, seemingly innocuous chromosome 22. In retrospect, it seems farcical, an *opera comique*, in which myself and Margaret, DeMarr and Sally, Jonathan, and indeed others yet to be named all dug away into the mystery of the abductions and what Max was. Everything was done in a corner. All presumed secrecy and discretion, all watched the others shiftily to calibrate their own theories and to check that they had not missed anything of significance. All – quite erroneously as it transpired – presumed the others to be looking for the same thing. And at the centre of this absurd web of slapstick intrigue stood Max, long limbed, Homeric, an Endymion asleep or rather napping in his cave, seemingly oblivious to his uniqueness.

And what did we find? Or perhaps more instructively what did we look for? Margaret and I looked for a trail that linked DeMarr and Sally's work on Max's 22 to the rumoured discovery of an artefact in the wood in Leicestershire and then back to DeSilva's mysterious familiarity with the alien DNA. My allies also involved Dena, and eventually (although more by accident than design) Daniel Lockwood. We were not so much a team as a loose conspiracy, an improvised coalition, slow to move and badly coordinated. Years slipped through our fingers. In the late autumn of 1993 I had contacted Dena Small and asked her to look into the background of James DeSilva. What she discovered was both illuminating and chilling. DeSilva had worked for many years in the US under the guidance of Samuel Davies, a polymath genius of 'independent' financial means. Davies was a virologist but also a computer programmer and the recipient of various generous US defence contracts. During the 1970s DeSilva and Davies had both worked together on something intriguingly known as the *Wild Fire Project*, based in Santa Fe, New Mexico. The project, funded for a while by the US federal government, appeared to involve a planned attempt to locate and make contact with alien life. Some of the evidence implied that Davies actually ran it. It was, however, disbanded in the early 1980s wherein it quickly vanished into a welter of conspiracy theories involving stories of aliens in cookie jars and secret vaults in the desert. By the 1990s it had been replaced by a civilian based voluntary organisation called SETI: the eminently respectable if not somewhat quirky *Search for Extra Terrestrial Intelligence*.

Further attempts to reveal what, if anything, *Wild Fire* discovered hit a very effective brick wall backed up in the final analysis by the US State Department. It was logical to assume, however, that it was *Wild Fire* that had first encountered the alien DNA molecule with its three tell tale amino acid bases, and that DeSilva's precocious schematic handed out to the technicians in 1993 was based on an earlier find. It certainly explained his odd emotional behaviour and the theory on body snatching: had he seen evidence of this before – an alien coda overwriting and modifying the human genome? Was it, backed up by the evidence of DeMarr's prints of Max's 22, a plausible explanation of what might happen to my son? DeSilva had been vague about the time frame of the process but utterly convinced that eventually the DNA from the alien chromosomes would compromise and transform Max's physical identity. Long I thought on this, gnawing at the old data sets like a dog with a bone. Would the changes we had all observed on Max's chromosome remain asymptomatic, or would they accelerate? Would they migrate to other chromosomal pairings in his genome?

Keeping close tabs on Max's 22 was, however necessary, easier said than done even with access to Margaret's staining technique and the facilities I had at my disposal. And here lay the principal irony of my professional life vis-à-vis Louis DeMarr and Max. From 1993 until early 2000, DeMarr and I were *colleagues* mapping and sequencing the very chromosome that set Max apart. We were also members of the committee that met infrequently to review (and allegedly share) data on the children's progress until the government disbanded it in 1999. Both of us were so situated as to use emerging and innovative technology devised for the Genome Project secretly and immediately on Max as soon as the opportunity arose. And I am appalled to confess that DeMarr beat me to it every time. It was partly a question of resources but it was also down to the fact that DeMarr had a lead on me that he stubbornly maintained despite my best efforts to close in on him. He knew that in some vague insubstantial way I was on to him from the beginning. He remained deeply suspicious of Max's arrival at Farndon Road and made frequent jokes about my motives for adoption. My decision to work with Margaret Relph so openly both at college and then on the Genome Project exposed the extent to which I now knew of her involvement. DeMarr assumed – quite rightly – that she would have told me about the plates, the staining technique as well as the information over DeSilva's protocol, and yet we both retained the lie that nothing was amiss. It was absurd.

DeMarr, always DeMarr. Frankly I grew obsessed with him. How I watched him, and how long I mused over the exact shape and dimension of his plot! In many senses he was more mysterious than Max: the enigma of

Louis DeMarr, flitting back and forth throughout those early years plucking Max's lean, sculptured cheeks with his plump mottled hand, playing the role of a generous, extremely wealthy and amusing uncle; watchful and over attentive, cautious about Max at all times as if he considered my son to be some sort of volatile chemical that might explode suddenly. And he was hard to watch. Tracking his research on Max was almost impossible since it was confined to a private laboratory in London which included his own dedicated staff, all loyal and devoted to their patron. What encounters we had on the Genome project were over polite and guarded. How it was that DeMarr and I managed to collaborate and compete at the same time is, in retrospect, beyond me, but that is what we did. There are photographs to prove it: DeMarr and myself lined up outside the Institute of Molecular Studies following our 'joint' discovery of cat eye syndrome (a rare recessive disorder on 22, the first real interest for months), another at a dinner in London following some other obscure find and once, distressingly, at Max's birthday party. In most of the photos I have of DeMarr there is always a slight tightness about the mouth as if he was on the point of laughing out loud, at me, at the whole farce of our work together, at having beaten me all along.

Yet although we never overtook him, and no matter how under-resourced and considerably poorer we were in comparison with Louis, Margaret and I managed at least to keep him in view. We had the slight advantage of possessing Max ourselves, 'in custody' as it were and with ready access to his genetic data, mostly hair, which he left threaded and balled in the bathroom and in his bed as if he was a large Labrador. Gathering Max's cellular debris together became a sort of strange hobby requiring stealth and some ingenuity and I often felt I was living out some dark fable, a sinister fairy story with a bad ending. Invariably Sally tidied up Max's bedroom before I got anything worthwhile, (presumably for her own and DeMarr's collection), and then as Max grew older and more attentive to his young man's hygiene, he became as much an obstacle to this compulsive harvesting as my wife. Yet however easy it was to prepare fresh karyographs for Max in those early years, their diagnostic value was limited. Margaret's ingenious stain continued to expose the telltale presence of the alien DNA. It also revealed the alarming fact that it was increasing in density over time like rings on a tree, but there the insights ended. In 1995, our best guess was that Max's 22 contained about 50 times more genetic information than it had in 1993, and that the pace of change showed no let up despite the fact that Max remained healthy and asymptomatic. With such a large amount of new material was it not both reasonable and logical to expect that Max should exhibit some functional differences from the rest of his peers? Some suitable change or transformation coded by the alien materials?

Max did have some slight differences, but they were by themselves small and innocuous. The annual health checks authorised by the committee showed that his body temperature was a consistent, balmy 40 degrees. He had exotic if stable blood chemistry. His plasma contained relatively high levels of nitrogen-15, an unusual non-radioactive isotope, as well as unusually high traces of hydroxyapatite, a vital component of enamel in teeth and some bone structures. Mysteriously he also contained high levels of the mineral Selenium which would have proved toxic to anyone else. Were these the only physical manifestation of Max's alien genes? One evening, deadlocked over the kitchen table while Max and Jamie systematically vandalised the Relph's garden, Margaret suggested that much of the additional information on Max's 22 could be junk; random bits of un-sequenced DNA without function or purpose. It seemed likely. The spreading alien coda was in effect writing rubbish, defective information without physiological consequence. I had been morose for most of the day, almost as if I wanted something to happen, something to shake things up. Margaret shared my anxiety.

'We need to advance beyond simply staining a karyograph, Julian. We need to isolate his 22 and sequence the modified DNA. If we compare it with a generic human 22 we might find something, a pattern or a purpose?'

It was an impossible suggestion given our resources although I suspected that DeMarr had already done it. Our conversation had been interrupted by Jamie screaming in from the garden with Max protesting his innocence behind him. The mystery seemed hopelessly obscure, and with no end or solution in sight.

Chapter 8

In 1996, Louis DeMarr struck up a friendship with none other than Professor Samuel Davies. The former director of *Wild Fire*, and DeSilva's old mentor, was in the UK on secondment to the Roslin Institute in Edinburgh, where he was assisting in the cloning of 'Dolly' the sheep. Rumour had it that Davies had pioneered a revolutionary new computer software program that enabled gene sequencing to be carried out with unparalleled speed and accuracy, and that this had been put to good use in the first successful cloning of a mammal from a somatic cell. The result of these experiments – genuine or not – generated a great deal of excitement and public interest in his work and in genetics generally and Davies received numerous invitations from British Universities to discuss his work. The software remained under wraps, being patented to the University of Maryland and what turned out to be Davies' own Computer Company. Fame and influence acted like magnets to DeMarr, of course, as did the prospect of using the software on Max, and he made the trek north all by himself and then brought Davies to Cambridge for an extended sabbatical like a trophy. It was a dangerous and ominous development, although I remained sceptical of the claims Davies made in public about his program and his brilliance. I met him twice, a strangely placid man, pink skinned and of indeterminate age, never free of Louis who fussed and flapped about in the background, over excited and demanding, as shameless as he was ingenious.

Despite the fact that any collusion between DeMarr and Davies would be catastrophic for Max, my attempts to prevent it proved slow and inept. That it was actually taking place was confirmed when entirely by accident (a late night drunken pass aimed at Margaret by one of DeMarr's doctoral students at a conference) she was informed that DeMarr and Davies were going to collaborate on a particularly novel application of Davies' software, something 'pioneering' and 'seismic'. Margaret was not clear whether this confession was an apology for having asked for sex or a further indiscretion brought on by drink but it proved to be true. Soon DeMarr and Davies (and to a lesser extent, Sally) were all holed up in London. By October there was disturbing evidence that Davies had accessed the Committee archives in Oxford having gained security clearance through Louis. Again I was late in putting a stop to this and although I did manage to misfile various data sets on Max and Jonathan I found incontrovertible proof that Davies was definitely interested in the children and in Max in particular. By 1997 there was no doubt that DeMarr was now cooperating with Davies and some sort of established US interest in aliens. DeSilva was still in Australia however, oddly out of the way and seemingly forgotten but if Davies had indeed been in on the discovery of the alien DNA through *Wild Fire* he would recognise Max's 22 immediately. He would realise straight away that Max was extra-terrestrial enough to merit a place in some secret bunker under the deserts of New Mexico, pride of place in any collection.

The prospects of Max being kidnapped not by aliens but by some strange black ops outfit in balaclavas kept me awake for months and drove me to tell Max repeatedly that he should never talk to strangers and that he must come home or call me if anyone showed the slightest interest in him – an absurd request in the light of Max's existence. Almost ten by now, and with a precocious understanding of my neurosis over his wellbeing, he typically ended up reassuring me that all was well. Would someone come for my son? Would Sally allow such a thing to happen? For two agonising years nothing happened, the signs of archival activity ceased and all appeared quiet until, in April 1999, my long-standing relationship with Louis DeMarr suddenly and spectacularly collapsed amid allegations of cheating and general dishonesty. Not surprisingly it concerned Davies' software. It was a complicated, public quarrel and it broke without warning.

Just as the UK team was about to announce to the world the complete mapping of human chromosome 22 – the first sequenced part of the human genome – it came to light that the US team had been granted access to a commercial beta version of Davies's software, and with spectacular results. Once this became widely known several other panels, including the British, applied to purchase the software but to everyone's consternation (except my own), the US authorities refused permission. Dena Small was able to confirm that both Davies and Louis had been instrumental in this, citing national security issues and concerns over intellectual property rights. Was such a strategy really an attempt to prevent me getting hold of it? To prevent me using it on Max? I had no doubt at the time. And that Louis would risk such public outrage troubled me greatly: the data he and Davies had acquired on Max was obviously invaluable, worth protecting at almost any price. Perhaps the software was indeed revolutionary?

There followed a week of international bewilderment. The Genome Project was a huge collaborative effort involving 88 countries and over 300 scientists. Restricting something as obviously useful as sequencing and mapping software was not only a serious affront, it risked delaying the successful conclusion of the whole project. When I mischievously pressed DeMarr to try and confer with his old chum Davies and try and persuade him to share, Louis exploded into a fit of quite unimaginable rage. Frustrated beyond measure I accused DeMarr of being spineless and supine to US interests which led him to empty a glass of decent red wine over my face. The incident rumbled on and culminated in another unseemly spat with DeMarr at a major international conference in Denmark in 2000. We had, thankfully, narrowly missed being jointly awarded the 1999 Nobel Prize for the Physiology of Medicine. DeMarr was sufficiently conceited to be devastated but I rather spitefully took the opportunity to retort to him, in public, that should he continue to assist his American friends in hording their secret software he might be consoled with getting the Prize next year all for himself!

I had, for once, judged the mood of the scientific community accurately: even the mainstream press ran headlines denouncing DeMarr's and the American government's lack of cooperation. It did no good, the software vanished completely. A few months later DeMarr retaliated by accusing me of plagiarising some work from his Cambridge laboratories. The piece involved was an obscure article on reverse transcription;

I took legal action; DeMarr could not substantiate his claim and was later forced to apologise. Later in August 1999 he wrote a long and emotionally unbalanced letter accusing me of trying to destroy his professional career and seeking to 'set him up' as a stooge of the US government, and of *Davies* in particular. It seemed a curious confession to make. I considered trying to reply but it seemed pointless and dishonest. Years later, I regretted not re-reading the letter carefully: on close inspection I am sure I would have seen it for what it was; a pompous, self-righteous call for help. We would not speak again until 2006. Given the public nature of the spat, and the unintentional publicity it afforded to the Genome Project as a whole, Max himself took a curious, ironic interest in the affair. I remember he once dangled an editorial from *The Telegraph* at me over breakfast, ingeniously entitled *Boffins at War*, which he then proceeded to read out slowly and precisely. He then concluded his citation with the unusual – somewhat understated – observation that he rather liked 'Uncle' DeMarr and hoped that we would remain friends. Sally, who had studiously remained out of the whole affair, glared at him with uncharacteristic anger.

After *boffins at war*, everything seemed to return to normal until, in the middle of the indifferent wet summer of 2005, we were plunged into a fresh crisis, this time by Max himself. I had gone to collect him from a routine eye appointment. I had actually forgotten him and had been languishing in my office marking Finals scripts when Max rang from his mobile. He had already tried Margaret. Glad to put aside *Elementary Cellular Biology II*, I drove the short distance to Summertown to fetch and then bundle Max off to his next scheduled appearance, like a pop star or a politician. When I arrived the ophthalmologist called me through to her office. She was a young woman scarcely qualified, eager and helpful and seemingly puzzled. Even as I sat down I had no particular sense of doom. After all Max had gone through almost every routine physical a normal healthy child can be subjected to, and always to exclamations of amazement and incredulity. I had seen dentists clicking their tongues in amazement at his bite. One had even said to me in a sort of hushed whisper that he had never seen teeth so rooted and so even. 'I hope to God he never needs them extracted. The eye teeth and the molars are rooted well into the jaw below the nerve line. They'd need dynamite!' So there was nothing in the ophthalmologist's behaviour that initially alarmed me. I merely anticipated more praise.

'Professor Grey, have you ever noticed anything unusual about your son's eyes?'

'Unusual? I don't understand –' I had felt vaguely taken aback. Max had beautiful eyes – strange, kaleidoscopic, variable, surely she wasn't referring to that?

'No – are they too blue?' It had been a semi-serious question.

She looked at me, a ghost of a smile on her lips, as if I was being deliberately irreverent.

'Max has fantastic eyesight actually and an astounding degree of peripheral vision, and yes they're very blue!' she coloured slightly. I felt mean as if I had been patronising her but before I could apologise she added quietly, 'but there is something odd about the retina, something I think that requires a closer look.'

'Odd? On which eye?' I felt myself tensing.

'Well both actually. It's probably an inherited characteristic, probably nothing to worry about. I don't think it's a pathology of any kind although there's something altogether odd about the irises as well. At first I thought it was my instruments, but there is a peculiar reflectivity there, an oddity in the pigmentation.' Her voice trailed away, bemused, *intrigued*. 'And his eyes *do* change colour.'

I said nothing. Eventually she looked at me and then, without the slightest idea as to who I was, suggested the possibility that Max might have cat eye syndrome. She asked me if we had any incident of it in the family.

'Max is adopted, and so I am not clear as to his family history,' I said evenly. My mouth was dry and I had dropped my voice to almost a whisper. I had been momentarily amused that she thought I was biologically related to the tall, dark youth sitting in the waiting room; hoodie up, long legs stuck out in front of him, stabbing his mobile phone.

'And besides, cat eye is most evidently manifest by a split or gap in the iris. Max has neither.'

She stiffened slightly. 'I'm sorry, I didn't realise that you were a doctor?'

'I'm a geneticist, as it happens,' I said. I tried to smile. I had not intended to sound condescending but I had. I was rather frightened, actually. We talked about referring Max for further appointments and I dutifully pretended to agree. Later as I drove Max to his sports club he asked me why I looked so preoccupied. I had apologised and said I was tired. In fact I was worried sick.

Cat eye syndrome was, of course, associated with a genetic anomaly *located on chromosome 22* and DeMarr and I had catalogued it in the late 1990s. Max did not have it, I was pretty convinced of my diagnosis, but the association with his eyes and his mysterious chromosome was clearly not a coincidence and was the first indication of some direct physical change or modification associated with the changes we had long observed on 22. After dropping off Max I immediately called Margaret and we met the next day near the Sheldonian Theatre just off Broad Street.

'When I come to think about it I *have* noticed something about Max's eyes over the years! I noticed it it first when he was in hospital as a boy!'

'Really? Such as?'

We were walking through the Clarendon Building like tourists, preoccupied, looking at everything and nothing. Margaret sounded sceptical.

'Something in the way that they catch the light. They *flash* sometimes. I've seen it occasionally and I have noticed that they change colour, Isn't that odd? I took a good look at his eyes earlier, incidentally: they *looked* quite normal, but what can this mean?'

That morning I had cornered Max coming out of the shower en route to his bedroom, half draped in a towel and puddling watery footprints on the floor. Once we had managed to part the thicket of hair away from his forehead I had held his face in my hands and moved it about as if he was a manikin, making him roll his eyes first one way then another. I had felt a sudden intense déjà vu, the memory of holding a small child's face in the Radcliffe with Jonathan looking on, ready to make his curious offer to me. Max's eyes had seemed fine, sharp, brilliant, and incredibly clear.

'Will I live?' he had asked, bored, but interested in that languid masculine way of his. I squinted into his eyes again for good measure. He was taller than me now, his body hot and powerful. I felt as if I was holding back some juvenile predator, beautiful; playful but dangerous. The image distressed me. We had laughed but before releasing him I had casually glanced at the muscles on his shoulders and torso; thick, elaborately defined; still dappled with water. Had I noticed these physical changes before? I thought of the gym and the exercise and his sheer energy. Were they altogether normal for a 17 year old?

'It can't be a coincidence, Margaret. It just *can't* be!' I felt short of breath, hysterical.

'The coincidence goes deeper than just his eyes, Julian,' Margaret said eventually, her voice almost inaudible.

'What do you mean?'

We had crossed the road and were window shopping outside Blackwell's, listlessly and without interest. To my irritation I saw DeMarr's recent textbook prominently on display in the window: *A Coded Life: The Discovery of the Human Genome.*

'Have you considered the possibility that whoever was behind the abductions and the experiment in 1993 *knew* that you and DeMarr would be working on chromosome 22, and that you would see the changes and work them out? That you would find cat eye syndrome, let alone identify changes taking place on your son's chromosome?'

I stood with my eyes closed recalling the moment I first found Max's plates sitting on top of DeMarr's filing cabinet.

'I don't understand?' Clues? The deliberate, slow unfolding of a map? 'When I found the plates the coincidence about 22 struck me immediately but then I nearly didn't find them, did I? And even so think what that means? That either I or DeMarr in part determined the experiment, or vice versa, and whichever way, in so doing determined that Max was meant to come to us?' I stopped myself mid sentence, shocked all over again and then I stammered 'But how does that explain DeMarr's behaviour? That he was supposed to collaborate with me, that we should have stayed friends?'

Margaret sighed and touched my arm.

'Perhaps? You were colleagues at the time, and close friends, Julian. Perhaps whoever was behind this misunderstood the degree of competitive research in terrestrial universities! Perhaps they had assumed you would always work together?' She had forced a smile. The conversation was surreal, ridiculous, but hadn't I dreamed of Max almost from the beginning, repeatedly visualised him waiting for me, and hadn't Jonathan whispered to me quietly 'you have been *given* a son?'

Margaret turned to me with sudden intensity.

'OK let's assume this isn't a coincidence about the eyes but rather an important clue as to what's happening to Max's 22.' She paused. 'Something *like* a recessive genetic disorder, something *like* cat eye? We might be able to make use of this discovery by looking at the *segment* of Max's 22, and comparing it with someone who has the actual condition? I mean that can't be hard, you sequenced the disorder yourself! We don't need the whole chromosomal sequence now – we know exactly which bit of 22 to look at.'

I frowned, momentarily puzzled. Margaret was intuitively sharper than me and was evidently already onto something. And then she said explosively, 'If only we could get Davies' software, or a version of it! Surely now after all this time they would let it go public! Is it *so* valuable?'

I shrugged and then suddenly her face took on a look of intrigue.

'What?' I said cautiously, sensing her mood and sounding oddly like my son. Margaret narrowed her eyes and then her face clouded, as if an idea had been suggested, scrutinised and then found wanting. She sighed irritably.

'Why don't I just go to Louis now and ask him for it, a personal request for a copy of the software?'

I looked appalled. The idea of asking Louis for help seemed almost obscene as well as highly risky.

'Margaret! Why would he cooperate now? He'd claim to no longer have it or say that it was impossible!' I sounded testy and bitter. I looked coldly at DeMarr's book cover again: elaborate, expensive, and clearly aimed at a mass market. Somewhat petulantly I wondered if it cited any of my work at all. His publicity photo showed him in authoritative black and white under a large brimmed, absurdly theatrical, hat.

'But *you've* never asked him, have you?' Margaret

suggested delicately, still following some strange compelling line of thought.

'No, no I haven't actually, but I just couldn't bear to. I mean, just imagine. It would be an open admission that we need him and more importantly, a confession that we still don't know what is happening to Max?'

Margaret sighed. 'Well perhaps he doesn't either?'

'What?'

'Know about Max?' She moved her hands expansively, 'Look it's obvious that whatever was going on between Davies and DeMarr broke down several years ago. Think about it. Louis meets Davies and they work together for a while, Davies comes here and sniffs about the archive, Louis and Sally lock him up in London and then – then nothing happens? It doesn't make sense! I suspect Louis tried to trick Davies like he did DeSilva, access the software and hide Max, but this time it didn't work. It's an old technique of DeMarr's! DeMarr might still be as clueless as we are, even with the data he has acquired?'

'And Davies? If Davies knows about Max why has no one come for my son?'

Margaret breathed in deeply and said with sudden determination, 'I don't know but seriously – I think you should ask DeMarr, Julian. I think you should ring Louis up, apologise to him and ask for the software! We're running out of time!'

'Margaret!'

'Or just pretend to apologise, do whatever it takes and do it soon! The changes to Max's eyes could just be the start of something!' She was holding my arm and in that moment I realised that she loved Max almost as much as I did. We walked back towards college and as we did so I became aware that I was trembling.

That evening I mulled over Margaret's odd suggestion. Was this just about pride in having to speak with and apologise to DeMarr? In effect, ask him a favour? Or was it about compromising my involvement with Max? Showing my hand? But hadn't my obsession with Max been compromised a long time ago? Then I contemplated Sally. Might it be safer to ask him *through* her? She was often in London, and still saw Louis frequently. Although she had remained studiously neutral since the 2000 *boffins at war* incident, she might mediate some sort of truce. I felt childish and rather petulant about the whole thing, but anxious, and Margaret was right: we were close to the start of something, I sensed it. I roamed about the house in semi-darkness, indecisive, anxious. Using Sally was an act of cowardice, and she would probably refuse then tell DeMarr about it anyway. Was it really possible that DeMarr was as stuck as I was?

Later, having thought myself into a stupor, Max appeared noisily in the hallway like a small storm and found me sitting in the kitchen. Usually after a brief conversation from the foot of the stairs he would stampede up to his bedroom, invariably with Jamie or more recently with a young woman called Zoë Craven, but on this occasion, alone, he had stuck his head around the door and narrowed his eyes at me as if he thought I was contemplating suicide or an act of random violence.

'Is everything ok?'

'Yes, Max. It's fine. Did you have a good day?'

Max ignored my question and concentrated on his own. 'You sure?' He then walked into the room, his hair wedged into a green hoodie and with various strange bands and bits of string tied around the wrist of his right hand. The sun had tanned his complexion to a deep bronze. He looked like a shaman or some splendid barbarian. He turned the kitchen lights on and looked at me suspiciously.

'Have you been arguing with Sally again?'

I winced, stung by the word *again*. 'Max! His accuracy

always made me feel so dysfunctional. 'I never argue with your mother! We merely ignore each other until one of us cracks first! You should know that!'

He snorted a laugh. I was struck again by his height, his size, the ambiguity of who he was.

'So are you about to crack?' he pulled a stool towards the table evidently intrigued, having decided to stay and observe me like an anthropologist.

'I *might* be,' and then suddenly I had confessed half, most of the story to him, my will weakened by his proximity and the hint of absolution he brought with him. 'It's actually about DeMarr – Louis DeMarr?' For a moment I wondered if Max would remember him.

'You're not going to make it up with him, are you?' Max sounded incredulous and almost angry as if he thought this was very unwise. I was surprised by his tone.

'Well, no – not *exactly*. I need something from him but I don't want to make the first move. I know it's pathetic but –'

'This is the guy who accused you of stealing his work?'

'Yes Max.'

'And you've been sitting here all night thinking about this?' Max removed the hoodie as if it was a helmet. He shook his hair free and the effect was startling, dramatic, like a peacock opening its tail. He seemed to fill the room now completely.

'Yes, I suppose I have.' I was consciously trying not to look at Max's eyes. For a moment Max was silent, his right hand flat on the table top, close to mine, as if he was about to summon spirits.

'Look, it's easy – just text him. Texting doesn't count. When Jamie and I fight he'll never speak first, but in the end he'll text and that's cool. It's the same with Zoë. When we fight she texts but keeps face, sort of?'

'You fight with Zoë a lot?'

Max looked at me and smiled. 'Not as much as I fight

with Jamie! But seriously – give it a go?'

'But I don't know DeMarr's mobile number. He doesn't look the sort of man who would have one, Max.'

My son made an exquisite, desperate gesture with his hands, like a magician and rolled his eyes. As he did so they obviously and very distinctively flashed. Luckily he was so outraged by DeMarr's lack of technological consideration that he didn't notice my sharp intake of breath. Instead he offered a compromise.

'How about a voice mail? I bet DeMarr has one on his office phone?'

'Max he might answer it!'

'Well just hang up, or better still ring at some stupid time like 2 a.m.!'

'OK. I'll think about it!' My distress over DeMarr and my love for Max stood momentarily in perfect equilibrium. 'It's not a bad idea, though,' I finally conceded. Max beamed a smile of devastating brilliance and then asked for a beer, a reward for his Zeus like intervention. My insistence that it was a school day made me sound mean and in the end we had one each. Later, when Max was lying inert in the bath surrounded by candles I dutifully rang DeMarr's office. It was late enough. I felt stupid, angry and embarrassed that Max would hear. I practiced my tone so I could sound dignified and not desperate. Several times I panicked and hung up before the voicemail cut in. In the end it was a wonder that DeMarr recognised my voice at all.

'Louis, it's Julian. I need your help. I need Davies' software urgently for a research project. I know it's a difficult request and that this is an extremely sensitive issue, but it's very important. If you can call me I would really appreciate it.' Before I finished there was the bleep and the line disconnected. I had forgotten to use the word apology. I contemplated ringing again and tagging on the rest of the message but I felt too exhausted. To my added irritation as I had stalked past the bathroom

Max shouted out brightly, 'How did it go?'

I gave Margaret an edited version of what I had done, blaming Max for the idea. I told her I was 'inspired' by his lessons in late teenage etiquette. I didn't tell her that Max had suggested it directly. She found Max's social skills very funny, and his reference to Jamie. 'They are so like a couple at times, it's just uncanny!' Although we both agreed that my ploy was unlikely to work, two days later a hire van turned up outside the Institute of Molecular Biology at Oxford containing a large delivery addressed to me. After some fuss about papers and authorisation, it was opened to reveal excessive amounts of new computer and laboratory equipment, the purposes of which were not immediately obvious, and a series of large envelopes containing what was, without doubt, Davies' software program. And there was more: DeMarr had also thrown in a serious amount of raw data, data on Max dating back to the mid 1990s. The mystery over what had motivated such generosity deepened when it transpired that DeMarr had sent us what was clearly a pirated copy of Davies's program, indeed the beta version that had caused the argument in 1999.

'It's a trap,' I muttered, pouring over some elaborate device containing a series of odd, unusual looking monitors. Margaret had, for once, not heard my cynicism. She looked up at me over a clipboard and an inventory.

'Where did he get this stuff, Julian?' I had shrugged, conscious that DeMarr was wealthy, suspicious that in some way he had stolen it from Davies.

It took several days to persuade the University to hand over lab space and install most of the equipment and by the time it was done Margaret was bursting with energy and excitement. And as if blessed with some dark serendipity the evening before the first test run, Max had the misfortune to get a ball kicked into his face, and returned home with a pile of scarlet tissues from the resulting nose bleed. I had instinctively gone to sequester some away but Margaret had nodded curtly in the car mirror.

'I've got some already.'

I had laughed humourlessly.

'If I had any moral consciousness left I'd be ashamed! Or I'd think we both had Munchausen's by Proxy.'

She shrugged. 'We do what we have to do, Julian.' We had then both turned to see Jamie watching us from the open car boot with animal-like stealth. I knew immediately he had heard us. We were growing careless.

Two days later – a week after the eye examination – Margaret called me at home late at night and said she needed to see me urgently. It was after eleven p.m. Disconcertingly Max had answered the phone.

'Dad! Dr Relph requires your immediate presence!' As I took the phone off him he pulled a mock curious expression and then stood quite close to me, watching my face intently.

'Margaret?' I looked up at my son who had not moved an inch. 'Max – do you mind?'

He raised his eyebrows ironically and padded off towards the sofa. Margaret asked me to make some excuse and get over to the institute. She sounded breathless, tense. As I pulled on my coat I was aware of Max still watching me expectantly. He was alone, with Jamie away and Zoë Craven on some family excursion. I warned him I might be late and not to stay up. I walked the relatively short distance towards the science park. When I met up with Margaret twenty minutes later she looked exited but also slightly frightened.

'What is it?'

'This *is* strange and rather alarming Julian, but we're

not to panic, ok?' She swiped us in to the main facility, walking close together, our arms brushing.

'What's up? Tell me?'

'Hard to know where to start, or which is stranger – the equipment itself, the data from Max, or the software! I mean I have never seen anything like this stuff!' We passed through another set of doors into a wide dim corridor with many rooms locked and dark about us.

'Margaret, you've done the sell, now just tell me!'

She laughed and placed her hand on my arm. 'I'm not sure that what you are about to see is a product of our new technology or an actual change to Max's 22. Given DeMarr's generosity with his earlier data it does look very much like the latter, that Max's changes are accelerating, but I need to do more cross checking. We can't jump to conclusions on one run of this equipment alone.' We had arrived in a deserted computer lab shaded by low pools of halogen light. It gave the place an odd relaxed feel like a bar in a resort. Margaret was monopolising a large amount of machinery, including a large LCD monitor with a split screen and various other mysterious devices, their operating manuals spread out about the table like cook books. Assembled, the technology looked both impressive, but to a trained geneticist surprisingly unfamiliar. I removed my jacket and draped it over the back of a nearby chair. Margaret composed herself, hands together and to her lips, her eyes closed and then pointed to the LCD monitor. 'Here goes. The image on the left is from Max. The image on the right is from a patient suffering from cat eye syndrome.'

I wedged my reading glasses up on the bridge of my nose and squinted at the display which showed two high resolution computer generated images of 22. I saw immediately the cause of the syndrome on the right screen: an additional chromosome inverted onto the end of 22's slightly longer arm. DeMarr had speculated that it was a replication error in which the duplicate was retained, so that there were in effect *two sets* of 22, one upside down to the other. I looked back across to Max's. In comparison his 22 looked perfectly normal. I looked at Margaret, intrigued as to where she was heading. She smiled beautifully.

'Quite different, yes? And there is no evidence that Max has the condition at all?'

I nodded cautiously, alerted by her tone. She then flicked the keyboard and dramatically enlarged the magnification on Max's chromosome.

'Good God!' I stammered, impressed. 'Is this Davies' software?'

'It is indeed, and you haven't seen anything yet! This makes the staining techniques of the early 1990s look positively medieval!' She messed about with the mouse, whizzing over panels and dropdown windows. Suddenly both chromosomes zoomed up like galaxies. The definition was astounding. Confidently typing the relevant keys, Margaret merged the displays so that the two images of 22 came together.

'The computer has used a complex variety of algorithms to sequence the long arm of Max's chromosome, the site of protein coding genes. On the cat eye 22, you can see the duplicate chromosomes retained. Now if you compare this to Max's, you see that the location of the duplicate matches the dark bandings on Max's 22, the site of the alien chromatin.'

I leaned in squinting. I recalled Margaret's expression outside Blackwell's recently: 'something *like* cat eye.'

'Now, hold onto your seat, Julian.'

There were more movements with the mouse, more dropdown commands and then I let out another small gasp. I was looking at the bandings under astounding, almost unbelievable magnification. My eyes swam about helplessly, sensing Margaret's anticipation without understanding. At first I saw nothing, and then gradually,

I saw it.

'My God!' I stood up involuntarily, pushing the chair back, my face flushed hot. I felt adrenalin spike my pulse. 'There has to be some sort of error? This is impossible!'

'No. It isn't Julian.' Margaret said quietly. 'I've been refining this for days – there's no fault anywhere. Davies must have designed this equipment to run the software as well, probably in the context of *Wild Fire* itself!' She looked at me searchingly. 'Astounding isn't it! Behold Max's *inner* beauty!'

It was both beautiful and terrifying.

In 1995 Margaret and I had theorised that the dark bandings on Max's 22 were made up of massive amounts of additional genetic material. We knew that much of it contained the amino acid bases from the original alien DNA. What set this new image of Max's chromosome 22 apart was the sudden vivid revelation that the amount of additional material was *far in excess* of what we had then estimated. There were *massive* amounts of it. The bandings were made up of layer upon layer of seemingly endless chromatin, vast matrices of genetic data carefully wound up within the bandings themselves and neatly stacked along the long arm of Max's 22, a microscopic version of the 'disorder' that defined the cat eye patient's 22, but instead of one inverted chromosome, Max had *millions*.

'This extra coding is *huge*! It can't be possible! This just doesn't make sense!'

Margaret shrugged as if I was being pedantic or un-necessarily dogmatic. I walked back to the screen, drawing in breath like a swimmer in difficulties and sat down again. I touched the mouse and scanned about randomly. Margaret put her hand over mine to steady the arrow on the screen which was shaking slightly. When she spoke she sounded astoundingly calm.

'I think we're looking at what are, in effect,

chromosomes *within* a chromosome. Or, in fact, given the number and the way they are arranged, whole *genomes* within one human chromosome!'

I glanced up at her sharply. She was close to the screen now, her face serious.

'But that's ridiculous! Its back to front – how could something so big be hidden on something so small?' I looked at the image again and thought suddenly of one of those strangely haunting Escher prints in which a geometric shape proliferates endlessly, growing smaller and smaller, until it vanishes into the grains of ink and paper and then starts again. I sat upright, cold in the large, dimly lit room and for a while I couldn't speak.

'The more I look at this, Julian, the more I am convinced that Max's chromosome 22 has been *engineered* to carry *nth* amounts of additional data; hybridised information containing both alien and human DNA, re-arranged and resorted into endless sequences. And this information is compressed in such a way as to take up hardly any space, like a zip file on a computer.'

'But entire genomes? Genomes of *what*? My voice wavered slightly. 'And for what purpose?'

'I've tried modelling some of them. I've isolated about 300 in the last day or so. They all appear to contain 26 chromosomal pairings, with between 1/3 or even 1/5 of their base amino acids derived from the alien DNA – the rest are definitely human. And there are millions upon millions of them. In short, Max's 22 contains multiple variants of a new hybrid humanoid species – I am certain of this now. It's as if he's pregnant, in a sort of genetic sense at least, and there is one more thing,' Margaret's voice was suddenly tense, as if she had rationed out the bad news and kept the worst until last.

'What?'

'There is clear evidence now that alien DNA has migrated from 22 to at least three other chromosomes on his human genome. It is likely that the proliferation we have witnessed on 22 will start again, although I can't be sure.'

I shook my head, sick with fear and old denial. 'Which ones?' I asked finally, as if it made any difference.

'The sex chromosome 23 and 2 through to 8. The budding is slight, but it is exactly the same process we identified in 1993.'

'So Max's 22 is a wooden horse of sorts after all, hiding hordes of secret genomes. Does this mean that DeSilva was right? That Max will change? Or hatch an army of aliens?'

Margaret pursed her lips calmly and touched my shoulder. 'He had a hypothesis. There are many others. This is a vastly complex experiment, Julian. Let's stay calm.'

'Can we stop this proliferation at all?'

Margaret made a helpless gesture with her hands. 'In *theory* – although how we can block the additional genetic material replicating without damaging Max's normal genome is literally rocket science. We'd need an entire research team and the budget of a small European state to stand a chance of finding it soon.'

I sat hunched in on myself. Were Max's flashing eyes the start of some monstrous transformation, long foreseen by DeSilva and foretold by his own mother? Margaret put her arm around me suddenly and unexpectedly.

'Julian, I told you not to panic! DeSilva was wrong about the retrovirus, he might well be wrong about this. If the aliens wanted to recode Max surely the procedure would have been simpler than this? And why take so long?'

I put my head back, close to tears. 'But look at the sheer number of genomes inside, and that's just on one chromosome – now it's spreading!'

'Julian! Forget the bloody Trojan horse story for just a minute!'

I half smiled, trying to nod in agreement. I straightened my shoulders and sat upright breathing deeply. I suddenly found I was thinking about Louis.

'Why would DeMarr make a gift of this, knowing what we would find? He must know this about Max already – he knew this almost *six years* ago?'

'Well he saw some of it,' Margaret corrected gently. 'The amount of material on Max's 22 has dramatically increased in the last six years, but you're right – he must know most of what we do.'

'And Davies? Look at this stuff? If this equipment is representative of what he has been hording up in the US since *Wildfire*, he must know more than anyone! And if so why has he left Max alone?'

Margaret paused, looking at me with sudden concern and then slowly shook her head. She had clearly thought about the same thing.

'I don't know Julian. Perhaps they're waiting for something? Perhaps they know how or when the experiment will end and are biding their time?'

I shrugged helplessly. For the first time I felt utterly without hope. It seemed a reasonable deduction but the idea that someone else knew more about my son than I did was momentarily unbearable. I looked at Margaret desperately. 'So what do we do now?'

'We run away together with Max,' Margaret answered after a pause. For a moment I think she almost meant it. 'But we'd have to take Jamie I'm afraid!'

I smiled weakly. 'And Max would probably insist on bringing this Zoë girl with him as well!' Margaret raised her eyebrows but then suddenly yawned.

'You need to get some rest! You must have been here for days, Margaret!'

'Well most of the week actually.' I wondered if her children minded or whether her husband ever complained. 'You are a genius, Margaret. I mean that quite literally! You must take all the credit for this.'

'*Julian!*' she scowled, standing up suddenly and gathering her things about her, powering down some of the equipment. We walked out, clicking off the lighting behind us. Just before the labs were engulfed in darkness Margaret turned to me with an unusual, rather frightened expression on her face.

'We talk and worry about Louis and about Davies. But if this is what the experiment was designed to do, if this is what Max is *for*, then surely the biggest concern is that the aliens will re-abduct him?'

I said nothing.

We walked on in silence, lost in our private misgivings. Out in the stairwell Margaret changed the subject, self-consciously and with some effort.

'Going from the sublime to the ridiculous, or rather, from the extra-terrestrial to the domestic, I think that Jamie has a *crush* on Max, actually.'

'A crush?' We strolled past the security porters near the exit. They waved at Margaret.

'Yeah, you know. It really isn't a surprise. I have a crush on Max, for that matter, as does the entire universe. But I think Jamie is gay and that the crush is more than casual male bonding.'

'Really?' I was still thinking of Max and aliens and the switch in conversation had momentarily thrown me.

'Has Jamie told you that? I mean about being gay?'

'Not exactly. He's only seventeen – he might not think of his sexuality in those terms yet. But he is more than just obsessed with Max. Has Max has never mentioned anything to you?'

'About Jamie? Well nothing specifically – I mean he talks about Jamie all the time! It's rather hard to know where one starts and the other ends!' I hesitated, frowning. Margaret was laughing.

'That's a good way of putting it!'

'Are you ok with Jamie being gay?' It seemed a curious

question to ask, as if I might not be. 'I'm not implying that-' I stumbled to explain but she laughed again.

'I know what you mean Julian. I'm fine with it. And I think he is as well. It might make things complicated for him but it's the 21st century for God's sake! Do you think *Max* will be fine?'

For a moment she sounded anxious.

'Good God, yes. I'm sure he will be. And he *must* know. I bet he even knew before Jamie! You know how uncannily perceptive he is! But I don't understand Margaret. I mean if Jamie has never mentioned this to you, what makes you think he's gay?'

I was curious, recalling the boys together, the way they argued and worked together. I tried to see them as possible lovers. Outside on the Banbury Road the night was surprisingly cool for late June. Margaret was hugging herself, a bag over her shoulder.

'Oh, it's difficult to say. Nothing too obvious and if I listed them they'd sound silly but taken all together, it's sort of obvious. And it's just the way he is when he's around Max or if he hasn't seen Max or phoned Max.' She smiled rather dreamily. 'Even after you've factored in the Max Effect! It's rather cute actually – and they do look rather good together! But I think for Jamie it's becoming serious. I think he might actually be in *love* with Max.' Margaret made the word serious, a definitive power. We both stopped and looked at each other.

'Max loves him just as much, I have no doubt about that.' I felt awkward and surprisingly uncomfortable, not so much over Jamie's sexuality but my general lack of observation.

'I know, I know – but not in the way that Jamie wants!' Margaret stopped and looked at me.

'Do you want me to have a talk with Max?' I asked anxiously, intrigued by her intuition, panicked at the prospect of bringing the subject up with my son.

'Good *God* no! I'm only mentioning it because I'm

worried that Jamie will get hurt. It's always difficult being in love with your best friend!'

Margaret resumed walking, having given the observation some indirect emphasis. I frowned and then asked if Jamie had ever mentioned Zoë Craven. The fact that Max now had a girlfriend must clearly have had some impact.

'Oh yes! I've heard all about Zoë!' said Margaret mysteriously.

'Is Jamie alright about it? God I should have realised sooner!' I recalled Max's enigmatic remark about fighting with Jamie and making up via texting. Had they been arguing a lot recently?

'I think so. He and Max had a long talk, apparently, and Jamie felt a lot better! You know how cool Max is about stuff like this. I mean I'm sure that this isn't the first time he has had to disabuse an ardent admirer!' We were approaching the start of Farndon Road.

'Margaret, I'm sure Max will be there for Jamie, I'm sure of it! I only hope that Jamie will be there for Max when we come to the end of this.' We lapsed into silence. I felt I had spoilt the mood, two parents talking about routine, normal adolescent stuff for a change, not about aliens or chromosomes or abductions. To my surprise Margaret slid her hand under my arm.

'You must worry about Max a lot? I sometimes forget what this must feel like as a father.'

I felt my throat knot with emotion. 'I worry all the time, and especially now, after tonight and of course I am not his father. I think I secretly convinced myself that whatever happened to Max as a child was in effect over – despite the odd loose ends – finished. Now I realise it's not even really started. And sometimes when I look at him, I feel – *almost afraid?*'

Margaret had not removed her arm from mine. It felt profoundly satisfying, reassuring, 'Afraid of what?'

'I don't know – his *difference*, that he doesn't know

173

what he is himself, I'm not going to mention James DeSilva's metaphor but – something inside Max is beginning to change Margaret, I have sensed it myself over the last year. I suspect that as he reaches adulthood the experiment will conclude as suddenly as it started. He is beginning to treat me differently as well, cautiously, as if he knows he is being watched or something.'

Margaret sighed thoughtfully. 'I know. I sense that as well.'

'Margaret what is he for! Who is he?' My voice carried, exasperated, desperate.

'I have no idea, Julian, but when I look at Max I don't see a weapon or a trick. I seen a beautiful young man, well brought up and well cared for, with extraordinary sensitivities, and I also see a small boy who would have died of cancer had he not been abducted and in some way modified, for whatever purpose. I have never believed in DeSilva's hypothesis, it just doesn't make sense. And whatever Max has that makes him different he is also human, remember that. He's a *gift*.'

'But from whom?'

We had reached the end of my driveway and, despite the lateness of the hour, Margaret discreetly released my arm.

'Does it matter?' We lingered facing each other reluctant to part company. I was preoccupied, thinking of Max with an intensity that almost physically hurt me.

'Remember me telling you a few days ago that I had checked Max's eyes, Margaret? He'd just come out of the shower. He was just wrapped in a towel. His physicality was astounding. I found his body almost intimidating. His vitality made me feel old, wasted and I do wonder if Max's physical size is linked to the alien side of Max. He has grown suddenly so tall and so muscular. Is it just my imagination? I wonder if I should discourage his gym obsession.'

Margaret smiled and shook my arm with her hand.

'Julian! Young boys grow! Remember we never knew his father. It could be a perfectly normal inherited characteristic. Jamie is quite beefy, but then so is Neville! And Jamie works out because he has some idealised body image stuck in his head, probably Max's! You have to step back a bit as they grow older, let them get on with their lives, have faith that they will do the right things! Even Max, especially Max!'

Faith was an odd word and yet it felt strangely appropriate, bringing me suddenly close to tears again.

'You're right. I'm too close to Max, too caught up in what he might be! I sometimes let my imagination loose on him. I've even recently started thinking about old Braedabarker and his talk on demonology, and Mrs Lennox –'

Margaret took my arm again, 'Julian, for God's sake, Max is not a demon! If he's anything he's probably an angel!' She smiled teasingly but my mood was oddly set to gloom and darkness.

'Aren't they the same? I mean don't they share the same ontological space? I used to liken Max to Ariel, did I ever tell you that?

She seemed taken aback. 'You really have been thinking about this haven't you? I think you did once, years ago, *The Tempest*? He would make a good Ariel!'

'Did you know that in Milton's *Paradise Lost*, Ariel sided with the rebellion against God?'

She shook her head, bemused. 'No, Julian I'm afraid I didn't!'

'Sorry Margaret. The simple fact is that if I lost him I would go mad. I mean literally mad with grief.'

'I know.' She stroked my arm carefully. 'Perhaps the time is coming when we should talk with Max directly? I mean he's no longer a child, and as you say, perhaps he is beginning to remember things; about the wood, about what he is?'

I nodded, incoherent with grief. Margaret looked at

me intently and then leaned forward and kissed me on the lips. 'Stop worrying! We've made a real breakthrough tonight. I'll call you in the morning – or rather later this morning!' I watched her pull away from me and walk off along the silent, empty street.

As I turned to walk up the driveway towards the porch I caught sight of Max against the window to Sally's office. He was dimly silhouetted from behind by the hall light and through some trick of perspective he looked quite menacing, looming up large like a stranger. Only the profile of his hair reassured me it was him at all and not some random, opportunistic burglar. In the same instance that I recognised him I also noticed that the window sash was slightly raised. He waved at me and mimicked looking at his wrist to emphasise the time, just gone 2 a.m. There was nothing furtive or guilty in his body language but I felt uneasy and compromised. Somewhat embarrassed I let myself into the house and walked through to the kitchen. After a few minutes silence there came a familiar creaking on the stairs and then sound of Max's bare feet on the kitchen tiles.

'We have school tomorrow!' I said, turning towards him, trying to disguise my sudden nervousness. 'And you know how your mother dislikes you being in her office!'

'Sorry, sorry, sorry!' Max patted my arm and then leaned down into the fridge. He was wearing boxer shorts and a T-shirt that had the words 'GYM RAT' stretched across his chest.

'But actually, Julian, it's Saturday tomorrow! And her door was wide open, inviting inspection!' He was holding a carton of milk close to his mouth. I frowned and passed him a glass quickly. He faked a look of contrition. 'Everything all right?'

'Yes, everything is fine Max. Sorry for being so late – Margaret has a new toy in the lab and she wanted to show off her skills.'

Max drank deeply, wiped his mouth with the back of his hand and raised an eyebrow. He had left a bead of milk in the corner of his lips like a pearl.

'Is that a euphemism for something?' He looked at me closely and then re-filled the glass. I was confused and still on edge. 'You're not hiding anything from me, are you, Professor Grey?' he said in mock seriousness. He half turned to put the glass down and as he leaned forward coils of raven black hair snaked over his face like question marks. For a moment I was too stunned to say anything.

'Like what?' I tried to sound humorous. Had he heard part of my conversation with Margaret? Our voices would have carried slightly, the window *had* been open. I felt close to panic. Max frowned. Curiously he seemed almost embarrassed as well.

'Well, you know – I mean -?' he shrugged and looked at me quizzically.

'Max, *I don't know*! So cut to the chase, young man – what's on your mind?' I nerved myself to look directly into his face.

'I mean, *Margaret*? You and Margaret. Jamie's mother and all that – you seem to be spending *a lot of time* with her, and Sally is spending *a lot of time* in London. Am I missing something?' My relief was almost palpable. Max was half smiling but I knew he was serious.

'Good God, Max! I am not having an affair with Margaret Relph! Believe me! She's just a very close friend and colleague! She has a work ethos second only to the Poles! But thanks for asking!' I sighed. He hadn't moved.

'But is everything alright between you and Sally?' There was an intensity to Max's body language that was unusual.

'Yes! Max I'd tell you if it wasn't!' I frowned trying not to get cross. He stood looking at me moodily, making up his mind slowly.

'But you and Sally have separated, haven't you?'

'Well yes, I suppose we have. Max look – it's complicated! And listen to me Max Lennox Grey!' I poked his sternum with my finger with each part of his name. 'If you think you can deflect attention away from your blatant transgression of Sally's office by interrogating me you are very much mistaken!' I was tapping thick solid muscle where I was pretty sure there ought to be just bone. It was disconcerting. Max's anxiety lifted suddenly and quickly. He cocked his head down to see my finger.

'Cool. I was just checking. From now on you and I need to communicate more directly!' he said, taking my finger in his hand and removing it slowly from the proximity of his chest.

'We – we do?' Something in the tone of his voice caught my attention. He remained holding my finger a fraction longer than he would normally have done. His hand was surprisingly cold. The effect was not unlike getting a small electric shock.

'Don't we communicate well?' I stammered. I had always prided myself on my relationship with Max, our sense of equality, and I sounded genuinely upset.

'Yes, but it needs improvement. I need to see more of you for a start, and you need to tell me about your personal stuff, like Sally, you know, the sort of everyday chat middle-class parents have with their children.'

'Sure.' I felt an odd flush of inclusion and then I narrowed my eyes slightly. The difficulty with Max was that, since about the age of fifteen, he had perfected a sort of sham sophistication that I found frankly bewildering.

'Perhaps we can take up a hobby together, like bowls or astronomy? Perhaps I could go to the gym with you!' I said slowly, playing along, trying to regain my footing.

'Why *yes*!' Max gasped in mock revelation, his eyes wide and his mouth open in surprise: his expression winded me. We both stood looking at each other vaguely nonplussed.

'Max – about the gym – I've been meaning to ask.'

'Oh God is this where you accuse me of taking steroids or something!'

'Are you?'

'Dad!'

'Sorry Max, but you have bulked up a lot recently. I mean it's impressive –' I stammered, lost, struggling for the right words, 'but are you sure that you're not overdoing it?'

'I'm fine – it's all natural I assure you.'

There was a silence. Max threaded long strands of hair away from a curved angular cheek, his mother's gesture.

'Is this one of those hugging moments?' I suggested, trying to mimic his irony but I sounded vaguely needy. He paused, screwed his face up in concentration and then said, 'No. Not yet.'

Later I had paused by Max's open bedroom door listening to him sleep. I had long acquired the habit of over interpreting him. Perhaps he had just picked up on the growing distance between Sally and I. It was pretty obvious by now. And he had clearly seen me with Margaret in the street; he might even have seen her holding my arm. I had obviously been spending a huge amount of time with her. And perhaps I did *like* her. I thought about her kiss, and her odd elusive comment about Max being Jamie's best friend. I walked up to the top of the house feeling irritated that Max had caught me unawares. He could be so skilfully manipulative when it came to my emotions. From the top landing I noticed that Sally's office door was still slightly open. I wondered if she had been back recently on one of her rare unannounced visits: had she said something to Max? I switched on the light and casually glanced about the room. It was sparse and tidy; a complete contrast to my own and to Max's. Sally had few ornaments, no photographs and one stark, mass produced Paul Klee print facing her desk. Her shelves displayed someone functional and to the point, a life without sentiment or clutter. I walked to the window, to where Max would have been standing. It was still open. I looked down at the deserted street, densely packed with cars, hunkered down like sleeping animals. As I turned to go I saw that the bottom drawer of Sally's desk had been opened and that someone had evidently ransacked its contents. There were paper clips on the floor along with some old-fashioned green treasury tags and several elastic bands. I looked about me cautiously, suddenly aware that several things had been moved and hastily returned to their place.

I crouched down slowly and opened the drawer. It contained a series of black folders and a bundle of long, blue, hard backed pocket diaries produced by Oxford University Press, the sort that had a week to a page. The first one was 1991 and the last was 2000 but they were not in order and the one nearest the top was 1993. I picked up the 1993 diary. It was an elegant, over-produced thing with a blue silk strip stitched into the small spine. The strip was marking the week beginning March 19th. Most of the days that week were filled with meaningless times and initials, linked to committee meetings but on the 19th Sally had written simply *Final Pairing. Max and Jonathan found in North West Leicestershire.*

I sighed, exhausted, and replaced the bundles. I then removed one of the black folders. They contained plates of Max's karyograph. I noted that they were the 'legal' ones that had been circulated to the entire committee – they still retained the faded blue memo sheet on the front. On the top of each sheet Sally had neatly written out Max's name and on close inspection, I noticed that some of the plates had gone missing.

Chapter 9

I had no idea why Max searched through Sally's office that night. Or rather, there were so many reasons why that I had difficulty knowing where to start. Was he finally aware of the very strange circumstances surrounding his adoption? Was he now embarking on some investigation of his own? The diaries seemed to indicate he had looked carefully at Sally's account of March 1993, such as it was. He had also looked throughout the room carefully and thoroughly. For a while I tried to find a suitable opportunity to raise the subject, to somehow insinuate the topic into our now frequent 'communication sessions' (as Max called them) but my nerve always failed me. Margaret had been right about eventually needing to talk with Max but until I had some coherent answer, some sort of explanation, what was I to tell him? And besides, part of me had always assumed that if or when Max started to remember what and who he was he would come to me, trust me, confide in me – but was this true?

The questions and doubts multiplied as the summer waxed and then waned, anxieties about Davies' data, concerns and confusions over DeMarr's motives, and, in the middle of such worries, I started to systematically dream about Max for the first time since 1993. It started innocuously enough. Usually I was standing in a room or space of intense tropical brilliance. The light was so powerful that I had no idea if I was suspended in a huge void, standing on something solid, or merely floating in a sort of luminous fluid. And there was a noise, a soft, subliminal vibration around me like the sound of the wind in trees at high summer or the sea. I tried to listen to it, to focus on the sound and as I did so I would see a shape form in front of me. It would loom out of the light, a thin curve at first, a line of darkness, like the disc of the moon appearing during an eclipse, like black ink in water, bleeding out into the surrounding brilliance. In the initial phase I would wake at this point. Later, as the dream progressed, I successfully willed myself to stay asleep and watch the shape take on greater form.

Eventually the line emerged from the dazzling miasma as the figure of a man, its outline dancing against the dappled glare like a mirage. He had his hands to his face, the palms shielding his eyes. I could see the muscles in the forearm, the long cords of veins and tendons, a tall dark skinned man in his mid or late twenties, athletic, implicitly naked and evidently desperately searching for something. For some weeks the image was anonymous, heraldic, oddly enticing, but then one night I noticed the youth's hair, knotted and gathered on the shoulders, like dreadlocks, some spiked and drawn down around the forehead and I instinctively knew it was Max and yet not Max either. Only in dreams can such a bizarre tension exist between *knowing* and yet not recognising. I would try to cry out. Try to shout his name, but subject to the laws of my dream world I could neither speak or be heard and invariably woke myself.

The dream stuck at this point for some time. On and off, not every night, but near enough, I would see this astounding version of Max looking for something. Some nights, this peculiarly hyper-masculine version of Max would not come at all and all I would sense was light and sound. And then one night, dog tired after a day of lecturing and presenting a conference paper to an indifferent audience, dream Max came right up to me. The sequence was the same as always, the brilliant light, the emergence of the young man, the hands to his head, searching. But on this occasion he materialised very close to me.

'Max?'

I looked at him, each sinew and muscle intimately drawn and separated, packed and bundled under the smooth dark skin almost as if he had been flayed. I tried to look into his face but his eyes were deep in shadow. I could make out his nose, the strong line of his lips. I whispered his name again. He lowered his hands slightly, and his hair fell forward. I looked at his chest, then down to his stomach past a boss of black pubic hair and rested my gaze on his feet. They were not human feet at all, more like a bird's, vaguely reptilian. As I looked up I noticed that he had a series of tattoos on the outside of his thighs, drawn up through the narrowed waist and out up onto his shoulders. Again, it was Max and yet not Max, too old, too dark, too male to be real. And while I was thinking this, trying to see him and communicate, to demand he speak with me he suddenly took my hand and placed it on the middle of his stomach just above his navel, palm down. I felt strong, padded muscles, the extraordinary yielding texture of his flesh. He said something to me in a language I could not understand. And then I felt beneath my hand the beating of small, tiny hearts. *He was pregnant.*

The first time I touched him I had screamed. My shock had been palpable, and it had taken me several hours to calm down and rationalise that the dream was only some metaphorical representation of what I feared about Max and his replicating genomes, some allegory of what Margaret and I had seen in the labs. Yet as if my powers of rationality had no real control over his magic, the dream un-nerved me. It was not just the bizarre aspect of Max being literally pregnant, an almost deliberate subversion of his powerful masculinity, it was the sense of his joy – of completion – that I felt when Max took my hand. The dream stopped developing at this stage, but would repeat itself endlessly. In some disconcerting way the image of Max in my dream distorted or changed my view of Max in the real world: they seemed to converge, with Max's physique, his manners and gestures, becoming almost ethereal. One afternoon I spoke with a vague acquaintance, an anthropologist from St Catherine's College. The conversation turned oddly enough to male initiation rites and she told me that fantastic representations of male pregnancies were a common symbolic feature of rites of passage, the passage into adulthood, the crossing of the threshold into death. I had tried to sound disinterested but the relevance of the topic to Max's real life struck me as ominous, strangely imminent.

And then, on August 15th 2005 I got a telephone call from Daniel Lockwood. I had not spoken to him for over ten years. There had been the odd card between us, a few letters, but nothing more. His had been the very last name I had expected to hear when my secretary called through to my office, sounding guarded and cautious as if she had a crank or some outraged parent on the line.

'Lockwood? Good God – yes of course, Miss Dear, put him through!'

His voice was entirely unchanged. I tried to sound

unsurprised, matter-off-fact. We exchanged pleasantries, he asked after Max and Louis and then he said simply and directly, 'I'm sorry to call you up out of the blue like this, but Jonathan has turned up.'

I blinked pointlessly, holding my breath.

'Hello? You remember Jonathan, the boy they found with Max?'

'Yes, of course, of course. Sorry. You mean he's at your *farmhouse*?'

Daniel laughed. 'No, good God no, but not far! I've tracked him down to a local squat, a disused house I own nearby.'

'What's he doing there, Daniel?'

'Well he seems to be casing out the wood.'

I sat up, concentrating hard. 'Really? How long has he been there? Is he alone?'

'Yeah, he's alone. And I think he's been here for about a week. I only recognised him by chance. What's been the score with him, Julian? I mean obviously he's no longer a minor, but he doesn't look in good shape.'

I felt a pang of guilt and shame.

'I'm afraid it's been a rather long, involved story, Daniel. He ran away from his last foster arrangements in Witney and since then, he's been in and out of juvenile detention facilities, you know – petty crimes, break-ins. I'm afraid my relationship with him broke down completely.' I left the rest unsaid. No doubt Daniel would make the connection and politely fill in the blanks.

'Jesus, that's really sad – I didn't know that,' he replied after a pause. 'So far he seems to have stayed out of trouble here. He hangs about on the bridle path and keeps going in and out of the trees, you know, where the mound used to be – the one DeMarr removed. He's digging about for something.'

I stood and walked around my desk to the window. With sudden, almost visionary clarity, I recalled the birch trees that clear March morning, elegant, mysterious, silent witnesses to the boys' arrival.

'Did you say digging?'

I leaned over my desk and discreetly closed the connecting door between my office and Miss Dear's. Daniel's voice had broken up on the line momentarily.

'Yes. I think he's looking for the alien artefact? The one I told you about in 1993. The one you said DeMarr denied all knowledge of?'

My face and neck went instantly cold. Daniel spoke with such obvious certainty. I had so long forgotten the rumoured device, buried it so deep under what had seemed more immediate, more tangible concerns, that its almost casual mention winded me. DeMarr *had* denied it, several times, and despite endless rumours, endless press reporting, endless allegations, the government had never acknowledged its existence at all.

'Julian, are you there?'

'Yes of course. Sorry. Yes I'm here.'

'Look Julian, do you know what this is about?'

'Daniel, I really have no idea. He could well be looking for the device but I never succeeded in confirming that anything was dug up in the wood. I've tried, several times.' I *had tried*, but perhaps not as hard as I might have done, not as persistently. The fear that I had missed something; some vital clue, made me sick with fear.

'Well if you want my views on this, Julian, there was something and Jonathan has come back to find it. He is orientating himself around where the mound was. He's definitely working to some sort of scheme, and he has a map – some sort of OS job?'

'A map of the wood?'

'Yeah – he's not very discreet. It's almost as if he wanted me to see. I actually challenged him this morning – asked him what he thought he was doing in my wood!'

'Oh my God – you spoke with him?' I sat down again heavily.

'Well yes, several times, actually. He's quite a likeable

fellow in his own, odd way. He obviously recognised me from 1993. He knows who I am. He even asked about you!'

My heart seemed to freeze and miss a beat, a sort of heart event. I heard the plastic phone snapping as I gripped it tightly.

'Shit what a fool – I'd entirely forgotten about the wood!' I whispered, but for my own benefit really, not Daniel's.

Daniel remained silently attentive on the other end of the line before he said quietly, 'You know there is something altogether odd about the place now.'

I narrowed my eyes like someone expecting a blow to the face or a sharp needle. 'Odd?'

There was another pause through which I could hear Daniel breathing, seemingly unsure what to say or how to say it.

'Oh it's nothing Julian, forget it –'

'Daniel please – it might be important.'

Another pause, another odd hesitation.

'Look, this sounds crazy but in the last few weeks or so the wood looks different, I mean – as if it's been changed physically in some way, and I just feel that there's something here, something in the trees.'

'Have there been more sightings?' I whispered, anxious that my voice should not carry.

'No, not yet and I've been waiting and watching for years Julian. Do you think they will come back – the aliens – come back for the boys? That the wood is some sort of rendezvous?' His voice was insistent again, almost angry.

'It's complicated, Daniel, and I can't tell you much over the phone.' Was it possible?

'Why don't you come up to Leicestershire? We can have a talk, perhaps confront Jonathan together – or do you want me to come to Oxford?'

My mind remained stubbornly blank, devoid of

anything except the bizarre image of Jonathan with a map, digging through the red clay soil like a sapper.

'Look let me think about this and I'll call you later today. Is that alright?'

'Of course!' said Daniel, using a tone I found hard to decipher. 'What about Riley? Mark Riley? Is he still alive? Perhaps he might know something about the device – he was very angry about the excavations, I remember – he wrote to me saying he'd complained to the Home Office or something. Julian? Are you there?'

Again for a moment the name meant nothing, some shadowy acquaintance, almost a ghost.

'Yes, sorry, yes I am here. I haven't kept up with Riley at all. I think he retired some years ago.'

'Ok, then why not ask DeMarr again – tell him that Jonathan has returned?'

'We haven't spoken since 1999, Daniel.'

'Shit – oh sorry – I mean, wow, I'm surprised. What happened?'

'We fell out over Max.'

There was a pause and then Daniel snapped back 'Look, I think you need to bring me up to speed, Julian – I mean something's going on isn't it?'

'I will, I will. Sorry. It's obvious that I have overlooked something here – I'll get in touch.' I hung up suddenly.

I had indeed forgotten about the wood, about the rumoured find of something alien. When I briefed Margaret later that afternoon I reminded her of the question I had posed at our first meeting in 1993 about alien technology.

'Do you really think something was found, Julian, something connected to Max?' We were in *Browns*, discreetly hidden by luxurious foliage, morose and unsettled.

'Yes, yes I do. In fact I'm sure of it, Margaret. And there is clearly a connection between the changed to Max and to Jonathan's return to the wood. It makes sense, as if the various elements of Max's mystery are realigning, coming back together in some way.'

'Well if that's the case we'd better change our approach. I can concentrate on finishing off the analysis of Max's 22 with Davies's gizmos. Perhaps you should go and meet Lockwood? But for God's sake be careful.'

Later I telephoned Daniel to arrange a visit only to be told that the police had moved Jonathan on later that very day. We postponed the idea of me visiting the wood and Daniel agreed to redouble his watch for any UFO activity in the area.

I decided to turn aside from Max for a while, from his intriguing, proliferating genomes, and go back to the morning of March 19th, 1993. I started with the newspaper clippings sent to me by Lockwood. I tried un-successfully to contact the journalists and then – despite my conservative instincts – I turned to the internet to scurry and dig through websites of either dubious credibility or outright paranoia. Nothing much – nothing reliable – except the *persistent* rumour that the find was some sort of communication device, something that was able to contact the aliens, a signal perhaps that the experiment was over?

Could it be true? Wasn't there some sort of logic to it? In the end I decided to conduct a sort of thought experiment which assumed that the device did exist, and that it was directly related to the experiment itself: to Max's genomes, a catalyst of some kind, a necessary part of the overall research plan, but there my thoughts stuck without proof or possible experimentation. And what galled me more than anything was the realisation that, like everything else, the device had already passed through the hands of DeMarr. I was reluctant to risk contacting him again and instead, set out to re-trace Jonathan's life after our emotional exchange at Bankside in 1999. It was a difficult, incomplete search, revealing the usual trail through rehab clinics, a juvenile detention centre near Bath, and then a series of casual labouring jobs. At one stage he seemed to have stayed in Bristol and then in about 2004 the trail petered out until Daniel's dramatic sighting in Leicestershire. Jonathan had never made much sense to me. He had been taken in error, his genetics had been unmodified, but the tag had remained stubbornly intact. He had effectively encouraged me to adopt Max, and now, suddenly, he had returned to the place where it had all started. Wasn't the obvious move towards Max now? Would Jonathan come looking for my son as we approached some threshold or event horizon, or would Max seek Jonathan out? I emailed Dena Small, renewing our acquaintance as much through necessity and cautiously informed her of what had been happening and my likely explanations. I wrote the messages up as disguised, elaborate hypotheses half expecting her to miss their point completely, but canny as ever she replied a few days later saying it seemed likely. I then turned to Mark Riley. Finding him turned out to be much easier than I had at first expected. I had long assumed he would have retired to the South Coast, and my guess was uncannily accurate: he had moved to Hove to play golf and grow roses. I had set aside an entire day to do what a computer search engine took just five seconds to accomplish: it even showed photographs of Riley chairing a rose competition and receiving his police long service medal. Mark had an email address. I sent him an affable, seemingly random note, pregnant with anxiety.

Two days after sending Mark a third, increasingly tetchy mail asking him to contact me, I returned home to find Sally kneeling in the front room, her face shockingly drawn and tight. She was wearing yellow marigold gloves and had a bowl of soapy water next to her. Her presence was entirely unannounced. When I walked in she was rubbing the carpet vigorously. The room was disturbed, a small table had been knocked to one side scattering books and magazines on the floor, and most surprising of all, there was a broken chair in the corner with its back snapped off. It was all very *film noir*. When I asked what had happened Sally appeared to be stupefied into a sort of trance. 'It's nothing,' she said eventually. 'How are you?' We greeted each other awkwardly as if we were meeting at a reception or in a queue. I hadn't seen her for ages.

'Where's Max?' I asked cautiously.

'He's upstairs, but I would rather we just forget this whole incident, Julian. He's apologised to me, after a fashion. I don't want to talk about this, darling.' Her voice had been close to breaking, rare in someone so contained, usually so unemotional.

'Of course. I never liked that chair anyway.' I was intrigued but not necessarily alarmed. She forced a smile. 'Good. Perhaps you can chop it up and burn it next door on the fire? All is well with you I trust?' We talked small talk. I had removed my jacket, waited for a discreet interval to elapse, and then sloped off to Max's room. I knocked and stuck my head around the door. He was lying on the bed looking up at the ceiling. His arms were pressed back behind his head, a pose of vast endurance.

'Hey?' Max looked unusually pale; his eyes lined dark as if he had marked them with crayons. For a moment I wondered whether he had been crying. I sat on the end of the bed. As I did so he sat up, hugging his knees.

'Apparently I'm not allowed to ask or talk about this but there's a perfectly good dining chair with its back missing in the front room, and your mother is deploying a powerful stain remover – can you help me at all?'

Max smiled slowly, with effort. I had rarely seen him so upset. I ran my hand up and down his shoulder, patting him as if I was encouraging or consoling a child. It was an anachronistic gesture.

'We'll talk about it later,' he said with rather chilling finality. We sat in silence and after a while I stood and walked to the door.

'Wait.' Max swivelled around and put his feet down to the floor. 'Are you ok?' The question surprised me. It was said with evident concern. I pressed the door too and walked back into the room.

'Yes, sure. Why? Max, what's the matter?'

'Nothing Jules, nothing.' He had started calling me Jules a lot recently, a subtle reconfiguration of our relationship.

Downstairs Sally had recovered herself and was preparing dinner. There seemed no immediate or obvious explanation as to why she was here. I feigned curious indifference. All I could elicit from her was that she was stopping over en route to some strange meeting in Birmingham. Max stayed upstairs and prowled about the bedroom (the floor creaked overhead with his heavy, purposeful tread) and then eventually went out for a walk, to return with his hair full of leaves. The weather had turned suddenly violent, with the wind well up and rattling the front windows. The mood inside the house was almost as tempestuous. Sally tried to engage Max in some sort of conversation but the incident with the chair cast a long and painful shadow over the eventual meal and, to my amazement, Max ignored his mother completely. He sat very close to me, so close in fact I couldn't use my fork properly. It gave what was a rare occasion now – a family meal – a strange rather sinister asymmetry, with Sally stuck up at one end, Max and me at the other. I was terribly, absurdly nervous throughout, garrulous and unfocused. I rambled on about work, politics, *anything* until Max ran his foot up alongside my shin as if trying to signal something. There was a gaunt silence and then Max said in a sort of growl.

'I'm being followed.'

Sally, deadpan, a fork elegantly half turned in her mouth looked at Max and then at me but remained silent. I looked up sharply, Max's foot now coolly against mine.

'Followed?'

Max nodded in confirmation and then, for some reason, poked me in the side. His tactility was legendary – it was another of his strange, beguiling oddities – but there was something dogmatic about the gesture that distressed me.

'When was this?' I tried to sound normal. Max and I looked at each other, frankly, almost painfully. I pointedly removed a leaf from the top of his head.

'Followed or stalked?' Sally asked finally, determined to have a part in the conversation. She poured herself some wine and ignored Max's mournful gaze at the bottle.

I blinked several times and said,

'Did you recognise who it was?'

'I think I did, actually.'

There was no doubt in my mind that he was referring to Jonathan.

'So who is this stalker, Max?' Sally asked with sudden animosity. She studiously avoided my gaze.

'It's some weird crack head dude I made a mistake of buying the *Big Issue* off some months ago, during the summer, and he's been following me off and on ever since.'

'On and off?' I said this too quickly, instinctively alarmed, and in quite the wrong tone. Max sensed some inner reaction, I could tell immediately. His face changed almost imperceptibly, like a dog catching a high sound.

'Since about May. He appeared to stalk me for a time, first spotted by my faithful shield bearer Jamie, coming back from Zoë Craven's birthday party, and then twice by Zoë herself. Then he disappeared and I forgot about it but now he's evidently back on my trail. I saw him this afternoon.' I was looking intently down into my lap calculating rapidly: Jonathan returned to Oxford, identified Max, went to the wood in Leicestershire and then came back?

'Have you spoken with him?' I asked, still looking down.

'Should I?'

'Are you sure it isn't Zoë's father, concerned about his daughter's wellbeing?' Sally said quietly, cutting her steak rather savagely. The table vibrated slightly and the glasses tinkled.

'Max, just be careful,' I whispered. As if to underscore the unfolding drama a particularly strong gust of wind shook the dining room windows.

'I'm always careful. He's probably half my weight. He's inoffensive, he wants more money I guess, I mean he's not going to snatch me off the street in a white van and rape me!'

'Oh good God! Max!' Sally exclaimed, downing her cutlery. I had rarely seen her so angry and so barely in control.

'Look Max, I know you *are* careful, but please if he follows you again I want you to tell me. Is that clear?'

'Just call the police, Max,' said Sally, as if I was not to be relied on.

'Ok. Perhaps I should stop buying the *Big Issue?*'

'You can stop buying the *News of the World*, for a start, snatched off the street indeed!' Sally seemed genuinely outraged. After we'd cleared the table, I tried to glean a few more bits of information from Max; the exact date of Zoë's birthday, when Max had first bought his copy of the Big Issue, or even his second, but Max had gone off on a tangent, asking if Jamie could come over and stay with us for a few days. Again, there was something disconcertingly prescient in this topic of conversation as if Max was baiting me. 'Jamie has started having panic attacks,' said Max, adult serious.

'I have those all the time!' snapped Sally, standing up and walking out towards the kitchen. Max followed her out with a surprisingly spiteful look. Their mutual animosity was quite distressing. I had rarely seen either in such an odd mood.

'I think he has OCD,' Max continued, to me only, his face close but his eyes on the door. He then picked up my wine glass and took a large gulp. I scowled.

'Don't make me complicit in this, young man, whatever this is!' I said quietly and firmly, directing my voice to where I thought his ear might be. I caught Max's scent, a deep smell of wood smoke and cold air. 'What's with all this animosity towards Sally?'

He flared his nostrils and looked so beautifully cross that I had to look away to disguise a smile.

'My animosity towards *her*!'

I tried to talk about Zoë Craven but he wanted to talk about OCD and drug therapies. The entire conversation was like a fencing match although I was conscious that his rapier was aimed at Sally, not me. Compromised by nerves I then made a serious faux pas.

'I really don't seem to know much about Zoë at all, Max, I mean, other than the fact you see a lot of her.'

'You speak to her all the time!'

'Do I? Well what I mean is that this seems to be a serious relationship, doesn't it.' I had raised my voice trying to include Sally but Max looked at me and said simply, 'I really *don't believe* you just said that!'

The evening was, alas, far from over. After dinner Jamie turned up and left with Max out into the storm after some protracted argument on the landing outside the bathroom conducted in stage whispers. Sally and I sat reading in the front drawing room like complete strangers. She still seemed irritated, with Max, with me, with the book she was evidently not looking at. Eventually even she bored of the pretence.

'He's strange, suddenly, isn't he? How long has he been like this, Julian?'

I peered over reading glasses in her general direction.

'He isn't strange, darling, this is unusual. I don't understand this mood – it's quite new. Have you been arguing?'

'Well I don't like it,' she snapped, ignoring my allusion to the chair. 'And what in God's name has he been eating? He looks much bigger than the last time I saw him!'

'You mean fat?'

'No, Julian, *not* fat – you know exactly what I mean!'

'It's the gym – he spends a lot of time, you know, working out – pressing benches, whatever it's called?'

She had turned back to her book, pensive, her mind preoccupied with something. 'Why?'

'Darling I have no idea. He wants to be fit?'

Sally was glaring at me as if none of this made sense. She went to resume her book. I remained looking at her.

'Sally you don't think that Max's stalker is Jonathan do you, by any chance. Jonathan Price?'

She looked up and I was surprised to see that the name actually didn't initially register. She then frowned dramatically.

'No I don't! Why would you think that?'

'I don't know – I just wondered.'

She looked suddenly suspicious, intrigued even. 'Julian?'

'Darling it's nothing. I just often think about what happened to him that's all.'

I resumed marking essays but I could sense her watching me. Then suddenly she stood up abruptly and went to the window. The trees was thrashing about in the wind, the air full of odd debris, bits of rubbish; a hat, plastic pots. Without turning to face me she spoke with sudden, urgent intensity.

'I've been offered the position of senior scientific advisor to the government. Louis is retiring at the end of the month.'

I glanced up at her rather owlishly. It was a significant if not largely titular post and she was eminently qualified for it. Louis had stayed in the saddle far longer than anyone else but the news surprised me. Had she come to Oxford to tell me this?

'Well that's excellent news!' I said with some effort. 'How is Louis, by the way?'

She turned her head and glared at me. 'You should ask him, Julian! I mean this stupid vendetta you two have going, it's ridiculous!'

I ignored her but felt the comment had a certain immediacy about it, as if it somehow my argument with DeMarr had been at the forefront of her mind. Then, without warning, she asked me about Margaret, an odd indirect question.

'She's fine, thank you.' We looked at each other, both in two minds whether to push on or back down. We were definitely on the edge of something, working our way around it, a Pandora's box of a conversation, unsure whether to open it or leave it closed. It was Sally who suddenly backed down, looked at her watch and then to my surprise announced that she was leaving.

'What now? Tonight? You've only just arrived!'

But she was strangely adamant. I offered to drive her to the station but she called a taxi. I walked down the drive to see her off, opening the car door for her.

'Sally we need to talk. We need to talk about Max.'

She seemed startled, looking up at me in the darkness. It was probably the first time I had taken her by surprise.

'I know, but not yet, Julian, not now. Soon.'

As she drove away I had the distinct impression that I would not see her again for a long time.

Chapter 10

The darkness was full of slamming gates and metallic rattles and overhead, the curious whine of cables. As I turned to walk back inside I saw a man sitting on a low wall opposite the house. I thought immediately of Jonathan, but he seemed too big, too contained, and it was only when the figure stood up I realised it was Max. Suddenly, inexplicably, I felt almost frightened by him. In the windy animated darkness he seemed utterly different, looming towards me, hands down into his pockets, his face hidden inside his hoodie.

'Max – what on earth are you doing? Where's Jamie?' My voice was sharp, angrier than I had intended. He had scared me and he seemed to sense it. He reached out his hand and touched my face. The gesture was intimate, aimed perhaps to reassure, but it made the encounter seem even stranger.

'I didn't mean to startle you Julian, sorry. Jamie's asleep.' He spoke softly. I could hardly hear him above the gusting wind. Behind us, a small red road sign blew down sideways and careened down the street.

'Max what happened with Sally? Did you have a fight?' We walked back together and then suddenly he put his arm through mine. I stopped.

'Max, you're frightening me. What is it?'

He stood, still hesitant. 'I need to tell you something.' His voice sounded strange, uneven. We walked into the porch and he sat down suddenly, pulling me down next to him with casual strength.

'It's about *DeMarr*,' Max said quietly. It was surreal hearing Max say the name. There was so much he could have said. Jonathan. Aliens. The wood. A device. I braced myself for some unanticipated revelation.

'What about him?'

'He was here this morning. In your study, with Sally.'

I sat anchored to my son's arm and I could sense Max looking at me in the darkness. I had a curious sensation that if he let go I would blow off into the gale.

'Tell me about the chair?' I said eventually. Again Max touched my face with his free hand without warning or purpose. I felt he was trying to make some form of immediate contact with me, like a medium.

'Promise me you won't get upset,' he whispered and sounded strangely like Margaret.

'I'm already upset Max, just tell me what happened.'

'Jamie was ill at school and they asked me to take him home. Margaret was in London and Jamie's dad was out somewhere so I brought him here, to this house. When we arrived I found Sally with DeMarr, searching through your study. Well, ransacking it almost.'

'Go on.'

'Sally was really mortified to see me – I mean – shocked! I asked them what they were doing, and she lied badly, *so badly*! She said you'd lost something and wanted it found quickly. It was *pathetic*! And DeMarr – he looked terrified to see me! I offered to run down to college to fetch you and they said it was alright but it was obvious they were doing something behind your back!'

He sounded genuinely, touchingly outraged. 'When I tried to call you on my mobile Sally took it off me and tried to send me to my room but I refused to leave your study and sat on the desk. Sally and DeMarr then went downstairs and started having an argument in the front room.'

More wind, more animated darkness. Max fell silent, waiting for me to catch up.

'Do you know what they were arguing about?'

Max sighed deeply. There was evidently more. 'Sort of.' he said, somewhat disingenuously. 'I stood outside the door for some time, trying to listen. Sally was angry, said she disliked being used, and that DeMarr should sort out his own quarrels. The argument seemed to involve some discussions about a guy called Davies, or Davids? An American? About some gift DeMarr had given to you and Margaret, some sort of software program and some equipment he had lifted from Davies? DeMarr said he had a right to see your data because without the software, you would never have been able to obtain it! She called him an idiot several times, and accused him of letting Davies take over his life, of spoiling *their* relationship, their own project?' He paused.

'Good God, Max – how long were you standing outside the door for?'

'About ten, fifteen minutes. I was sitting on the bottom stair pretending to text Jamie having retrieved my phone from the kitchen. I would have heard more but then Sally came out and caught me obviously listening. I think she thought I was relaying it to you line by line. *She went ballistic*, said I was spying on her and sneaking about, that I had always spied on her, intimidated her, and that I was working with you!'

'She *said* that? Working with me! Good God! What a preposterous idea!'

'Yes,' Max said curiously, slowly, as if it all still puzzled him. 'And then she said that she didn't know who I was any more.'

'And what did you say?'

'I said she was a liar and, and an adulterer.' I felt him verbally wince. 'Well, I called her a whore actually.'

'Ah,' I said. 'And how did that go down?'

I heard him snort a laugh; embarrassed.

'Not well but I was well fucked off with the whole thing by now.' Max swore causally, a recent development. 'Then it got *really* heavy. DeMarr seemed worried that I would say something to you, that I would tell, and kept patting my shoulder like I was a pony and that I had to be discreet, *dear boy, not tell, mum's the word*. I *had* to keep quiet about this unfortunate incident otherwise terrible things might happen, blah blah blah and before I knew it –' Max's voice lowered slightly, swallowed up by his anxiety. I leaned into him my ears straining,

'I *hit* him.'

'You *hit* Louis DeMarr?'

'Well no, actually,' said Max thoughtfully, 'I threw him into the chair.'

Despite myself, despite the horror of what Max had told me, I almost started to laugh. The image that came to my mind was momentarily priceless. 'I see. And what happened after that?'

'I'm not sure. Sally went very silent and then said she would call the police unless I went to my room. DeMarr just lay crumpled up on the chair, eyes wide, trembling – he seemed terrified.' Suddenly Max started to laugh, apologetically.

'I'm sorry. It was sort of funny. He looked like something out of *Wind in the Willows*, the sketch of Toad after the collision with the automobile. Do you remember the drawings? Except not so much enthralled as terrified.' I knew exactly what Max meant. It was an apt image. Amid all this disaster I laughed too, DeMarr as Toad. After a pause Max continued.

'I went to help him up and he made this horrible sound as if I was going to stab him or something, I apologised and, slowly, everyone calmed down. It was actually really horrible and unpleasant. What really shocked me was my *strength* and my anger. DeMarr is, what, 120 kg? I just threw him like a doll. It was ridiculous!'

I breathed out deeply. I could imagine Max doing it, effortlessly, almost on a whim and it seemed to make perfect sense that Max had no idea of his strength.

'Do you have any idea what any of this means?' Max asked suddenly.

Should I tell him? Tell him everything? Or was this story, like his earlier tale of the *Big Issue* stalker, some sort of test, a way of finding out how much I was prepared to trust him? I sensed him waiting for at least some semblance of an explanation.

'We'll talk in the morning, Max. This is all very distressing. Remember our conversation some weeks ago about messages on voice mail and the etiquette of keeping face? This is about that. DeMarr did give me something I needed urgently for my own work. I was surprised at the time, although now it seems that DeMarr had a very clear motive.'

'Is this about the cheating thing? Him stealing your work?' said Max.

'In a way, yes.'

We stood up. Max removed his arm from mine and we walked into the house and into the hallway. At the bottom of the stairs Max turned to look at me intently.

'Can't you at least give me some idea what they were looking for, in your office? It seemed incredibly important?'

I had been about to go into the garden room. The question surprised me. I chewed my lip, tired beyond endurance, anxious, deeply in love.

'Genetic *data*. Once, many years ago we collaborated

on a project, Max, and then we drifted apart. We tried to find a series of answers to the same question but in competition with each other. At one stage, Sally and DeMarr seemingly agreed to work together, but –' A lie, an omission? An allegorical version of the truth? Max listened intently, as if he was weighing each word. And then he asked gently, 'This is all about chromosome 22?'

Again we looked at each other, Max's distressingly adult stare; my own evasive hooded eyes.

'Yes.' I was so tired I could no longer be shocked or surprised. So Max knew? He had used a generic term for 22. He had not said *his* 22. We parted without further comment.

That night I lay awake pondering the events and what they could mean. Clearly something had cracked off with Davies, something serious enough to force DeMarr to send me his dated but still highly advanced software and then come looking for the data, but why the curious delay – almost six years? At least I could finally see a clear motive for DeMarr's action: it had been some sort of insurance policy to retain access to information that he presumably no longer possessed or had never fully been allowed to share. Data on Max's chromosome? Something else? And then of course there was the sudden revelation of Max's stalker. There was no doubt in my mind that we were closing in rapidly on some sudden revelation, some endgame, but as yet I was still entirely clueless as to what any of this meant and if and how the device fitted in. I confided in Margaret over lunch at college next day, my fear pouring out in a series of incoherent emotional rants. She sat next to me, stoically stabbing a piece of fish, preoccupied with my fears, listening attentively. I suddenly felt I was profoundly abusing her patience.

'Look. We have to do one thing at a time, Julian; otherwise we'll just go to pieces over all this. Have you heard from Riley yet?'

'No, he clearly isn't interested. The emails are getting through. Perhaps he can't answer them, perhaps he's afraid?' I massaged my temples aggressively. 'Now I think we should track down Jonathan. If he is a vendor for the *Big Issue* perhaps I can find him myself? He's definitely come straight from the wood to Oxford to meet Max.'

'I agree Julian, but there are quite a few vendors here. We could check out the centre and down towards the station? Is it possible that they've already met up?'

'Yes, or at least it can't be ruled out. Max is oddly secretive at the moment. He seems to be out an awful lot and there is something about his behaviour, something different, like the evening he went through Sally's office, almost as if he wants me to know he is finally aware of himself, aware of what is happening to him!'

'Then darling let's talk to him! You said he mentioned 22 himself – perhaps Max is asking for help!'

'But what help have we to give? If we tell him what we have found it might scare him to death, and we still have no answers! And I'm afraid to compromise him.' I leaned back in my chair sighing heavily. Was that is – or was I simply afraid of finding he was already preparing to leave, to complete his mysterious mission all by himself? What if he knew something terrible, deadly? I sensed Margaret's implicit disagreement. 'And it's not just his absences, Margaret!' I sounded plaintive. 'Even when he's at home he's on his mobile or his computer murmuring with someone on MSN, and then going off on mysterious errands at all hours. It's like living with the *Great Gatsby*!'

She laughed, shaking her head gently.

'I even followed him the other night.'

'What?' Several of our colleagues looked up from their meals and stared at us. Margaret looked self-consciously about her and then at me.

'Julian I think we need to step back a bit and stick to a single plan, solve one part of the problem at a time – it's not that dissimilar from lab work!' She then started to smile and whispered theatrically; 'Where did Max go?'

'He went to meet *Jamie*, of course. I was just being absurd.' I felt myself blushing. I told her the sordid adventure: Resolved to tail Max following a late furtive departure from the house, I had given him about a five-minute head start before slipping out like an assassin. I had quickly caught up with him on Woodstock Road, a dark wedge of shadow dipping and peaking under the streetlights, predictably on his mobile. I had half jogged to keep him in sight, exaggerated, cartoon-like, trying to make as little noise as I could but aware that I must have looked both stupid and suspicious. When I got to Plantation Road, he'd vanished. Appalled at my failure I stood loitering about indecisively until I made a guess that he had turned right to head towards Walton Street. I walked on briskly, thinking myself streetwise (he was doubling back somewhere, an odd but sensible precaution) but when I got to the junction between Plantation Road and Leckford Place there was no sign of anyone. Easily discouraged I had set off back home only to encounter Max *approaching* me in the company of Jamie, deep in discussion. Startled, I had leapt into a driveway scuffing my knee and tripping a security light. Jamie didn't notice but Max, with the sensual acuity of a shark, looked up and, despite the gloom said with chilling interest:

'Dad what are you doing?'

When I finished the saga Margaret was laughing so much her eyes were red and puffy and we had made so much noise that we had felt it prudent to leave the senior common room and retire to my office for coffee. Retelling the story oddly cheered me.

'What must Max think!' she said, slowly getting the better of her mirth. We were configured about my office much the same way as on that first fateful interview over ten years ago. She seemed to sense the *déjà vu* as much as I did. She took my hand and held it gently.

'Julian, why are you so convinced that Jonathan and Max will come back together? I mean I understand the pattern, the symmetry between the end and the beginning, but for what purpose? To be retaken? But Jonathan is normal – except for the tag?'

I held her hand in mine and found I was caressing it, thinking vaguely of Sally's interest in Margaret and recalling Max's nervous interrogation about our relationship. I suddenly realised I loved her, a strange irrelevant thought in the context but quite clear and discernible.

'I'm convinced they're linked, by the wood, and by this mysterious device, somehow, in some way! I think we've missed two really crucial parts of the puzzle. I think Jonathan went back to Leicestershire this year to find what DeMarr found in 1993, and is now in Oxford because he has to tell Max sometime, remind him who he is, explain something – as yet I don't know. The wood and the device are part of this experiment. It can't be a coincidence that Jonathan shows up now just as Max's 22 starts going into some sort of overdrive?' We arose and stood incautiously by the window holding hands. I sensed her looking at me.

'Damn Riley! Where is he!' she said with sudden intensity. 'OK, let's concentrate on Jonathan. I can make a start tomorrow and in the meantime you can search Max's bedroom – again!'

'Margaret!'

She produced a mock frown but we both knew full well that I had become something of an expert. We walked towards the door. I had to give a lecture over at Schools and would now be late.

'I really do feel guilty about this now you know. It's not like Max is ten and I have some sort of parental right! Do you check up on Jamie? *Did you* check up on Katherine?'

'Katherine, yes – it was easier with her. Jamie has always been more complex, more secretive. I agree that, in normal circumstances, the ethics are complex. I mean I would have been very angry had I found my parents snooping about my personal things, but the world was relatively more straightforward then. And once you start looking you are never prepared to deal with what you might find! When I found Jamie's private collection of male *erotica* I have to say I felt initially very embarrassed, then just very guilty, then vaguely curious and then just angry that he hadn't told me!'

We both laughed, instinctively holding hands and yet conscious that Miss Dear was watching us intently through her open door.

The following day, while Margaret scoured Oxford scrutinising *Big Issue* vendors and buying up a large stash of the magazine, I went through Max's room and made two very important discoveries. Under his bed, amid a sort of graveyard of lost socks and rubber bands I found an OS map of the Leicestershire wood. It was old, worn and well folded and had been marked by either Max or Jonathan in red and blue biro. It was probably the map that Daniel had seen Jonathan working from recently. The area where the mound had been situated was covered in crosses, as were specific areas at the opposite end of the wood. I took this as pretty clear evidence of collusion. Did it mean that *Max* had been to North West Leicestershire as well? Or had Jonathan given him the map to plan some later joint operation? Yet the most shocking discovery concerned a blue hospital identification tag, wound up tightly in the back pocket of a pair of Max's jeans in the bottom of his wardrobe. Max had never been inside a hospital since 1993. I smoothed it out and squinted at the small blue label. *Max Lennox d.o.b 23.7.87. Adm 12.2.93.* It was Max's tag from Great Ormond Street. He would have been wearing it when he was abducted. Yet Max and Jonathan had both been found naked, covered in nothing but blankets later traced to Bristol Children's Hospital. The only possible explanation for Max having this now was that he had been given it by Jonathan. Had it been in the wood someone would have found it by now, and had it been with the device it would presumably be with DeMarr?

Later that evening Margaret called around to tell me that Max's stalker was indeed Jonathan, she had found him standing in Carfax, literally under our noses, outside the HSBC bank. Typical of her resourcefulness and stamina she'd hung about and managed to follow him back past the station where with some effort, she discovered he was living on a boat moored up close to the Thames looking across to Osney Island and North Street.

The next morning, at the strangely early hour of 5.30 a.m., I received a telephone call from Mark Riley. Far from ignoring my emails he had been on some family business in South Africa. After a breathless chat he invited me down to the South Coast immediately and, with relative ease, I cancelled my appointments and left just after 10 a.m. I met with Riley pottering about a wide long garden full of rose beds. He looked exactly the same as in 1993 except his hair was snow white and thin. He still smiled a great deal, his face well lined and affable.

'Bizarre really when you come to think about it.' We had gone inside, away from a thick grey drizzle that seemed suspended permanently in the air like fog.

'When I first started growing roses I used to prune them in March, then in late February, and now I prune them before Halloween! Astounding how mild it has become down here. In a good year I can get three or four flushes out of each bush!'

'Really?' I had never grown roses and never pruned anything. After rattling about a well-organised, rather stark kitchen, Mark Riley produced a two-tiered cake stand and poured the tea.

'You can't be too gentle when it comes to roses, Professor. There is an old proverb that says you should let your worst enemy prune them! You can *kill* some varieties, however, if you *are* too harsh.' Riley drank his tea with evident joy. We were surrounded by framed photographs of what appeared to be a large and extended family, although he evidently lived alone. We looked at each other with interest.

'Well, it is *very, very* good to see you after all these years, Julian. Of course I've seen you occasionally on the television, and your old friend DeMarr! How is he? Still wearing his flamboyant shirts I hope! Still trying to flirt?'

We both laughed and I reluctantly gave him a brief synopsis of our argument and the end of our friendship. He seemed to know something about it.

'Often these foreigners don't quite understand plagiarism, Julian. I mean, especially the Italians. When my daughter was at university you know she alleged that her tutor published whole chapters of her Msc dissertation in a journal without citation! When she collared the tutor he said Italians did it all the time! There was a dreadful stink about the whole thing! But I'm sorry to hear about DeMarr. I can't profess to know him well but he was a likeable man and very amusing even at the most difficult and frustrating times. And God knows there were lots of those!' Had it not been for the fog-drizzle the view from the windows would have been spectacular, out along the bay towards a distant French coast.

'Anyway, I'm sure you haven't driven all this way to hear my view on academic citation or roses!' He stood up with particular agility and went to a bureau. He rolled down the lid and removed several blue files and a series of letters.

'After re-reading your emails I had a root through my old notes and log books, made a few calls and *jogged* the brain. The woman you were interested in was Judith MacMillan who worked for the National Radiation Inspectorate, which is now part of the Environmental Agency. Unfortunately she died in 2000, somewhere in Australia, some accident or other. As you may recall we had more agencies working on this case than we had fighting throughout the entirety of WWII! I have however managed to track down, through a friend of mine, the initial report MacMillan submitted in June 1993.' he handed me the first blue folder. 'But it's pretty speculative. It was MacMillan's team that found the evidence that something was buried in the mound.' He sat down, holding the other letters close to his chest like a hand at cards.

'Then there is a device?' Bizarrely the confirmation that it existed startled me. I had never seen the report.

'Most definitely, although I have no idea what it is. I tried my best to stop the digging, Julian. I was pretty outraged at the time because I was still running the formal investigation and the wood was an official crime scene. But one fine morning DeMarr turned up, excluded my forensic team from any further operations and brought in spooks and earthmovers. And Lockwood, you remember Lockwood, yes? Well, Lockwood rang to say they were digging up the wood! By the time I got there it was too late. Typical ruthless spook efficiency! I complained all the way to the Home Office I can tell you!'

'DeMarr?'

'Yes, in person, all of him, tweed coat and gloves, the lot!' and then Mark handed me a document. 'This is a letter from some Minister for something or other. It confirmed that the case was being taken out of our jurisdiction on the grounds of national security. It states quite plainly that in the light of evidence found in the mound, and under advice from the principal scientific advisor to the government, there was no choice but to take this 'regrettable' decision!'

I scanned the letter quickly. There was no mention of what the evidence was. The letter was dated May 4th 1993. The committee would still have been in constant session. I felt an old anger stir within me.

'I wonder how they found it? And do you know where it is being kept?'

Riley looked at me, faintly amused by my tone, as if I was contemplating some sort of heist.

'When you read MacMillan's report you'll see that she noted that there was a strong magnetic field surrounding that end of the spinney, and that several planes flying into the East Midlands Airport had reported navigational errors. They would have flown close to, or over, the exact location where the children were found. It's probably what led the spooks to it. For years it was kept at the MoD.' He was evidently enjoying himself. 'Curious, isn't it?' he mused.

'It certainly is! I should have acted sooner! There were endless rumours but no evidence – I put it all down to public hysteria!'

'Don't be too hard on yourself. You were rather preoccupied and more to the point why should it occur to you that DeMarr would hide it?'

'Nothing was found at any of the other sites?'

'No. After Macmillan's discovery I know for a fact that every location was scanned for tell tale magnetic profiles like the one over the mound. They all came up blank.' Riley looked at me, his friendly eyes glinting in the dim, cosy room.

'So the wood was more important than all the other locations?' I asked cautiously.

'Or Max and Jonathan were more important than the other children?' Mark pursed his lips. 'Is Max well, Julian? I don't need to know the details of course, but clearly you've come to me for a reason?' I sat chewing my lower lip for a while, perplexed.

'Max is well for now, but I'm worried, Mark. I'm here for lots of reasons probably. Firstly, because the committee I chaired was not presented with all the facts or the full cooperation of the authorities. Secondly because Jonathan has returned to Oxford and has, I suspect, struck up a friendship with Max. I also know from Daniel Lockwood that Jonathan returned to the wood earlier this year and was digging about, looking for something; I am guessing the missing device. Of all the mysteries that surround this case, Jonathan and the device are the two I can least explain.'

Mark looked at me, intensely interested. 'Good God. How astounding! Have you seen the boys together?'

'As good as.' I put my hand into my jacket pocket and removed a small envelope containing Max's hospital tag and the OS map. I trusted Mark enough to show him both although there was no need yet to burden him with the ever-present mystery of chromosome 22. I gave him the envelope.

'I found these in Max's possession. The tag is from Great Ormond Street where he was admitted having been transferred down from Scotland. The map is the one Jonathan took with him to the wood. Lockwood saw him with it.'

Mark looked suitably intrigued. He opened the envelope, glanced at the contents and whistled through his teeth. He then proceeded to spin the tag about in his hand for a while, absentmindedly. 'Well, well, well. You're still in touch with Lockwood then? He was a sensible fellow.' He paused thoughtfully and then looked at me sharply. 'Do you think Jonathan is a threat? Do you think or suspect that he is involving Max in this, against his will? Coercion perhaps?'

'No, it's not that. I think Jonathan and the device are *really important*, Mark. Although none of the children could recall anything of their ordeal, I think Jonathan has started to remember, something at least, perhaps he never actually forgot it! I think that this explains the trauma in Jonathans life, and I think he has *sought out* Max for a reason because well, because Max is the experiment,' I was thinking out loud really, trying to articulate a series of theories that had been slowly coalescing in my mind all autumn. I felt Mark's gaze burning onto the side of my face. Then I said, quietly, to myself 'I think that Jonathan is *still in touch* with the aliens who abducted them.' For a while neither of us said anything and then finally Mark broke the silence.

'Well, I must say, this is a rum business from start to finish, Professor. This device obviously makes more sense to you than it does to me, so I won't press you on it but I was saving the best until last!' He handed me one last set of letters, tied together with a green treasury tag.

'What's this?' The letterhead was covered by a large red TOP SECRET block stamped across the typing.

'It's a provisional chemical analysis of the device itself. It was an appendix attached to the provisional report I showed you earlier. It's well above my head but you will understand it, I'm sure.'

Taken aback I found that the papers were trembling in my hand. Mark tried to look modestly indifferent to my obvious shock. The documents consisted of several dense computer printouts, old dot matrix fonts on yellowed paper, the sort that had perforated edges. I put my glasses on quickly and standing up leaned into the bay window. I scanned through the sheets and felt myself tensing with excitement.

'Interesting?' said Riley, as if he was keen to share the discovery. Even at a cursory glance the significance of the find was obvious: the device was made up of ribose, the building block of both the DNA and RNA molecule. There were other chemical signatures as well: ones I had seen before and almost in the same quantities: nitrogen-15, hydroxyapatite and selenium. I looked up, firstly into the grey fog and then at Mark.

'It contains almost the exact same chemistry as Max's blood. It has his chemical smell all over it.'

Mark frowned and remained looking unsettled.

'And that helps?'

'Mark this is a huge breakthrough! Are you sure you don't know where the device is now?'

He shook his head sadly. 'Alas no. The MoD archives were closed some years ago. It might even be with the Americans. Once its existence was widely known you can imagine what sort of organisations wanted their noses in the trough!' I instinctively thought of *Wild Fire* and Davies. 'Perhaps Jonathan might have some answers?' he suggested suddenly. 'Having found it gone from the wood, he might now be looking for it himself – he's a resourceful fellow if I remember? Does he live in Oxford?'

I mentioned the boat. Mark looked impressed at my information and then vaguely cunning. 'We could pay his boat a visit? Have a snoop about?'

'Isn't that illegal?'

Mark pulled a sort of DeMarr face, a sort of mock surprise.

'Not necessarily. We could finesse the point with some help from the local constabulary; I have a few old associates bored in high places.'

I jumped at the idea instinctively.

'That would be really helpful!'

'Excellent!' Mark replaced the tab into the envelope along with the map and passed it back to me. I went to hand him back the reports but he asked me to keep them all. We talked for a while longer, mostly about Braed-abarker. Mark was unaware that he had died of cancer and he was also surprised to hear that Sally and I had separated. As we walked into the hallway he suddenly asked if I had a photograph of Max. I obliged. I carried a picture of Max inside my wallet, cropped badly to fit in next to my driving license. It was recent, taken earlier in the year and he was looking mysterious, enigmatic, his head turned to one side as if he was listening to something invisible standing behind him.

'Good God! Is that Max!' he seemed genuinely incredulous, no doubt recalling the small boy on the mound. 'God he looks astounding! How old is he? Eighteen?'

'Eighteen next year.'

He returned the photograph. 'Three daughters myself and two with children now, all girls. I'm rather glad I never had a boy, actually.' He didn't elaborate.

I stood in the doorway and shook hands. I walked down the sloping path towards the driveway. The fog-drizzle was lifting. The sharp smell of the sea hinted at its vast, invisible presence all around. I felt relieved to have made the journey, relieved to have seen Mark and finally clarified something. I climbed in the car and made my way back towards London. It was mid afternoon, and away from the coast the light stayed gloomy, a sort of battleship grey. As I approached the motorway I had a curious and indistinct sensation that I was being followed.

Riley did not waste much time. Literally the next day, just after Max had gone off to school, and as I and Margaret sat working through the data on the device, Riley rang to say that he had arranged with the local police for a visit to Jonathan's boat and would be outside my front door within the hour! It was a bitterly cold, clear day, with bleak sunlight angled low at every turn. Margaret left with Macmillan's initial report while Mark and I walked to our destination, chatting amiably as if we were on a hike. We quickly passed by the railway station and then turned left past the Westgate Hotel, arriving suddenly in a strange part of the city: anonymous, abandoned, a backdrop of warehouses and sheds up against the river. At the end of Mill Street a small yard opened out into an exposed grey-blue landscape of waterways and bridges, with a variety of boats moored up tightly into the bank and below a high wall. A majority seemed deserted and cocooned in tarpaulins, the remnants of forgotten summers, but others trailed smoke and were clearly occupied.

'*Very* Braudel,' said Riley clapping his hands together in the cold. The brilliant sunlight bleached everything of colour. I thought rather bleakly: so this is where Jonathan lived. This is where, exhausted with cold after standing around all day selling his magazine he returned to sleep and dream, and dream of what? Max? Me? Aliens? Had Max been here? At that moment a patrol car appeared behind us, smudging the gravel and parked up at the entry of Millbank Street. A man and a woman in uniform climbed out and ambled towards us, the man yawning. A radio caw cawed like a bird through the open passenger window. 'Ah yes, back up,' said Riley rather whimsically.

The prospect of confronting Jonathan was bad enough – I was genuinely afraid of his reaction – but in the presence of two uniformed police officers the whole adventure seemed suddenly quite monstrous. Luckily however the houseboat was empty. After a few boisterous knocks the PW picked the door lock with disturbing ease and we filed down through a narrow kitchen galley and into a long sitting room with sofas converted to beds. It was surprisingly clean and tidy, with the tables lifted down and the bedding rolled up on each pallet. Behind a bathroom a narrow corridor led to two other cabins. One was more chaotic than the other, and decorated with a series of UFO posters and pictures cut out of magazines and newspapers.

'Here's our man, I think!' said Riley. I stood to one side while the officers piled in and worked it over for me with a dull, mechanical efficiency. My eyes immediately caught sight of my own photograph as well as one of DeMarr, glued over the narrow, dirty window. Both were from the science pages of *The Guardian*, 1998. There were other snippets of print plastered about randomly, some were from *New Scientist* and other serious magazines, others from more random, specialised, UFO circulars and the written confessions of abductees, the factual co-existing with the fictional in a bewildering colourful collage. On a small makeshift desk Jonathan had colour coordinated about a hundred felt-tip pens and crayons, meticulously and obsessively in long rows. Apart from a sense of chaos everything seemed clean. I stood feeling overwhelmed. Rooting under a single, hard bed, the policeman unearthed shoeboxes containing endless photocopies of articles on the human genome project; my own modest contributions to the mapping of chromosome 22, and extensive coverage of our near miss at a Nobel prize. There was also, intriguingly, a lot of material relating to Dolly the sheep and nuclear transfer as a technique for cloning. The policeman then picked up a small globe, painted with stars. It was broken near *Ursa Major*.

'I bought him that – for his 12th birthday.' I said, quietly touched that he had kept it. The two police officers looked at me curiously. Jonathan seemed obsessed about shoeboxes: some he used as filing drawers, the rest he piled up all neat and empty like a form of installation art.

'Quite a collection!' said Mark, following my gaze and smiling broadly. He had pulled on a pair of plastic gloves, the sort that surgeons wore, and was skimming through Jonathan's bedside table neatly and with some respect. Suddenly Mark made a small exclamation. 'Julian, look here!' He fished out another shoebox up from the floor labelled DEVICE. It contained a mass of newspaper clippings related to stories and rumours of the 'alien artefact' excavated from the wood in 1993. Some of these reports I had seen myself on my tentative sortie into the web: some were new. The most recent cutting – dated in September of this year – referred to news that the British government had passed on the device to the US in *April 2005*.

'Useful?' queried Mark, scrutinising me closely. I nodded at him bleakly. The policeman left the room and started working his way through the rest of the boat but with an air of boredom.

'Yes. I think it's very useful. At least I can double-check some of these sources myself.' I looked at the date again: why had it taken so long for the Americans to get it? Then suddenly the policewoman said 'Oh yes!' and passed me over yet another shoe box. It was filled with photographs, neatly organised by date and meticulously labelled, and at first glance, all of Max.

'Good God!'

On close inspection the box contained well over a hundred photographs of my son. The earliest one had been taken in or around 1996, and the last one was taken about a month ago, outside Farndon Road. It showed Max talking with Jamie in the driveway. Jamie's face was cast down, Max was touching his shoulder. It looked oddly posed, symbolic, very *Burns Jones* like. They made a striking pair, one dark, the other fair. For a strange moment it was like looking at a still from a movie.

'Who is that with Max?' asked Mark.

'Jamie Relph, Margaret's son. They go to the same school.' I flicked through the rest of the pictures at random. It was difficult to grasp the sheer number and the effort that had gone into taking them!

'It's incredible! I mean I guessed that Jonathan had

recently returned to Oxford but this looks like he's been coming here for – *years!*' I gasped, horrified that I could have been so inattentive as to have never seen or noticed Jonathan. Several pictures contained me or Sally, blithely unaware that we were being stalked.

'It's surprisingly easy to get sophisticated equipment these days, Prof.' said the policewoman, sympathetically. 'If they've been taken with a zoom lens there's no reason why you would have noticed him in the vicinity. He could have been a good distance away. He might even have got some other guy to take them.'

'Good God!' I said again, pathetically, looking at a picture of Max outside Green College walking with me. He was wearing shorts and I was wearing some bizarre, vaguely absurd hat with a wide brim. Only on close examination did I realise it was actually DeMarr. There were other shots of Max at Blenheim, running through the gardens, Max at parties, Max on his own, his satchel slung over his arm his face inscrutable.

'Good looking kid – this your son? Should be a model,' said the policewoman. At the back of the shoebox behind the last and earliest photo were a series of sketches, on plane folded A4 paper, sketches of trees – birch trees, well drawn, their barks delicately shaded. Riley caught my eye and looked at me, the inclusive look of a man who had been with me at the beginning.

'How very interesting,' he said as if I had found some sort of antique.

'What shall we do, Guv?' the PW asked Mark. Mark turned to her, his eyes and lips thoughtful, and then quickly back to me.

'Julian? Shall we take these? Along with the clippings and stuff? We could keep an eye on Jonathan now, try and catch him when he next feels the urge to snap a photo of Max?'

I sat down on the end of the bed. I had no real idea. Jonathan had followed Max almost from the beginning, and he had also, more to the point, followed me and the work on chromosome 22. Why? Because he was obsessed? Or because he too was waiting for something? It was intriguing but also still so inconclusive. I had somehow hoped to find more, a journal perhaps, explicit signs? I felt the PW watching me intently.

'At the very least isn't this a case of an invasion of privacy, even if no threat has been made?' she suggested as if this might encourage me to do something.

'But no law as such has been broken –' Mark was rubbing his lower lip with his finger, thoughtfully. 'Privacy is a bit of a dog's breakfast I'm afraid in tort law, and it's not as if we can do him for trespassing. My suggestion is that you take these and keep them safe. It might provoke him to doing something further and we can then detain him.'

'Could we take him in for questioning?' I suggested but then thought it inappropriate, pointless, too confrontational. My fear of seeing Jonathan alone almost overwhelmed me.

'For what, exactly?' asked Mark not unkindly. 'Although there's nothing to stop you staying behind and having a chat with him?' he looked at the broken globe on the table. 'I mean he knew you quite well once, and from the amount of material he has hoarded on you he seems to know about you even now?' Mark raised his eyebrows at me and smiled knowingly. Did he sense my anxiety, my sense of shame? There came the sound of someone lifting up the engine hatch and then, after a wobble and shake to the boat, the sound of a stick being rattled in the fresh water tank under the tiller. Eventually the policeman returned, empty handed.

'Clean as a whistle.'

'Ok, Julian, we'll depart and leave you?'

'Mark, I can't thank you enough –'

'My dear man, don't mention it. It was good to see you again. And do let me know how the whole business pans out? Yes?' He turned, hesitating in the door. The two officers had walked forward and the boat moved oddly, inertial, gently nudged down and sideways by their motion.

'Be careful Mark.' We shook hands. 'This may sound a touch theatrical but I did have the sense that I was being followed when I returned from Hove.'

To my discomfort, he nodded but said nothing.

I waited for about an hour, perhaps less. The cold grew intense, numbing my feet and legs. For a while I read randomly through Jonathan's extensive archives; looking over the various theories that people had 'blogged' up concerning the abduction. Most were mad, others intriguingly accurate. Yet the longer I waited the more I lost my nerve: was this such a good idea? Would it not have been better to be on the outside, knocking on the door like a regular visitor, instead of actually sitting on Jonathan's bed like some sort of sleuth? Jonathan had always been prone to paranoia; God knows he was difficult enough at the best of times. As I neared the threshold of retreat I heard feet clamping down into the bow, the move of the boat again as people walked into the galley and various bits of outraged conversation with lots of swearing. It was quickly evident that the occupants were aware that their home had been searched. Next minute someone stood in the cabin doorway opposite me, an outline in the darkness, a yellow-orange glow of a cigarette, end on, around the mouth. I rose from the bed, trying to look calm and polite, unaware that I was virtually invisible. A male voice said 'Fuck!' and ran back and then after a brief commotion someone flicked a light switch on and I stood blinking, looking at Jonathan and behind him, a gaggle of youths, a women with a nose piercing, a tall thin black youth with dreadlocks holding the cigarette in his left hand. For a moment, Jonathan's expression was utterly enigmatic, but it signalled recognition, perhaps even shock.

'It's ok. Leave us. I know this guy.' he said eventually with unexpected authority.

With some hesitancy, and more curiosity than ill will, Jonathan's friends backed away and returned to the front of the boat. Jonathan stood looking at me, his face blue-red with cold.

'You broke into my fucking house?'

'Not exactly Jonathan. I came with Mark Riley, who in turn came with some police from the local constabulary; I needed to see you, I needed to find out what you know.'

'Riley? Fuck quite a reunion! Shame you didn't invite Louis DeMarr and *your wife*!'

'Or Max?' I snapped back.

He glared at me with sudden anger and slammed the door closed behind him. He threw a baseball cap onto the bed. Beneath it his hair was cropped very short, reddish, his skull visible. It made him look oddly monkish: and yet he looked dramatically better than the last time I had seen him

'What do you want?'

'I've told you. I want answers. You've been following Max, you've been following me. You've been to the wood. You obviously know about the device, you know what Max is for, what is going to happen to him –'

'And you *don't*?' his tone was incredulous, one of utter disbelief. 'You really *don't*! After all this time?'

'Jonathan.' I tried to sound calm, measured but tears were suddenly close to the surface, stinging my eyes. 'Max is my son, whatever he is, and Max is changing, at the genetic level and now possibly at the physical level. Please, you have to help me!'

'Ok, ok. Just calm down man.' Jonathan's voice was suddenly soft, almost affectionate. 'And I haven't told him anything. He *can't* know – not yet. Not until it happens.'

'Until what happens? Jonathan, for God's sake – what will happen to my son?'

Jonathan sat down heavily on the narrow bed, rubbing his face with large, raw hands. I could hardly breathe. 'Sit down, Julian.'

I sat on the edge of the bed as if Jonathan was a patient. He looked at me, not unkindly. 'You took your time coming to me, seeking my help. I'd almost given up on you!'

'You could have come to me, Jonathan! You knew where I lived and the last time we met – well – I thought you wanted rid of me.'

He smiled, a pleasant smile, at some memory, something long ago. 'Perhaps I did. We haven't got long. The experiment will terminate when Max is eighteen, July 2006. He'll return to the wood and he'll need the device.'

'Or –'

'The experiment concludes but Max dies.'

I closed my eyes in horror. 'You know this? How?'

'I know *shit loads*. I've heard things, voices in my fucking head – voices that told me to go back to the wood, that told me where to look, told me that the time was coming when I would need to stay close to Max!' Jonathan tapped his head dramatically.

'Voices?' for one intense moment I thought he was mad. His eyes were wide and the pupils dilated but then I understood he was referring to the tag in his head.

'Then you do communicate with them?'

'I wouldn't put it quite like that.' he snapped. 'You were supposed to be running the show! It was supposed to be *your* committee! How come you let everyone walk over you! Especially bloody DeMarr!'

'What do the voices say, exactly?'

'They tell me to find things,' Jonathan said, struggling to regain his composure. 'They help me remember. They led me to Max's hospital tag amd then, to the mound –

which of course had gone! I was supposed to find the device and keep it safe for Max until he needed it.' Jonathan looked away from me, agitated, upset. 'I keep trying to explain to them that it's gone but they don't hear me, they don't respond – they keep on and on about the wood and the mound!'

'Jonathan, listen to me. When did the voices start?'

'*They've never stopped!*' He winced as he said this. His hands locked together around his head as if his skull was about to explode. He leaned away from me, holding himself like something injured.

'I don't understand, Jonathan.' If I did the implications were too horrifying.

'Sometimes I hear them; sometimes they go silent – for weeks – sometimes years. But they've always been in my head since I was found. They usually speak a language I don't understand, but it's about Max, always Max! Sometimes the tense is different as well, or wrong, as if Max is gone or yet to come. But I can tell his name in any language! They represent Max in so many different ways, I mean – shit! There's one symbol, like a line, a strange line! A dark black crescent, surrounded by light!' he looked at me. He seemed almost hysterical. Instinctively I thought of my dream.

'It was the voices inside my head that begged me to let him go to you, to allow you to adopt him, they *wanted you to adopt Max* –' He had suddenly started to cry, tears welling silently down his face as if to recall his separation from Max caused him physical pain. I had gone cold, nauseous. I put my hand to my face as if somehow I could wipe this all away, his loss, the horror of being abandoned. I sat listening to Jonathan sob but I felt remote, far away in another universe, unable to comfort him. Again the image of Max was in my head, the impossible youth, his hands to his face, searching for something.

'Do you know what the experiment is for?'

'Yes, sort of. A lot of what I see is fucked up, Julian. It doesn't make any immediate sense. It never has. I don't know who *they are* but Max is their saviour, and he is coded to remember them when the time comes,' he spoke slowly, carefully.

'Coded?'

'Yes. It's part of the information on his 22.' said Jonathan without any particular emphasis. 'The aliens are desperate, afraid, and alone.' He looked up at me in sudden puzzlement 'They *came from Earth*, Julian. They came from Earth and left a long time ago and in their despair they came back to find help.'

I stood up from the bed afraid I might be physically sick. After years of nothing, guesswork, poking about in the dark, random confusing clues and bits of data, suddenly here, in the most unlikely of places, came this sudden, astounding rush of information. Jonathan watched my reactions curiously, almost apologetically.

'They told me that they had come back here because they were *dying.*'

I stood perfectly still, every nerve focused on what Jonathan was saying.

'Dying?'

'Yes. Coming back here and looking for the children was their last hope of survival. They'd been here before, many times, always looking, always searching.'

'A disease?'

'No.' Jonathan closed his eyes again, hard, as if he was trying to remember. 'Not really. No. They are very, very *old*, childless, no – more like,' he struggled for words, 'Infertile?'

'*Sterile*,' I whispered to myself. It was not a question. I saw in my mind an outline of Max's 22, cleaned up in my imagination, free of the fuzz and blur of intense magnification. And then in one extraordinary flash of intuition I understood what it was they were trying to do. I saw the experiment and its purpose in astounding, shocking clarity. I heard the youth in my dream, the youth who was Max and yet not Max, say to me '*I am pregnant*'. I saw the vast swarm of genomes nestled along Max's 22 racked up like eggs. The revelation stunned me. For a moment I could not speak. I stood forward, away from Jonathan looking fixedly ahead, trying to remain calm, to not scream or call out. Eventually, fighting down a rush of panic, I asked carefully.

'Do they have a name?'

'Yes. They are known as the Seeth.'

'Did you ever recall seeing them, Jonathan? Can you remember what they look like?'

Jonathan looked pained.

'No, *not really*. Sometimes I think they're like us, humanoid, upright, sometimes I recall them as different. I mean very different, like animals or trees, or things that fly. Or sometimes like stones. Or just colours? Sometimes I'm not even sure they have any form at all!'

'Like ghosts,' I said, my voice a whisper.

'Yeah, or dreams,' he said intelligently, watching my expression. He must have seen my epiphany. 'You understand it now, then?'

'Yes. Thanks to you, to what you've just told me. You've just nudged the whole astounding experiment into some shape at last!' I covered my face in disbelief. When I removed my hands I was looking at the mosaic of newspaper cuttings Jonathan had used to cover the window. I felt relieved now, perhaps even sad. The answer had been staring at me in the face for years. Like everything that is intuitively, naturally right, it now seemed obvious. It seemed astounding that I had not worked it out before. I looked at the young man keenly.

'In 1993, DeMarr speculated that the experiment had been designed to hybridise two distinct, but related species. The theory did not make much sense, for various, complicated reasons, and we were then distracted by James DeSilva, a virologist, who was obsessed that the children had been infected by something: a weapon, a virus to recode the children's physiology into some entirely new species. Now it looks as if Louis was closer to the truth. If the Seeth originated from *Earth*, then we would no doubt share a genetic ancestry with them. There would be differences, such as the unknown amino acid base pairings in the DNA, but there would be much commonality. That is why they came back. It is that commonality they are desperately looking for.'

'To do what, to breed?'

'In a manner of speaking. For whatever reason, the Seeth obviously became infertile and no longer capable of sexual reproduction. And you said they were very old – implying that they had not reproduced for many years, possibly centuries? I think that somehow, in some way, they *devastated* their own genome. Either through accident or, God forbid, some bizarre technology. However they did it, they brought their species to the edge of extinction!'

Jonathan continued to stare at me with clear, wide eyes. For a strange, fleeting moment, there was almost a passing facial resemblance to Max, to the way that Max looked when he was startled or surprised.

'And Max is the answer?'

'I am pretty convinced now that the reproduction of genetic material inside Max's 22 is an elaborate attempt to repair the Seeth genome by sequencing endless hybrids of human and Seeth DNA. They clearly knew which part of their genome was damaged: they only inserted into the children *five chromosomal pairings* of what looks like a basic genome consisting of twenty-six pairs. Max's 22 literally contains millions of re-sequenced chromosomes. And it would appear that only children suffering from *Ewings Sarcoma* provides suitable hosts and in only one did the process of repairing actually begin.' I looked at Jonathan utterly convinced that, in outline, this was what the Seeth were doing.

'Which one of the millions of genomes is the right code? All of them?' asked Jonathan quietly. He had followed my explanation implicitly.

'I don't really know. They will probably need them all to ensure that the subsequent gene pool is deep enough to avoid mutation. I presume that the Seeth will return and extract them from Max in order to re-populate their planet through some very advanced form of gene therapy.' I shrugged. 'But where does the device fit in? Perhaps this harvests the hybridised genetic data?' Its chemical composition suggested this but Jonathan's assertion that it was necessary to save Max and not the experiment still bewildered me. I felt a nag of doubt, a sense that I was still missing something. As if he could read my doubts, Jonathan nodded his head and said quietly, 'A storage device yes, but it harvests Max's genetic profile and not the Seeth genomes.'

I looked at him blankly. 'Jonathan are you sure that is what the voices say?' Why extract Max's genetic data from an alien and not vice versa? Jonathan was watching me desperately. 'I don't know. If you don't understand, why should I!'

I sat down again trying to rationalise, organise what I now knew. What was I missing? And then, with a sudden wave of terror, I realised that not only had DeMarr been broadly correct in his theory, *so too had DeSilva*. Jonathan saw my look of horror.

'What is it?'

'Good God, no! Wait! There are no Seeth hosts, no surrogate pregnancies! The experiment actually transforms Max into the host!' I looked at Jonathan. I felt wet and clammy. 'A host pregnant with an entire race of new hybrids?' The symmetry between the start and the end state of the experiment loomed out at me. 'Yes, think about it, almost the exact reverse of how the experiment started, a child containing five pairs of alien chromosomes becomes a Seeth containing millions of genomes!'

'But why?' and even as Jonathan asked this I understood the bold logic of what was being done, the sheer audacity of the experiment as well as the strange inability of Jonathan to communicate with the aliens: *it was because they were already extinct.*

'Because the experiment is in fact automated in some way, Jonathan. The Seeth are already dead, they were probably already extinct in 1993. Max must therefore be entirely recoded to save them – and in doing so his data – his own humanity – has to be totally cannibalised to restore the Seeth, just as DeSilva suspected. But for some as yet unknown reason the experiment devised a way of saving Max, through the device. It takes Max into 'storage' – before his data is completely re-sequenced into the emerging hybrid. It's the equivalent of copying his human genome onto a hard drive so it can be restored later, copied before it has been modified beyond recognition.'

'Why would they save Max's identity even after the experiment had succeeded?'

I gripped my head in my hands, desperately trying to think: why indeed? An act of compassion? And had the aliens targeted me because their automated experiment had presumed I would know what to do with the device? Was I expected to know how to regenerate my son, after he had in effect regenerated the Seeth? Or would Max be taken by the experiment itself, in some mysterious, inexplicable way? Back to some dead world? And wasn't this all missing the shocking point that we had lost the device and had no way of retrieving it?

'We have to stop the recombination process on Max's 22 as quickly as we can!' I said hopelessly, feeling an intense surge of anger.

'And destroy an entire race?' gasped Jonathan.

'Why should my son sacrifice himself? He was never given a chance!'

Jonathan was silent for a time and then softly touched

my arm. 'His life was spared once, Julian. He would have died years ago without the Seeth, and the Seeth have devised a way to save him. Perhaps he is precious to them?'

I looked at Jonathan as if he was deranged. 'They're going to hatch a pregnant Seeth hybrid inside him. Even if you trust them to restore Max, or if we have the ability here to clone him and bring him back, it won't be Max!' I stopped, close to breaking. In my passion I recalled Mrs Lennox and her strange belief that Max was already a copy in 1993. That her real son had been taken and never returned. 'And if they love him so much Jonathan, why isn't he supposed to know? Why haven't they told him!'

'Because it will terrify him, and because the Seeth plan – had *planned* – for him to gradually become self-aware. The tag, remember?'

'But Max has no tag Jonathan, not anymore. You were the only child to retain it.'

'This will change soon. When his tag regenerates he will start to remember and he will know what to do. Besides, he knows a great deal already. He's followed me to this boat, broken in and stolen a map and his hospital tag. Like father like son.'

'So you haven't *met* him?'

Jonathan seemed embarrassed, almost awkward. 'Not yet, not to speak to. I keep putting it off, he's a bit overwhelming – and look at me – I am hardly the guy he would befriend until he starts to remember. And then there's that blond guy Max hangs around with all the time, he really dislikes me.'

'Jamie?'

'Yeah, Relph's kid, the guard dog!'

'But surely Max *recognises* you?'

'Perhaps – he is starting to remember – as the genomes recode the memories will start as well as the realisation over what has to be done.' I thought of the image of Max in the window of Sally's office at Farndon Road, the diaries scrutinised and hastily returned. The timing all seemed to make some sense. We sat in silence again and listened to the distant movements of Jonathan's housemates. I wondered what they made of my visit, of Jonathan's obvious recognition of me. I was still stunned by what I had discovered and suddenly tired beyond belief.

'If the device was so important to Max why in God's name was it left in the wood for DeMarr to find? It just doesn't make sense? Did you have any contact with it? Can you remember it at all?' I said eventually, anxious that my questions sounded like an accusation.

'I've never seen it. The Seeth returned to the wood after we had been found – a few weeks after.'

I blinked at him. 'The second sighting? Bugger! Lockwood wrote to me about it just after the committee started its work. They – I mean the ship, the experiment – came back with the device?'

'I guess.'

'It seems so random, Jonathan. Did it forget to leave it the first time, or in some odd way change its mind about Max?'

'Perhaps it panicked, rushed everything. I think everything was sort of going to shit by then?' He stared at me and then glanced down, sniffing loudly and rubbing his nose. Had I not in 1993, sifting through the evidence, thought much the same: that whatever had been done to the children had been rushed, done in a hurry? I stood up, sighing, and tried to focus on the simple task ahead of us: the near impossible job of finding the device before Max reached his 18th birthday.

'Jonathan has DeMarr got the device? Does he know what it is? Has he worked out the experiment? Have the Americans?'

He scowled at the flow of questions as if I was interrogating him. He jumped up and prowled about his room and then turned to his desk and started to touch his pens and straighten them out.

'Davies and the alien hunters know about Max, they've been following him recently and they suspect that D-Day is his eighteenth birthday – they've been on to the Seeth for years, but you know that already – but perhaps they don't know they're extinct, if you're right about that part: they want the Seeth to come for Max and communicate with them. I don't get DeMarr at all. I never have – or your wife for that matter. DeMarr's been sniffing about me for years, double dealing, hiding things, scheming behind everyone's back! And he *hated* you! He used to come and see me at Witney, lots of presents, lots of money, walks in the woods and loads of questions: did I know what Max was doing, did I know anything about the wood, had anything else been left there? He vanished completely for years but then he turned up suddenly at Bristol in 2004, having tracked me down somehow. God was I fucking shocked to see him! All smiles and chuckles, walking into my squat with a bag of sugared almonds as if I was a ten year old. I was going straight and on probation, and he was the last guy I wanted to see. And the same old questions, about Max, but new ones as well: this time about the tags, and a new twist to his obsession with the device: What was it? What did *it do*? How was it related to the experiment? Did I know it contained specific chemicals very similar to Max's, like I was a fucking bio-chemist or something!'

Again I was intrigued by DeMarr's delay. Why had he ignored the significance of the provisional report on the device for almost ten years? Or had he, like me, simply ignored or forgotten about it?

'One thing's for sure: DeMarr is not working for 'Dolly' Davies! He hated the Americans from the beginning, and he never trusted the alien brigade as he called them. He was always trying to throw them a false trail.'

Suddenly my anger and frustration over Louis fell flat.

'If that's all true shouldn't we approach him, Jonathan? He has oddly helped me in the past – for whatever reason –'

Jonathan was shaking his head vigorously as if I had suggested something quite shocking.

'No way! Whatever he's up to isn't any good! He's in the US as we speak!'

'But he's less of a threat than *Wild Fire*!'

'I agree, but he compromised Max years ago and he hasn't got the device any more – it's gone to the US!'

'Are you sure about that?' I recalled the articles in Jonathan's shoebox. 'Is that information reliable?'

'I'm afraid to say it is.'

'Shit!' I said, uncharacteristically. 'This just keeps getting worse and worse!'

'Yeah? Then brace yourself for this: DeSilva is back from Australia. He met up with his old mate and buddy Davies at a conference in the Hague.'

I felt as if someone had just put a gun to my temple: to Max's.

'How do you know that?' I asked pathetically.

'I told you, I know shit loads. DeSilva finally worked out DeMarr's little deception in 1993 over the plates and Max's 22 and was apoplectic with rage. It's probably why DeMarr's done a runner, you know he's a coward at heart!'

'Why didn't Davies and DeSilva get together sooner? Davies would have known that James was on the committee.'

Jonathan shrugged, disinterested. 'Probably for the same reason you didn't cooperate with DeMarr?' It was a rebuke and I justly deserved it.

'Jonathan what are we going to do!'

He looked up at me suddenly, perhaps shaken by the

tone of my voice or by his sudden inclusion.

'We have to get the device back. It's pretty simple. Or build another? If the hard drive metaphor is correct, you can do that, can't you? Aren't you a genius?' The idea that I could casually construct a replacement was momentarily as ridiculous as retrieving the device from the Americans. I almost laughed.

'The tags and the device, are they related? And do you have any idea when Max will complete his transformation?' I asked randomly, thinking of the changes to Max's eyes over the summer. I felt hysterical, insane. My entire world, fragile and improvised for so long, had suddenly and instantly collapsed.

'I think they're both biogenic components of the experiment – I am not sure when Max will change – we need to keep an eye on him.'

'We have, Jonathan, for almost twelve years!' I breathed out desperately and yet the image of us together suddenly touched me deeply, the realisation of Jonathan's long vigil was almost a source of hope. With sudden decision, Jonathan ended the interview.

'Look, it's getting late. You'd better go.' He spoke abruptly and for a moment I feared that his old hostility had returned, but he was evidently hungry.

'You'll meet with me again?' I asked desperately.

'Of course, of course we'll meet, but you mustn't tell Max anything yet? However difficult – do you understand?'

'Yes. I guess so.'

'Are you still in touch with Dena Small? With Braedabarker?'

'Braedabarker's dead, Jonathan.' I was surprised he didn't know that. 'But yes I am still in touch with Dena – is she safe?'

'Yeah, she's cool. She knows a lot about the alien crowd and the first contact spooks. She might be our one real chance. Brief her if you can? She might have some idea where the device is. I am sorry about Joe. He was kind to me.'

I stood up slowly, my legs stiff with cold and cramp.

'Jonathan what about Sally? Do you know how she's involved in this?'

He looked at me rather gently. 'She's mysterious. She seems to have left DeMarr's conspiracy some time ago. Hasn't she just become principal science guru?'

I nodded. We were walking forward towards the galley. Several people were eating quietly. They looked outlandish, rather New Age, but attractive in an aggressive, predatory sort of way. As we passed through towards the door I tried to look amicable, like a visiting Uncle. I thought what curious friends Jonathan had made over the years. Once outside in the cold night I scrambled up the ladder and turned to see Jonathan looking up at me pensively.

'Listen, don't come here again – it's dangerous. I'll contact you. And don't tell Max anything –'

'But what if he asks, Jonathan? I can't deny it – I can't lie to him! And he might know things that will help me!'

'You've been lying to him for years, Julian!' for a moment he sounded angry. Suddenly he seemed to relent. 'If he asks you something then yes, answer him: remember the Seeth chose you as much as they chose him!'

The statement no longer surprised me.

Despite the lateness of the hour – it was past 11 p.m. – I called in on Margaret. I was desperate to just be with her. Neville answered the door. Despite my long friendship with his wife, I hardly knew him.

'Oh hi, I thought you were Jamie.' There was a deliberate pause. 'Do you want to come in?' He seemed a bit bemused. We walked into the hallway, a long narrow passageway that led directly to the kitchen. Margaret was upstairs in what had been Katherine's room. He shouted Margaret's name up the stairs, and then added mine – as if we were children and I had called around to see if she was coming out to play. I wondered if the apparent sarcasm was intended. He left into the nearby sitting room. I could hear the unmistakably clipped, animated commentary and roar of some sort of sporting event from the TV. Margaret leaned over from the landing above and called down.

'Hey! How did the police raid go? I've been calling you all evening. Come up to my eerie and we can drink some of my elderberry wine.'

I removed my shoes. I felt excited at the prospect of telling Margaret, at sharing what I knew, and yet devastated at the prospect of reliving the horror of Max's fate. Jonathan's conviction that we could save Max now seemed wildly misplaced. Margaret seemed to sense my despair.

'Julian, what is it?'

I walked briskly up the stairs. She was standing looking down at me, her face cautious, composed now to receive bad news.

'Jonathan knew – well he knew enough – for me to work out what the experiment is for.'

Her face registered the news, and then, suddenly the shock. 'Oh my God!'

I nodded, not trusting myself to speak. She took my arm and we walked into her office.

'How was Jonathan? Was he alright?'

'Yeah, yeah he was fine.' I took deep breaths through my mouth and tried to fight back the fear, the sheer sorrow of what I now knew. 'He's completely transformed, kind, intuitive: I think he must have taken a biology degree by correspondence or something!'

'Tell me everything.' She steered me with care to a small sofa and gently pressed me down into it. I was still in my coat. I tried to impose some sort of order in my mind, some sequence to the explanation. For a moment it seemed impossible, as if in trying to assert some linear causality violated the intricacy, the complexity of what Max was for. Eventually, slowly, like a witness recounts a crime, I reconstructed the revelation, the luminous moment at which Max and his experiment had been revealed to me. By the time I had finished – with several interruptions – including a snide goodnight from Neville – we had moved downstairs and Margaret was slumped at the kitchen table, a glass of claret in her hand. She seemed pale, distracted. For a while no one seemed able or willing to speak.

'I just have nothing to say – I mean what can you say!' she said finally.

'DeMarr used to call everything astounding, can you remember?'

She nodded. 'Or fantastic. He liked that as well. I have to say if I had I not seen with my own eyes the complexity of Max's 22 I would think you were mad, that we were both mad, delusional! I always knew Max was special, I see it every day, but this: Max as the saviour of an entire race?'

'Do you think it's right, Margaret, do you think my deductions on this are sound?'

'God yes! I mean the theory fits everything we have observed ourselves – right down to the last replicating genome! The probability that the Seeth are dead and that the experiment is running itself is rather weird – and what happens to the new hybrid Seeth once it has formed? Does it stay here, with us on Earth? And the device – does the experiment expect us to know what to do with it?'

'If the Seeth are dead, their planet destroyed, perhaps this is their new home?' I said darkly. I sat, shell shocked, looking into the middle distance, a man caught in headlights. I thought of Jonathan's touching certainty that I would be able to cook up a new device from scratch.

'I just don't know, Margaret. We're still missing vital parts of the experimental design. The Seeth came from Earth, they predate us in evolutionary terms, perhaps that gives them a right to come home?' I thought bleakly of DeSilva's obsession with invasion, colonisation. Perhaps in some backhand way he was right after all. *Had* they come home?

'There might be more answers in the wood, Jules. Didn't Daniel Lockwood tell you he thought it strangely altered, and didn't Jonathan imply that Max will be compelled to return? Doesn't that sound like a rendezvous, a return trip?! We still don't have the complete picture, Julian!'

I nodded slowly. 'I agree but however complex the actual endgame is, we need the device, and we have just over nine months to find it! It must take priority over everything else.'

Margaret sighed deeply and I sympathised with her evident feeling of hopelessness. 'Any ideas *how?*'

'Jonathan suggests we get hold of Dena. I suggested we contact DeMarr but he thought that a bad idea!' My head fell back into the sofa rest. 'You know what really eats away at me, Margaret, is the fact that I thought that DeMarr was stupid! I mean I liked him, he was a good friend, amusing to have about, a bit tedious – what with all that nonsense about being foreign and immensely rich – but I realise now that I never took him seriously as a scientist. He used to challenge me on that you know, he used to say "you think I'm pedestrian, don't you my dear?" and even when I denied it I secretly thought, yes, I *do* actually, you're a big fat fake!'

Margaret laughed.

'And now he has run rings around me, massive orbital rings as big as Jupiter – Jesus!'

'Julian, DeMarr is a very capable man, I never thought him stupid but he is odd, and the incident in your study with Sally is even odder. Desperate times call for desperate measures – we might have to go to him yet, or even to Sally, despite Jonathan. DeMarr had the device for years, and didn't you say he's in America? Perhaps he's looking for it as well? If he has split with Davies and DeSilva, doesn't that make him an ally?'

The suggestion made me wince but Margaret was right.

Chapter 11

There was no real time to recover from Jonathan's singular revelation; to work out a scheme aimed at retrieving the device, no time to catch breath. The very day after my visit to Jonathan's boat the government ordered the committee archives to be removed immediately from the Institute of Molecular Biology in Oxford and sent to a secret location in central London. I received a telephone call from the director, incoherent with anger, but by the time I drove over to the offices the process was in full swing. When we finally succeeded in rousing an official action by the University the vans and lorries had gone and the matter was effectively closed. The only thing left to do was to write a letter of complaint as the former chair of the 1993 committee protesting the move. Later I wrote to all the former committee members as well, including somewhat bizarrely my wife. I acted impulsively through fear and anger. My letter to DeSilva was returned unopened, Dena replied supporting my outrage and emailed later to say she would help in any way she could. Louis ignored me but to my surprise Sally responded rather directly and in such a way that cast further intrigue over her entire involvement with Louis. Firstly, and in her official capacity, Sally stated that the archives had been removed on the grounds of national security. Had she instructed this? Did her current post give her that much power? She reassured me that the archive would be reopened to authorised use as soon as it was re-housed at a secure site. Then, disconcertingly, and evidently in her capacity as my estranged wife and Max's adopted mother, she enclosed the following postscript in pencil.

I understand that you have made contact with Jonathan. Evidently by now you know about the device. It is currently in Pasadena, California. It was sent there following repeated requests from the Americans in April 2005. Prior to that, it was kept in London and then at Cambridge University under the safe keeping of Louis. He knows a great deal about it. Perhaps you should ask him about it when he returns from the US? He is not quite the demon you have made him out to be. We are, as I am sure you are aware, running out of time for Max.

The information on the device was obviously genuine, confirming the evidence from the website found in Jonathan's cabin. I passed the note to Margaret who seemed as bemused as I was, although as always more optimistic.

'Perhaps Louis is over the Pond trying to retrieve it?' she said dryly and with Max-like irony, but before we had time to even digest this, what it meant about Sally and what she had been doing over the long years, Max took suddenly and spectacularly ill.

He returned home after a football game that evening complaining of a cold. He didn't eat much for supper and went to bed early complaining of a headache. For someone who had never been ill I was immediately anxious. Before I turned in, Max was running an absurdly high temperature and was hallucinating; the room was full of giant lizards stuck to the walls, something was chasing him. He didn't seem to recognise me and when I successfully calmed him he clung to me with such force that he almost broke my arm. He was burning up. Then to my horror he started speaking in some sort of sharp angled language as if he was literally possessed. Nothing I could do seemed to help. At 2 a.m. I called an ambulance. He was in convulsions by the time the paramedics arrived. I sat with him on the short drive to the John Radcliffe, holding his hand although he kept asking for me as if I was not there. When we arrived at A and E it seemed so distressingly familiar that I thought for a moment that I was suffering my own hallucinatory flashback, as if we were back at the beginning of all things. Competent, calm people swarmed over my son and within minutes – vaguely conscious – Max was tubed and wired. I jostled along with him, adding bits of information and from what I was able to gather they suspected some sudden infection, possible meningitis, or some sort of septic shock. Later, the evidence that he had taken ill after a football match, encouraged some speculation that he might also be suffering from concussion.

It was all utterly terrifying. By 4 a.m. his temperature was down and he was deemed to be in no immediate danger, but I stayed close to him, dozing next to his bed in a small bay sealed off by blue nylon curtains. At 7 a.m. I finally called Margaret and within minutes she arrived along with Jamie. It was a weekday. He was obviously missing school, and there had clearly been some argument about this since Jamie looked both angry and, on seeing Max, devastated, as if he was already dead. I left Jamie holding Max's hand tightly in his own and walked into the corridor with his mother.

'Julian you should have called me!' We were holding each other unashamedly.

'It was late. There was no need to get you out of bed as well. There was no need to scare us both, but God I am terrified, Margaret.'

'Shouldn't we find Jonathan?' She whispered, but I was conscious of the proximity of Jamie back in the bay. She sensed me looking at him.

'He insisted on coming. He would have come on his own if I'd have let him!'

'That's fine – he deserves to be here. Max would do the same for him. I'm sure Jonathan will know. He has an uncanny ability with regards to my son.'

'Tell me what happened?'

I told her as best I could. After we finished she seemed composed but pale. I looked about us carefully and then whispered. 'It might be the tag? Jonathan implied it would regenerate, remember?'

Before Margaret could reply we were joined by a middle-aged male doctor casually, if not haphazardly dressed, his tie loosened and with a stethoscope over his shoulder. He had black curly hair that was greying at the temples. It made him look of indeterminate age and strangely villainous.

'Are you the parents?' he asked glancing at me as if Margaret was invisible.

Margaret extended her hand moving forward. 'Margaret Relph and Julian Grey, Max's father,' she said curtly. The doctor nodded, still looking at me, a flicker of recognition in his face. We shook hands.

'*The* Professor Grey – the geneticist?'

I acknowledged my fame – or perhaps my notoriety – with a certain degree of awkwardness.

'Yes. That's correct. What is wrong with my son? Is it serious?'

The doctor's face had relaxed somewhat as if my

identity allowed him some liberty in skipping some of the usual parental warm ups. I recalled how Sally hated telling parents bad news. She invariably got someone else to do it. She always said it took too long, and after fitting in all the necessary caveats to avoid confusion or litigation no one understood exactly what had been said anyway.

'Well – it's a real privilege to meet you!' he said surprisingly and then he looked in Max's direction as if remembering why I was there. 'Dr Hawking. Well the bottom line is we don't know exactly what is wrong with your son. He appears to be suffering from severe exhaustion brought on by either some form of infection or possible concussion? His temperature has come down a bit, but not much. His blood pressure is high, although that, too, seems to be coming down. His respiration is fine, heartbeat elevated but dropping. Frankly I want to keep him in observation for a while and run a few tests,' he paused. I saw Margaret wince, grinding her teeth. I glanced at Jamie and beckoned him over. He discreetly let go of Max's hand. He had been crying. I asked him about the football match but he categorically denied that Max had hit his head or been injured in any way. Hawking rolled his head back and forth as if his neck was stiff. 'We've done X-rays on the neck and shoulder; we'll have them back any minute.'

'Will you need to do a scan?' I asked. Hawking narrowed his eyes as if I had suggested something vaguely untoward. 'A scan – of his head? We might, yes, although it doesn't look as if one is necessary at the moment.'

Hawking was then distracted by a nurse and Margaret said quietly but firmly in my ear, in full view of Jamie.

'Julian, for God's sake, we have to get him out of here as quickly as possible!'

I glanced at her in horror. She was right but Max was ill – where else was I to take him – to Jonathan? Jamie looked at his mother in complete bemusement. He looked back towards Max, his complexion white.

'What's going on – what's wrong with Max?'

'I don't know darling, but he's better than he was.' Margaret shot one more look of warning in my direction and turned to comfort her son.

Hawking returned and stood by me, his ID badge flashing in the overhead lighting, *David Hawking MD*

'Prof-'

'Julian, *really* –'

'Julian, we're having problems finding medical records for Max. Have you moved recently into the area, or changed addresses?'

'No. But Max has never been hospitalised since he was six and he's never really seen a doctor. Well, I mean a GP.' I sounded and looked evasive. 'He's never been ill. He is also adopted. His original name was Max *Lennox*.'

'Ah, ok – that's probably why we can't find anything, then.' He drew closer to me, conspiratorial, 'I have to ask you, is he taking recreational drugs at all?'

The question surprised me. For a moment I thought of caffeine, alcohol but then said: 'you mean like cocaine?'

'No, no – well – I was actually referring to his physique: have you any idea whether he's been taking steroids for the gym?'

I breathed out with relief.

'Good God no – I see what you mean – no, it's all his own, I mean – it's *natural*.'

'Ok,' Hawking seemed satisfied. 'I had to ask you because of his age. I couldn't help noticing when I examined him – Sorry,' he added, as if he had accused me directly. 'He is in remarkable shape. What does he bench press, by the way?'

'I don't really have any idea.'

'Righty ho. We'll get to the bottom of this incident. It isn't necessarily serious.' He walked off again. Margaret put her head around the curtain, Jamie was standing behind her, placated to some extent but I could see he was still upset.

'What was that about?'

'He wants to know how much Max bench presses!'

Jamie managed to laugh and even Margaret smiled. Suddenly Max was awake and asking for me, groggily aware that he was not at home. Jamie was smiling and pretending to have something in his eyes. He kept blowing his nose and then he went off suddenly to be on his own. Jamie's condition seemed to distress Max more than the realisation that he was in hospital.

'Where am I?'

I leaned my face close to his, trying to look reassuring, confident.

'You're in the John Radcliffe, you took ill.'

'Ill? Oh. I can't remember anything. Am I alright now?' he sounded genuinely curious, surprised. I tried to look calm and parental and yet ever since Jonathan's revelation, I found looking at Max difficult, a sort of test. I was afraid that he would see in my own eyes the knowledge of his own uniqueness.

'Julian, just relax. It's alright – I feel fine now! Go and see if Jamie's ok would you?'

Margaret and I stayed with him talking in strangely subdued tones until they removed him to the observation ward. At the last minute however I was seized with an irrational fear that as soon as my back was turned, my son would be taken.

'Look, Jamie's missed school already. Perhaps we could ask him to stay with Max? I'm sure I could persuade Hawking to allow it? I could tell him he is Max's brother.'

'They look totally unlike each other and they're the same age! Besides, Jamie will start to suspect something – he's bound to – he's already suspicious.' We were walking slowly and reluctantly back towards the entrance, Jamie was ahead of us silent and distressingly unhappy.

'Margaret, listen. I know I'm being sentimental perhaps, but we need to trust in their friendship. I know that their relationship is complicated –' I glanced up at Jamie and lowered my voice, stopping to turn to Margaret. 'Max would trust Jamie with his life, and frankly at this particular moment, so would I!'

She seemed taken aback, either by the observation or my tone. 'Julian, under the provisions of the 1993 committee report the hospitalisation of any of the children could well trigger quarantine or detention – you know that!' She looked helplessly at Jamie who was now standing some way away, Max like, hands in his jean pockets and with his shoulders slightly hunched forward. He was watching us intently. 'If Davies turns up what good will Jamie do? Call Sally!'

'He can call us! I have to try and get hold of Jonathan!'

'Then let me stay!'

Jamie coughed loudly and glared at us both. 'Are you guys coming or what?'

Margaret sighed. 'Ok, ok. Go and ask him Julian, I'll be in the car.' She touched my arm and then paused. 'You're not proposing to tell him, are you?'

'Of course not.'

Once Margaret had disappeared into the car park, I beckoned Jamie over to some seats. To my surprise, he started crying again as if he suspected I was going to tell him something dreadful. It took me some time to calm him.

'Jamie I want to ask you to do something for me, for Max?'

'Sure.'

I looked at him carefully. He had his mother's eyes and colouring, Nordic blond hair inclined to curl, cut short and, either by design or accident, strangely spiked. He was handsome now in a very English rather preppy sort of way, broad shouldered, tall. It was disconcerting to see his face wet with tears.

'I want you to stay here with Max, ok? I don't want you to leave his side at all until I come back. If anything happens –' Jamie's eyes – a clear winter grey – narrowed suspiciously, making me pause. 'If anything odd happens I want you to call me immediately or your mother on the mobile?'

'But what do you mean, odd?'

I was running my tongue around my upper lip, a gesture of anxiety or impatience, a well-known habit much commented on by Margaret. Jamie seemed to recognise the tell tale sign as well.

'What's going on, Julian?'

'Jamie nothing's going on, it's just that I need time to organise my day and I don't want Max left alone. Will you do this for me?'

He was so unlike Max, so volatile, always ready to go off on some blazing tangent; it was like trying to pull a young horse into a starting gate very much against its will.

'Will I be allowed to stay? I mean what about visiting hours – is this allowed?'

'I'll talk with Hawking.'

We walked back to the observation ward. I took some time to find Hawking and to persuade him that Jamie *should* stay. Eventually and obviously somewhat intrigued, Hawking relented and allowed Jamie to sit quietly in Max's bay. I left him whispering with Max and as I walked away I thought of Jamie as a curious anagram of Jonathan, as if the experiment had somehow summoned up another child to stand guard over my son, to love him.

On my return home I set about trying to find Jonathan, and I tried several times to call Sally. She was not on any of her numerous numbers and I was afraid to leave any voicemails. By the afternoon Max was well enough to speak with me on the phone and plead for his release. He said that Jamie was comatose and needed sending home but I managed to convince him that we would sort it out later. Feeling calmer, I commandeered Max's digital radio and listened to Radio Three in the bath, morosely sticking my toes in the taps and then at around 5 p.m. I drove with Margaret back to the Radcliffe. To my relief Max was sitting up in bed looking much better. Jamie was almost exactly in the same position I had left him. He looked exhausted, his attractive face coated in a sheen of sweat.

'Have they said anything to you Max, suggested anything?' I settled down on the chair next to Jamie while Margaret stood at the end of the bed and started going through the charts.

'I'm not sure. Hawking keeps devising new things to do to me as if I am his pet project!' Max's vague sarcasm was back. I took that as a good sign.

'He's being thorough, Max.'

'He's obsessed with phantom head injuries,' snapped Jamie rolling his eyes. Clearly he'd been interrogated several times about any so-called accident. Max was looking wilful.

'Look I'm much better, really. It was just some sort of flu thing! They're going to let me out, right? I mean you have to make them, Julian!' As if on cue, there was a rustle behind me and Hawking appeared, all smiles, nodding at Max appreciatively. It was almost the end of visiting time.

'Any developments, Dr Hawking?' Hawking fussed about the end of the bed, looking at the charts as if he could sense that someone else had gone through them.

'No, not much I'm afraid – which I am inclined to believe is good news! Did you know that your son has a resting pulse of 42!' he said brightly as if my son was not there.

'No I didn't.' We made some small talk and then Hawking walked me out towards the nursing station. Max caught my eye and made a mock snarl. Hawking seemed rather hyperactive. Once out of earshot he turned to me confidentially.

'He's fine really but I've found some curiosities in the blood chemistry that don't make much *immediate* sense.'

I tried to remain calm, stoical. I made a sort of indifferent sound, a noncommittal clearing of the throat. 'Such as?'

'Well for a start he has a high nitrogen content in his blood, and also high levels of calcium and the compound Androstenol.'

I narrowed my eyes, the name was unfamiliar to me. It's presence in Max's blood was new.

'A steroid?' I recalled Hawking's interest in Max's body and the question about recreational drugs.

'No. It's a hydro-carbon. It's usually associated with sandalwood.'

I looked genuinely bemused. 'Really?'

'It's a pheromone.'

'Do you think this is causing his illness?'

Hawking stuck his lower lip out, thoughtfully, in a way that curiously reminded me of Louis DeMarr. 'Not exactly, I think along with the other oddities they're just idiosyncratic to Max! The nitrogen worried me initially but I checked his kidney function and it's fine. Given his training priorities it's probably caused by a very high protein diet. He'll need to watch that over the years, incidentally. Androstenol might be dietary. But it doesn't make much sense.' I faked a laugh but then Hawking said with intense interest. 'Has Max ever had any surgery to his head?' The comment seemed precise.

'No, not since I adopted him.'

'Ah yes. Quite. And you were obviously aware that Max Lennox was diagnosed with cancer at the age of four?'

They had evidently found Max's records. I felt irritated and shaken. Max's cancer had spread to the right lobe of the brain. Hawking would know that as well.

'Yes. *Ewing's Sarcoma*. You're not suggesting it has returned are you?'

'No, no I am not. Sorry Julian, I'm not usually this speculative. At the moment we have lots of symptoms but all without any obvious cause. Max has no infection, he has no obvious pathology, and everything points to some sort of head injury. I asked Jamie – his *brother* – repeatedly about the football game. Sometimes patients are not aware that they received a hit to the head, especially in contact sport. Incidentally, why did you suggest a scan earlier, this morning?' It was rather skilfully done, I thought: disguising the key question at the end, as if Hawking was a clever lawyer.

'Honestly there was no particular reason. Have you done the scan yet?'

'No, not yet. Max is very uncooperative about that – does he suffer from claustrophobia?'

'No. He probably resents the fuss!'

Hawking laughed rather boisterously as if I had made a very good joke. 'Look, go home and have a good rest. Come back tomorrow and we'll see how things have progressed! He's quite happy – and already a bit of a star on the ward!' I said something non-committal, vacuous. 'And send Jamie my regards, Julian. I'm not sure what your instructions to him were, but he never let Max once out of his sight!' There was a further hint of intrigue in his voice. I went back and said good night to Max who played up spectacularly over having to stay another night. For one moment, I thought he would literally walk out himself. I told him I would definitely fetch him out tomorrow morning. He looked at me rather mournfully and then gave me a rather European peck on the cheek.

'Ring me if you need me, Max. Ok?'

Our eyes locked momentarily, although mine were the first to pull away.

'I'm not supposed to use a mobile in the wards, Dad. They have signs you know.'

'And since when has that made a difference?'

When I got out to the car there was a slight hint of drama as if Jamie and his mother had been arguing again. Jamie was leaning low on the backseat with Margaret in the front, and when I appeared he shot bolt upright.

'Everything ok?'

'Yes, Jamie. Hawking sends his regards.' I caught his face in the centre mirror. 'You are a wonderful friend to my son, I know you love him very much and it means a huge amount to me as well as to him, obviously.' Jamie's face was emotional, barely in control. He nodded quickly and then leaned back where he could not be scrutinised. Margaret smiled at me, tired but encouraging.

'What did our new best friend Dr Hawking want?'

'He's convinced that Max hit his head on a wall or a pine tree!' but my eyes said something else to her.

'Jesus,' gasped Jamie.

'And the usual body fascist questions – Jamie you must get Max to tell me more about the gym! People ask me and I'm expected to know these things, so that I can claim to live in the same world that he does!'

To my relief Jamie laughed and leaned forward, his mood lifting. We dropped him off on Walton Street and then Margaret and I returned to Farndon Road to resume our conspiracy. If Jamie thought this odd he didn't let on. As soon as we were inside I leaned against the door, exasperated.

'Hawking suspects something – I could see it. I don't think he's seen a single patient today other than Max! They know about his cancer and the name of his bio-logical mother.'

'He does seem keen! Where are all these incompetent

NHS doctors I keep reading about?' Margaret pointed to a bottle of wine.

'Well, it's *Max*, isn't it! The Seeth picked a boy incapable of being inconspicuous – they may just as well have stuck wings on him!' The hall phone rang. I felt my heart race. Was it Sally?

'I'll get it.' Margaret walked through, picked it up, and said her name as if her being here was the most natural thing in the world. There followed a few exclamations of gratitude and surprise. After a while Margaret reappeared. 'It was Zoë. She wants to see Max. Can she visit with you sometime tomorrow?'

'Yes, of course. If they keep him in that is. Incidentally, did I embarrass Jamie in the car just then?'

Margaret was pouring the wine.

'I don't think so. He'd just thrown a grade A tantrum about being kept in the dark over Max!' She handed me a glass. 'I thought it was a really sweet thing to say, Julian. He's really upset – he thinks Max is going to die or something!'

'He's been a brick to Max, he really has.'

She sighed, leaning forward on the table. 'We have to be careful, Julian. Jamie is very sharp, very attentive – he's beginning to ask rather leading questions.'

'I know. He reminds me of a brilliant technician I once met who devised a very innovative staining technique!'

We both laughed.

Later, alone, I retired early but not having Max in the house was eerie, and kept me awake, anxious and abandoned. I read for a while, dozing with the light on. Just after 3 a.m. I was aware that someone was in my room. I had been dreaming and as I came around I noticed that the hall light was on and my bedroom door ajar. I then sensed someone sit down on the bed on Sally's side. I could feel their weight and the slight depression on the mattress. For a moment I even thought it was her, but then I knew intuitively it was Jonathan. I moved casually, obviously, rising up to see Jonathan sitting with his back half turned to me, thinking, distracted. He clearly saw nothing unusual in visiting at such an hour and in such a bizarre manner. I wondered if it was a form of revenge for my 'breaking' into his houseboat.

'Thank God you're here. Max is in hospital,' I said thickly. My face felt crumpled, rolled up like a carpet.

'I know. I have to go to him.' Jonathan looked at me with a sort of defiance as if he anticipated my objection. He was wearing his standard fare sports outfit as if he had jogged over for a chat, although he was holding his baseball cap in his hand.

'How did you get in?'

'You left a key under a tile in the porch, for fuck's sake! Besides, I'm good at getting into things.' I was aware that the room was intensely cold.

'Jonathan: is Max's illness connected to the tag? You said it might happen soon?'

A frown clouded his face, an odd momentary look of pain. 'Yes. Max's tag is regenerating. That's why he is having difficulties with his temperature and his ability to sleep. It should synchronise on its own quite quickly. I didn't think it would make him so ill or that it would require him to be hospitalised. Afterwards he might well hear the Seeth.'

I had reached for my dressing gown and walked towards the door. I thought of my own dream, of the bizarre idea that a dead race would soon communicate with my son.

'But we can't leave him in hospital, not in that place!'

'Let's go to my study, Jonathan, there's a fire in there.'

After a momentary pause in which he looked briefly around the bedroom, Jonathan slipped to his feet and followed. I noticed he had removed his trainers. I also noticed that outside my door on a small hall table was the shoebox containing the photographs of Max.

'I don't need them now. You may as well keep them.' Jonathan said somewhat evasively.

I switched on a gas fire and put some lights on. When I offered him a drink he declined suddenly as if shocked.

'I never touch it now.'

I apologised for my thoughtlessness.

'There are people at the hospital, people from the government, people *watching Max*, trying to touch him. Americans.'

I stood rooted to the spot. 'How do you know this? Have you been there?'

'Someone has to watch over him!' Jonathan snapped. Then he relented, suddenly. I was surprised by an apology. 'Sorry, Julian: it was upsetting to see him, to go back to that place. He is at risk there.'

'I know that and I'm as distressed as you are. Will he recover enough to come out soon?'

'I think so – I might be able to help him – I might be able to speed things up a bit.'

'In what way?'

'I have a tag already – I might be able to assist Max's – I'll have to touch him.' Jonathan seemed unsure but was clearly following some idea through. He looked at me with renewed urgency.

'We can't risk keeping him in there for long! We have to get him out of that hospital!'

'I agree, Jonathan, but it's nearly 4 a.m. – we can't just waltz in and fetch him!' I suddenly remembered the scan, and Max's strange reluctance to have it. As if reading my thoughts, Jonathan whispered quietly

'If they scan him we're completely fucked! They'd lock him up straight away!'

'Quite.'

I ran my hands over my face. 'When did these Americans arrive? Did you see Davies?'

'No – I didn't see Davies – but Sally was there.'

'Sally!'

'Yes.' Jonathan scowled as if I was being particularly dense. It was too early in the morning, too cold, to deal with any of this. Everything had happened so fast, my final grasp of the experiment and the device, the archive, the illness. I felt old and suddenly remarkably *incapable*. Jonathan took some sort of pity on me because the next minute he was standing by me trying to sound reasonable.

'I don't know what she's doing, let's not judge her yet. She's escorting people from the US Centre for Disease Control around and I saw her talking with Dr Hawking.'

'Good God!' I had a fleeting image of Jonathan pressed flat against a wall, conspicuous in his tracksuit, sleuth-like, spying on my wife. I had no idea how he did it!

'Any sign of DeMarr?' I wondered for a moment if the news that he was in the US was a lie, some sort of cover.

'No. No sign of DeMarr. Look – we have to go first thing tomorrow? Yes? We'll leave at 7 a.m.' Jonathan sounded oddly authoritative and yet there was none of his old anger. He was picking up odd things from my desk. He looked at a photograph I had of Sally still, the 'professor and professor' one, and then his eyes fell on the small white pebble. He touched it, holding it in his hand, looking at it through half closed eyes as if it could talk to him.

'Can you remember Max giving that to me?' I asked, moved to see him touch it.

'Of course I do!' he smiled at me. I had so rarely seen Jonathan smile that the effect was rather astounding.

'How are you going to help Max tomorrow? Max is in an open bay under observation, you can't risk anything that will attract too much attention!'

'I just have to touch him, perhaps not even that! Come on let's get some sleep!' Bewildered by the subtle transformation in Jonathan's character, I dutifully went back to my room. Jonathan said good night and went downstairs where he walked into Max's room and closed the door. It seemed the most natural thing in the world. Before I turned back into my bedroom I saw, under Max's door, the nightlight go off. Caliban did not fear the dark.

In the short hours left to us I slept a deep, dead sleep of utter oblivion. It was complete and dreamless as if I had been buried deep under the ground with my eyes and mouth stitched together. I had set the alarm for 6.30 but was awoken earlier by the telephone ringing, infinitely remote despite being next to me on the nightstand, far off in another house, another universe. When I finally picked up the receiver it was only to hear the ominous click of the caller disconnecting. I felt my way to the bathroom and took a hot shower and when I emerged feeling vaguely human, vaguely well, the house was still in cold darkness. Jonathan, surprisingly, was still asleep. I made us both coffees. I waited to see if he would shower or wash, or need the bathroom. Instead he merely laced his trainers back on and announced he was ready. Outside, the cold clear air revived me but Jonathan dithered and shook violently. I gave him one of Max's coats, a large black duffle that half buried him and, with the hood up, gave him the appearance of a nun. Once inside the car Jonathan seemed oddly contemplative, calm; unusually placid. He looked into the middle distance like someone who reminisces, who sees things that no one else does.

'How's this going to work again?' I asked as we parked up, some way away from the white modernist façade of the Radcliffe. I felt nervous, self-conscious of Jonathan's appearance. The hospital glowered out at us, set in the ochre browns of bare winter trees. He didn't answer. We walked into the main reception area where I wanted to suggest he removed his cap but thought better of it, anxious to prolong his silence and not antagonise him. At reception I was informed that Max had been moved from observation to ICU. Shocked, we followed signs written out in bold, official lettering, only to run into the ubiquitous Dr Hawking.

'Thank God, Julian! I've been trying to call you at home. Max's condition suddenly deteriorated about three hours ago. He seems to have gone into a coma-like state – well actually – a form of narcolepsy. It's not in itself serious and we could revive him easily with stimulants, but I am utterly mystified! I took the precaution of moving him here to be on the safe side.'

I glanced at Jonathan who was standing just behind me but he showed no response. Hawking indicated an awareness of his presence by an inclusive smile, a sort of benign flicker in the corner of his eyes.

'Have you scanned Max yet?' I asked, trying to not sound too accusatory.

'No scans!' muttered Jonathan.

'No – not yet – we'll do it this morning.' Hawking had darted a glance at Jonathan and then at me.

'Can I see Max?' I asked quickly, eager to forestall some sort of unpleasant revelation.

'Of course. I'll take you to him – but,' Hawking looked directly and a little pointedly at Jonathan.

'He is an old friend of Max's,' I said. Hawking gave me a peculiarly sharp glance, the look of a man who knows he is being deceived. 'Let me guess, an older brother?'

We walked deeper into the IC unit. It was quiet, subdued, and full of the soft hum and bleep of complex, anonymous equipment. It felt like we were in an engine room or an airport control tower. Max was in a bay, with a plastic oxygen mask on his face, his complexion now ghostly white. He looked remote, like a sculpture and quite lifeless. Jonathan started moving his hands about impatiently and muttering something. I had to get Hawking away somehow.

'Can he hear me?' I asked, distractedly. Max was

wearing a blue pyjama top I had never seen before. Someone had tried to comb his hair but failed: it was spiked up and over his face.

'Yes, I'm sure he can – it's important that you talk to him. He seems to be dreaming, you can see his eyes moving under the lids and he seems to respond to loud noises! He is clearly aware of his surroundings – he just doesn't want to wake up!' I touched Max's cheek – it was icy. My eyes were distracted by a large collection of cards and flowers on a nearby window. Hawking followed my stare.

'They really shouldn't be here, but the staff on the other ward insisted we have them. The registrar will hit the roof! Have a few minutes with Max, reassure him.' Hawking turned to me. 'I'll give you some privacy.' He drew the curtain around Max and left. Immediately Jonathan started unplugging some of the machines.

'*Jonathan!*'

'We can't work with all this shit over him – keep an eye out for that fucking Doctor!' He removed the blood pressure and the heart rate monitors. He then went up to my son and took Max's right hand in his, curling his fingers through Max's, pressing hard palm to palm. After this he looked a little indecisive, and then, with his other hand, he touched the top of Max's head. The whole scene looked both absurd and disturbing as if Jonathan was about to exorcise my son of demons: or raise him from the dead.

'Jonathan – perhaps we should leave it. If he's going to recover himself it might be safer than attracting attention like this.' I looked anxiously at the curtains. I felt ridiculous, even embarrassed, and afraid that either Hawking or Sally would suddenly appear behind me. Jonathan ignored me, his eyes tightly closed, his lips moving as he spoke to himself, to Max. Max's face lay beneath his, calm, angelic, his eyes sweeping in arcs under the closed lids. Fleetingly, somewhat randomly, I wondered if the REM induced state was somehow linked to the Seeth, to how they communicated with Jonathan and how they had planned, somehow, to communicate with the rest of the children even though they were now extinct. Tags to the brains, some state of altered consciousness? The language of dreams? Nothing seemed to be happening. A nurse walked by outside, her silhouette startling me as it rippled over the drawn curtains.

'Stop fussing!' hissed Jonathan. And then suddenly, Max moved. He arched up from the bed, pulling his lower back in, and raising his chest and shoulders. He breathed in deeply but erratically, as if he was suffocating. I had a distressing image of a drowned man being revived. Jonathan seemed to fall forward slightly, his face contorted as if in pain or confusion.

'Jonathan!' but as I stood close by I suddenly felt a curious sense of calm, of reassurance, as if Jonathan was literally lifting my son up out of darkness. I thought of Braedabarker's insistence that the children were meant to work in pairs. Jonathan was supposed to be doing this – he had almost – in an odd sense – lived for this.

Max's chest rose and fell, he murmured something, a name, something unintelligible. Then suddenly Max made a sort of sneeze, a half choke, and a white viscous fluid bled from his nose profusely.

'Oh my God! Jonathan!'

'I have it – it's ok!' Someone was bound to hear this. As the liquid poured out of Max's nose, it solidified quickly and darkened almost like oil. I ferreted about the pockets of my coat for a handkerchief and wiped Max's face. Was it blood? It had a strange, very sharp chemical smell to it. Max's breathing suddenly appeared to return to normal and he sank back down, pulling Jonathan off balance slightly and then to my intense shock, both Max and Jonathan screamed in unison. Jonathan sprang back into the curtain while I knocked over a sheath of cards and a plastic jug of water. In an instant the curtains were snatched back on two sides, and Hawking appeared, followed by two nurses. I could see him frowning, smelling the air, picking up the still acrid, rather visceral smell of the fluid. Before he could say anything however, Max screamed again, a solo performance this time, since inexplicably and at remarkable speed, Jonathan had gone.

Hawking grabbed my son's arm and tried to restrain him, clearly thinking that he was having some sort of seizure. The nurses closed in, but then Max said with evident surprise and a certain coldness, 'What the fuck are you doing!'

He seemed disorientated amid the confusion, but he saw me clearly enough and seemed suddenly, immediately returned to health.

'Julian? What's happening? Dr Hawking, let go of my arm, man!'

'It's ok, Max, it's ok,' Hawking said, quite matter of fact, releasing him slowly.

'Max! –' I came forward relieved, emotional. 'It's fine – your condition deteriorated during the night – you've been brought into ICU.'

Max seemed stunned by the news.

'ICU?' and then he touched his head as if he had a shadow of a pain. His mouth was dry and evidently sour. I handed him a glass of water. He took it and as he did so he looked at me with a look of complicity. I recognised it instantly, a soft residual glow in both eyes. He seemed to collect himself.

'I was having a dream,' he said evenly. As the sense of emergency passed, some of the staff moved away. Hawking, his hands in his pockets, looked at me again before sitting on the bed and addressing Max.

'Was it a good dream?'

'Sort of,' he smiled rather coyly at Hawking. Max did

one of his slight side to side head movements which I realised meant he rather liked Hawking.

'I screamed because I thought I was suffocating. I had a sensation that my lungs were filling up with fluid,' he lowered his voice. 'It was so realistic!' he glanced up at me.

'Was Jamie here? I thought I saw him?'

'Yes, he's gone out for some fresh air –' I looked at Hawking who, conscious of the lie, remained affable.

'He evidently got distressed,' he finished for me.

Max looked down at his hand, which I was now gripping quite painfully. 'Guys can I go home?'

'Now, now, not quite so fast. I haven't finished with you yet! Let's see how you progress for a few hours and see what all the fuss was about?' Hawking caught sight of a sort of papery smear just under Max's nostrils and down his chin.

'Perhaps it would be better if we took him home and, if necessary, referred him to outpatients?' I said rather pointedly, not keen for a fight, but determined to discharge him as quickly as possible. Hawking looked at us both as if we were part of some elaborate confidence trick.

'Well let's see shall we, a few more hours?'

Hawking and I walked back down to the entrance level using the stairs, trotting down side by side. I sensed him glancing at me, waiting for me to confess to something. In the main lobby we both spied Jonathan sitting holding his head, his baseball cap down, and a plastic cup of something at his feet. He still wore Max's coat.

'There's *Jamie*.'

'Ah yes. Yes.'

Hawking laughed. 'I am not entirely sure what happened just then or indeed what exactly is going on here. But I'll call you this afternoon once we've looked over Max; if his vital signs are ok and his appetite returns I don't see any reasons why we can't free up a bed tonight.'

I sighed with very evident relief but Hawking remained looking at me.

'There is one thing I need to tell you, however: Max's mother is here. She arrived late last night. I was unaware that Sally Grey is now the principle scientific advisor to the government.'

'Yes, well – it's a rather obscure post. It was held for many years by Louis DeMarr.'

'Yes, yes,' he was distracted. 'What I mean Julian, is that she seemed to be here on some sort of *professional* business. She brought a rather comprehensive group of experts with her. I *would* have called you –'

I looked at him curiously, wondering what had obviously stopped him. He left the sentence hanging.

'Did she speak with Max?'

'Possibly, I wasn't here and when I resumed my shift Max was unconscious by then. I do know that Sally spent a great deal of time with the registrar and that she has obviously been to the hospital before –'

I pressed my lips together. Hawking had made the connection between Max, the children and the abductions. I sensed it intuitively.

'She has, yes. In fact, we both worked here briefly some time ago. What did this group of experts want?'

'Tissue samples from Max. I thought it highly irregular, but she said she was his mother and my senior and the registrar seemed to agree! Professor Grey seemed to be supervising the whole thing. I reassured them that I had seen no sign of infection in Max at all. Do you have any idea what they were looking for?'

Was Sally working against Max or protecting him? I was watching Jonathan who hadn't moved, his head down as if in prayer or meditation. Several people on seats to either side were looking at him with some concern.

'Julian – is there something special about Max? I mean – his cancer for instance?' Hawking hesitated, trying to keep his curiosity in check. 'Look I don't wish to pry but he was one of the children who was abducted in 1993, wasn't he?'

Before I could say anything Jonathan fell forward, head first, onto the floor in one abrupt movement as if he had been switched off. I ran forward with Hawking close by me. When I reached Jonathan his face was white, his nose was bleeding and his eyes seemed swollen. The blood seemed normal, not white, nothing to over-excite Hawking's already keen interest in the case.

'I'll take him home – he hasn't eaten,' I said as calmly as I could. Jonathan revived quickly when he saw Hawking trying to take his pulse.

'Fuck off!'

'Jonathan!' I helped him up. He seemed groggy as if someone had punched him in the head. We stood together while he recovered. I held his arm. Again I was shocked to note how thin he was. I could feel the bones beneath his clothing. Hawking reappeared with a cup of warm, sweet tea.

'Here, drink this *Jamie*. I'll be in touch with you, Julian. Anything that comes up I'll call.' He was looking at Jonathan intently who didn't appear to notice he'd been called the wrong name. I acknowledged his concern.

'I would really appreciate that. Max might still be at risk,' I said cryptically. Hawking nodded at me knowingly. He turned and then paused, feeling for something inside his back pocket. 'Sorry, I almost forgot. Sally gave me this –'

He produced a note on yellow X-ray paper, folded into a square.

'Oh, thank you.' I took it from him rather pointedly, mystified. Hawking had been ubiquitous, helpful, caught up by Max like a moth in the light: he had not been unfriendly. I tried to be appreciative.

'Look Dr Hawking, it's complicated.'

'So I gather. I'll call you.' He nodded at Jonathan and then walked off back to my son. After a while, as the attention around us began to ebb, we walked slowly out to the car. Jonathan seemed particularly fragile but better, indeed almost serene. I wondered if the regeneration of Max's tag had lessened the Seeth voices inside his own head? Could Max now hear them? Were they already speaking to him? Could Max hear Jonathan now?

'Jonathan, I can't thank you enough. You were right of course, you clearly speeded up the process – will it have any consequences for Max? I mean the tag?' He didn't answer me. He seemed tired, exhausted. We crossed a broad driveway where the ambulances and emergency vehicles swung in towards A & E and admissions. I saw several cars with elaborate, foreign number plates drawn up in a space clearly prohibited for parking with their engines running. Two or three men stood about, obviously security for someone or something. One of the car doors was open. Jonathan turned to me and half whispered.

'We are close to it now – we have to plan to get the device back and quickly.'

Before I could acknowledge the point the group of men parted and suddenly, shockingly, I recognised Sally standing with her back to me talking to a tall grey haired man, his hand resting on the top of the open door. It was *Davies*. He was wearing a big, expensive looking Kashmir coat and a tasteful woollen scarf; very East Coast, very Bostonian. They were both looking away from me, back towards the main entrance of the hospital, deep in conversation. Sally was gesturing with her hands, describing something. I screwed up my eyes to get a better look. As I turned to resume the walk to my car I recognised someone else: someone sitting in the car looking vaguely bored, waiting for Davies to either get in or close the door: it was *James DeSilva*. I slipped into the car my heart in my mouth. I felt a sudden urge to go and literally take Max home with me immediately.

'Jonathan, what shall we do?'

'Read your note,' said Jonathan, his voice flat. He was leaning back looking through the sunroof. He seemed suddenly very young. I removed the yellow paper from my pocket and dutifully opened it out. Sally had written in a quick neat hand.

Dear Julian.

I was contacted late last night and asked to escort Professor Davies and a team from CDC to see Max who was admitted to the John Radcliff hospital. We were later joined by James DeSilva. The 1993 protocol was triggered by Max's details being entered on-line and the fact that Max has been under observation for some time. Davies' team was authorised by the same protocol to remove tissue samples and analyse them, and also to undertake a series of body scans: in effect, to screen Max much as he was screened during the time of the committee. I will endeavour to ensure that any changes or anomalies that MIGHT have taken place do not compromise Max's safety but I am no longer confident of my abilities to do this. You must plan a contingency to take Max into hiding at any stage between now and his eighteenth birthday. We are under considerable pressure from the Americans to hand Max over. It is also important that you are aware that the British government has worked out a contingency plan to arrest Max under a faked viral cover story. When necessary they will announce that our son is infected with a dangerous pathogen and alert the public accordingly. I will try my best – when the time comes – to counter the propaganda but it has been authorised by COBRA and I suspect will be genuinely believed. As for the device, Louis is in the US now trying to find out its location.

Sally.

We drove home in silence. Jonathan actually fell asleep. As he lay strapped in next to me, his head to one side, I felt something very close to love for him, the same desire to protect and share his life as I continuously felt for Max. The note from Sally hummed with secrets, with things not said but for the time being it reassured me that I was not alone, a satisfying thought however inexplicable and only partly dented by my anxiety over DeSilva's return to England. Back at Farndon Road Jonathan stayed in Max's room for a while, in a sort of stupor, half way between exhaustion and meditation. There was so much I wanted to ask him, but in the end I let him alone. After an evening meal he slipped away into the winter darkness like a ghost.

Early next morning Max was discharged without fuss, and allowed to return home and then, after a day or two of stalking me about the house, to resume school. He had been embarrassed by the attention he had received, and was anxious to either kick a ball about or do some push ups: but he was also changed in some odd, subtle way. Neither of us spoke directly about the hospital but it further altered our relationship. Absurdly perhaps in the circumstances I waited for Max to tell me who he was. Slowly, superficially he resumed his old habits. Zoë came over and stayed with him for the first weekend, apparently angered by her exclusion and his seeming reluctance to call her. By way of compensation they spent an entire day in bed together which I dutifully condoned by leaving for a long and quite unnecessary walk. Jamie, too, seemed different towards me, more cautious and attentive, watchful and for a time I sensed some of the old animosity between him and Zoë. There was one final act of drama. On the day that Max resumed his schooling Hawking called me at college. He informed me that although there had been some confusion over the taking of an MRI scan, the result was normal. There was some evidence of scarring around the pituitary gland but it was well healed and had probably occurred in childhood. He didn't ask or speculate what might have caused it and I didn't ask him to elaborate on the confusion. Max's blood chemistry remained 'intriguing' (his word) but nothing that merited medical concern. He asked me to send Max his regards.

Two days after Hawking's call I came across an old internal A3 envelope in my College mail marked TOP SECRET. I recognised it immediately. It was one used by the committee in 1993. My name – typed on a label – had been stuck on the front. When I opened it I found it contained a high resolution printout of an MRI head scan: frontal and in profile. The subject was male – the canines, the frontal sinuses, and the ridges above the eye sockets made that reasonably clear – and I immediately, subliminally recognised it as Max. And clearly revealed, deep in the soft tissue of the brain level with the eyes and the bridge of the nose, was a strange H shaped tag linked to the bony shield around the pituitary. The date, indexed on the original scan, was clearly visible on the printout: *November 19th 2005*. There was also something odd, different, about the tissue in the frontal lobe. It was vastly more crenulated than before and seemed larger in proportion to the rest of the brain as a whole. I stood with the print trembling softly in my hand. Signs of a tumour? Some sort of pathology – or of some other Ovidian transformation? I recalled Hawking's use of the word confusion. Someone had obviously substituted an archived scan for the one taken just over a fortnight ago. Hawking had been tricked into seeing the last image taken by the committee in 1999 just before it has been disbanded. The tag had long gone but the scar tissue would have remained. Now it had re-generated and was considerably larger than before. And Max's brain was also changing. There was no doubt. I put the glossy sheet of paper back into the envelope and placed it along with the original recommendations of the committee and the report from the Japanese team on the alien DNA in my office safe. The urgency of finding Max's device flared up inside me. And for the first time in years I felt a sort of love for Sally, for her cold, precise brilliance: for who else would have the opportunity, the audacity and skill to substitute the scan but her?

Part Two
25th - 27th June 2006

Chapter 12

I couldn't sleep. It was too hot and I just couldn't stop thinking about stuff: Max, Jonathan, *Max*. In the end my head hurt. I got half dressed and MSN'd with Katherine, telling her what I was going to do on my birthday and why. Typically, she thought my plans overly dramatic and unnecessary. She said people didn't 'come out' any more – it was apparently Eighties – they just got on with their lives. I was too tired, too distracted to argue. I replied that I wanted people to know what I was and how important it was to me and she said – not unkindly – that everyone knew anyway! I typed 'brb' and went to fetch some water, admittedly crestfallen by her views. When I got back we talked about her work, her boyfriend, London, and then suddenly Kat asked me if I had anyone 'significant' in my life. Jesus – as if! I reminded her that I was seventeen and still at home. She typed out LOL and then asked immediately about *Max Grey*. It was typical of her to make a connection and I felt a familiar slightly sick feeling in my stomach at the mention of Max's name.

'He's *straight*,' I typed back. 'And my best friend, and he's going out with the legendary Zoë Craven.' I *nearly* typed 'And there's something seriously wrong with him,' but I sat crouched over the keyboard holding my hands together. She sent her condolences, stating he was beautiful, sexy, funny and very smart and therefore couldn't really be a boy at all! Did he know I was gay?

I typed back yes cautiously and then paused again, with my fingers over the keyboard like a pianist, overwhelmed with grief.

Max had been the first person I had told about being gay, late last year; sometime in October, and I was still unsure how he'd taken the news. In fact, I wasn't even sure he was my best friend now, but a stranger, some weird impostor. I felt my diaphragm buckle under a wave of despair. I tried to change the subject but my sister seemed oddly preoccupied with Max. She asked about his dad, and then not surprisingly about the 'weirdo mother' who she'd seen on the news recently and then, as if making some implicit connection, she asked me if I knew why Margaret had suddenly and so dramatically gone off to the US a few weeks ago. I said it was to do with a sudden slot opening up at conference, a paper she'd really wanted to give. Katherine said it seemed so unlike her and then suddenly announced she had to go to bed in order to start an early shift, a 'suicide watch' job that she really disliked. Before signing out she urged me one last time to avoid any 'speeches' or dramatic gestures about sexuality! She sounded just like my mother typing that. I could even hear the tone of her voice in my head. I was to send Max her 'special' love.

I logged off and shut down my computer. Once the motor and fan stopped the room fell ominously silent. It was just after two in the morning by now and my room was still stuffy, the curtains drawn back and every window and door open. The weather in the last few weeks had been weirdly tropical, unbearable. I had just under a week left at school and then the holidays and then University – back to Oxford if I got the grades, Max to Edinburgh! The idea of being parted from him took my breath away. I felt like I wanted to scream or smash something. To say Max had been growing on my mind recently was a massive understatement. I had been preoccupied with Max *for years* but in the sort of way that you're preoccupied by a house you've lived in and grown up around. Max was like that: a part of the landscape, ever-present even when not consciously recognised. Recently though, I had recognised him a lot. I had started to *see* Max and what I saw unsettled the natural order of things. In fact, for the past few months I had become completely obsessed with him and now with *Jonathan*. Jonathan. Who the fuck was Jonathan? Max was definitely straight. That was obvious and had always been obvious although it had not prevented me daydreaming several situations in which I discovered that this was an elaborate disguise! But Max's straightness and the whole Zoë Craven 'thing' was actually cool, bearable even, but what wasn't cool was what I had seen Max and Jonathan doing on zombie boy's boat. I mean what the fuck had that been about? What had I seen exactly? A huge vast storm of anger and jealousy exploded in my chest. I paced about the room like some caged animal but worse than being angry was being scared. And I was now really scared. I tried to concentrate, calm myself, to breathe deeply, to explain Max to myself all over again.

I undressed and crept off to the bathroom. No one was about. I brushed my teeth with slow precision like the hygienist at my dentist, up and down and then to the side, spitting foam into the sink. I was still thinking about Max when I curled up on top of the bed naked with the heat viscous about me. Max Grey. Or as he was officially called Max Lennox Grey, which I thought made him sound like a movie star, perhaps a spy, or an artist. Max Lennox Grey, a short thumb sketch of beauty, a few curvaceous lines thrown across a vast white canvas, known throughout the school hierarchy as the eighth wonder of the world; the boy who spoke in scarcely audible grunts and who was, to borrow a phrase from my Mum, adept in 'the strategic use of silence'. And someone I loved almost to destruction.

I had told Max I was gay while sitting in the library at school. He had been leaning back in his chair looking through *New Scientist* like other guys look through *Autocar* or a porn mag. When he failed to respond, I thought he might not have heard and so I repeated my revelation in a deliberately underhand sort of way. But he had heard of course. Eventually he said 'really?' or something equally non-committal as if being gay was optional and then, when I had been struck by a spasm of panic and asked him if he minded, he had laughed and said,

'Jamie, why the fuck should I mind?'

I'd scanned his face for some hint of a reaction, some revelation, a phobia or a secret desire. I felt like a sort of satellite scanning Max from orbit prior to rushing off to analyse the data: alarmed, disinterested, and intrigued? I had known Max since I was seven. His father worked with my mother sometimes rather too much and too intimately for my Dad's liking. Max used to joke that such parental excess made us half brothers! We shared the same interests and the same hobbies and for much of our schooling had even been in the same classes. Inside all of my memories of me was Max, a complementary image of myself as if we were joined at the hip. Max had shoved me out of trees and dragged me out of ponds.

Max had broken and then repaired my favourite toys. I once stuck a pin through his hand and he had once tried to strangle me. Max saved me and sometimes, rarely, I saved him. And as I grew up and began to unpack my sexual desires about who I was and needed to be it was not surprising to find that Max was at the centre of them all, the hard kernel of truth like that last indivisible character at the centre of a nest of Russian dolls. I loved his eyes, wide and dark, blue for the most part, sometimes grey, and occasionally; weirdly, a sort of moss green, narrowed, perplexed, as if he had caught the scent of something and was about to run off and kill it. I loved his Boss Model cheekbones and how they made him seem classy and *foreign*, but most of all I loved his crow's nest of hair, oily black and twiggy, either heaped over his forehead, or sometimes, long and chaotic across his neck like one of those 1970s pop stars. It was a mystery like no other. Did he ever cut it? Why did it always smell like linseed oil or dried summer grass? Did he ever use *product*? Actually, I also loved his shoulders, their wide sweep down to his waist and butt and recently I had taken to sneaking a look at his throat and thinking what it would be like to kiss or lick it. God it was all so desperately sad!

Telling Max I was gay was the closest I could get to saying I loved him; a sort of code passed under a closed door between us asking him if he felt the same, a euphemism for wanting to touch him, to kiss him; for him to want me in the same way? But of course he didn't. In one sense it didn't matter I guess. I mean where did love stop and sex begin, and were they the same? Jesus! And Max loved me. He'd actually told me that after one of my mega tantrums over Zoë last year. He'd told me slowly and carefully in that seriously weird way he had, all measured and metro sexual but then, as if sensing my dilemma, he'd asked me if I would stilll feel the same if he was ugly, or short, or spotty and into model train sets? I'd replied that he wasn't any of these things but, oddly insistent, he'd pressed home the point that my desire was superficial and missing the point of what he was! A pretty boy? Straight? I'd found the point he was trying to make obscure. Perhaps he'd been hinting at something else, something altogether sinister. I sat up in bed suddenly. Sometimes my love for him really scared me, I mean scared the shit out of me, as if it would escape from my chest like an animal. I felt hot and breathless. Perhaps I had a heart condition? I lay down again in agony, wide awake and buzzing with anxiety. Everything was such a mess.

'You're the first person I've told, Max, I mean *officially,* about being gay.' There was no reaction to his outward show of casual, chilling beauty: the sort that had driven Lucy Phillips of the lower Fifth to Prozac, a beauty that herded most of the school to either side of him, like Moses accidentally and unintentionally parting the Red Sea. Even the formidably talented Zoë Craven felt unable to entirely master the Enigma that Was Max: she had confessed it to me, naturally enough, asking me what she should do about it.

'Max. Do *you* mind?'

Sensing my anxiety, he had looked up and said '*What?*'

That was a really Max thing to say, by the way. He said '*What?*' a great deal, and always with a fantastically sharp sense of grievance as if someone had deliberately muttered a personal insult just out of earshot. Another quintessential Max characteristic was his tendency to respond to external stimuli at glacial speed no matter the urgency of any question or request. It was known universally throughout the sixth form as *Max Time.* Slowness. Silence. Max was a guy of few words. He was more a guy of presence, of mood like one of those minimalist Japanese gardens, all boulders and moss and

and dark pools of silent brooding water. It wasn't what Max said it was what he didn't say, and how he didn't say it.

'Max I've just told you something really important about myself and I could do with some sort of reassurance?' I waved my hands about his face. Or had I meant to say reciprocation? Frowning he put down the magazine with cold precision.

'Jamie what do you *want* me to say? I am really pleased for you – no, really! I am. But should it change who you are to me? What I think about you?' I narrowed my eyes sensing a trap. It was also typical of Max to make something that seemed self evidently simple suddenly sound incredibly complex. And then he added gently, 'Jamie just relax! I sort of knew, man!'

I had blushed and Max had laughed, a single bark like a fox and then he had gently pulled my ear. For someone so cool and decidedly Alpha in the school male hierarchy, Max was astoundingly, even shockingly relaxed about touching. He was forever doing it, picking things up, feeling or rubbing your arm or face, as if he thought and communicated through textures.

'You knew?' I smiled at him. It was my stoical smile, forged through great pain, a sort of face I imagined Sylvia Plath had when she wrote poetry: *once one has seen God what is the remedy*? Max frowned slowly, creating an illusion of sunlight behind racing clouds and then he smiled whimsically as if I was a *difficult* friend. He returned to his magazine and then asked in his special third parent voice, 'Have you told Margaret yet?'

I pulled a face, and he frowned again, and then flashed another smile at me, notching the power down a bit and merely blinding my sight this time, stopping my heart-lung function and most of my central nervous system.

'So how did you know? When did you suspect?' I asked, embarrassed to be pushing the 'me me me' agenda quite so shamelessly but already panicked and thinking:

has he seen me looking at him. Is it something in the way I touch him now, speak to him? Is it all obvious?

'Suspect *what?*' Max asked as if he had already forgotten the entire conversation. 'What *is it* with you this morning?'

'Nothing Max, nothing at all. I've just revealed my true form to you that's all, the inner me!' For a moment he had looked at me oddly, his blue-grey eyes wide and steady, an odd cautious look, like someone who had not quite understood.

Max's response to my revelation had been strangely complex and indirect as if he was preoccupied by something else, or worried about the allegorical note of my love and what it meant for our friendship. And with his changing mood came the sneaking realisation that Max probably found this gayness embarrassing, distracting, or – worst of all – that Max had secrets as well. Secrets he was not willing to share with me. Although at nearly eighteen I remained for all intents and purposes the definitive authority on Max, the guy his ex-girlfriends cornered for insights and consolation; the one his jock friends used to contact to confirm Max's personal whereabouts and consult his calendar or interpret his mood – I was slowly realising I didn't actually know who Max was at all. Not anymore. And who the fuck was Jonathan Price? Where had he suddenly appeared from? Years of Max to myself and then – from nowhere – *zombie boy*. My stomach churned up again all acidic and hollow and I sat suddenly upright in bed, like a guy who contemplates how far he might have to run to throw up safely or fetch help. Max wouldn't go away tonight. He stayed in my mind like an anxiety, a flashing persistent SOS winking on and off, on and off. Actually it had all started with Jonathan. I was pretty sure everything was fine before that *bastard* had appeared like some omen crowding out the sky, right as rain, and then…

When Max met Jonathan: The movie. I'd been there at the opening night. It was almost biblical, or like the opening of a Greek tragedy; Oedipus on the road to Thebes: the beginnings of a prophecy. Last year, sometime in the early summer, Max had gone to buy *The Big Issue* and this skinny, baseball capped wreck of a human being shoved the magazine in his face and then stared at Max in sheer terror as if he'd come across Michael the Archangel on a shopping trip. I mean I could understand the terror, of course, that was the *easy part*; the *normal* bit. I had even expected Max to say 'Fear not!' but he had noticed Jonathan immediately. I knew that look. A deep, odd, glow in his eyes, a sort of déjà vu like they'd met before? I watched as they carried out their little transaction as if the *Big Issue* was a giant euphemism for something else. Max deliberately overpaid him for the magazine and then walked off but just as we drew up alongside Magdalen Church he turned around again and looked back at Jonathan.

'You gave him too much money, Max. Shall I get it back?'

'No it's cool.'

'Then what is it?'

There had been an ominous pause like the twitch of a witness at an identity parade. 'Nothing man, come on!'

Two or three days later, walking home after Zoë Craven's absentee birthday party, we had run into Skeletor again. It had been early evening. Max had been doing something mysteriously heterosexual with Zoë in the garden most of the afternoon and I was pretending to be indifferent to the fact that he had obviously put his clothes back on in a hurry. We were coming up from the Botley Road towards the train station and it was near the Blackwells building that I had recognised Jonathan.

I recognised him before Max, naturally. And what was even weirder was he was obviously following us. He was so fucking indiscreet that it was sort of comical.

'Your *Big Issue* friend is returning your extra change, Max.'

Max, with what appeared to be a scratch down his neck and a bite on his throat, looked over my shoulder and then at me.

'God that's really weird! So he is!' but did nothing about it and seemed to forget him immediately. Jonathan followed us towards the top end of Walton Street and then disappeared into the coach station, slinking about, Gollum like.

There was no mention or sighting of Jonathan again until after a bewildering, crisis-filled autumn we ran into him selling his magazine in Carfax one Friday afternoon sometime in October. It was like something out of *Ground Hog Day*. Jono boy had the same baseball cap on and his cheap, aid agency issue tracksuit. Either it was the same one he wore earlier in the year or he had a wardrobe of identical outfits. Max had bought another magazine but this time Jonathan had been calmer, more measured in his response and they had both exchanged a strange look of complicity, a sort of conspiratorial nod that made me certain they knew each other. I had tried to make light of it, but Max sensed my interest and was vague, non-committal in his replies. And typically he never denied knowing this guy. To my shame I had stormed off home in a temper, angry, upset, and suddenly inarticulate with all the emotional shit I was starting to carry within me about Max. When I had got home Mum had been about, all alert and attentive. She could see I was upset and that it was probably Max related. She asked a few questions and I had let the matter drop but she was definitely on to me now – I could sense that as well. Later Max had texted me about physics and revision but obviously to see if I was still pissed at him.

Then suddenly, as if Max's growing secrecy wasn't enough, he suddenly took ill, horribly ill and things started to get definitely weird. For a start Max was never ill, I mean, seriously – *never*. No colds, no flu, no measles or mumps – jack shit. And then suddenly he's being rushed off in an ambulance in the dead of night with an impossible temperature of 43! Something to do with his head? His dad has been sweet to me – I like his dad a lot – but he's also been acting weird lately as well, like asking me to stay with Max and follow him everywhere, not let him out of my sight until he got back, like a bodyguard. What had *that* been about? And all that strange whispering and tugging with Mum, as if they were having some affair, or arguing over something to do with Max that I didn't know about? Once I actually heard them suggest they took Max out of the hospital, despite his condition, because somehow he wasn't safe? In danger, I mean – *in a hospital*? Anyway, I had sat guarding Max from some unknown threat (mostly likely the mad doctor who had taken to Max like a duck to water) suspicious that my mum and Max's dad were definitely up to something, odd, furtive, but now sort of serious. Nothing made sense. And then, after a strangely dramatic recovery, Max really began to change, especially in his behaviour towards me. He started dropping out of things we'd done together for ages. In early March he stopped coming to astronomy classes every other Monday on the *pathetic* excuse he needed to do more homework for his exams. This was such bollocks I was offended he even bothered lying about it. When I ran into his dad at college and actually asked him the lie was exposed straight away: Max was *out* somewhere on Mondays but his dad obviously still thought we were going to astronomy classes together. I said we were, of course, out of loyalty but it was clear that Max lied to his parents and he now lied to me. Tactful investigations revealed he wasn't with Zoë or playing football either. Where did he go?

Then, *much more seriously*, about twelve weeks ago, Max changed his habits at the gym. The gym was a way of life for him and also for me, for pretty obvious reasons of course. Astoundingly well made and athletic, Max hit the weights at about sixteen and then ripped his way up the scale like some secret Olympian. He really started to cut up and shape himself. It was pretty awesome but on reflection also vaguely sinister. And just as Max took on the form of some mega gay porn star he went all weird about what he wore and where he changed and showered, becoming all prudish and evasive.

This was all bewilderingly un-Max like. Max had never been one for modesty. He'd always had a body that most guys would have killed for and body snatched, and in some vague, roundabout way he knew it but without being icily vain like all the other fit boys at school. Yet the more he sculptured his body, the more cautious he got about revealing himself. Wasn't it supposed to be the other way around? Wasn't the idea to show it off, indifferent to the stares and the distressing effect a body like Max's had on people trying to change in or out of their kits, aim their deodorants correctly, or not get caught looking? Oh no. Max now arrived in his gear and left in it like a major public figure anxious to avoid the paparazzi or being perved on by some hidden webcam. And by May the gear consisted of a sort of giant woolly hoodie and baggie trackies. I thought this was mightily fucking weird. This had to be about me. Clearly he must have noticed me dogging him up in some way although I had tried to be cunning and thought I had been. On a particularly hot day recently I disguised my disappointment as a general concern over hygiene.

'What's with the *purdah* outfits in the gym? I hope you don't think I've been getting off on you or something?' We had been sitting on a bus, swaying and lurching as it staggered through Abingdon back towards Oxford.

'*What?*' He removed the small earpiece of his iPod and looked at me.

'Max look – do I make you uncomfortable?'

He had looked at me, initially puzzled, evidently clueless as to my drift and then he looked very cross for a moment, his dark face drawn down like a boy in a Manga cartoon, the hair neon black and snaking.

'Jamie don't go on! You're not the centre of the fucking universe!' Yet he had relented almost immediately, putting his wide hand over my knee in a killer grip.

'I am totally cool about you, Jamie – I just want to shower at home – stop making such a big deal about everything! It's not all about you, man!'

I looked at him suspiciously but the feel of his hand touching me made any immediate counter attack impossible. The subject of gym wear and showering was thus dropped.

Then, very recently, Max started wearing sunglasses. This was surprisingly un-cool for Max since they were not the sort of wrap around, *Matrix* ones, but the full-on Michael Jackson type. They made him look dangerous, like a drugs baron. No one said anything about this of course, and some guys even started to emulate him. He wore them indoors and out and although he had several pairs confiscated by the teachers he seemed to have an unlimited stash of them somewhere because they were renewed almost immediately. It was at this stage that I had begun to really worry that all this shit *wasn't* anything about me and my quest to be at peace with my gayness, but all about Max! At first I suspected steroids and drugs, having read a leaflet left in the school gym. After reading it several times I checked things out on the web and I decided that Max showed all the signs, personality change, obsessive habits, but it still didn't seem right – Max would never use drugs. Then I decided he was terminally ill and not telling me. Had he been diagnosed with some horrible condition in the wake of his illness last year and decided to hide it? I tried several times to mention the shades but in the wake of the gym gear controversy I began to sound like some jilted girlfriend, of which Max of course had a large number. I did not have exclusive rights to be consulted over what Max wore, and persistent whinging only just made matters worse. But I couldn't help it. It was like some form of OCD. And all the time Max became more and more remote and sort of sneaky with it as well.

If things were bad by now, they suddenly got worse after my last Maths exam, I mean seriously worse, *off the scale* of all possible worseness. I had come out of the exam hall to see Zoë standing by the door clearly waiting for me and suspiciously unescorted by her usual posse of women. She seized the problem immediately and by the balls so to speak.

'Jamie, what the fuck is wrong with Max?' She was intelligent, very good looking; *occasionally* nasty.

'I have no idea,' I lied letting my anxiety slide as we walked out into the sun. I liked Zoë, although I was insanely jealous that she had unfettered access to Max's body. 'Why, what's up?'

'I think he's seeing someone else,' she said with such certainty that a chilling fog instantly cut off my vision.

'No way!' I was so genuinely alarmed that the denial sounded entirely plausible. Zoë looked momentarily relieved. For some stupidly absurd reason I was thinking of Jonathan, of course, while she was clearly thinking of another woman, possibly that weird Christian girl Max had hung around with two years ago!

'I just hope you're right but look, there's something

wrong with him though, *definitely*. Have you seen him at the gym recently? I mean, in the raw?'

I sensed something vaguely leading about the question. I said I had, in a very matter of fact way, as if Max's nudity was an occupational hazard.

'He's not done anything *weird* to himself, has he?'

We had walked towards the Sixth Form centre. I had felt my stomach tighten at her tone, at the question. *What the fuck?*

'Not that I know of – why?'

'Nothing –' she stopped then, thinking furiously. 'But he's being very hands off – I mean, *physically*?'

'Yeah?' I tried to sound all knowing. In reality, I was close to hyperventilating. I nodded slowly but, disappointingly, she didn't elaborate.

'Jamie, sort this out? He might have had some sort of *piercing* or something –'

The thought of Max with some gay boy tat on his abs or pectoral had made me almost expire on the spot. No way!

'Sure, leave it to me.'

Zoë was sort of complicit in my obsession about Max. Perhaps she thought it was an advanced form of male bonding, but she was a candid bastard and sort of eerily prescient in the way girls could be. She knew I was gay because I was pretty sure Max had told her. I said I would deal with it and that she should relax and she had sighed theatrically as if I would do it there and then:

'You're a good guy, Jamie.'

My proposal for sorting this out was to confront Max directly. There was no other option now. At the time, watching Zoë stride away from me like Athena it seemed to require merely picking the right moment and ambushing Max as I had so often done in the past, or persistently wearing him down until *Max Time* finally collapsed. And what better opportunity to pick than

Monday evenings, *astronomy*, and Max's evening about town? Despite Max's absence, I had still been attending the fortnightly classes, held in St Edwards School, just up the Woodstock Road. They were about to finish for the summer. By now – exams almost over – what homework could Max conceivably have left? If I got to his house early enough I might even catch him going out on his mysterious trip. It was a sort of plan. At about 7 p.m. on the day of reckoning I sauntered up towards Max's house. It appeared empty. I say appeared because the Greys had a doorbell that either never worked or, cunningly, could never be heard from outside. I rang it several times and then clattered the letterbox. The noise was swallowed up in the hallway.

It was a big, red-bricked house with a high slate roof and a front door on the side reached through an elaborate wooden porch like the entrance to a church. Max's parents had separated some time ago but his father and Max had stayed on in the house despite it being ridiculously large, or perhaps because of it. Max's dad could afford to stay and perhaps he was waiting for his wife to come back? In the meantime he had allowed the place to degenerate rapidly. The gardens were overgrown and the woodwork was chipped and peeling. Some of the third floor windows were without curtains, and the guttering at the front of the house had come away from the wall. It had a slightly eccentric, spooky look about it. It was, without doubt, the sort of house that Professor Grey ought to have lived in: a mad Scientist turned recluse, and his beautiful, athletic and *mysterious* son. Max was adopted after all, so he was definitely mysterious! I rattled the door and rang the bell but nothing. Fantasising about Max was a way of life now, I did it most of the time even without thinking, a necessary substitution for the real thing.

I walked back down the steps and stood by the porch momentarily at a loss. There was no plan B. I realised at this stage that I had not adopted a particularly sophisticated approach to this problem. As I moped about wondering whether to go home or not I noticed that on the bottom of the porch steps, placed neatly alongside several bags and official looking papers, was a lidless shoebox stuffed full of what appeared to be photographs. One rather large one, sticking slightly out from the rest looked like a photograph of Max; I could tell the top of his head anywhere in the world, in any light. Looking around me I stepped forward and, bending down as if to tie my trainer I took a closer look. I was sweating like a rapist by this stage and my chest felt airless. The photos were mostly black and white ones, badly focused, oddly composed, and *all of Max*, well mostly. Some had clearly missed Max and taken pictures of trees, street lamps, moving cars. I leaned down cautiously, intrigued by the large print. Max was looking away from the camera, his face profiled, his hair a black cloud spiked and contoured. It had been taken recently and it made him look insanely sexy like a photo op for a magazine. I flicked through the rest of the pictures, quickly, breathlessly. There were literally hundreds of them. Random, quirky shots as if they had been taken by accident, or during an earthquake, or with a very shaky hand. And they seemed to cover a period of about five or six years, perhaps longer, because in some of them Max was quite young and the picture had cropped in his mother, and sometimes his father. There was even one of me, standing quite recently in the driveway, having had an argument about the gym! I skimmed through them quickly, my hands sticky with anxiety. And then I realised why they looked so strange. Whoever had taken these clearly hadn't wanted to be seen and probably hadn't. That's why Max was never looking to camera. He hadn't realised he was being filmed. What the fuck? Then I heard a noise, a sort of metallic rattle, coming from the back garden.

I jumped back and looked instinctively, furtively, towards the sound. Intrigued, I walked through an open, unhinged gate past a flight of steps down to a basement and towards a long conservatory that ran out into a jungle of lawn. At the far bottom corner of the garden, partly hidden under fruit trees, Max's dad was burning stuff in a metal incinerator. Piled next to him were several tell tale shoeboxes full of papers like the one containing the photos. He had his back turned to me, and despite the warmth, he was wearing a light blue cardigan. He was hunched in slightly, thinking about something: what he was burning, probably, or whether the neighbours would complain about the smoke. I had that instinctive realisation that this was not something I should necessarily be witnessing but before I could do anything he suddenly turned and saw me.

We both looked pretty shocked to be honest and then, so as not to look sneaky, I had started to walk towards him, asking him about Max. For a moment he looked alarmed, almost as if he didn't recognise me. Eventually he replied that Max had gone out. We talked on a little, random stuff, fake as hell as if he hadn't seen me for ages. I hung about for some reason as if Max was hiding behind a bush or in a tree deliberately avoiding me. It then occurred to me that Grey intended to burn the photos of Max along with all the other stuff down by the front door. Max's dad asked me about my mother, her trip to the US, about whether I had heard from her yet? And all the time his eyes kept moving towards the incinerator as if he had a body in there. After a while I made my excuses and walked down Woodstock road, towards town, past Green College and eventually past Grey Friars and *Browns*. I felt really oddly upset to be honest, as if I had caught my parents having sex or witnessed a murder. Grey wasn't usually as strange as this, although he could be pretty weird. He seemed afraid of something.

I walked about thinking about the photos, the incinerator, Professor Grey, Max and then suddenly I realised that something was happening – to Max and to the people around him – something really sinister. The revelation hit me like one of those cheap magic eye tricks in which suddenly amid a mass of dots and dashes you spot the Eiffel Tower. It had all been so fucking obvious! Not just the illness at Christmas, but other stuff before, like the time when Max and I had been arguing about Zoë just off Plantation Road quite late and then spotted Max's dad hanging about some guy's driveway on the opposite side of the road as if he had been following us! Or the time when Max came home with a nosebleed and I saw my mother pocket the bloody tissues in a small plastic bag and squirrel them away, with Grey whispering something to her, just out of earshot. God I had been blind! Or possibly self obsessed. And the more I walked about the town the more I got a really scary idea that my mother's sudden and mysterious trip to the States had something to do with Max as well. Or was I now officially mad in some way – had Max made me crazy?

I should have gone home really, after the bin incident and the photos and my failure to corner Max and fulfil Zoë's quest. I should have given up the whole idea, but the fact that Max was in town seemed to fixate me and I was so unsettled by my train of thought I thought the walk would do me good. I texted Zoë and asked her if she was with Max. The reply came back pretty instantly that she was alone but did I have 'any news for her?' The prospect, the hysterical certainty he was with Jonathan made me literally nauseous but determined. I wondered about town for ages, my head surging this way and that, thinking, thinking, thinking. I am not exactly sure how far I walked. In the end, I found myself near Westgate, having walked right round the centre and back up by the ice rink. It was there that I saw Max with Jonathan. It was entirely accidental.

Of course I had suspected Max had been in contact with Jonathan ever since the New Year. I had actually seen them together, in a café on the High Street talking with distressing seriousness, looking at a folder or something. I had even seen Max give him *money*. This time however, this time was *different*, because I felt different about the whole thing. I was crossing New Road heading towards the lane that short cuts past the back of St Peter's College through to George Street when I saw them, standing on the opposite side of the road. It was a clear, vivid evening. Jonathan was wearing tracksuit bottoms and a light coloured T-shirt. He looked healthier than usual though, less thin and sharp around the elbows. His face was covered by his baseball cap drawn down low on his forehead. I paused, conscious that I might be seen, but Max was talking and Jonathan was moving and twitching as he listened in that crack head way of his. I felt sick and miserable. They were clearly at opposite ends of the body language scale: Max hardly ever moved and Jonathan moved all the time. As I stood watching them they suddenly turned in unison and walked off towards the Botley Road. My mind was completely empty for a minute. Dead. It just kept repeating a one-line code. Max was in danger, something really serious, blackmail, sickness, drugs? I felt close to throwing up but then I just felt incredibly fucking angry, a huge energising rush like road rage, aimed partly at Max but mostly at Jonathan. I turned around and followed. I was so pissed off I didn't really think about it. The light was so brilliant it was a miracle they didn't see me but I suddenly didn't care. As I stalked on, I thought it ironic that, like Jonathan last year, I was following Max now, as if we had swapped places in Max's affection. The stupid thought stuck into me like a knife.

They passed the train station on their right, heads down, deep in talk, Max slightly stooped because of his height and probably because Jono boy was muttering. They then went under the bridge and turned left just before Osney Island. There was almost no one about now except a few people outside the Westgate Hotel and some kids on skate boards. I waited a good two or three minutes on the corner of the main road and then followed. At first I thought I had lost them but all the streets here were grid-like, boxed in between the river and the Botley Road, and so I was pretty confident I could find them again and indeed as I neared what appeared to be a dead end, I saw them entering a yard that backed onto the canal or possibly part of the Thames. It was quiet and deserted now, the light beginning to mellow slightly and the heat abate. I could hear the sound of water everywhere, heavy and consistent, like a sluice gate or a weir. It was weird, like being in a dream sequence. I was completely torn up inside, a horrible raw pain that made me feel physically unwell. I fantasised about killing Jonathan. He was pathetic, gaunt and I was in good shape, taller and stronger. I could snap his neck and say he'd fallen. When I eventually turned into the yard I was horrified to find that they'd vanished completely. Then I realised that they had climbed down into a *boat*. Several were moored along a curve of embankment in front of me, steep as a cliff. Jesus – the idea that Jonathan lived on a boat definitely figured.

Then I heard Max laugh. It seemed to come from under the ground. For a split second as I stood there holding my breath, my nerve failed me. What the fuck was I doing here? And if I was found what would Max say? I knew of course. He'd look at me with that quizzical frown, the one that profiled his cheeks and made him look like some casual Michelangelo sketch, a work in progress, and then he'd growl 'Jamie?' as if I were being possessive and unfair. I stood with my eyes hot and itchy with tears and my mouth doing some weird tremble. I walked back away from the embankment and sat where I could keep an eye on them while attempting to get a grip, to have one last go to rationalise my jealousy. The air was heavy with the ripe green smell of river water. I considered staying here until their little liaison was over and then just saying 'Hi Max!' as if I stood around in boat yards all the time, casual and indifferent.

It *was* possible to confront Max, I'd done it often enough. It required skill, like creeping up to a large tiger and pulling its tail. You had to blind side Max, and before he could respond, land the first accusation. But as I sat there and grew calmer I just felt stupid and more wretched than ever. As my anger left me. all I had to confront Max with was the enormous despair that Max had sensed in me before and clearly disliked; thinking it unfair, undeserved, hopeless. What I was doing would only make him dislike me. I picked at the edge of the stone step I was sitting on, clawing out the stone cement until my fingers bled. Then, with one final effort I got up and walked along the edge of the moorings. I tried to look like I was out exercising some fucking imaginary dog, a last tactical scan in enemy territory before I ran for cover.

There wasn't much to see at first, just the tops of the boats, a chimney and a few pathetic looking plants along the roofs, dried out in the heat wave. There was a strong smell of cannabis, like cat piss and I thought I heard a radio on very low. I couldn't see into the windows because they were too close up into the wall of the embankment itself. But as I got to the end of the boat I came across them suddenly. They were sitting in the stern where the tiller would have been. A wave of cold panic hit my face. Max had his back to me and for a moment I couldn't see Jonathan until I realised that Max was holding him tightly in his arms, pressed up close against his chest as if he was a rag doll. It was astounding how accurately I saw all this as if I was looking at an enlarged photograph through a magnifying glass. Max had a grey low-necked T-shirt on and the back lay stretched over his shoulders. Because of the intensity of the embrace, the material on his arms had snared up on his broad triceps and there was some white tag of a label just below a stud of vertebra at the base of his neck. The exposed skin between the shirt and the massed cords of hair was tanned deep brown.

I saw all of this and then, entirely on remote, I walked past them and kept going, walking slowly and evenly and re-joining the street without looking back. I just kept moving trying not to think or scream but just concentrate on the pavement in front of me and the way the tiles sloped and angled on the uneven ground and how some had pits of moss in between them and others hadn't. It suddenly mattered a great deal. I was so deeply shocked I didn't actually lose it until I got to the bottom of Walton Street, opposite the bus station and then I thought I would actually collapse, stop breathing. I sat opposite Worchester College for so long that some woman asked me if I was alright and it was only when I went to reassure her that I was fine that I realised I was crying; I mean full on girlie crying like I'd just seen the world blown out like a candle. The image of them together was stuck in my brain like a movie clip, repeating itself endlessly, flickering on a loop. *Max holds Jonathan.* I hadn't seen Max since then. He'd been off school for the last few days and I hadn't called him, hoping he'd sense my outrage and text me. He didn't and that made things almost impossible to bear. And the movie clip had gone on and on repeating. I'd then MSN'd Katherine but once chatting had lost my nerve to ask her to help me, to tell her I was sinking head first like the fucking *Titanic* and needed rescuing.

I heard a clock strike 2.30 a.m. The heat in my bedroom was so heavy and thick that I started to panic that I couldn't breathe properly. I so wished Mum was here. I could talk to her about most stuff. Mum had guessed about my feelings for Max. She hadn't said anything directly, but she had hinted at things sometimes, over the last months especially: she probably knew before I did. She'd always start with 'I really like Max you know –' as if this would lead to an avalanche of confessions from me and when we were together recently I had caught her looking at Max oddly, an expression of worry and love that I now realised was partly aimed at me. If only I could tell her about the sheer *darkness* inside me, the anger at being excluded, lied to? It was destroying my friendship with Max and it was destroying me. Suddenly I realised I had to do something immediately, urgently, some desperate procedure to dig out the pain.

I grabbed my mobile phone and went to call Max to demand an explanation but then, suddenly, I rang his father. I had his number stored under Max's, mostly because I usually had to remind Max's dad about stuff to do with school and lifts home or Max's whereabouts. What I was doing made no sense to me at all but I still did it. I didn't even think about the time and the fact that I would be waking Max's dad in the dead of night. I sat up against the headboard of the bed expecting the voicemail to cut in at any moment, to hear Julian's deep rather hesitant voice asking the caller to leave a message. I was already composing one vague enough to cover various scenarios from Max doesn't love me to something weird and dangerous is happening to your son. There was a distinct crackle as someone picked up, an odd electric silence and then a voice said loudly and expectantly 'Hello!'

The voice was very *awake*.

I felt momentarily stunned and then stupidly asked for Julian Grey as if I was a crank and wasn't sure I'd called the right number. The voice confirmed Grey's identity with a slight trace of anxiety but when I told him who I was he seemed oddly excited and started asking again about my mother. Had I heard any news from her? Was she alright? It was as if he'd been up all night waiting for her to ring him!

I screwed up my courage and said I was calling about Max, to warn that Max was in danger. It sounded so fucking stupid saying it straight out that I thought he would laugh or get cross, but he seemed to know something already. When I started to explain I lost control of the lip again and started rambling with my voice all over the place. Jesus! He asked me to calm down, quietly and gently, and his odd show of affection just made matters worse. I was crying again and rambling because in one shocking instant I realised that his dad *knew* something was wrong. I sensed it. I asked him to meet me and at first the poor bastard thought I meant literally there and then, but he finally suggested *Browns* and said we could meet after school. He suggested this with infinite care like someone arranges a meeting to tell them dreadful and horrible news. But at least he had agreed to meet and for the moment I felt less mad, less terrified. Rather abruptly I hung up in case he had second thoughts.

Chapter 13

I slept somehow and at some stage, wedged between lucid dreams of Max's dad burning papers in his garden and scary sepia-like visions of Max running through dark fields. Both were distressing but the fields one was worse. When I jumped awake I had the distinct feeling I'd dreamed it before. Max was sprinting ahead of me for dear life and I was behind him trying to keep up, aware that something – or lots of things – were not only chasing us but also beginning to close in and gain on Max. I had tried to shout a warning but I suddenly lost my footing and stumbled forward. As I fell, I caught sight of a flash of grey pelts and several large dogs – wolves actually – streaking past me. I'm sure they were wolves and I think I screamed but that might not have been in the dream. When I emerged on the landing it was 9.40 a.m. and my dad was just about to go off to work. He looked suitably appalled at the time and my condition. After a vague and incoherent lecture about being nearly 18 and therefore an adult with responsibilities, he drove me to school and dropped me off with some sort of improvised packed lunch. I had tried to point out several times that I didn't need to go to school but he seemed reluctant to leave me in the house alone. He was off to Birmingham and obviously feared I might hold some sort of spontaneous party.

I should have faked an illness. Mum would have let me stay at home. Actually, I was ill! Apart from his anxiety about the house, Dad also seemed uncannily preoccupied with Max as well. This was *unprecedented.* Once in the car, he had started on Max immediately as if he'd fucking rehearsed some speech all night. He used strange euphemisms like, 'I know that Max is *very special* to you Jamie,' and a new, potentially disturbing variation on the lines of 'Jamie, you can talk to *your mother and me* about anything, you know that, don't you? I mean about anything, Jamie?' I wondered if I was somehow manifesting an outward sign of my mental turmoil? A rash perhaps, or the word MAX written on my forehead. I reassured him that all was well while trying not to scream or have a panic attack. I twitched forward in my seat and asked Dad if he thought Max was weird. The question clearly startled him and took him perilously off script.

'Weird as in?'

'As in strange? Mysterious?'

Dad frowned and chewed his lip, a bad sign usually. He then seemed to think very hard and then said carefully.

'I think Max is very special, Jamie. He clearly means a lot to you.'

I resumed classes like one resumes life after a bereavement. I was scared about seeing Max and *losing* it, scared about not seeing him, scared that I'd tell him I was going to meet his dad at *Browns* and that I was onto him at last. Almost the first person I ran into was Max himself, manifest like some god, sitting on his own and waiting for me. And he looked incredible, even for Max. He'd discarded most of his uniform and had no bag and no books. He wore a shirt unbuttoned almost to his navel and out at the back. I wondered if Zoë had ambushed him or demanded some random physical inspection. I didn't risk looking at him and we had some random exchange en route to some optional study skill class, my eyes glued to the floor. When I did look at him, I thought I might burst into flames. His exposed throat was darkened by the sun, knotted at the base into a surreal dune scape of padded muscle like the bottom of some sandy tropical ocean. And if this wasn't enough every time he moved, his shirt exposed the curved discs of his pectorals at me, smooth and dark beneath the white cotton. The only way I could hold onto my resolve to be pissy and unmoved was to think of Jonathan.

For his part, Max seemed utterly oblivious to any transgression whatsoever and kept asking me what the matter was. And then he started apologising for something, anything, on the working assumption he'd clearly done something to upset me and his typical generosity made me feel wretched and ungrateful and worse than ever. During class he sat behind me with his legs unconsciously sprawled under mine and kept making tiny paper darts and putting them behind my ear. He then started nudging my arm, like a dog nuzzling for attention.

'What's up with you? Jamie? Hey? Jamie?'

He wasn't even wearing his shades. I tried to visualise him kissing Jonathan and recalled the tone of his dad's voice on the phone last night so I could concentrate my sheer fucking rage on him, like sunlight through a magnifying glass, but the proximity of his body, his smell, his attention, was too much for me. In the end I turned around and glared at him. My expression seemed to sting him slightly.

'What?'

His eyes seemed tired, darker than usual, delicately smudged blue black in the corners near the bridge of his nose as if he was wearing henna. It gave him a dangerously erotic look, like a Hindu deity, that seemed to scold my face. My eyes skidded off his and down his face and the trimmed sideburns to the floor and then my desk. I mumbled something insensible.

'Jamie?'

Evidently perplexed, Max leaned very close to my ear and whispered loudly,

'Why are you being such a *bitch*?' There were several titters from nearby desks and the teacher – mid way through a discussion on University life and the challenges ahead – glanced up nervously. But Max persisted in looking bewildered, *hurt* even! Why didn't I just ask him outright? About Jonathan, about who he was and what they did together? Why couldn't I just ask him if he was alright and believe his answer and let it go!

It was like this all morning, Max playful, at ease, as if nothing had happened, me knotted up with anxiety and anger but also doubt. Then I started to have serious misgivings about my planned visit to *Browns*. Like the dream in the fields with Max and the wolves, the idea that I was going to confront Max's dad with some deep-seated conspiracy over a pot of tea melted away into the clear hot air like an apparition. I was deranged, unhinged by love and some ill-defined lust, borderline psychotic. Surely, the best thing was to confront Max calmly and rationally without any chick moments of tears or hysteria and during lunch break I was presented with a brief window of opportunity. Max had crept up on me as I sat watching a five-aside football match. He had managed to get right up close, in full *ninja* mode, and had then shouted in my ear at point blank range. I had sprung up startled, discarding my remaining food in the air.

'You *bastard*, Max!'

'Checking out the talent?' he breezed, picking up a boiled egg from out of the grass. I had complained and he had laughed. Below us on an artificial grey surface a gaggle of boys ran after a ball unenthusiastically. They looked pretty uninspiring.

'Yeah, right – a real *stud* pen – how are you – feeling better?'

'Better?' he pushed me along on the bench and then sat with his thigh quite close to mine, close enough for me to feel its heat. I stayed where I was expecting him to move away slightly but he didn't. He could be such a manipulative bastard when he wanted to be.

'Have I been ill?'

'You know, the sinister shades, and the 'I have a migraine' routine? You had me worried there for a moment. I thought you might be coming down with something?'

'I'm ok – God you're worse than my dad, for fuck's sake – he's been nagging a lot recently.'

'Has he?' I narrowed my eyes as some poor guy fell over miles from the ball and for no apparent reason as if he'd walked into an invisible object.

'What's he been nagging you about?'

It was unwise to lie to Max. He had a sort of sixth sense about these things and he knew most of my interrogatory approaches, including the feigned indifference strategy. Talking about his Dad also risked me giving myself away, mentioning the phone call, or God forbid *Browns*.

'Strange stuff. He's very emotional at the moment, especially around me.'

The comment seemed odd and unusually serious.

'Perhaps he's worried about you Max.' I nerved myself to look at him and found he was watching me carefully, his face beautiful but remote.

'Have you spoken to him recently? Jamie?'

I felt myself stiffen suddenly. 'No, not for ages.'

Max remained looking at me for a moment and then he put his hand along the bench behind me and left it there. It was an expansive gesture unconsciously done, almost an act of reconciliation. I was also vaguely hoping someone would see it. I swallowed hard and breathed in sharply through my nose as if I was about to dive into deep cold water.

'Max –'

'What?'

'There's something going on with you and I don't know what it is and I don't want to pry or be jealous or possessive or unreasonable-'

'Jamie –' He had moved his hand off the bench and suddenly put it across my back, his fingers anchored around my shoulder.

'But you don't tell me anything Max, you've never told me *anything* about yourself or about what goes on in your head and I am worried sick we're drifting apart and- ' I stopped suddenly, my voice unsteady and my chest tight with pain. Why could I never keep to the point? Why did I ramble? I expected some rebuke or flare of temper but Max sat there in silence with his arm around me in full view of the universe as if this was the most natural gesture in the world.

'Jamie what the fuck are you talking about? *No one's* drifting apart – is this about us going off to different universities or something? Is this still about Zoë?'

'It's *not* about Zoë, Max. It's about you. No, it's about us! It's about you keeping secrets from me.'

Slowly he removed his hand and slid it over my upper back like a caress and then he stood up slowly. I felt I'd stabbed him hard in his chest without need or warning.

'Jamie –'

'Max *don't*! Don't tell me I am over-reacting or just being hysterical! Something is going on! I've always confided in you about everything – I mean I'd trust you with my life but you, you don't trust me at all! With anything!'

He played with his hair, absentmindedly twisting the fringe out and then brushing it back. I'd hurt him and I instantly regretted it. I felt my face flush with shame. Max remained standing and then wedged his hands into his trouser pockets. I caught a flash of his pant band white below the flat wall of his lower abs and above his belt buckle.

'Is that what you really think?' he asked eventually, his tone neutral. For a very brief moment, I didn't recognise his voice at all. I tried to think of something to say, something reasonable and measured to pull us back in from the abyss but Max suddenly turned away. As he turned I noticed his eyes flash. I mean they suddenly glinted silver in the way that lenses in a pair of binoculars catch in the sunlight, or the way an LCD screen shimmers when you move it. It was quite dramatic and Max seemed to sense it as well. There was a long black silence. I closed my eyes tightly. God why did I always fuck this up?

'I want to help you Max.'

Carefully, afraid perhaps his eyes would misbehave again, Max looked up at me slowly, as if he had a physical weight on his head. He was now a dark shape, self-contained, brooding like a cloud. For a moment he was utterly inscrutable.

'I know you do, Jamie. I know that.' he paused. 'We ok for the gym tonight?' He sounded almost defiant, daring me to say no. It was almost a form of emotional blackmail. We stared at each other, perhaps startled by each other's intensity, the air of sudden crisis.

'Yeah, sure. 7 p.m. I'll meet you there?'

He nodded but his face was preoccupied, guarded, as if he had come close to the point of telling me something and then suddenly changed his mind and drawn back.

I was almost late for Professor Grey. In the end I had to run through Ratcliffe Square, up Broad Street and passed Balliol, panting like a bloodhound. When I got to *Browns*, Professor Grey was sitting inside looking anxiously about as if he'd been stood up. He was wearing a very old herringbone tweed jacket, despite the heat and his grey hair was particularly professorial, heaped up, bone white, randomised. He'd ordered himself a pot of some curious, rather foul-smelling tea and was reading the menu. I cantered in and made my apologies. Despite having spent all afternoon working through various stratagems, as soon as I saw him I felt entirely at a loss as to what I was actually going to say. He ordered me some coffee and teacakes as if I was twelve years old and he was my Uncle. We sat for a while in polite silence. I had sudden premonitions of disaster.

Browns was full of parlour palms and tourists – most of the undergraduates had gone down by now. As an icebreaker I explained briefly, breathlessly, why I was late. Julian tutted several times and then I felt like I had something stuck in my throat and kept having to drink loads of water. In the end Max's dad said to me very sweetly
'Jamie, relax you look terribly anxious. It's fine. Tell me what's bothering you and let's see if I can help? Yes?'
I sighed expansively, shaking my head. I apologised for calling him last night so late but he said he was wide awake and in his study and that I could always call him whenever I needed. I thought he seemed sad and I remembered Max's earlier comment about his emotional state.
'Julian –'
I felt insanely nervous. Luckily my coffee arrived and caused a minor distraction behind which I tried to regroup, to think of Jonathan, Max, his weirdness, his flashing eyes.

'Please don't tell Max about this, Julian. I mean I should really talk to him but I've tried and he won't tell me anything!'

Professor Grey nodded sagely. 'He can be very stubborn, even obstinate, but you must know that by now. I mean you must know Max better than anyone else –'

'But that's the point!' I exploded suddenly. 'I don't! I mean, look: I should! But he's hiding something from me, his *body* –' My voice suddenly sounded guilty as fuck, a bit too high and I felt myself blushing uncontrollably as if I was about to tell Max's dad I watched his body all the time. I winced visibly and tried to start again, 'We spend a lot of time together but recently Max has become very private, and sort of secretive, and I think he's in trouble but won't tell me?' I looked up at Julian realising how bizarre and stupid all this must sound. Then I added rather pointlessly, 'I think he's on drugs or something!'

Grey's eyes had fallen away from me and he was unfolding and refolding a linen napkin in front of him as if he was about to make an origami figure out of it. He seemed to be sorting out something in his head, like a chess player contemplating a move. Had I embarrassed him?

'And then there's this guy Jonathan, Jonathan Price? He's some tramp, some dude selling the *Big Issue* up at the top end of Carfax. He and Max have been seeing each other, and I think that has something to do with what's happening to Max. I've seen Max give him money.' I said this ominously and then closed my eyes feeling that I had ratted on Max for no good reason except jealously and greed. Still his dad played with the napkin, his hands fussing over the material, mottled and long fingered. He was probably thinking I was mad or whether and at what stage he should call my father.

'Jamie, Max is fine –'

'Julian, don't lie to me, please. I am Max's best friend.' My mouth felt strange and dry. I had gone to speak of love but had stopped myself, afraid I would be misunderstood. I was predictably and pathetically close to tears already.

'I *know*,' said Grey quietly. 'We both love him very much, Jamie.' He then leaned forward struggling to speak. 'And so does Jonathan. Max and Jonathan have known each other a long time, Jamie.'

'Yeah?' *What*!

'Have you met him? Jonathan?'

I was staring hard at the table in shock. I hardly heard the question at all and Max's dad repeated it quietly, insistently.

'No. Not really. I mean I was there when Max met him last year but I've never spoken with him. Sorry.' I frowned, surprised I was apologising. Then Julian asked me if Max and Jonathan had met often.

'Yes, quite a lot recently –' I was confused now, unsure whether I should confess to stalking Max or keep quiet. I suddenly realised that Julian was as interested in their relationship as I was.

'I saw them together last Monday evening after I called around to see if Max was in. The night you were burning *stuff*.' I glanced at Julian's eyes but he was looking through me, still thinking of something else. So disconcerting was his stare that I almost turned around and looked at the table behind me.

'Who *is* Jonathan? How did they know each other? I think he has some hold on Max, Julian. I think he might even be threatening Max in some way?' I tried to say the word blackmail but couldn't.

Julian sighed deeply and then looked at me intently, his pale blue eyes troubled.

'It isn't what it seems, Jamie. I mean the meetings and the money, it isn't drugs or anything illicit. Max knew Jonathan briefly before my wife and I adopted him.

Jonathan was fostered about the same time, although he is older than Max, in his early twenties. He has been less –' he paused, and seemed to struggle for the right word – 'Less *fortunate* than Max. In fact Sally and I had initially intended to adopt them both but, well, how I wish to God we had.'

I felt myself go cold. I stammered something incoherent, a sort of startled mew. This information made my feelings of jealously *infinitely* worse. Jonathan was no longer some random stranger. He was part of the mysterious pre-Oxford phrase of Max's life, a part that pre-dated me!

'Does Max remember him?'

'He didn't at first, I think. However, Jonathan clearly remembered Max – he's hard to forget, of course! And he may well have come back to Oxford to find him after all these years.'

'Back?' It seemed a precise word to use, heavy with meaning. Julian looked slightly alarmed and then nodded sharply, his lips pressed tightly together. I suddenly realised Max's dad was stonewalling me and badly. He was also probably regretting having agreed to meet me. My frustration gave me sudden courage.

'So Max is fine?' I said with a trace of sarcasm in my voice. 'So why the odd behaviour at the gym, why the box of photos outside your door? Did you take those? Have you been having Max followed?'

Julian showed a trace of irritation or panic, it was hard to tell which. 'No, no Jamie I haven't been following Max.'

'Who took them?'

'Jamie they're family photos, I was sorting out the house!'

'And at the hospital just after Christmas, when Max was ill. You wanted me to stay with him – you asked me!' I was surprised to hear my own anger.

'Yes I did.'

'Because –'

Julian put his hand to his forehead and started to massage his temples. 'Jamie, please. I was worried that something was happening to Max, that perhaps his cancer had returned?'

'*Cancer?*'

Max's father seemed to start slightly as if he had been caught out or forced into an error.

'Max had cancer?' I thought of his eyes and his body. *Was* he hiding some sort of illness?

Julian looked about helplessly for some sort of distraction, a waiter, another customer, then he looked at me desperately.

'When Max was a small child he was diagnosed with a rare form of bone cancer that spread to his brain –'

I was feeling sick now, my mind wheeling about like a flock of gulls. I remembered the A & E doctor pressing me about some accident on the pitch, whether Max had concussed his head.

'When was this, Julian?'

'The early 1990s. We adopted him after it went into remission. And he's been perfectly well since, except for the illness last year. It just shocked me Jamie, that's all, and I wanted someone close to him that he, that I, trusted. I'm afraid to say that the sight of him in hospital, especially at the Radcliffe, was very distressing. It was very good of you to stay with him that day. Your mother thought it a dreadful imposition!'

'It was nothing,' I whispered. My mind was racing and whirling so much I could hardly hear anything. *Especially* at the Radcliffe? Max's dad looked as wretched as I did and yet to my own amazement I pressed on with my interrogation.

'Did Max meet Jonathan in hospital? Was Jonathan ill as well?' Perhaps they had met in some kid's cancer ward, experienced some intense bonding session through a shared illness? Something pretty weird must have happened to possess Jonathan to seek Max out, even with the Max effect, years later.

'No. Jonathan had been misdiagnosed, a mistake,' said Julian vaguely and again seemingly against his better judgement. Suddenly he tried to assert himself.

'Jamie, listen to me. I understand how important Max is to you. Max is going through some sort of identity crisis at the moment. It's not uncommon with people who have been adopted. Meeting up with Jonathan is a tangible link with his past and I think he is intrigued but also slightly frightened as to his former life.'

I was concentrating on the crystal candleholder in the middle of the table. Was this possible? It seemed feasible. 'Has he tried to contact his real parents, Julian? Are they still alive?' I thought the word real sounded accusatory.

'I don't think so. Max never knew his biological father and his real mother died recently.'

'Norma Lennox?'

Julian showed a flash of surprise and gave me another one of his minimalist Prussian nods and then he asked one of his odd questions 'Has Max ever spoken to you about his real mother, Jamie?'

'No, not really. I mean *sometimes*.'

Wasn't that the problem? That Max never told me anything personal about himself? I sat leaning back in my chair, winded with the revelation that, obsessed with my own identity I had been completely oblivious to Max's past and his own current spirit quest. But why had he never asked me, invited me in, confided in me! A great inky black storm of anger and resentment clawed up my chest and for a while I couldn't speak or think. I saw Julian look anxiously at his watch.

'Sorry, Julian. I've been stupid about this,' I said eventually. Professor Grey looked at me and smiled weakly.

'You are the least stupid person I have ever met! Please don't be angry at Max, Jamie. He hasn't knowingly excluded you from this.'

'Hasn't he?'

Julian caught the waiter's eye and then paid the bill. The teacake was uneaten and so as not to offend I wrapped it up and put it in my pocket. Outside on the pavement the afternoon heat was intense and oven-like. We walked together to the corner of Little Clarendon Street and as we went to part, he asked me about my mother AGAIN. Had she called? When would she be back?

I drifted home exhausted and very sketchy, still convinced that Max's dad was lying but no longer clear as to why. Nothing made any sense. Perhaps he was as excluded as I was from Max's recent musings over who he was. The revelation over Jonathan was shocking and yet obvious now, as was Max's own need to find himself (and god was that ironic in the circumstances of our relationship) but something still didn't add up. Something was still wrong. And cancer? Wasn't Julian's estranged wife some leading expert on children's cancer, is that how they met Max, as a patient? I tried to solve the problem as if Max and Jonathan and his dad were all parts of some mathematical equation. I texted Max to remind him about the gym. Perhaps I was too tired to go? Max's recent workouts had been pretty terrifying and I was liable to fall asleep as soon as I lay down on a bench. He texted back almost immediately saying he'd see me later. He added an x at the end of the message, a sure sign he was feeling guilty over something or preparing me for bad news.

I drank some milk and then sat in the kitchen feeling pathetic and deeply sorry for myself. Dad had plastered almost every available surface with notes as if I couldn't be trusted to cook a meal or switch on any appliance without destroying the house. I went upstairs and lay on the bed and tried to have one of my mother's power naps but when I closed my eyes all I saw was Julian's puzzled, worried eyes moving about over his napkin, the same guarded movements I had seen in the garden the other night. Thinking over the *Browns* incident I thought typically about some of the questions I should have asked but hadn't. I mean, for fuck's sake, was Grey seriously trashing photos of Max? And they were so *not* family shots! I'd seen them! I sat up suddenly, jumped over to my desk and switched on my computer, determined to utilise the two principal sources of teenage crisis management: *Wikipedia* and *Google.*

I started out with Julian but there was far too much on him to make a quick search feasible. Most of it seemed either to do with Oxford, the Genome Project or citations from very obscure academic papers. His wife was more promising. I quickly got to her homepage, which listed her interests under a series of headings all helpfully hot linked to further sources on the web. I followed child cancers and found myself on two additional links: leukaemia and *Ewing's Sarcoma*. Clicking on *Ewing's Sarcoma* took me to several entries on bone cancer and eventually back to Sally Grey's entry at Great Ormond Street. I then Googled *Ewing's Sarcoma* and ended up on a bewilderingly detailed stub from *Wikipedia* and a series of further links. It seemed hopeless but the very last reference was to a *Wikipedia* article entitled JOHN RADCLIFFE 1993. I sat bolt upright in my chair, conscious of the time and my own sense of dread. I opened the link and found a list of newspaper articles referring to the abduction of 24 children that had occurred in March 1993. My eyes scanned rapidly over the screen as I paged down frantically. All the abducted children were suffering from cancer but when they were found they had all been miraculously cured. They had then been taken to the John Radcliffe for tests and observation amid tight security and the rumour of alien invasion before being released in July. I paused, sick with excitement.

Hadn't my mother worked at the Radcliffe in the early 1990s? Some freelance labwork? I recalled her once telling Max how she had met his dad there, just before he was adopted. I scanned madly for photos or a list of names. All the children had been found in pairs, ten boy-girl combinations with one pair of boys and one of girls. The heat in the room was oppressive like a weight pressing down on me. I realised I was breathing in strange short gasps, dizzy, with small white dots swarming in front of my eyes. Still no names, nothing that seemed to tie the children to a given identity and location but then, at last, a paragraph from a local Leicestershire newspaper, *The Hinckley Times*, dated March 21st 1993, a front page story citing a Detective Inspector Mark Riley declining to identify the names of the last two children to be found, two boys, somewhere in a wood in Leicestershire. All Riley would confirm to the intrepid reporter was that the boys were well and that one was, unusually, not only older than all the other children but had also been free of cancer prior to being taken: *a misdiagnosis.*

Chapter 14

It had been a mistake seeing Jamie. I had been unprepared for his emotional intensity and the clarity of purpose that it lent him. Tired and overwrought I had allowed myself to be blindsided and he had extracted more information out of me than I had intended. Not a crumb of our conversation would have gone to waste. Like his mother, Jamie was intuitive and quite imaginative. He missed none of my discomfort and had probably stored up everything I *hadn't* said and was even now sifting through it carefully with all the cold fury that came from Max's rejection of his trust. Why had Max never mentioned his cancer? Why talk about Norma Lennox but not the hospital where she in effect abandoned him? My son's rejection of Jamie seemed to be sudden and rather callous, but what in his position was he to do? If Max knew now what was before him, as surely he must, how and in what ways could he confide in Jamie? What could he tell him that Jamie would understand or make Max's imminent departure more bearable? Max's deceit with me was telling but at least I had the consolation of knowing that we were both complicit in it, as if it was an elaborate game of double bluff: Jamie had only recently started to suspect something was amiss, most likely motivated through his jealousy over Jonathan, and Max's sudden coyness about his physical appearance. It seemed so unfair! As I walked home through the heat and glare of late afternoon I pondered to what extent Max and Jonathan were now scheming up something themselves, some plot to either retrieve the device or to go quietly and without fuss to await what? Max's final transformation? It would be typical of Max to want it that way, to avoid the emotional excess of parting. Would he go quietly in the end? Would there be a part of him that would want to stay here with us and with the life we had given him, myself, Sally, Jamie? My sorrow over Jamie was surprisingly intense and distressing. For a moment, it even eclipsed the prospect of losing Max himself. Should I warn Jamie myself? Perhaps that is why I had gone to *Brown's* in the first place. Perhaps I hadn't been blindsided at all.

Again, instinctively I took my mobile phone out of my pocket and looked to see if Margaret had returned any of my messages and texts to her! Nothing. I checked it stupidly to see that it was in credit, not broken, switched on. I had been doing this all week, obsessively peering at the keys and the screen. What could have happened to her? The last message I had received concerned a meeting with Dena Small over four days ago. It was to have taken place in Boston. What could have gone wrong? I turned into the driveway and paused to look at the house. It seemed oddly abandoned and in disrepair with the garden overgrown and windblown, browned out in the heat. I suddenly realised that I had to speak to Max now, that I had no choice but to tell him what I knew, to tell him I had failed. I pushed open the porch door, tomb-like. Max was back from school. I shouted some non-committal greeting as I walked in and went upstairs. His shirt lay thrown casually across his bedroom floor, and his kit bag lay on the bed, half-unzipped, smelling of sweat, stale clothes and shoes. From the bathroom I could hear the roar of the shower and a radio. I was intrigued to see that he had tided his room up and then shocked to notice that a holdall and some plastic bags lay hidden under the bed. Then ominously I saw several envelopes on his cleared and tided desk, one with Zoë Craven's name on, and then another with Jamie's. I paused waiting to hear the water stop but decided I could best manage the coming encounter downstairs. It would look less like an ambush, less like my now habitual stealth and spying.

I returned to the kitchen and then I sat down, exhausted. Eventually, Max appeared towelling his hair. It hung over his face in great cords of slick blackness, thick as kelp. As Jamie had rightly predicted he was wrapped up in a sweatshirt and tracksuit bottoms despite the weather. His feet were bare though. As he walked in, I looked at them a little too intently, thinking of his feet in my dream, bird-like. He followed my gaze thoughtfully down to the floor.

'What is it?' he asked quietly.

'It's incredibly hot out there Max, aren't you over-dressed?'

His feet seemed normal. He smiled slowly at me, hesitantly, as if he was trying to sense my mood. I still felt bizarrely angry on behalf of Jamie as if Max's deceit was my responsibility.

'If I didn't know better I'd think that you and Jamie were coordinating your strategies!' Max said carefully, sitting down and stretching one leg out to put on a sock. His face had caught the sun. He looked astoundingly powerful.

'Actually I saw Jamie today, Max.' I tried to hold his gaze but found I looked away first, off towards the French doors and the sight of the incinerator standing abandoned amongst the fruit trees, blackened and stained like a space capsule after a fiery re-entry.

'Today?'

'Walking up St Giles. We had quite a chat.'

My voice sounded rather tight and accusatory. I could see from Max's expression that he had picked up my tone and seemed puzzled by it. After he finished with his socks he collapsed into the back of the sofa, his hands on his knees scrutinising me, sleek cheeked, his hair over his eyes. They were intensely blue, almost violet, the colour of caution.

'That's weird. He must have walked back from school. He was in a strange mood today, even for Jamie, as if he was hatching some secret. He's been *especially* moody lately.'

'He told me he was gay.' I lied to give myself some cover, an excuse to hack a route directly to the subject at hand.

'Did he?'

I tried not to smile at Max's obvious sense of intrigue. He was suspicious now and attentive, sitting forward. 'He told me ages ago, finally! I'd been waiting for about a year!'

'You *knew*, of course?' I got the blend of complement and sarcasm just right. Max smiled hesitantly as if I was teasing him, a revelation, like the sun.

'I know *everything*,' he said carefully. 'I knew ages ago and so did you. Come on, it was pretty obvious. All that possessiveness over me and Zoë, the fact that he went out with the most attractive women at school all at once and did nothing with any of them! The chick music, the mysterious magazines under his bed with someone else's name on the address label!'

I laughed appreciatively at his attention to detail. Max narrowed his eyes, cat like. 'But of course when he did finally tell me I looked dutifully surprised and God have I tried to be supportive! But he's been a bit obsessed since!'

'Then you don't mind?' I looked at him again with a certain anger. 'I mean, it doesn't cause any tension between you, knowing he loves you as he does?' Max looked surprised and glanced down at the floor for a moment. When he lifted his face up he seemed stung by my tone.

'Why should I mind? I love Jamie; if not quite in the way he wants me to. I'm not interested in having sex with him, and I think gay men often mistake love for sex, and sex for intimacy. And I've told him that endlessly!'

The sophistication of the answer surprised me and yet it was so typical of Max. I closed my eyes and leaned my head back.

'He would do anything for you Max. He stayed with you when you were in hospital, for instance. He would have stayed all week if they'd have kept you in! And, like his mother, he is astoundingly clever. He's an asset.'

'I know,' Max said quietly, sounding suddenly upset. He put his hand under his chin and with his elbow resting precariously on his knee scrutinised me hard and now openly with some alarm.

'Are you angry? Did you and Jamie talk about *me?*'

In radically different circumstances; in a parallel world perhaps, Max's question would have been comical. And it was said with such obvious disregard for his omnipotence to my life and work that even in my despair I could barely suppress a smile. Yet knowingly I had brought us both to the moment I had long dreaded: my confession that I knew what he was or was becoming and could not save him. I was surprised to see the extent of his shock, to see him stiffen slightly and look at me with an expression not unlike one of Sally's. There was no going back.

'He's worried about you. He thinks you're unwell and hiding things from him.' I spoke slowly and carefully, painfully close to breaking down. Huge waves of fear and resentment seemed to fog my vision.

Max sighed and sank back into the sofa, his legs apart, one foot tapping repetitively on the floor like a nervous tic. He seemed almost relieved.

'I see. And what did you tell him?'

We sat staring at each other. I had thought of this conversation often, especially in the last few years and certainly since Max was released from hospital. I had rehearsed it endless times but it had never started with Jamie and already it had gone wrong, off course, veering away.

'That you were fine of course, that you have no secrets, and that he had nothing to worry about.'

There was a silence and then urgently, both leaning forward, both visibly un-nerved, we spoke together. Max stopped first and stood up. He put his hands on top of his head and walked towards the French doors, his face inscrutable. He stood with his back to me.

'You came into my room last night, didn't you?'

'Yes.'

'What did you see?'

'Enough. I saw enough, Max.'

Max nodded to himself slowly, sorting something out in his head. 'Ok, I thought you did, but I wasn't sure. I thought you were a dream. I've been dreaming a lot recently, about my adoption, about the wood, about the Seeth. They talk to me.'

'Max we have to talk. Do you know what is about to happen to you?'

'Sort of. I mean, yes, yes I do now.'

'Then how does this end?'

Max turned and walked back towards my chair and

stood looking down at me deep in thought as if he was trying to phrase something carefully and precisely. Eventually he said;

'Listen. I have to go and see Jamie now. I was going to tell him something tonight, not exactly the whole *I am an alien* bit, but something. I mean I realise he's been following me, and I know he's been preoccupied with Jonathan. I never wanted to hurt him. When I come back from the gym, we'll talk, yeah? I'll tell you everything I know and you can tell me?' He put his hand on top of my head and brushed my hair, typically inverting my relationship to him, the son consoling the father. 'We cool?'

'No –'

'*Dad*! Don't make this any harder than it is.' He leaned down and kissed my forehead, a premonition of absolution and then he quietly walked out into the hall. I heard the front door click shut and the house fall back into silence.

I sat immobilised with grief. Max seemed to have already accepted his fate, indeed even prepared for it. I wondered where Jonathan was and whether I should call him and at the precise moment the telephone rang. I leapt up and almost ran into the hall. Snatching it up I said without thinking, 'Margaret?'

There was a silence, an intense hesitation, and then I heard a voice I had not heard for many years. 'I'm afraid it isn't, Julian. It's Louis.' For a moment I was not sure I could breathe properly. I was stunned, almost paralysed. Eventually I was just able to say 'DeMarr?' as if I knew hundreds of Louis'. He must have sensed my disbelief because he added, apparently without humour 'Yes dear, Louis! Louis DeMarr – your former student, friend and ally!'

I recovered my nerve. 'Is that so? What can I do for you? I tried to sound firm but not unfriendly, not too relieved either despite the fact I had been trying to contact him for several months.

'Well *my dear*, as always I think it's rather what I can do for you!' I went to interrupt, irritated but he cut me off curtly. 'I want to meet with you, tonight. I want to put my cards firmly on the table. Perhaps you don't know this yet but several of the children, or should I say now, *young adults*, have taken seriously ill? Three have been hospitalised. Max is in danger, Julian, and I can help you.'

My whole body was tense, analysing every word, every syllable.

'Louis I am not the slightest bit interested in meeting you. Max is fine – he's just left to the gym and there is nothing wrong with the children for God's sake, how could there be?'

'*Think carefully*, Julian,' DeMarr said suddenly, sharply. It was almost a hiss and yet for a moment his voice carried a tone almost of panic. 'I don't *have* to ask you this. Frankly you do seem to have been anxious to meet me or at least speak with me since on my return to Cambridge I found a lot of letters from you, my dear. And by now you know very well that I could simply stand by and watch as Max is taken into protective custody under the 1993 protocols. As you once said to me in happier times, the State is a *marvellous* thing, and the State is very much against you, Julian.'

I leaned my head heavily on the banister holding the phone away from me as if it might explode. The heat was thick, meditative, heavy with late sunlight.

'What do you want?'

'I will come over to see you, tonight, *alone*. I shall not bring the police or my old friend Davies. Indeed I shall not bring any Americans whatsoever. We can then have a long and inclusive chat about our separate research projects, about your son actually, and what we have found about him. And don't bring Margaret or anyone else either. I then propose that after the necessary preparations, we have an exchange?'

'An exchange?'

'Yes – we both have things the other wants. And I have always been willing to help you out, as I am sure you remember.'

I let the reference to the software alone. Of more immediate interest was the obvious fact that he was referring to the device. If he had just returned from the US was it possible that he had brought it with him, or at least some news of its whereabouts? I was trying to think hard, trying to work out what DeMarr could possibly want from me. Max? I clasped my hand over the mouthpiece of the phone. I was looking at nothing, thinking about nothing, listening so closely to DeMarr that I could almost visualise each individual word. I had an image of him sitting in a long, impressive office with a necktie, triumphant, immensely pleased with himself. Except the image didn't fit what I was hearing. DeMarr's voice contained an undercurrent of tension, and the *absurd* lie about the other children being ill. Something was wrong.

'Very well. I'm not entirely sure I know what you want, but come to my offices in College –'

'No, no Julian, I was thinking of something a little more *intimate*. I will come to the house. I will be there at about 10 p.m. I would like to see Max there as well. I shall of course be discreet, I mean there will be no need to interview or examine him, but I want to see him with you.'

It seemed a curious pre-condition. I agreed.

'Good, excellent. I look forward to seeing you,' and at that DeMarr quietly terminated the call. I gasped, as if released from some sort of spell. An exchange? Then I felt my mobile vibrate in my pocket. It was a text from Margaret. She was just about to depart from JFK and would be at London, Heathrow in the small hours of the morning. I phoned her back immediately but the call went straight through to voicemail. I texted her a short, urgent message to come straight to the house regardless of the time. I texted her that DeMarr was likely to be here as well and then added that I planned to have the conversation with Max. I baulked at mentioning Jamie.

I took a power nap on top of my bed. I did not expect it to work in the circumstances but in fact I fell into a deep cloying sleep and awoke at 9 p.m. I sat up, drugged and light headed, hungry and disorientated. I took a quick shower and then went downstairs to get something to eat and I was in the kitchen cooking an omelette when Max and Jamie clattered into the house together. I was taken aback and for a moment looked it. Max pulled a face which Jamie half saw: evidently things had not gone the way my son had planned and yet despite some unforeseen complication I had to warn Max about Louis. Jamie hung back by the kitchen door as if he was embarrassed to see me so soon after *Brown's*. He looked frightened.

'Jamie, come in!'

'Hi. I think I'll use your bathroom.'

I took Max's arm. 'Any luck?'

'No. I just can't!' Max closed his eyes and seemed exhausted, genuinely flustered, a rare sight. 'He knows about the children, he knows I was abducted!'

'Then you have to tell him! Tell us both!'

'This isn't fair!' I was shocked to see Max so emotional, almost close to tears. We were talking in loud whispers.

'Max, Louis DeMarr will be here any minute!'

'What? Did you call him?'

'No, no. He called me. Something's wrong. He's coming alone to make some sort of deal?'

'A deal?' Max swung around, tense, and his eyes flashed brilliantly and mysteriously. I noticed how the irises held on to a strange silver sheen. It made him look exotic and quite dangerous.

'Don't stare, dad.'

'Sorry. Does that hurt?'

'No, it doesn't. What kind of deal?'

'I have no idea Max, but he may have news of the device. He may even have it with him?'

Max pondered this carefully. I could see his jaw working, the muscles trembling and flexing.

'I doubt that. But he may well have some information on it. He had it long enough.' Max glanced down. I had a sudden impulse to hold him but as I put my arms on his shoulders there was a movement behind us and Jamie reappeared, his face pale, angry. Max composed himself quickly and efficiently but having seemed to sense my mood he took my hand in his, squeezed it rather painfully and then let it go.

'Jamie, you want a beer? Dad?'

'Sure. I could do with one.'

Jamie nodded curtly. Max bent down into the fridge and brought out a pack of *Stella*. I could feel Jamie staring at me, but concentrated on the table as if it was some mysterious new addition to the room. At that precise moment the doorbell went. Max said 'Shit!' with quiet understatement and moved towards the hall.

'Max! Leave it, I'll get it.'

'No it's ok!' He was already ahead of me. Jamie stood aside to let him through the door. As Max passed he gently stroked Jamie's stomach with the knuckles of his hand.

'Max, go easy on him!' I said cryptically.

'What's going on?' Jamie glanced after Max and towards the front door. It occurred to me that Jamie might well be expecting Jonathan to appear. 'It's an old colleague of mine, Jamie.' I followed my son out into the hallway. Max had the door open and he and Louis were staring at each other with a sort of horrid fascination.

'Louis, Louis, come in –' I stood next to Max and tried

to smile. Max smelled hot like an overworked machine. Louis stood, his coat over his arm, looking quizzically at Max and then at me.

'Hello Louis!' said Max suddenly and with devastating charm. 'Let me take your coat!'

Louis narrowed his eyes as if sensing some sort of trap but after a slight pause moved forward. He handed Max several items as if my son was a beautiful footman at some private club. As he walked through into the hall Louis caught sight of Jamie.

'This is Jamie Relph,' Max said in anticipation, 'Margaret's son. My *very best* friend!' I saw Jamie wince slightly. Louis was looking at Max with a strange possessive gleam in his eye. He nodded in Jamie's direction. 'Ah yes! *Margaret's* boy.' He looked at the two young men. 'How you've both grown!'

'Come in here, Louis –' I gestured to the room overlooking the front garden. As I did so I saw Max give a beer to Jamie and head towards the stairs. 'We'll be in my room if you need anything,' he said to me directly, his eyes on mine, a sort of code.

'Ok, sure, thanks Max. We'll eat later.'

'Yes, a last supper?'

I ignored the remark and as I went to follow DeMarr I heard Jamie say plaintively 'Max what the *fuck* is going on in this house!'

I closed the front room door and leaned against it. DeMarr was standing by the large windows holding a framed picture close up to his face as if he was extremely short sighted and for a moment I watched him unobserved. The last six years had not been kind to him. He had gained weight. He was still foppish in his appearance, extravagant even; I could see the dull chain links of a fob-watch laced across the front of a brilliant blue waistcoat, but his face was curiously jaundiced, heavily lined, almost swollen. He did not look well. Aware of my attention, DeMarr walked back towards the fireplace and replaced the picture carefully on the mantelpiece. I looked at it slyly. It was a group shot of the chromosome 22 group taken in 1999. I was sitting in the front row, with Louis looking boorishly into the camera next to me. We were both grinning inanely.

'A long time ago.' I said un-necessarily. We had so much to talk about, so many things to say: I suddenly felt incapable of speaking; too exhausted, too lost.

'To you, perhaps. To me it seems only like yesterday, Julian.' DeMarr looked expectantly at a decanter of brandy half hidden on a bookshelf. I made a vague gesture towards it.

'Help yourself –' Ought I to thank him for coming? How much could I pretend to still like him? I was curious to sense that perhaps part of me still did. Had I missed him? Had he brought me the device? DeMarr moved rather too eagerly towards the liquor.

'You look well, *trim*,' he said, patting his paunch with one hand self-consciously while with the other hand he gestured to a second crystal tumbler. I declined.

'Max is impressive. He's grown considerably since he threw me at a chair. Do you ever wonder what happened to the small elfish boy we found in 1993?' DeMarr cocked his head up towards the ceiling. 'How old is he?'

I did not want him talking about Max. I tried to disguise a tone of loathing.

'He will be eighteen in a few days. You know that.'

'Do I?' DeMarr glanced up at me with his hooded myopic eyes. He seemed genuinely bemused by my hostility. 'Well he obviously works out, as the Americans say!' DeMarr made an odd, quirky laugh and sat down opposite me with a certain stiffness as if he was in pain. There was a corpulence to his body that was not natural; that made him look almost bloated, beetle-like. From upstairs came a heavy thud and the sound of male laughter.

'I spent some time recently in the US, Julian, with some colleagues of Professor Davies. In the US almost everyone *works out*, even the fat ones! A truly bewildering habit of the young! Each campus and research centre across the land has a huge gymnasium full of shiny chrome and metal – astounding! But once you're over 30 you're finished, no one looks at you. You cease to exist! Isn't that odd?'

'What do you know about Max, Louis? Why are you here?' I was half listening for further sounds upstairs, the revelation that Max had told Jamie who he was. DeMarr was looking at me intently, carefully.

'You know why I am here. I am here because of your adopted son. I am here because he is the only *successful* outcome of the abduction experiments, the purpose of which was evidently to insinuate into human chromosome 22 genetic material from an alien species and reproduce it en mass. And I am here because I have something to offer you. Something that you will *need*, or rather, that Max will need.' As he spoke he watched me like a hawk, every movement, every gesture as if he feared I might attack him.

'And you know all this how, Louis? Because you hid strategic information from me while I was chairing a committee set up to investigate the abductions? Because you lied about a device? Because you then went on to clone genetic material using techniques borrowed from Davies? And I don't need anything from you DeMarr. Not now, not after what you have done to me and to my son.'

He stared at me for a while.

'Julian, I understand that you are upset but try to be rational about this. I think you should hear me out at some length before you make some hasty, emotional decision. It is obviously true that I deceived you about

Margaret's discovery, and that Sally and I incubated a series of cloned chromatins as early as 1994-5. Davies did indeed help me around 1997 – if that is quite the right word – with some of the more intricate aspects of somatic cloning: but that led me to a place I did not necessarily want to go. And you well know that I retrieved something from the wood in 1993, hidden in the mound, but it does not follow that I set myself out to destroy you or to harm Max. And as for helping you, have I not helped you before?' He looked down at the drink in his hand; hard, focused, as if he suddenly thought I might be poisoning him. He then said urgently, 'Max is in danger, terrible danger, and so are you!'

'It's a little late for this, Louis, isn't it?'

Again there was a brittle standoff. I changed my mind about the drink. It seemed pointless faking a nonchalance I did not feel. As I poured myself a shot, DeMarr's glass appeared in the air close by, demanding attention, already empty. I refilled it reassured that he evidently needed alcohol as much as I did.

'So why is Max in danger, Louis? Because he contains a killer virus? Because he's DeSilva's Trojan horse ready to disgorge its army? Because he's *different?*'

'Max *is* a Trojan horse, Julian, like it or not. You've seen the data? Davies is convinced that he constitutes a major biological hazard.'

'The wooden horse was a stupid metaphor then and it is now.' I said sharply but no longer with any real conviction.

DeMarr shrugged. 'I'm inclined to agree my dear but Davies rather liked it. Curious how bio-chemists are prone to classical metaphors: he later coined another, perhaps a more accurate one, or was it an allegory? Max and the sowing of dragon's teeth, with fully formed aliens springing up from the ground, or worse, from the ingested remains of humans, aliens *returning home!*'

'Is Davies so senile as to believe that?' I smiled

contemptuously but the information disturbed me. I thought of the strange exoskeleton I had observed on my son last night, the dark mottling on his temples, like the skin of a lizard, like something growing inside him.

'Louis. Perhaps it would be best if we started at the very beginning. And you said on the phone that you needed my help? As for the device, you know as well as I do that it was sent to the US last April. So, unless you have managed to persuade your ex-friend Davies to part with it, an unlikely occurrence given the apparent state of your working relationship together, or have some startling insight that allows us to get around its absence, you have nothing to offer me except more lies.'

Louis looked up at me surprised and strangely troubled. The room was cast now in a deep, pleasing shade; cool after the long hot day. I tried to contain my sense of outrage, still shockingly real after all those years. 'So?'

DeMarr stirred himself and nodded his head gently as if amused by my tone. 'Very well. Let me begin. Let me sit upon the grass and tell you my sad story, Julian. Of failure, of *bewilderment*? About the staining techniques, the extra plates? Young Ms Relph?' He smiled whimsically. 'It was DeSilva who started it, of course. Not long after I approached him to take up a place on the committee he presented me with a secret protocol, first drawn up by the US government in the 1970s when they were looking for little green men –'

'*Operation Wildfire*. The search for alien genomes. Where DeSilva met Davies.' I interrupted dryly.

'The very same. He was so terribly coy at first, hiding his schematic inside his pocket like a piece of pornography. He said you weren't to be trusted and that I was to report to him if I found anything resembling a DNA molecule containing three distinct amino acids.'

'How did they come by it exactly?' I was genuinely intrigued. 'Did *Wild Fire* actually find any aliens?'

Louis laughed. 'No, nothing quite so dramatic. The first DNA samples were found on Earth, actually. In cattle mutilations in the US I believe, and then, somewhat obscurely, in an ape colony in the Congo. *Wild Fire* was for a time disbanded but then in 1993 when the US intelligence agencies heard of the British children taken from their beds it was quickly back up on its feet! They rightly guessed that the children had been modified with the same alien DNA they had deep frozen in California. You had no idea how often we nearly lost control of the committee, Julian! All this rot about the UK-US special relationship! It made me proud to be a European and not part of some Anglo-Saxon feud! Every day poor humble DeMarr would have to parry some nasty little demand from the US State Department, or prevent some hit squad swooping in, aided and abetted by DeSilva, determined to remove the whole investigation to New Mexico or somewhere equally absurd! And all that rubbish about alien invasions! But DeSilva was paranoid my dear, quite – what do you say here – *off his trolley* – over the whole thing! What he had seen during those years in the US had obviously spooked him. Anyway, I signed his protocol and charmed him with Margaret and cut a singular path all of my own!'

'Astounding! You double crossed him? You found the DNA and hid the evidence?'

DeMarr was indiscreet enough to smile at me rather impishly.

'Why?'

'*Julian*! The answer was right there, under our noses. Twenty-three terminally ill children *cured* of cancer and not just leukaemia, or some other managed condition in which the poor creatures had to be bombarded with radiation or chemicals every year, but actually *cured*!'

I felt at a loss. And then slowly the extent of DeMarr's conceit – and my mistake – began to emerge.

'You were interested in finding the *cure* for cancer?' I

gasped, incredulous.

'And why not? Why not me? You said yourself, many years ago, that I was a brilliant bio-chemist – and I was, Julian! I am! Indeed in a while I hope that my brilliance will become clearer to you than ever before. Yes a cure for cancer! Think firstly of the fame, my dear Grey, and the money! And then think of the relief that I would bring to the world. One in two of us will have a brush with cancer by the time we get to our sixties. For many of us it will be fatal. But someone had cured it, Julian! Easily, almost thoughtlessly, like someone turns off a light. I simply had to re-trace how! And my God, sir, I was determined! But I couldn't do it on my own, firstly I needed DeSilva's little schematic, then I needed Sally and for a while I needed Margaret, and I had to work fast before either you or the American's got their hands on my data! Of course DeSilva was far more dangerous than you and considerably more cunning! Especially after he managed to snaffle the Japanese report from under our noses!'

I felt the hairs stand up on the back of my neck. I had been *utterly wrong* about DeMarr's motivation. Max himself had been almost entirely incidental to his initial research. DeMarr pressed on.

'I mean, good God! Had he found my data he would have locked Max up in some high security prison or probably killed him there and then and grown his remains on a Petri dish! So before you start blaming me for betraying Max, credit me with keeping his identity safe in 1993!'

I leaned forward, stroking my chin, trying to absorb DeMarr's revelation, tasting it, trying to tease out whether it was true or just another fabrication. I nodded grimly to myself. 'Thank you, although it appears your caution was largely self motivated! But Louis, I don't understand why, armed with the positive identification of the DNA contained in the Japanese Report, DeSilva didn't go on to find Max's 22 all by himself? He's a virologist for God's sake!'

DeMarr smiled his self-congratulatory smile again and drained his glass. 'He is indeed, and a good one, but he's not good in experimental design, and he has no patience. Firstly he was thrown by the sudden disintegration of the alien chromosomes, and secondly he was obsessed with viral activity. He was looking for conventional signs of infection in keeping, I think, with his earlier experiences of the DNA from the *Wild Fire* years where, from what I can now surmise, the experiment on cattle and apes did indeed use retroviral agents. But the biochemistry of the experimental design on the children was quite different, far more sophisticated even if it evidently involved the same basic material. You see Julian these aliens have been experimenting on Earth *for years*! And clearly they had changed their techniques along with their subject. The net result of chance and negligence was to make sure that DeSilva never noticed Max's small, innocuous and proliferating 22 even though he alone knew what he was looking for!'

I slumped back into the chair, momentarily speechless. 'So while DeSilva was looking for aliens and invasions you were looking at cancer?' It still seemed impossible. 'Why did you assume that the DNA molecules were part of the cure?'

'Well, Jonathan for a start. *'No cancer, no chromosomes'* and it seemed a fair place to start given the circumstances. But of course I needed someone specialised in cancer itself and who better to turn to than Sally.' Louis then added with curious urgency 'I never wished to harm Max or to expose him, Julian, and neither did she. You must believe that. Sally and I worked as much as we could without involving anyone else, but ambitious as we were the problems were far too complex, far too advanced. Later when I used Davies and his considerable experience, I *tried* to be careful and, how shall I say, *obscure* about everything – and Sally never condoned what I did.' He sounded sour then, bitter and as he hitched himself into his seat I realised with sudden clarity that DeMarr was seriously ill.

'Did you confide in Sally because you were sleeping with her or because she was genuinely interested in curing cancer?' I asked eventually. His inference to their shared sense of ambition had not surprised me.

'*Both*, Julian. But in the first she was slightly more disingenuous than in the second.'

'I don't understand?'

DeMarr barked a laugh, oddly amused.

'Of course you don't! That's my point! I am not an attractive man, my dear Professor, neither now nor back then. And I was never particularly young. As I am sure you know, Sally's usual type is younger and considerably more physical; you know full well what I am saying. But I was after all the principal scientific adviser to the government, a role I rather enjoyed and one that Sally coveted. It was not without some prestige and a little influence. And you know how much Sally likes these things,' he sighed, deflated.

'So you used each other?' It seemed a curiously cannibalistic relationship well suited to them both.

DeMarr's eyes narrowed momentarily as if he considered the feasibility of some brutal aside but then thought better of it.

'Let us just say she grew disinterested, Julian, impatient perhaps and leave it at that. There is no need for us to become *indecent*.' He stopped, trying to recall his thoughts. 'But at first of course she was wildly enthusiastic and extremely cooperative. Not long after the committee stood down we cloned the extraneous genetic material that had budded on Max's 22 so we could examine it more closely. It was a bizarrely complex process, and I sorely missed DeSilva. We incubated a batch in my labs at Cambridge.'

'You succeeded?' I asked. I recalled Sally's single question written on Max's plate all those years ago: 'incubate?'

'Of course! It allowed us to get a very close look at what had happened to Max's 22. After a period of 'budding' specific alien-human gene sequences started to parallel 22 in a way that was reminiscent of cat eye syndrome – can you remember – a replication error in which the chromosomes divide but do not separate? Except on this occasion endless chromosomes – eventually, as you know, entire genomes – began to gather silently over the years. The replication process was so well designed, it was breathtaking! At first I thought it really was some form of retrovirus but it was too controlled, too systematic: no mutation, and no viral shredding, no immune response from the host. Like cancer, but not cancerous! Here surely was a clue – a major insight – to what had cured the children in the first place. If only we could isolate the actual agent and then replicate *that*? It was Sally who devised an experiment in which we injected material from Max's 22 into a cancer tumour, a mouse at first, and then various larger creatures, horses and cattle, apes. The results were at first miraculous!'

'The tumours went into remission?'

'The tumours *vanished*, my dear, almost immediately. On close examination, we discovered that the cancer cells had been completely recoded, with the modified genes from Max's serum reconstituting normal cell division. Furthermore, Max's silver bullet even repaired the damaged gene sequence that gave rise to the tumour in the first place! It was astoundingly complex and yet so simple, so beautiful!'

I gasped, interrupting. 'It cured the cancer at the genetic level?'

'Absolutely. As if what was contained on Max's

chromatin were hordes of clever nanites, *willed* to repair and re-sequence DNA, to innovate, to improvise! They could even distinguish between redundant, junk DNA, and the original missing base pairs needed for a particular repair job! Can you believe that! But clearly several important gene sequences needed to be damaged to trigger the reaction in the first place! As we both suspected, cancer was the trigger for its own cure, or rather the trigger that initiated the alien DNA search and rescue mission in the first place!' And then DeMarr's expression changed slightly, an anticipation of doom. Something had evidently not worked.

'What happened? What went wrong?'

'I'm not sure it ever went right, Julian. Getting the cure to work at all was curiously random. Often as in the majority of the children the genetic material failed to make any impact. And if it did work, immediately *after* the cure the modified chromatin would begin the same strange proliferation of hybrid genetic material, attaching them to a pre-selected chromosome, which varied from species to species. In the equine genome it was always on chromosome 30, in the mouse it was chromosome 7. Humans it was evidently 22. But unlike Max's condition, the accumulation of extraneous material was neither controlled or gradual: it resulted in a virulent form of cancer that killed the subject within days. At first I suspected it was to do with the obvious mismatch between Max's cloned material and the various experimental hosts: they were hardly compatible, horses, mice, humans, in all the results were identical. Cure and then virulent tumour. I suspect that Max's survival is to do with his genetic inheritance, his uniqueness, or some particular compatibility between his genome and the alien DNA. But it could be anything,' he added helplessly. 'And remember we never found out who Max's biological father was. There was one other interesting phenomenon.' DeMarr's voice was suddenly tired and flat.

'And what was that?'

'The whole sequence I have described – initial cure, chromosomal proliferation and then virulent cancer – only took place if we used cloned material from Max's chromosome sampled between April 18th and the 22nd 1993. Any time after that, *nothing* happened at all!'

'Really?'

'Yes! An intriguing insight again, a specific window of bio-chemical agency! Sally and I were quite dispirited by now! We desperately needed a virologist, someone with access to vast sums of money and equipment which would allow us to get down to the individual codons on the DNA! There was a limit to how much I could use the facilities at Cambridge and not arouse suspicion, especially given my links to the committee, and there was you of course, sniffing about, asking questions, watching all the time. It wasn't as if I could put in a research bid! I thought about re-approaching DeSilva but the risk was too great and he was in Australia by now and so I turned to Davies who was working on dear old Dolly the sheep and on his super computer mapping program!'

I scoffed slightly, causing a cloud of irritation to wrinkle DeMarr's domed forehead.

'I suppose it didn't occur to you Louis, to actually check out who Davies was and whether he knew DeSilva?'

DeMarr ignored me and sat leaning back into the chair with his legs thrust oddly forward. 'I went up to see him in Edinburgh you know, 1995 or 1996, I begin to forget the dates. You and I were busy as bees with the Genome project. I realised you were up to something, Julian, although I confess to having not the slightest idea what it was. And I had always been profoundly sceptical about your reasons for adopting Max and knew that you were keeping secrets from me. I even considered the possibility that you had agreed to work with DeSilva, but I knew you too well. Anyway, I had to stay focused.'

'And so was Davies useful?' I asked, my voice heavy with dark sarcasm.

'For a while, my dear Julian. Davies' software was astoundingly accurate as you know now for yourself. He allowed me to use a prototype. I went back to examine Max's 22, at specific intervals after it first became contaminated, to see if it could cast light on the specific chemical sequences that allowed the alien DNA to proliferate. I tried to eliminate any changes made to Max's chromatin by the cloning technique I had used in the first experiments. I even went all the way to see Mrs Lennox to get an original sample of Max's DNA before he had been abducted! And good God was that hard work! But nothing. It had to be about *technique*, about the way in which the alien DNA had been initially incorporated into Max, and then from Max into a third party – we were doing something wrong! Reproducing something that was affecting the outcome, putting something together in the wrong sequence, *something!*' he sighed explosively, as if it was too much to recall even now. 'In the end, desperate, I showed the raw data to Davies himself, hoping he would use his influence to get me more money and lab time and more access to his technology. I needed to find the molecular basis of the recoding process down to the last protein! I could not have made a worse mistake in my life. Americans! And worse still, American virologists!'

I had already anticipated the direction in which DeMarr was taking me. It was my turn to refill my glass. The room was now in a deep blue darkness. I put on a small desk lamp before resuming my chair. DeMarr was shaking his head to himself as if he was still bewildered, all these years later, at the error he had committed.

'When Davies got his hands on the information,

Julian, there was a most frightful fuss. I mean, really! He had some sort of cerebral orgasm! There is no other word. He demanded to know where I had got the original chromatin from and to tell him who or what the original host was. I was pretty sure he recognised it immediately for what it was, but I couldn't be too sure. Of course he had given me access to the software, helped me out, but there was no way I was prepared to reveal Max's identity. I tried to pamper Davies, inviting him to Cambridge, providing him with endless supplies of college port, trips up the river, you know – put him off the scent – but in the end he soon found out who Max was!'

I moaned irritably. It was so typical of DeMarr not to think something through like this, to put his ambition before his responsibility!

'DeMarr, for god's sake! It can't have been hard for Davies! He would have known about the committee and it wouldn't have taken him long to realise that DeSilva was a member, or to find the right child!' and even as I spoke I remembered my discovery of the file request forms in the Oxford archive, summoning data. Davies must have started working behind DeMarr's back almost immediately.

'So once Davies identified Max, he took it from there I presume, and on his *own*?' My voice was sarcastic again.

'You are spending far too much time with moody teenage boys, Julian: you are starting to sound like them! But you're right. He did indeed! I was jilted, suddenly excluded from his data, his software, his refinements of my own data! And Sally was suddenly far less accommodating than she had been. She had cautioned me that I had bitten off more than I could chew on approaching Davies. She never cared for him and thought him sinister. And God was she right about that!' DeMarr stood up, stiffly and with effort and walked towards the window overlooking the lawn and the road.

'Davies went right back to the beginning, Julian. I mean to *Wild Fire* and the whole alien mystery. As such he was intuitively much closer to the alien dimension than I had ever been. I have to confess that part of me never took it seriously. But Davies could 'see' more than I ever could. Not only did he recognise the telltale DNA bases, he realised straight away that the alien experiment was *designed* to do just this! To hybridise alien and human DNA and to find some sort of match! And more to the point, everything had Max's signature on it.'

'How is that possible? How could they know?' My voice was scarcely a whisper. DeMarr shrugged.

'However we explain it, it was Max's uniqueness that prevented the cure being transplanted across species in a stable manner, and also why Max's cancer has never returned. It was Max they were looking for all along. The cure was for him and him alone. Other species had been tried, *apparently*. And then that was it. DeMarr cast out! Abandoned! And Davies holed up in Maryland with the best equipment that money could buy! I tried to work on my own – scrape together some students, throw my own money at it – but it was no use. All I could see was that something inside Max was maturing nicely. Then, by some bizarre coincidence, I received your strange answerphone message last year, requesting the software. And I thought what a strangely transparent excuse – another research project! But then I thought *why not?*'

'Why not indeed – knowing no doubt how far I was behind you!' I added, trying to make a sort of joke. 'But tell me, Louis: apart from the cure for cancer, did the experiment, did Max himself, not intrigue you at all?'

'No, not at first. I wanted access to raw data on the process, the minutia, not the big picture.' He smiled sadly at me as if this had been a mistake too.

'So you gave me access to Davies' software in the hope that I might replicate useful data which, via Sally, you could just turn up and borrow?' I clenched my jaw. Max, of course, had caught him literally in the act, like a common burglar. For a moment DeMarr looked vaguely sheepish, almost embarrassed, if such an emotion were still possible for him.

'Something like that, yes.'

'So if you drew a blank with the cure and the Nobel Prize of the century, what did Davies find? Do you have details Louis?'

DeMarr was seated again staring down at his lap. He looked strangely senile for a moment, as if he had forgotten who he was or why he was there.

'Davies proposed almost the same theory that DeSilva had blurted out in 1993, although he now had much more evidence, and with some of my ideas about a breeding program added in willy-nilly. He speculated that the genetic modification to Max's 22 would eventually impact on Max's physiology and change him. That he would become completely alien, and he knows – as you do – that the process will be complete in a few days' time.'

I breathed slowly, thinking of Max upstairs and the ridges of bone breaking through on his shoulders and upper back.

'And for what purpose?'

The question seemed to surprise Louis.

'The usual Davies obsession. Alien invasions, bodysnatching, some grand galactic virus – I have no idea Julian and I was never particularly interested. The amount of material inside Max's 22 was far in excess of what was needed if such a purpose was indeed the intention of the experiment. But I think Davies has a theory about that as well.'

'He does?'

DeMarr shrugged as if what Davies thought was of no consequence. 'He thinks Max was chosen to design the perfect biological weapon, the alien equivalent of patient zero. He believes once he has changed the aliens will return to collect the hybridised entity and begin some form of occupation. He suspects that the aliens need human bodies as hosts!'

I sat rigidly in my seat, my head buzzing. 'Is there any evidence for that at all? It's a preposterous suggestion!' We were back – indeed we had never left – the Trojan horse metaphor, Max now safely inside the citadel, with the rest of the army massing outside the city gates ready to swarm.

'Quite, but you saw DeSilva that night in 1993, and Davies is no better: slightly more urbane perhaps and less inclined to sweat, but driven by an interest not in Max at all but in aliens. They want Max as bait – they want the Seeth themselves when they come for their new hybrid: that part is at least accurate, surely?'

The word froze my blood, disguising DeMarr's odd tone of doubt. Had it been a trick of my imagination – had DeMarr actually used the word, hissed out the name. *Seeth*. He scanned my face looking for a reaction. I tried to blank him, but for a moment I was sure that my shock was quite visible.

'The Seeth?' It was Louis' turn to laugh, vaguely contemptuously.

'Oh come along Julian, the game is up, for God's sake stop blustering!'

I sighed explosively and sank my head back into the armrest. Was Davies aware that the Seeth were already dead? Were they? Why would Max and Jonathan be compelled to go to the wood if the Seeth had long perished? I tried to think of Max as a threat, some sort of preliminary assault, but it still made no sense. It never had.

We sat in the summer gloom with the house oddly silent about us. There was no noise from upstairs, no music, no sound of Max pacing about. I wondered if the boys had left without me noticing them. I looked at my former friend and student, his shape indistinct in the gloom.

'What do you know of this device, Louis? What does Davies know? Isn't it odd that it never occurred to you that it might be part of the experiment itself, or some necessary component for your claim to fame and a cure?'

'Ah, the device,' he snorted, a strange tired sound. 'Another of my – or should I say our – momentous mistakes. To be honest Julian, I wasn't convinced it was alien at all, at first: it looked so innocuous! And what with MacMillan waving magnetic charts in my face as if she'd found oil and the press crawling all over the wood, tree by tree! Frankly I thought it was a hoax. After some cursory examination I had it stuck in a vault somewhere in London. Then, as my own experiments bogged down in the conundrum of Max's 22, I *did* venture to take a look at it again, and yes it did occur to me that it was vital!' DeMarr's eyes glinted at me playfully.

'What does the device look like?' I asked, suddenly curious.

'It is a heavy cylinder composed mostly of carbon, 15-20 cms long, about 10 wide, solid and quite unmoving! It made no sense to me and when I risked asking Jonathan about it years later he didn't seem to know it existed at all. But he wouldn't have – as you probably know – it was left a few weeks later, the 'second sighting' in late March 1993.'

'But didn't the provisional analysis alert you to the fact that it might be related to the tags, ribose for God's sake?' I still had Riley's stolen summary upstairs in my study, one that presumably DeMarr had commissioned. He looked impressed as if I had pleasantly surprised him.

'How did you know about that?'

'Mark Riley obtained a copy of MacMillan's report,

and a summary of the device was attached to the back, presumably after the original had been shredded.'

DeMarr laughed amused. 'Indeed I should have realised – but as I say – it made no sense to me and I certainly couldn't see it fitting in with Davies' theories of what Max was for! Now I realise that, in some inexplicable way, it is designed to harvest Max's human genome before the hybridisation process destroys all informational trace of your son.'

I was aware that Louis was glaring at me. 'You *knew* that I presume?'

'I know everything,' I said curtly, conscious that I was paraphrasing my son.

'The experiment itself? What Max means?'

I laughed to myself, at DeMarr, at the whole surreal conversation, at the astounding revelation that I had beaten DeMarr in some small way and yet I was struck by the odd coincidence that we had both arrived at the same place and almost at the same time, a place of failure, as DeMarr had said himself, of bewilderment. After an initial pause I told DeMarr what Jonathan had told me, and what I had, like some curious bard, recited to Margaret. I told the story of how my son was going to resurrect a species from extinction. I even – despite myself perhaps – told DeMarr about what I had discovered last night while examining Max as he lay spread out beneath me, unconscious, exposed to me at last. As I spoke I watched DeMarr closely and although no longer confident in my ability to perceive anything of his real intentions, I think he was surprised and yet knowing at the same time. When I finished speaking I was sure that he had experienced exactly what I had felt in Jonathan's cabin last year; the sting of discovery and yet the joy of recognition. For a long time he did not speak. When he did it was with obvious difficulty.

'Good God! This is – this is – this is *not* what I had

expected, Julian!' DeMarr struggled to his feet unable to contain himself, to stay still. He walked about the room seemingly at random, his hands clasped together. 'I can scarcely comprehend it, and yet, and yet it has been staring at us in the face for years!' His voice was emotional.

'Us?' I said rather needlessly. He ignored the taunt and said my son's name in an odd, haunted voice to himself, to me. He glanced up at the ceiling.

'Does he know? Does he know what he is?' DeMarr's voice shook and trembled. It was curiously frightening to see his reaction.

'Yes. I think he has gradually become self aware since he was hospitalised and his tag regenerated.'

'Does he meet with Jonathan often?' The news of the tag did not appear to impress him. Evidently he knew already of Sally's purloined scan, I wondered if she had told him.

'Yes, I think they are colluding in something, the device, the need to go to the wood.'

'Good God,' said DeMarr again. 'But if the Seeth are extinct as you suppose, and this whole experiment is somehow bizarrely self running, why go there? It doesn't make sense? I cannot have missed something else – some other device or artefact?'

'I agree – the actual end is obscure. I intend to ask Max tonight if he knows. He appears to have packed ready for his final journey.'

'If Max is returning, then the Seeth must still be out there as Davies suspects, ready to collect their hybrid and your son's genetic code, although how and why save Max?' DeMarr sounded bemused, deeply intrigued.

'I still don't know. But doesn't attempting to *save* Max cast serious doubt on the whole alien invasion theory? I have no idea how this ends and anyway, all this is beside the point: we confront the single dilemma that the device is not here. It's in the US. You gave it away!'

DeMarr blinked at me and then said quietly 'I did not *give it away*. That is unkind, Julian. I have made errors, I have lied to you, but I did not *betray* Max.' His expression was shocked and rather raw. He kept muttering 'It doesn't make sense, it doesn't add up, Julian! Why did they come back with a device – why even bother to design some form of instrumentation that saved the host once the Seeth hybrid had been regenerated and repaired? Why even repair the genome in this way? Why did they need to invade the whole human genome?' DeMarr paced about, rambling softly, asking the very first questions that had come to my mind as I had sat with Jonathan that night.

'I have no idea. Perhaps their own genome was so wasted, so compromised, it was the only way to save themselves. Perhaps the five chromosomal pairs inserted into the children in 1993 were not, as I then presumed, the most damaged part of a bigger Seeth genome, but the only part that remained intact?'

DeMarr looked at me with horror and then again, up towards the ceiling.

'It seems so haphazard, Julian, coming back, almost as if they forgot to leave it in the first place, too messy, rushed?' We stood together in silence. I thought I could hear Max and Jamie shouting, laughing at something, but I couldn't be sure. I looked sideways at DeMarr who was staring ahead remote and seemingly fearful.

'Yes. A race panicked by the immediacy of their own species death, literally running out of time, or the strange automated hiccups in an experiment running on after its creators were gone.' I looked at DeMarr with sudden, odd affection. 'I had hoped you had it on you, Louis. When you said on the phone you wanted an exchange I thought that however improbable, you'd managed to steal it from under Davies' nose.' It was impossible to disguise my disappointment. 'Although I was rather curious as to what I had that you wanted so badly.'

Louis turned to look at me gradually and with the odd stiffness I had noticed earlier. I was shaken to see in the dim light that his cheeks were wet with tears.

'Louis? What is it?'

'I am a treacherous old bastard, Julian, as desperate in my own way as you are. I came this evening intent on tricking you one last time, it's such a habit my dear, so ingrained.'

'To pretend you had the device itself?'

'Yes, more or less.'

'In exchange for what?'

'Fresh samples from Max. I'm sure that you now understand why. The bio-chemistry of the experiment's end phase mirrors the beginning: I suspected as much and from what you have told me I now know. For the next few days, as Max's genetic coding polarises between human and Seeth-human hybrid there is a hope that I can find from fresh samples that elusive window I saw in mid April 1993, one last opportunity to grab Max's silver bullet!'

I was amused, oddly touched by his confession and yet appalled that even now Max could be of so little consequence to him. He sensed my rebuke. 'But it seems so immaterial now after what you have told me, the revelation of Max was unexpected. I had not expected it. I had almost *forgotten* Max.'

It was a strange remark. It made no immediate sense. Louis turned towards me his face almost lost in darkness.

'Did you ever dream of Max, Julian?'

'Dream?' I felt my spine tingle.

'Yes? Dream.'

'Sometimes.'

He nodded his head, quietly, to himself. 'I did. Strange, distressing dreams, curiously intimate, indeed in their own way rather shocking. They started after Max threw me across this very room.' He was watching me again, intently trying to interpret my expression.

'Pregnant?' I said simply, a sort of code.

'Indeed. How very odd this is, how very odd it has become. I really didn't give the device away Julian. You of all people know how spineless the British can be when it comes to the Americans. Davies found out about the device when he met up with that MacMillan woman in Australia. It is astounding how, given the size of the planet, bio-chemists so frequently run into each other!'

'When was this?'

'Around 2002. The US started pressuring the British almost immediately for information on it. I tried to stall them but in the end, well you know the rest. In 2005 they took it and since then I've been in the US almost continuously, trying to get my hands on it, to work out what it does. Now I know.'

'Do you think there's any chance we can get it back, Louis?' It was an absurd question and he seemed to smile at my naivety.

'No, I don't. There is a remote possibility that we could try and engineer some form of substitute but its very simplicity is baffling. And we don't have time, obviously.'

'Can we stop the experiment concluding in some way by treating Max?' I asked desperately. Louis limped back to his chair.

'No, not without killing Max and the Seeth as well. The coding of Max and his emergent host is too complex to separate given our current understanding of genetics, and there is so much coding anyway. No. It couldn't be done.'

I returned to my seat slowly and in much distress. 'Are you sure Davies is still unaware of what the device is really for?'

DeMarr peered over at me. He looked very tired now,

probably drunk.

'Definitely! He may well have made a connection between its composition and Max's chemical smell as it were, but I doubt he has really understood it. He will interpret its use in the light of his singular misunderstanding of what the Seeth are trying to do – that is a great advantage to us – you must have faith in Davies' sheer conviction that the aliens are out to destroy, colonise or conquer us. Even if Davies has worked out that the experiment is designed to repair and propagate their genome, you can be confident that he has elaborated some horrible theory as to how its restoration requires the entire destruction of humanity! You know Americans dramatise everything! From what I can gather he is convinced that the device is some sort of communication system. He has rightly guessed that Max will go back to the wood. He believes that without the device Max will be unable to contact his abductors. So he plans to bargain I think.'

'Shit.' I said quietly.

'One thing is certain however, I don't think he knows or cares much about Jonathan. Both he and James have over-looked Jonathan completely.'

'Really? But Davies would know from the committee archives that Jonathan had a tag; that he was the only child to retain one?'

'Possibly – but his genome was always normal, human and I suspect Davies might have discounted him as we both did as some sort of error. I am certain that Davies doesn't know that Jonathan returned to the wood last year.' There was a loud bang upstairs as if something had been dropped or overturned. Louis looked at his watch, putting it close to his eyes in the dark. 'I had better go soon, Julian.' He paused, gathering himself together oddly, his hands clasped about his chest. 'Will you give me samples of Max's blood?' The request seemed oddly defiant, as if despite his surprise, part of Louis had remained focused on the real purpose of his visit, or was he desperate? I snorted a sort of laugh. What DeMarr had come to in effect steal or cheat from me he now asked openly and without shame. I didn't answer him.

'Please Julian.'

I felt angry, and desperately, desperately sad. 'Why! Why should I help you now?'

'Because I am dying, my dear.'

The silence of the room was for a moment so intense that it literally rang in my ears like tinnitus.

'What?'

'I have pancreatic cancer. I was diagnosed in the US and despite some relatively advanced treatment it is ripping merrily away through my digestive tract without any real hope or reason. I have reached that invidious stage where the treatment is only marginally less painful than the illness.'

'Oh God, Louis. Louis I had no idea!'

'Of course not, only Sally knows. But it's quite hopeless, six months at best and you know how hopelessly optimistic the medical profession can be! Observation affects outcome. I probably have less than two months. Give me the samples, Julian. Ask Max to give them to me, give me one last chance?'

'Is there time?' I asked without thinking, unconsciously aligning Louis' dilemma with my own.

'Probably not.'

I stood up and walked over to help Louis up from his chair. The hint of illness, implicit from his arrival, was obvious to me now.

'Don't fuss, dear. I'm fine,' he shooed my hands away. 'I have done you a great injury, and Max as well – a painful disintegrative death is probably my just dessert.'

'Louis, I never wanted to lose your friendship. I was jealous of you at times, and irritated, but I admired your abilities and I always tried to help you! I didn't want this.'

'I know, I know. It is a tragedy that I resented your patronage and yet in some senses craved yet more.' We walked with difficulty out into the hall.

'I'll talk with Max. Are you staying in Oxford?'

'All Souls, a last exercise of my fellowship rights to cheap bed and board.' He turned to look at me urgently. 'Will you come tomorrow?'

'Yes. Yes I will see you tomorrow.' I retrieved DeMarr's coat from the banister and opened the door. Louis seemed suddenly much the worse for drink, unsteady on his feet, confused.

'Do you want me to walk with you?'

'No, no, my dear. I shall be fine.' And yet he stood on the doorstep reluctant to leave.

'In all the science, Julian, in all the bewildering detail, I wonder if we have missed what really is going on here. The *mystery* of it? Of Max himself?'

'Perhaps.' My answer was vague, unsure as to what Louis was getting at. He walked slowly down into the porch, stopped and then slowly started to walk away. Before he disappeared he turned to me once more and whispered, 'If he is going to risk returning to the wood, there must be something there, Julian? Something we've missed. If the Seeth are indeed dead, then your theory accounts for everything except the wood itself.'

Chapter 15

I couldn't get away from my computer or the compulsion to keep searching. It consumed me. Once I tapped into a link, there was literally tons of shit on the web about the 1993 abductions and several direct references to Norma Lennox. Apparently, she had gone mad and died in some sort of facility around 2001. I felt sick with fear and I have to confess, a sort of wild excitement. Part of me still resented Max for not telling me any of this but how could he? Where would he have started and would I have believed him? If I had, I would have been freaked senseless – about as freaked as I was now. And sitting in my bedroom sweating and tapping out keys, I knew that Max had excluded me to protect me and that thought moved me both to tears and to anger. I tried to focus on how I would confront Max. I had to do it immediately. I took some protein shakes for the gym and ran off through the hot early evening, late, desperate; my life unreal now like a dream. When I arrived, Max was already in the free weights room calmly doing his bench presses as if he were entirely normal.

I stood behind his head and watched him drop the barbell back on to the brackets. It was hard – almost impossible – to look at him now. It was as if in having made the connection with the children and the aliens he was utterly transformed, too perfect, too enigmatic to be human and that somehow, in some undisclosed way, his beauty was now dangerous. Max sensed me watching him and looked up. I instinctively avoided his eyes, a stupid slippery move on my behalf that made me look suspicious.

'Hey, there you are!' When I dared myself to regain eye contact Max's expression had already changed, clouded over and bemused, and the implied reproach seemed to pin me up on a wall at a single glance. 'What?' he growled, leaning up, his arms angled under him like hinges.

'Nothing. Sorry I'm late Max, I fell asleep.' I squatted down and started messing with a bottle of water and a towel needlessly, full on OCD style. I felt incredibly nervous and scared.

'Yeah? You ok?'

'Yes, honestly. I didn't get much sleep last night.'

I forced myself to stop fussing and stood up. 'Let me warm up man, I'll join you in a bit.' Max nodded in slow agreement but he had sensed something. I felt his gaze knifing my shoulder blades as I made my way through to the CV machines and the runners. I set the treadmill for twenty minutes but stopped after fifteen. When I found Max again he was still flat benching but on a Smith Press. I sneaked a look at the plates. He was pushing well above his normal weight with ease. Veins on his broad forehead and in his neck snaked out, vibrant; like wiring. He did ten and then stopped, his arms out above the top of his head.

'OK, Jamie what's wrong? You've been weird all day! Do you want to ask me something?'

I stood over him looking down, narrowing my eyes so my field of vision was fuzzed by my own eyelashes.

'No.' I said quietly although my voice was very unsteady. I had this weird sensation that I was visibly trembling and that everyone in the entire gym could see it. Max looked serious and remote as if he sensed my dishonesty and was puzzled by my hesitation. I felt he was looking through me, touching the inside of my head, the roof of the mouth, combing his long fingers down my nose and cheek. I started to blush.

'You don't look well, Jamie,' he said softly after a considerable pause.

'I'll be alright in a minute, Max. I'm troubled over issues of identity.'

'Your own?'

'No actually, surprising as it may seem, *yours*.'

He leaned up, swung his legs around the bench and sat upright, alert, bristling with curiosity now. He cocked his head to one side and observed me as if I was a complete stranger.

'Mine?' he sounded genuinely puzzled and for a second I doubted what I had seen; Max's dad, the websites, Max hugging Jonathan.

'Yes! When I told you I was gay Max, you were the first person I told and I needed you of all people to know. Because I trusted you. I trust you with everything.' I could feel my anger welling up from somewhere near my navel.

Max leaned forward, his arms on his knees, his hair snaking slowly down over his forehead, He shook it away, dog like, but he was thinking hard. He glanced up at me carefully,

'And I love you because of that Jamie, your honesty, the way you are with me.'

'But you didn't reciprocate that trust! You never told

me who you were!'

He put his head down, looking at the floor, his broad shoulders hunched as if he was in a sort of crash position.

'And don't say it's because I never asked you either, Max, because that's a crap answer.' I added quickly for good measure. Through the thick spears of hair, I saw his face smile faintly. Bizarrely he seemed more amused than angry. When he lifted his head to look at me he was almost grinning.

'Jamie, can you remember when we first met?' He narrowed his eyes playfully. The question took me aback. Suddenly Max seemed *much* closer to me somehow, almost inside my head. I felt myself beginning to panic slightly.

'You mean like at primary school?'

'Yeah!' he said dreamily. 'When you broke my arm!' Max beckoned to me to pass him up the weight on my side of the bench. As he took it off me, his fingers quite deliberately brushed against mine.

'It was an accident,' I said eventually.

'Was it?' he growled cryptically, suddenly handing me back the weight. 'Come on, let's go. I sense you're on a mission.'

Max did not shower afterwards but waited in reception until I had finished drying off and changing. When I emerged, he was talking with some men at the counter and with Bryan the owner. They were all talking about his physique and his shoulder routine. I could tell without even being in earshot. Max had a small notebook with him open on the main desk and they were all copying something down from it and looking at him appreciatively as if he was a prize race horse. Almost all the respect I had at the gym was as a result of my relationship with Max. 'Hey, you're Max's mate, right?' said Bryan once as if I had no identity of my own and when I said 'yes', I became immediately privileged. I walked up to the counter and waited while Max politely, rather coyly, disengaged himself from his fan club. Once out in the hot stale air we started straight for home, past Worchester College and into Walton Street. We were silent, lost in our own thoughts. Why couldn't I just come out and say it! About us, swifts screamed and dived overhead through the thick air and the pavement was still hot from the long summer day. We stopped outside my house.

'Want to come in?' I tried not to sound too eager, *desperate*. Was he in a hurry to get home? Would he see Jonathan tonight?

'Nah – I need something to eat, I'm really hungry! And I told Dad I'd have a few beers with him.' Max started to move away from me, his kit bag swung up over his shoulder, his hand gripping the strap and bunching the tendons in his dark tanned forearm. I pushed open the gate, the prospect of confronting him too overwhelming, too unreal. There came a sudden dread that I would not see him again, that he would just go without a word. The thought was random and stupid but so incredibly real that I turned back quickly. Max had stopped as well and was watching me intently as if he could sense my despair.

'Jamie, come and eat with me, let's sort this out.' he said with sudden decision. It wasn't even a question.

'Sure? Yeah, hold it – I'll leave my stuff here –' Max must have seen the change in my mood. Jesus! It was instantaneous. It was rather pointless trying to hide it. As we resumed walking, he suddenly said

'Dad said he met you today – running down St Giles?'

I felt my face heat up without warning.

'Yes! That's right!' I left the sentence unfinished. The routes through endless lies and half-truths stretched out around me like competing algorithms. Which one to take? The big lie or some small aside, an omission, or the truth? Direct and in his face?

'Julian was pretty vocal about you earlier! He seemed to imply we were not as close as we should be? Or were?'

I faked a laugh – a bad one, I thought – a sort of hyena bark, high with anxiety. 'Did he? Does he think we're no longer as friendly as we were. I mean, as kids?'

'Yeah, I think he does actually.' said Max, without any particular emphasis.

And then I said in a full-on needy voice *'You* don't think that, do you? That we're, I mean –'

Max stopped walking. I went to apologise but Max said suddenly, explosively,

'Jamie, what the fuck is wrong with you today!'

'Nothing is wrong, I mean everything is wrong! Jesus, Max I have no idea what you think about anything!' I sounded angrier than I had intended. Max jumped slightly and then scrutinised me in a way that was almost physically painful.

'Is this about Jonathan?' His face was dark, flushed from the gym; he literally shone out at me.

'No!' I said with such petulance that Max smiled again and then tried to look angry, and then I said. 'Yes ok it is. It started with him. Max I saw you with Jonathan the other night! And I've seen you give him money – I know he's involved with you in some way – I saw you on the boat, *holding him,* and today.' How far could I go? What if I told him what I knew and he denied it? What then? Max did his *boulder, dark water, moss* routine – and then he looked *disappointed,* like I'd promised to behave and hadn't. I hated that look. It cut through me like a knife.

'You don't fucking trust me, Max, and that's the truth! And now I know! But I had to sneak about and find it for myself! I know everything!'

I had not intended to shout or swear but had. Max suddenly looked incredibly pissed off. I did a half U-turn determined to go home but Max stood in front of me and next minute he had a sort of killer grip on my arm. He pulled me right up to him. The gesture was suggestive of profound violence. I wondered what it would feel like to be hit seriously by Max. He looked right into my face with such intensity that I braced myself for him to strike. He suddenly scared me.

'So you're following me now! You followed me to Jonathan's houseboat?' Our faces were close; Max's eyes were brilliant and clear, almost luminous. And I could see now that apart from being angry he was also *afraid*. In all my life, I had never known Max afraid of anything. His reaction, the proximity of him, the feel of his hand on my arm, froze my outrage in its tracks. His fear was infectious.

'What choice did you leave me with, Max? And I wasn't following you deliberately, well not at first. I called around to see you last Monday. Then I just went into town upset because you've been lying to me for ages!' He went to say something, his face flushed, but I interrupted him. 'And I saw you outside Nuffield College, near the Castle Mound. I just had to know what was going on with this Jonathan dude, why all the secrecy, why you wouldn't confide in me! Max – you're hurting my arm!' At that precise moment I wanted to die. I could not win anything now: if Max told me it would be because I had bullied him into a confession; his trust would not be a gift, something offered to me willingly, but something snatched, demanded, stolen from him. Max looked at his hand curiously as if he couldn't quite recall grabbing me. As I stared, I noticed an intricate blush of patterned specks had appeared in his hairline, banded like a rash. I was pretty sure they had been absent at the gym earlier. He sensed me looking at something.

'You are so demanding, Jamie,' he said very quietly and with surprising calm. 'God you're remorseless.' He let me go. His fingers had left white band marks across my skin. A couple with a young child walked by us watching carefully as if we were two stray dogs about to fight. The women gathered the child protectively between them and as they passed I saw the man glance at Max and then at me.

Max sighed deeply and with real anguish tilted his head up in despair. Through the neck of his hoodie his throat arched away from me, thickly veined and boned like some exotic bloom. I stared at his Adam's apple; knuckled in between two lines of muscle.

'It's not who I am Jamie. That's not what this is about. It's about *what* I am and what I have to do,' said Max addressing the sky. 'And I excluded you because I could not bear to bring you any harm, Jamie, to hurt you, to distress you, because you are, next to my father, someone I love very, very deeply!'

I stood blinking at him. Suddenly, everything had gone very quiet and still, like an image frozen on a TV or a monitor. Max was looking at me and to my horror I saw tears in his eyes, the lids glistening. I was so shocked that I couldn't move or speak.

'So what do you know?' he whispered to me eventually.

'I know you and Jonathan were abducted, Max. I know that you were found together in a wood in the midlands and that everyone said you had been taken by aliens. I know that my mother and your parents have been watching you for *like* ever! I also know that some serious shit went down in the hospital last year when you were ill.' I spoke rapidly, fearing a distraction, a rebuke, a Max denial. 'I know you are involved with Jonathan now because of this, because he came back to Oxford to find you.'

'Jonathan –' Max whispered affectionately, remotely, as if he had been long dead and I had invoked a memory.

'Did you know that Julian and Sally were initially going to adopt both of us? That Jonathan could have been my brother, and that, perhaps, if he *had* been adopted, he might have had a better life, off the streets and free of drugs? An expensive, life changing education? Comfort, *me*? But in the end they chose me and me alone.'

I closed my eyes, momentarily blinded. Max had seen me cry a lot. Usually in temper, later in a sort of displaced emotional excess over him, but I had never seen him so upset, so distressed.

'I knew some of that, yes.' I said trying to sound like I wasn't bawling; that I had been placated, that this was some sort of everyday reasonable conversation. 'You never told me.' It wasn't a reproach but it sounded like it. Something in my head was *screaming, screaming, screaming.*

Suddenly Max touched my face, his index finger brushed gently down the line of my jaw as if he wanted to see if I was real. It was more curious than affectionate, a bizarre gesture. I moved my head back suddenly.

'And what do you think that Jonathan did after he was abandoned, Jamie? What would you have done? Turned aside, forgotten me? No. Jonathan waited – he watched and he waited and then he came looking for me. And even now, he's doing something rash and dangerous, almost purely instinctive, trying to help me! He has no choice in this, of course. Nor do I.'

I took Max's hand in mine and moved it from my face. Surprisingly his long fingers snaked through mine and remained holding it.

'Max what is happening to you? I'm sorry for being jealous, I'm sorry. I know it's stupid, that it drives you away!' I started to sob, a real, full on end of the world performance. I couldn't help it. Something within me had snapped. I felt horribly embarrassed. Fuck knows what this must look like but I felt almost as if I was outside of myself anyway, watching us both. Max seemed calm now, more in control of himself but I kept thinking, what does he think of me, what is he thinking? People could *see* this! I tried one last desperate effort to contain my grief before it ripped through the whole world and tore it to shreds.

'I'm your best friend, Max. I have always been your best friend, and if you can't trust me with something as serious as this, whatever this is, then that means *nothing*.' I looked hard at the toggles on his hoodie.

'Why do you have to make this into a test, Jamie, for fuck sake!' he said softly. 'It's *because* you're my best friend, because you are so important to me, that I can't involve you in this! You have free will, Jonathan and I don't!'

I breathed deeply and unevenly. 'But I *want* to be involved in this, Max. I want to show you how much you mean to me – please don't leave me out of this! I would do anything for you, go anywhere – you know what I *feel* about you!'

Had I gone too far, said too much? Had I exposed myself? My mother once told me that once you put words out into the world they could not be taken back or forgotten. They took on a life of their own, a meaning independent of your will. Max sighed and then inexplicably put his arms around me. We remained in full view of the entire universe.

'I know what I mean to you, Jamie and how you feel about me. I *see* it every day. And sometimes it's frightening!'

He released me. I stood next to him, my heart screwed up so tightly that I felt on the verge of a heart attack. Someone shouted something from a passing car.

'But I don't see what I mean to you, not any more, Max, that's just it. I just don't see anything! I *should* do –'

'Because you look at the wrong things, Jamie. You always have! Come on, I have to speak with my father.'

I looked at him, bemused by his comment. 'What do you mean?'

'Jamie! Come on!' He had walked away from me and half turned, his hand outstretched towards me as if I was a difficult child.

I stumbled after him. 'Max will you tell me everything?'
'Oh for fuck sake! Yes! Yes!'

We ran into Max's dad almost immediately. He was incinerating an omelette and the house stank of smoke. I played it all cool and collected despite the fact that the palms of my hands were all sweaty and I looked as if I had been mugged. Max gave me a few nanoseconds in the hall to 'pull myself together' and then breezed into the kitchen in full assault mode, although his eyes still looked red. Julian seemed utterly mortified to see me and I hung about in the door desperate for a piss. It was probably nerves. I went down to the basement and used the toilet and then splashed cold water in my face and down my neck. I looked at myself in the mirror and my pupils were wide and dilated as if I was on drugs or something. I leaned on the sink breathing deeply. When I got back into the kitchen Max and his father seemed to be having some sort of weird, understated argument. Julian had his hands on Max's shoulders and looked as if he had been about to shake his son. Max towered over him, powerful, suddenly seeming quite different. I coughed nervously and then someone mentioned beers and just as I was about to come out with some icebreaker comment about the weather the doorbell went. I was surprised to hear it work actually and was pretty astounded by how loud it was. Max turned around and squeezed past me and rubbed my stomach playfully, reassuringly. I felt a stab of panic that this might well be Jonathan. Julian seemed to stress out as well and went after Max. He told me he was expecting some work mate or something and by the time I walked behind him Max was beaming at this old dude standing in the hall, taking his coat. He was a bald, yellow looking man wearing almost as many clothes as Max did at the gym. I'd seen him somewhere before. Max introduced me with a certain heavy sarcasm and then literally put a can of lager in my hand and pushed me up the stairs. As Julian closed the front room door he looked up at Max with a sort of complicit guilt.

'What the fuck is going on now? Who is that guy?'

Max grunted something but continued pushing me up the stairs, half playfully, half seriously. Once inside his bedroom he partially closed the door and stood listening intently. After a while he turned to me.

'That's Louis DeMarr, one of my Dad's *former* colleagues and your mother's doctoral supervisor.'

'Really?' I said mostly out of politeness. I didn't have the slightest idea why Max knew this or what it had to do with the current crisis. I sat down on the bed and as I did so I noticed that there was a holdall on the floor, like Max's gym bag but bigger, and looking about I saw other numerous signs of packing. Max finally closed the door, stood for a moment in a strangely heroic pose and then started to pull off his hoodie in one seamless curve of movement, like an archer loads an arrow and then draws the bow. I clicked open the can of lager.

'Put that down a minute and come here.' said Max firmly as if he was in a hurry. His assertion was casual, appealing, but definitely new.

'Sorry?'

'Jamie!' he half whispered as if I was being dense. 'There is no easy way to tell you this so I had better show you.' He looked irritated now, a normal look for me of late, as if I were being awkward and deliberately uncooperative. I stood up and walked over to him cautiously. Under his hoodie he wore a tight cotton T-shirt that seemed spray painted onto his torso. It was astounding how much he had defined and separated lately. All the heads of his bicep had been worked out perfectly. Most guys only do the tops so they had a sort of *Popeye* look, thin arms and a sudden bulge. Max's arms were massive with all the muscle groups meshed together and integrated, with the biceps running up into the sheath of triceps and then curving up into the back of his shoulder almost like plating. Max was watching me judging my mood. He still looked unsure about the whole thing.

'What is it?' I said, bewildered.

'Just don't obsess about this, Jamie, ok?' Then Max did something very, very disturbing. He removed his T-shirt.

He removed it in another quick, rather cat-like gesture, despite his size, the sheer bulk of him, as if he made a habit of taking his kit off in a hurry. I heard the material stretch and spark with static. There was a hot smell and I could feel Max's body heat on my face as if he was a hot metal plate. All the blood in my body seemed to be in my face and neck. What was he doing? I looked at his face, his eyes fuzzed over with a mane of black spiky hair and then down over his chest, taking in the astounding sight of him, looking for clues.

'You can touch as well, *within* reason.'

I frowned, bemused, as if Max was deliberately taking the piss out of me, setting up some elaborate test and then I saw, suddenly and distinctly what he had been trying to hide from me, from Zoë, from his father. I saw that his body was changing. On both sides of his neck, and across the top of his shoulders and into the side deltoids, ridges of bone had started to form. They had not yet broken the skin but they were clearly visible, like the patterns of waves embossed over wet sand by the passing tides. I stumbled forward and taking his arms extended them out as if he was a manikin and in an instant, the bones became much more visible.

'What the *fuck* are they?'

I tried to touch him in the right way. The bones felt odd, cartilage-like, with some movement beneath the muscle like gristle. Max cocked his eyebrows up and then he turned around slowly, inviting further inspection. With his back to me he dutifully lifted his hair and showed me the dark lines that radiated down across his upper back into the shoulder blades. For a moment I thought I would do something stupid, fuck this up badly by fainting or throwing up. But the realisation that Max was finally *asking* me to help screwed up my concentration into a tight, controlled beam of energy.

'Does it hurt?' I whispered. I ran my hands over his back, brushing him as if he was scared and needed comforting.

'No.' Max's voice was scarcely audible. 'It itches.'

I closed my eyes tightly and then opened them again. The upper spinal vertebrae seemed bizarrely separated, buried between thick ridges of cartilage and then rising up out of the ribs of muscle like some strange ancient structure. On closer inspection the dark lines that had appeared on his upper back were made up of millions of small freckles, flat like moles, but perfectly patterned like bands on the plumage of a bird. They were clearly symmetrical like the ones I had observed on his face. I moved him into the light from the window and he obliged, allowing me to drag him forward.

'It's beautiful,' I said stupidly and Max laughed, turning around to face me. He seemed relieved.

'Is it now?'

I pushed my hands through his thick hair, brushing it away from his temples on the pretence of wanting to look at his eyes. The strands corded around my hands, strong as ropes.

'And your eyes – they flashed at school today – is that why you were wearing the shades?'

'My eyes are a bit complicated. They seem to be triggered by a specific emotional state, anger, fear, but this – look at this – this is pretty awesome.' He looked about him expectantly and said mysteriously, 'Although I'm not sure the room is dark enough yet!' Max removed my hand, which was still perilously attached to his hair, and going to the window drew the curtains and in the gloom I saw a strange luminous shimmer over Max's chest and shoulders.

'Max, what is happening to you?'

'Now look at my eyes!' He leaned in close to me. His irises were outlined in a strange florescent blue-green, vibrant and shimmering, the eyes of some ocean dwelling creature, something indescribably old and wise. They were breathtakingly, changing shade and hue like variable stars. And yet the sudden realisation that they were possibly not human suddenly scared me. I backed away

'Jamie, don't freak out. It's still me – for the time being that is – touch me.'

I traced my right hand over his front shoulder, down towards the curve of his chest and the dark brown nipple. As I did so a snail trail of light followed brighter against the dull background glow. I ran a finger across his throat and for a moment a white luminous line stood out and then slowly faded.

'Fuck! Did they do this to you, the *aliens*?' I asked.

'Yes.' he said after a pause.

'So you're an alien now?' I said, the comment absurd, stupid, but seemingly undeniable.

'Well not exactly. Not yet!' He sat down on the bed with his top still off, chewing his lip thoughtfully. 'But it's only a question of hours now.'

'Hours?' I sat down on the floor. 'I don't understand.'

'The aliens abducted the children because they wanted a sort of donor.'

'A donor?'

'Yes – someone to bring them back from the dead. For years the process has been working through my genome and now I am beginning to change into someone, something else.'

'Like Kafka's beetle?'

He laughed again. 'Yeah right. Something a little bigger and with some attitude!' Max patted the side of the bed next to him. 'Come here,' he said again with his strange new authority.

I sat next to him, side on, unable again to look at him, to see him so close to me, so open. It was far more shocking than his secrecy. Suddenly he turned to face me and again took my hand in his.

'Jamie I am not going to be here for much longer. I have to go away.'

'Away?'

'Yes. For a long time perhaps. But I will come back, ok? I promise you that and in a moment I will make the same promise to Julian.'

I looked at him in horror. 'They're going to come for you? They're going to take you back?'

He looked at me and nodded slowly. 'In a manner of speaking, yes.'

'You *know* this?'

'As good as. I was planning to leave tonight, actually. I have to return to the wood, the wood in Leicestershire where I was found, before I am completely hybridised.'

I was aware that I had my mouth open, but I was unable to speak. For a moment the image of Max holding Jonathan ignited in my head but this time it was different. This time I understood. They had been saying goodbye to each other. The room was slipping into the soft blue cool of evening, dark with the curtains closed.

'Can I come with you?'

He smiled with great pain and suddenly affectionately started spiking up the front of my hair, looking at it intently as if he was designing a new style.

'No, you can't. You have to stay and be patient and look after my father? Ok?'

I drew a circle on his hard stomach, mesmerised as the pattern faded. Then in between his pectorals, slightly to the left, I drew an improvised heart, a sort of circle.

'You have to do this, right?'

'Yes, despite the fact it scares the shit out of me! The experiment is nearly over. When I was a child I had cancer, Jamie. I was very ill. I spent a lot of time in and out of hospital and eventually I ended up in London under Sally's care. By then I was five and it was terminal and there was no hope, really.'

'*Ewing's Sarcoma* – I know. I was reading about it earlier.'

Max poked my chest playfully. 'Then you know that if it were not for the abduction I would have been dead long ago. I would never have met you, Jamie. Not Julian, nor Zoë – no one.'

'How much does your father know?'

'Most of it by now but I need to find out exactly how much. He's probably reproaching himself for not having worked it out sooner but he knew I was different from the other children. He's been watching me for years. My difference is *one* of the reasons he adopted me in the first place.'

'Yeah? To study you?'

Max shrugged, indifferent, forgiving. 'At the beginning, perhaps. But he has protected me and cared for me. We love each other a great deal and telling him will be hard.' It sounded so weird hearing him say that, as if Julian was his son.

'What do they want from you? The aliens?' I felt I was suffocating, that there was some horrible weight on my chest and throat.

'To live again.'

'I don't understand?'

'I'll tell you over dinner, with dad. For the moment there is one more thing I have to show you. It's not all doom and gloom! Jonathan and I have been experimenting, and *no*, not in that way!'

I tried to smile but felt like I had some sort of facial

paralysis. 'Experimenting?'

'More lizard magic!'

'What?'

He jumped up off the bed with remarkable agility. 'This may distress you, Jamie. You see, I hear and see other people's thoughts. I can even visualise their memories and make them into something tangible.'

He looked carefree, absurdly excited. 'Here, come on, stand up!'

'You're telling me that you're telepathic or something!' My attempts to fluff the words up with sarcasm failed. My voice wobbled. 'Obviously not mine?' Coming in the wake of the luminous skin, the flashing eyes and the bones, I was surprised I sounded so sceptical.

'Yeah.' said Max casually as if it was not a thing to boast about. 'Especially yours! Don't get stressed about that either, OK?'

I leaned forward with a groan, burying my face in my hands. All of Max's weird, penetrative glances of late now made sense, his odd smirk, his knowing grimace.

'Oh fuck. Is there a range limit to this ability?'

Max laughed loudly enjoying my discomfort and hooked his arm around my shoulder in consolation. He shook me gently. 'Come on, stand up. And don't look so ashamed! It's all perfectly natural I'm sure Jamie. And try and remember this isn't about you, Jamie, or about what you want to do with me, to me, or to some of my clothes, it's all about me!'

'I don't believe this! *Max.*' My mouth and throat were dry and burning.

'Me, me, me! Me and my special powers! I want to try something out on you! *Non-physical*, you understand.'

I looked across at him. His mood appeared to have changed completely, the fear, the anger gone. He was literally aglow with excitement. How could he be, knowing what he did? My face felt swollen and red. I stood up and Max looked comically serious all of a sudden.

'Ok, ok. What's your clearest, most vivid memory of your childhood?'

'Can it involve you?'

'Yeah – so long as it's a *real recollection* and not something you've made up!' he said with coy suspicion. 'And clean!'

'Ok. Conway Castle, Wales – two, three years ago – the geography field trip!'

Max looked at me, trying to recall the event. Then he snapped his thumb and finger very loudly. 'Yes! Good choice! The gale! Mrs Bloomfield and the near massacre of the lower Fifth!'

And then we both said together 'The helicopter!' and laughed.

'That was a *great day*, Jamie! Come on –'

'Max?'

'Keep thinking about it – and give me your hand. I have to touch you.'

Max took my hand again and held it tightly. I tried to close down my thoughts – the feel of Max's hand, the calluses on the top of his palms, his smell, aliens, children and concentrate on the memory: a geography field trip, glacial processes, raised beaches, and then something unbelievable happened. I saw the sea. But I didn't just see it or smell it, I was there! Max's room had gone, along with the house, the street, Oxford. I shouted out in fear and amazement. As I did so I was standing next to Max again in the summer darkness of his room,

'Shit!'

Max burst out laughing at my expression. 'Ok, let's try again. Try not to scream, man. Think about that moment with particular detail, when we stood trying to spit into the wind! Remember, and I'll try to come with you! I think once we're in, the memory becomes self sustaining unless you break it.'

I took his hand again and this time we were transported immediately with the room sliding away around and over us both. We were standing on a series of rocky outcrops surrounded by green deep running seas. The strength of the wind was astounding, blowing in land, pinning us down against the rock. I felt the sharp threads of spray stinging my face. In front of me, in a great curve of ocean, a dull wide bay lay wreathed in mist and cloud. I was aware of Max's grip on my hand and then suddenly next to me, his blue-black hair snaking madly about his face, Medusa-like, was Max. He was shirtless, his body tensed and his brown skin dimpled with the cold. He held up his arms and shouted with joy. Suddenly we were hit by a wave of cold spray. We both screamed, half in terror.

'Max! Max, how are you doing this!' I shouted across at him but the wind shredded my words. We looked at each other in disbelief, and then he started laughing, real whoops of joy.

'I'm not entirely sure!' he screamed at me. 'I have a tag in my head. It regenerated while I was in hospital, it enhances my brain – or this Lizard dude's brain is just so much bigger!'

Again, the reference to lizards was strange, seemingly random, but before I could process the results I heard the sound of the helicopter trying to close in as it had tried that day, two years ago because Mrs Bloomfield had panicked and called the coast guard. I tried to see it but as I turned away from Max's face I caught sight of the sheer drop below me, down into the churning sea and felt my legs give way. Suddenly there was total blackness and I realised we were back in his room. We were both wet and shivering violently. 'How can we be wet?' I gasped and the fact that we had actually been back and got wet by my own memories of the sea *really* freaked me out. I stumbled back, overwhelmed, suddenly terrified. Max folded his arms over his body and started to rub himself warm.

'The aliens gave you this power?'

Max, panting slightly, put his hands on his knees and bent his head down, as if he had been sprinting. 'Phew – that was good! That was astounding!' He sounded like he had just found how to work some new toy or software. 'It's the first time I've tried to do that with someone else!' He seemed to hear my question at last. 'Sort of. It's not why I was taken, it's more a sort of tool kit – it's part of the original Seeth genome.'

I tried to concentrate on my breathing, trying to relax, but either from the cold or the shock I felt as if I couldn't breathe properly. Max saw my distress, perhaps he sensed it.

'It's ok – Jamie – it's ok. Shit! sorry I've been really stupid!'

I began to feel myself close to hyperventilating. I stood back, trying to get my breath but I felt that my chest was stuck. Max put his right hand forward and touched the side of my face.

'Jamie,' he spoke slowly. 'It's fine, you're fine. It's just shock. You'll be ok.' He prodded my forehead with his fingers and indeed the panic subsided, ebbing away, with the cold, and the feeling of vertigo.

'I was showing off. Sorry. I've taken this in slowly over the last few months, gradually and mostly with Jonathan's help. And I just throw you in at the deep end without any real warning! But you *wanted* me to tell you and we don't have much time!'

I nodded, totally numbed.

'Telling you has been a huge relief for me, to be honest. I should have told you a long time ago.' Max sighed deeply and pulled his hair back from his face, a quintessential Max gesture. His eyes were still glowing but they were no longer scary or even strange. 'You forgive me?'

'Only when you've finished telling me!'

He put his eyes very close to mine so quickly that I jumped. He took my hand suddenly rather firmly and the room winked away from us and we were standing out in the open air. It was a very early spring morning, chilly but clear. Overhead, through the fine black veins of branches, the sky was grey-blue, the colour of Max's normal, human eyes. It smelt of fresh rain. A blackbird called from a nearby hedge, a thread of sound running through the stillness. On all sides slender birch trees stretched away from us, sentinel like, observant. The sense of peace was heavy and absolute.

'This is where Jonathan and I were found. This is an image that Jonathan gave me. He returned here quite recently. This is the place where I must go, where I was going to go to tonight.' His voice stopped abruptly. It was cold in the wood, the light brilliant, holding out the promise of a beautiful day. And then suddenly the wood vanished and I was standing with Max in his bedroom with Professor Grey framed in the open doorway to the bedroom.

For a moment we all stood looking at each other as if surprised that we had converged in Max's room. Julian's face was lined and exhausted and he, too, looked as if he had been crying.

'DeMarr has gone, Max.'

Max moved slightly away from me. 'Any news of the device?' he asked his father mysteriously, affectionately.

Julian shook his head and Max sighed. 'So what did he want?'

'To exchange stories? Fresh tissue samples from you, and oddly enough, to ask for your forgiveness.'

'Really?' Max frowned, picking up his T-shirt and pulling it down over his head and then he added gently. 'He's dying isn't he?'

Julian looked at Max for a long time. It was not a hostile look but strange, as if suddenly he seemed no longer to recognise his son. Eventually Julian breathed in deeply and opened the bedroom door. 'We haven't much time Max, but I presume you know all this?' He glanced at me as if trying to see how much Max had told me, how far from normal I had strayed in the last few hours and whether I was holding it together. Then he spoke to me, softly.

'Margaret is on her way, Jamie. She will be with us by the early hours I hope.'

The confirmation that my mother was deeply involved in Max's conspiracy no longer surprised me. I followed Max and his dad out onto the landing. As he went to descend the stairs, he suddenly asked Max if he could hear voices.

'Yes, in a way, a requiem,' Max said with a trace of sadness, 'I'll tell you all about it.'

In the kitchen Max busied himself with getting some food as if it was just any other evening. I stood watching him bend down into the fridge to retrieve some steaks wrapped up inside a plastic tray. His father was standing with his back to us looking out of the darkened window with feigned interest.

'Beef all round?'

'Sure.' I wasn't hungry at all but anxious to play along, to sustain the illusion that everything was normal.

'Are you hungry, Dad? Steak?'

'Yes, of course.' Julian pulled out a chair and sat down with strange elegance, hitching up his cords and straightening his hair a bit as if he was about to give evidence. 'How did you know that Louis is dying, Max? Did you read his thoughts?'

'Yes. Or rather I could sense it when he looked at me. It was weird, seeing him see his own death.'

There the sizzle and smell of meat cooking and although the room fell silent I could sense Julian worrying, moving things about in his head, re-arranging things. I sat down, mute, feeling invisible and overwhelmed again. The black line of panic that had receded in the last few hours was back again, ringing me in, pressing down on my head.

'Where's Jonathan, Max? Shouldn't he be with us?' I asked urgently.

'He's off on official business! We've come up with a plan,' Max said cryptically, and then in a lighter tone, 'But first of all tell me about DeMarr, Julian?'

Julian put his hands together and kneaded the palms together anxiously. 'God I missed so much, Max. I entirely misunderstood his involvement. He wasn't really interested in you at all. He was interested in curing cancer, in getting a Nobel Prize and personal fame. Now it's rather personal. He's dying of cancer and wants one last shot at experimentation!'

'Poor DeMarr.' Max caught my expression, perhaps even my sense of exclusion. 'Dad, fill Jamie in while I get the meal sorted, and be careful – he's been doing his own research!'

'Like his mother!' Julian smiled at me faintly and then told me his son's story, and through Max's his own. In some way it was also my story I guess, and my mother's, and it was definitely Jonathan's. It took a long time and I interrupted several times to get things sorted in my head; dates, places, bits of science. Julian talked about the experiment, the abduction of the children, and the Seeth's long search for compatible genetic material. He talked about the importance of Max in his university lecturer's voice as if Max was absent from the room and not sprawled out next to him, his hands wedged behind the back of his head, nodding now and then in emphasis or slight disagreement. Several times during the narrative I looked at Max out of the corners of my eyes as if he was now some sort of mythical creature like a unicorn or a Minotaur, or to see if he had physically changed during the conversation. On one occasion he caught me and smiled mischievously, stabbing my foot with his. Finally – about 1 a.m. – there came the sound of a key in the front door, a commotion of bags and cases, and my mother appeared, exhausted, tense, but comically in urgent need of cab money. No one had any to hand but eventually Max produced some cash from his kit bag, mysteriously rolled up inside one of his trainers. Margaret ran out to pay and when she returned she looked at us all suspiciously.

'This looks ominous?' but she seemed amused, relieved. She turned to me and then to Max.

'The cat is out the bag, Dr Relph – or should I say the alien?' he said affectionately.

'You've *told* Jamie? Everything?'

'Yes. He left me little choice and besides, I should have told him ages ago!'

Mother did not seem entirely overjoyed by this news but nodded anyway. She put some of her stuff on the table and the floor and then leaned down to kiss the top of my head. I sensed she was angry in some way. Max stood up, touching Margaret's arm, 'You look exhausted – can I get you something?'

'Some coffee Max, some coffee would be great. So how long was DeMarr here for?' She went up to Max's dad and they hugged each other quietly, intimately. I tried not to look surprised or taken aback. Julian became self-conscious. 'DeMarr is still in Oxford – in All Souls. He's staying up until tomorrow. He wants to meet me for breakfast!'

'You're not going, are you?'

'That's one of the things we need to discuss,' said Max with quiet authority. Margaret looked suitably intrigued but sat down. Julian briefed her over DeMarr's various revelations. She appeared to know some of the news, but some of DeMarr's schemes clearly surprised her.

'Well, the cancer story is just – well – it's completely left field! If it's true – it's pretty amazing but as far as his relationship with Davies is concerned, it's much as Dena told me recently in Boston. And DeSilva *hates* Louis!'

'How is Dena Small?' Max asked suddenly. 'Does she know anything about the whereabouts of the device?'

'Yes and no' said Margaret. 'She hasn't got the necessary clearance to get access to it, but it's in California. The good news is that no one seems to have made any obvious connection between it and Max's 22. They still think it's a communication device or some sort of beacon to re-establish links with the abductors.' She took the coffee from Max. 'Much of what DeMarr has told you is true, Julian, Davies just wants his hands on Max to bargain with the Seeth.' She paused, blowing over the mug to cool the hot liquid. Julian turned to look at Max intensely.

'Max – am I right about the experiment? And are the Seeth dead? You mentioned a requiem?'

'Yes,' replied Max, not looking up. 'They have been extinct for centuries. The experiment has been running itself. The voices that Jonathan heard – that I hear now – are echoes – recordings, voice mail from a dead race, and of course that is why no one saw anyone physically abduct the children.'

'How can it run itself?' Margaret asked.

'I don't fully understand yet.' Max sat with his head to one side like some astounding oracle. 'I think Seeth technology is – *was* – both biogenic and temporal. They communicate through dreams and visualizations, I think they had the ability to dream time somehow, to operate and act upon their environment without instrumentation?' He shook his head, 'But I can't yet be sure.'

Julian's face was ashen white; lined, suddenly very old. 'That makes some sense to me. I dreamed about the genomes, about *you*, so did DeMarr. Perhaps Sally did as well. But what I don't understand Max, is that if the Seeth have perished why are you returning to the wood? What is there that we could possibly have missed?'

'There is a ship,' Max said gravely. 'The ship that returned Jonathan and I in 1993 and then came back with the device weeks later. It's still there, waiting for the experiment to finish.'

I felt everyone stiffen and tense, even Max. Margaret looked around us all, disbelieving.

'But where, Max?'

'Above the trees?'

Julian nodded slowly to himself in implicit agreement. 'Ingenious! Oddly enough Lockwood sensed it. Last year when he telephoned to tell me that Jonathan had returned to the wood, he said he felt there was something above the trees. He also said he felt the wood was different somehow, he didn't explain, couldn't explain, but it now makes sense.'

'The ship is hidden somehow, entirely invisible. It will re-materialise when it senses my tag, and my *smell* of course,' Max said simply. I looked completely bemused but again Julian seemed to accept the idea without difficulty.

'The pheromone Dr Hawking found in your blood last year?'

'Yes,' said Max.

Margaret frowned heavily, looking at them both for some clarity.

'Once I have transformed into a hybrid, I will secrete androstenol and the ship appears. It will proceed to take the hybrid home. If I have secured the device in time, it will take Max *as well.*'

'Ah,' said Julian. A look of profound misery swept his face. 'I did not quite understand that part. Is that part of the experiment?'

'Yes,' said Max ominously. No one spoke. I looked at my mother and then at Julian.

'I don't get any of this, this is your home!' I said almost desperately. Max leaned forward and put his hand on my arm.

'This is *Max's* home, and it will be again. But I am becoming a Seeth-human hybrid impregnated with millions of genomes. DeSilva's metaphor of an army was wrong – I am rather a sort of hatchery. The original Seeth genome was itself so compromised that all of my human DNA will have to be cannibalised to re-start the race.'

I looked at Max and then at his father. I felt stupid, lost, the information again overwhelming me. I sensed by mother's grief and felt I had missed something vital, shocking.

'But what happens to *you*, Max?'

Max lifted his head slowly and looked straight at me, his face inscrutable. He then glanced in the direction of his father, a soft, rather coy gesture.

'I will be destroyed, unless –'

'Unless, just before the hybridisation is complete, just before the final human chromosomes are re-configured, we manage to copy Max's genome into a biogenic carbon based device,' Julian whispered. 'And the device will be taken for you to be regenerated by the Seeth? Is that it? Why? Will you be kept there? Will you return?'

'Kept?' I repeated loudly, aggressively. Max's eyes looked suddenly exasperated. I recalled Max telling me softly that he had to go away and that I was to wait patiently.

'Jamie! Please! I will be returned when my job is done.'

'Your job done?' asked my mother slowly.

'They wish me to live amongst them for a time, after their restoration.'

'You know this?' Julian stood up abruptly, the chair scraping back on the floor. 'How? The voices? This is part of the experiment?'

Max shrugged, his first real gesture of confusion, but my mother – who had sat quietly tapping the table with her hand attentively – nodded with sudden decision.

'It makes sense, Julian. The hybridisation of the Seeth

genome with human DNA will fundamentally change the Seeth race – they'll all be human Seeth hybrids from now on, much *closer* to us. If they are successfully restored, they will be quite physiologically different from their former selves, and perhaps psychologically they need Max to assist them understand being half human, being different?' She smiled at Max faintly, but I thought her face looked tight, afraid.

Max nodded hesitantly. 'I think that is right. I will be replaced by a female host, who will in effect, propagate the first regenerative cycle, but I am still needed because their subsequent life cycle as hybrids will be very different from what it once was.'

'How will the female host propagate the genomes, Max? Do you have any idea?'

'She will lay eggs,' said Max quietly. 'Millions of them and then she will somehow regenerate me through a form of surrogate pregnancy.'

'Astounding,' said Julian. 'The Seeth are monotremes, egg-laying mammals?'

But before Max could reply, I suddenly exploded. 'This is just mad! All of it!' I stood up abruptly making everyone in the room jump as well, Max included. 'How do you know any of this will work? What if it fails? Who then restores you? How do you know they will keep their word and bring you back? Max?'

Julian looked at me, his face devastated with grief and exhaustion. I thought for a second he was going to rebuke me but he actually said, 'Jamie's right, it doesn't make sense – the time scale – it's literally astronomical. And if you are restored, you'll be a clone Max, you won't be my son – your own humanity will be gone.'

Max sighed again. I wondered if whether talking about it scared him, reminded him of his imminent departure, his imminent change.

'Father you're thinking in conventional terms, in *terrestrial* terms: look at what the Seeth experiment has already done! I can feel the Seeth entity inside me, she has memories – she is coded to fulfil this mission! The device was designed for me, to copy my genetic code, my memories, my habits, my obsession with gyms and Jamie's tantrums, everything!' Max moved forward and rubbed Julian's shoulders. 'This isn't just about the science of regeneration, it's also about *faith*, isn't it? I have to have faith that the Seeth will be restored and that they in turn will restore me! They gave me my life once, and I am sure they will give it back to me again! In a sense they *want* to be human!'

My mother's face crumpled slightly, and she put her hand over her mouth and looked away. Seeing her close to tears really, really shocked me. I sat down rigidly in my chair. Max's dad stood now and walked around the table towards the sink units.

'So what do we do? We don't have the bloody device? What about Davies? He knows about the wood. He may not know that the Seeth are dead, but given what Max contains and what he can do to Max's emergent hybrid, it doesn't really matter!'

I looked at Max in fresh horror. 'You mean we don't *even have* the storage device?'

Max flashed me a look, familiar to me from happier, more normal times, and ignoring me turned to his father.

'Davies knows a great deal, but as Louis told you earlier, he is blinded by his own prejudices. He knows about the wood, but he doesn't know about Jonathan, and he certainly has overlooked the fact that my tag has regenerated – thanks largely to Sally!' It was the first time he had mentioned his mother's name.

'Have you spoken with your mother?' Margaret asked this, cautiously.

'Yes. As I said earlier, Jonathan and I have come up with a plan.'

'And this involves Sally?' Julian turned slowly and

faced us.

'Yes. We have to *appear* to bargain.' Max ran his hands through his hair, streaming it back away from his face. The dark patterned lines were thickening on his scalp. He seemed to be changing quickly.

'Bargain with what?' asked my mother sharply, suddenly alert.

'With me! Davies and DeSilva want me very much, but not as much as they want the Seeth!'

Julian clenched his hands together behind his head. He went to say something but Max interrupted him gently. 'It's the only real option we have left –' he looked at his father almost apologetically. 'You know this, you've been considering it yourself! It was *Jonathan's* idea actually: it works on the basis that Davies thinks the device is a sort of intergalactic collect call! We've persuaded Sally to convince Davies that Jonathan can use the device to communicate with the Seeth just as well as I can, to tell them it's time to fetch me home. The proof will be when Davies scans Jonathan's head and sees the tag – and Jonathan has some powers of his own – we can impress him if we have to!'

'Powers?' asked his father.

'But his genome is normal –' interrupted Margaret.

'His powers come from me. Together Jonathan and I are very powerful: we have abilities, telepathy, telekinesis, the ability to alter the structure of objects. It's as if his tag is a relay of some kind. Once he teases Davies with his abilities, I don't think it will matter that his genome is human.'

'Good God!' Julian gasped.

'I've seen some of this,' I added quickly, sheepishly, as if I was half boasting. There was another silence but this time edged with sudden hope.

'But how does reuniting Jonathan with the device help? He can't simply walk out of a secure facility with it? They might even take Jonathan to the US!' my my mother frowned, puzzled.

'We are very powerful together. Jonathan merely has to touch the device to bring it to me, along with himself, and anything else he is touching at the time. The tags and the device are made from the same basic technology. The plan is for me to get to the wood and wait, to loosely coordinate my arrival with Davies handing Jonathan the device – hopefully there will be enough *Max* left in the hybrid to transfer and – well you know the rest.'

My mother looked remarkably sceptical. Julian resumed his strange pose by the kitchen window. I tried to focus my eyes on the clock and found it was impossibly late – almost 4 a.m. – and quite light outside. Eventually Julian said quietly, his voice shaking slightly. 'So this is it? You leave for the wood now and wait?'

Max didn't answer for a while. 'More or less.'

'Would you have said goodbye?' I said stupidly, referring to myself, to Julian, my mother; to everyone who loved him. The words blurted out without me thinking. Max winced slightly as if I had hit him without warning.

'I'd left you all letters,' said Max very quietly looking at the floor, embarrassed perhaps, ashamed, or just very sad. It was hard to tell.

'A *letter*?' I said and for a moment despite all I knew and understood I felt full of darkness again, the sheer enormity of being left behind. Max sighed, a plea. I bit my lip hard, catching the inside of my cheek. I felt my mouth fill with blood.

'You plan to go alone, despite the prospect that the wood is covered, and the fact that Davies knows that the transformation is imminent?' Julian asked, his voice flat but measured, as if he was evaluating some sort of impersonal project. Outside the windows the air was full of birdsong and light, the fine blue whiteness of another hot summer day.

'Yes.'

'Is that wise, Max?' my mother asked quietly. 'As the physical changes increase you might well suffer from convulsions, possibly even toxic shock and what of your appearance? What if it suddenly and quite dramatically changes? I presume you'd intended to leave at night?'

'I can't ask anyone to go with me – it's too dangerous – and given what will happen to me – too frightening!'

Julian went to speak, obviously to volunteer but Max intercepted him. 'No! You are too well known, as is Margaret.'

'Then what about Lockwood?' Julian said urgently. 'His farm looks over the site of the wood and he still owns the land – he knows a great deal about this and if Davies had overlooked Jonathan, he might well have no interest in Daniel!'

Max hesitated; the idea clearly appealed. 'It's a terrible thing to ask of him! And surely the farm is watched?'

'I'll go with you' I said loudly, dramatically. 'I'll meet this Lockwood dude, go to the wood. I'll go anywhere.' I stared at Max angrily, defying him to say no. Typically he looked pained but before he could say anything Julian said 'That's not a bad idea. You could keep an eye on Max and make sure he doesn't take ill, rendezvous with Lockwood and go to the wood. If Davies really thinks Jonathan will use the device to call in the Seeth to come and fetch Max, he has a vested interest in letting you get that far.'

'Like a trap?' said Margaret suddenly and then she said, in her special killjoy voice. 'I don't think Jamie should go.'

There was a brief stand-off. I felt my temper flare up but before I could respond Max put his hand on my knee. His fingers felt incredibly cold, like ice. Margaret tutted and sighed.

'Max this is madness!'

'I want to go – I have a right – I have a right to be with

Max at the end!' I said simply and to my immense relief I sensed Max nod gently, an affirmation.

'He can come with me to Leicester and then, if he wants, he can come back to Oxford once I am with Lockwood. Or he can come with me – he is my best friend, Margaret.' Boxed in, my mother finally relented. 'Has Lockwood agreed to any of this yet?' she said rather coldly. 'You haven't spoken with him since last year?'

'No, I haven't but I think in some odd way he won't be surprised.' Julian half turned to look at us, 'And he will help. I trust Lockwood, I did from the moment I met him. And like Jamie's, Lockwood's involvement would reassure me somehow. After all he was there at the beginning.'

I looked at my mother and tried to look encouraging, brave even. However un-enthusiastic she was about it she quickly rallied. She, too, stood up from the table now.

'Ok, ok. But this isn't a game, Jamie – it's deadly serious. The people who want the Seeth Hybrid have access to the State which means that you have to be as anonymous and as informal as possible, we can risk using mobiles but not for long, and you must get to Lockwood as quickly as possible.'

'Can't mobile phones be tracked via the SIM cards?' asked Max.

'Not yet, not with any reliability. Texting is good but no landlines.' She turned to look at Max almost in awe, almost as if he was already a stranger, someone almost beyond her comprehension.

'Sure,' and then Max added practically 'We'll need money!'

'And we go what, now? Immediately?' Suddenly I was so tired I could hardly focus on keeping my head up. The adrenaline of the last few hours was almost spent.

'I think you can both rest up a bit – we need to get in

touch with Lockwood.' Julian seemed suddenly animated. He looked up at the kitchen clock and then at me, at Max. 'I suggest Jamie calls Lockwood from a pay phone. It's too risky if I contact him.'

'And what if he's not at home?' I asked.

Julian shrugged but didn't answer. 'I'll get his contact details: keep it brief Jamie – say you're coming to Leicester with an old college friend. I suggest you take public transport, a train, pay cash at the station,' then Julian paused. 'And presumably we just wait here?' It was a poignant question. I had a sudden vision of Max's dad sitting in his kitchen with my mother, waiting forever.

'Not just yet,' said Max softly. 'I want you to go and see DeMarr. I want to give him something.'

Despite his exhaustion I saw Julian's face narrow with interest.

'I don't understand Max? I'm not entirely sure that DeMarr can be trusted even now.'

'I want you to give DeMarr some of my blood.'

'Max, he hasn't time now to resume his work – it's too late for Louis,' gasped Julian, surprised or irritated by Max's request.

'Please,' said Max with odd intimacy. 'It will distract you for a while, and it might throw Davies off slightly if he sees you meeting with Louis. He has been as confused over Louis as you have!'

Margaret looked about her, at me, at Max. She looked at Max for a long time and sensing her watching him, he walked over to her and hugged her. Neither spoke but stood embracing for some time. My mother looked quite small and diminutive next to him. When she disengaged I saw her cheeks were wet. Julian left into the hallway and after a while, returned with Lockwood's phone number and address on a small card. He gave it to me. 'After I have sorted out Louis, I will try and get to the wood as soon as I can,' he said, studying Max's reaction, not mine, fearing a protest but Max said nothing. He turned to me.

'I'll see you in a few hours, Jamie. Let's say 9-ish. I'll call around.'

It was nearly 7 a.m. when I got to finally lie down and by then everything felt completely unreal, too bright, too quiet, with no noise or sound corresponding with what I saw or tried to hear. It was as if my head was full of cotton wool or water. I stripped down to my boxers, lay on the top of the bed, and fell quickly into a series of light, insubstantial dozes. I dreamed vividly of Max, his taut male belly swollen with children, then of aliens, tall narrow stick insects that lived in trees and then I dreamed of Max running through the fields again, dark and sleek like a giant cat. Someone was shooting at us. I jumped awake but quickly fell back into the shallow, warm waters of lucid dreaming. I was with my sister helping her to pack a suitcase by standing on it. It seemed to contain bits of armour. Katherine was very scared and kept telling me that Max was a dragon and that I had to stab him under his throat. And then within no time at all I heard my mother knock gently on the door. She appeared with coffee, placing it carefully on the table next to my bed, left without speaking and then reappeared carrying some things before sitting down next to me, close up as if I was ill. I tried to focus on her, the room, the simple fact that the world had changed utterly.

'You ok, Jamie?'

I felt like shit, actually, worse than if I had stayed awake: I should have gone for a jog. My eyes wouldn't stay open and I felt drugged, remote, as if I was in the bottom of some dark well looking up into brilliant sunlight. My stomach was knotted up on itself, full of air. Sensing my feelings she handed me my drink. 'Here, try this! My super power brew.' She propped me up on several pillows. I noticed a case with clothes next to a small canvas bag, like a satchel. For someone who was jet lagged and had probably not slept for over twenty four hours or more, my mother looked remarkably on the ball.

'Have you been up since we got back?' I asked. My mouth tasted foul, parched. The coffee burned my throat.

'Yes. I find it better to just keep going in situations like this, at least at my age. If I lie down now I will go out like a light for hours. I used to work like this at the lab in my technician days! We lived on coffee and cake! I've taken a shower and some food. I feel vaguely better. Jamie –' she paused, the tone of her voice neutral.

'I'm going with him!' I had anticipated one last ambush. Then I said, without warning, as if in explanation, 'I *love* him –'

I blushed at the confession but she didn't look surprised. 'I know. I've always known. Have you told him?'

'Yes. I *think* –' I couldn't exactly remember. So much had happened, so much had been suggested and explained it was hard to remember. I'd said a lot last night to Max, with him standing, half naked, vulnerable, different. 'Perhaps not in so many words. But he knows how I feel. He sees it'

'I'm sure he does.' She brushed my hair back, thoughtfully. 'And Max has always loved you, Jamie. I have no doubt about that.' She still sounded guarded about something, as if being in love with him did not automatically qualify me to go off to Leicester with him, to risk my life.

'Yeah, I guess.' *In his way*. I leaned back and looked up at the ceiling. I could still see faint luminous stars stuck around the light, a gift from Max years ago. I remembered how we had argued about how to arrange them. I wanted to put them up in a hurry. Max had insisted we made proper constellations out of them. So

Max like.

'The fact is I'm ashamed of how I behaved over Jonathan, mum. I know that Max was trying to protect me, but being excluded from him was terrible, just unbearably painful. That's why I have to go now! Whatever the risk.' I thought briefly of Zoë. How would she feel when she found out? Had Max told her anything? I guess she would just get her letter, a final parting missive from a departed lover.

'I know, I know darling. I do want you to go, really, I do. I know how important Max is to you, I'm just afraid it's dangerous, and that whatever happens, you'll get hurt, emotionally if not physically –' she paused, unsure how to proceed. It was a conversation I know she had been trying to have with me for some time.

'Because Max is some sort of messiah alien? Or because he's straight?' I asked.

'Well both, obviously, but I think the messiah alien bit is the main problem.' She stroked my hair again. Usually I disliked this, it made me feel about ten or something, but we were both upset and I found it soothing if not vaguely suggestive of further bad news.

'Because?'

'Because there is a distinct possibility he will never come back from this.' She said this so suddenly and with such conviction that I immediately lost my temper.

'What are you trying to say?'

'Jamie, think about this. We have no idea how or when Max will return.' She looked at me desperately. 'We don't even know where the Seeth lived, you know yourself the distances involved – even if all this goes to plan, I mean the Seeth plan, let alone ours, none of us may live long enough to see Max return.'

'But –' all the points were utterly valid. In the clear light of day the idea that Max would be contained within some sort of biogenic pencil case and then returned to us made absolutely no sense whatsoever.

'But he said the Seeth would save him! He told us himself!' Anger, fear, love swelled up in my chest. How weird, how horrible would that be to see Max in say fifty years time, still about the same age as he is now, but without any memories of his previous life as a human? To see Max and for him to not recognise me at all? 'They wouldn't do that!' I felt water pricking behind my eyes again, distorting my voice. My entire emotional response to everything now seemed to involve bawling. 'It's about faith.' I said pathetically, borrowing Max's word. The word was so small, so inadequate. It meant absolutely nothing to me.

'I know. No one has more faith in Max than I do, Jamie. But I just want *you* to be prepared.'

'Ok, I will!' I drained the mug and stood up quickly to get dressed. Margaret stood as well and went over to the window to give me some privacy and to collect her thoughts.

'What's in the bag? I won't be gone that long, surely?' I tried to sound calm, humorous, anything but angry.

'I've collected some medical supplies for you to take along.' She walked over and retrieved the small satchel. 'There are some syringes, and some vials of morphine. I have also included some sedatives, some anti-nausea shots, and some drugs in case Max goes into some sort of allergenic shock.'

'Shock?'

'Yes. Any sudden changes to Max's physiology might send him into respiratory failure or cardiac shock. I'm sure the Seeth anticipated these changes, but I think it's best to be prepared for the worst. If he starts showing any distress, especially difficulties in breathing, inject him with the red phials: they're clearly marked. Make sure the syringe has no air in, and inject directly into the vein. Do you want me to show you?'

'No, it's fine.' Max had plenty of veins in his arms. I stared at them most days. Yet the sudden idea that I would fail Max terrified me, more than Davies and the alien stuff.

'Ok. The morphine is in the blue phials. Max's changes may cause considerable pain. Administer it with caution. See how much pain he can bear, but it will give him some relief and it will help him sleep if he has to. There is some other stuff here, antibiotics, some stimulants, mostly tablet form.'

'Where did you get this stuff from?'

'Katherine, mostly, but it's amazing what you can get on the internet these days! As I said earlier, we have been planning for every possible contingency. And Jamie, for God's sake, be discreet about all this – if your bags get searched they'll think you're a drug addict!'

I put my arms around her, suddenly, impulsively. I was surprised to find that I was taller than her. 'Sorry for being a bitch,' I said quietly. 'I know you are only trying to help me – I know you've lived with all this longer than I have. It's just that Max has been in my head for ages now – I mean – *seriously in my head*, like nothing else I've known. Explaining it to myself has been bad enough.'

'I know, Jamie. I know,' she whispered this, caressing my head. 'I've known for the last few years and I've tried to talk about it with you – but you've been very evasive, hard to crack!' I felt her smiling on my shoulder. I suddenly felt insubstantial, transparent, no longer part of a world that operated properly and safely, a world devoid of aliens, a place in which my mother knew everything and where pain could be consoled.

'Why did they choose him? Why Max?'

She hugged me tighter, closer.

'I have no idea. Clearly, the Seeth hoped to find a compatible genome here; they were from Earth after all. But we know so little of Max really – I mean – in terms of his family. Max's biological mother never cooperated in telling us about his early life. We never found any evidence of his father. Julian and I have considered – *let's see* – east European, southern European, native North American, central Asia. I tried to find any ancestral markers in his genes, but nothing – it's complex. Julian once argued that Max was of Inuit descent!' She laughed to herself. I didn't know the word. I looked at her blankly.

'It's a far northern grouping of native North Americans –' she laughed again at my expression.

'It was a joke, Jamie – Max's complexion is too dark and he's too tall.' She smiled to herself and lifted her head from my shoulder. 'And you think that you're obsessed with him, Jamie! Julian and I used to make up a new ancestral lineage for him all the time! We used to have an Ancestor of the Month spot! Seriously!' She smiled and we walked with the bags out and towards the stairs.

'Perhaps he had an alien for a father?' I suggested whimsically. As we reached the bottom of the stairs, my mother drew out a purse and started removing bank notes. Quite a lot of them.

'Mum – can I ask you something about Professor Grey?' She stopped, mid count. I was pretty sure my dad was out at work. I couldn't hear the TV, or the shower.

'Of course.'

'Are you having an affair with him?'

She hesitated and then resumed counting but for a moment her expression was pained. 'No. No I'm not, Jamie. Has Max ever suggested that?' For a moment her disappointment was painfully obvious, even to me. Before I could answer, we were startled by a brief, idiosyncratic rattle of the letterbox. It was eight forty five. Margaret brushed past me and opened the door and the house flooded with oblique, brilliant sunlight. The sheer dazzle hurt my eyes and then I was aware of Max standing a few feet away, a smudge of darkness, holding a bag over his shoulder. For one fanciful moment it seemed that the light came from within him. He was wearing a blue hoodie and blue canvas jeans. His hair was wet, chaotic as ever, jet-black, a rushed shower. Max looked at me with clear wide awake eyes as if this was just another school day.

'Hey –' he looked at me, at the bags, then at Margaret. 'Ready?'

'Ready.'

He stood back, away from the door, the two white corded ear pieces to his iPod dangling from his neck. I walked out alongside him, still faking normality. Margaret gathered herself with some effort. She seemed suddenly very emotional now.

'Have a safe journey, Max.' she went to say something else but stopped, breathing in deeply.

'Margaret I know, it's fine. Everything will be fine.'

She wouldn't look at Max but instead said to me quickly, 'Call Lockwood on the way to the station? If he's out then I guess you just head to Leicester and then the wood?'

'Sure.' I felt the card with his phone number curled up in the back pocket of my jeans.

I had expected her to kiss me, kiss Max, but instead Margaret clicked the front door too and was gone, quickly, urgently, as if she could contain herself no longer. When I turned Max was at the gate, waiting for me.

Chapter 16

I tried to call Lockwood twice; the first time he was engaged and the second went eventually to his answer phone. We walked slowly and indirectly towards the train station as if we were tourists circumnavigating Oxford, taking in the sights. A third call however, from the proximity of a butcher's shop in the Covered Market proved successful if not a little ominous. Initially Lockwood was very uncommunicative and took some persuading I was who I said I was. After a weird question and answer session, he started to agree to meet us at the train station at 3 p.m. but there was still an odd tone of hostility. Max hovered about, impatient, constantly on the point of taking the receiver of me, mouthing instructions.

'Three p.m.'s too late man! He needs to meet us off the train! Tell him to get to us earlier!'

I made a semi-cross shrug, missing something Lockwood was saying. Max crowded in behind me to take the phone, but Lockwood had disconnected the call.

'He sounded weird, afraid. Who is this guy again?'

Max nuzzled into my back as he put the receiver down. I thought he would be angry but he was smiling.

'He's the guy who found us in 1993. The guy who rang Dad about Jonathan, last year.'

'He sounded scared,' I said again. Max had wandered off and was looking up at a skinned bloodless carcass hanging from a hook. 'Come on, let's go.'

Max bought train tickets with cash and as we waited, we tried to look as inconspicuous as possible. We even went through an elaborate charade of sitting on the London platform and making sure we were spotted by at least several CCTV monitors doing so. We got so engrossed in this ruse that we almost missed the Birmingham train. I hated trains and Max of course knew this. He managed to get me a good seat on the end of the row and near the door as if I was some nascent OCD patient and he was my principal carer. I tried to remind myself that I was looking *after* Max. I thought about my mother's anxieties earlier, her reluctance: perhaps she thought I would be a liability to Max, actually slow him down? Max took a window seat and wedged himself in between the table and the wall, knees up. A middle-aged man looked at us rather irritably, especially as Max piled in, folding up his long limbs like some sort of collapsible chair. Then he scowled when Max produced a mobile phone and glared at a sign – stuck on the window – forbidding their use. Max had smiled at him, apologetically, telling him that the phone was off. He even showed him the switch. Most kids would look patronising and cocky doing this, Max looked like he was being especially helpful. The man had snorted and resumed some crossword puzzle on the back of his paper but within half and hour Max was helping him with the clues and the man was telling Max about his job, his wife, his hobbies – *Jesus*.

I sat, moody and on edge, worried about the carriage getting too crowded, worried that I had left my peak flow meter at home and that I had no inhaler, worried that Max was too visible, *too* Max like. We were supposed to be travelling *incognito*, anonymous. And all the time the alien shit was rattling around my head. Once out into open country I felt myself beginning to relax slightly. I kept an eye on my luggage, especially the satchel, anxious that the needles would somehow announce themselves, or knowing my luck, fall out everywhere. Then my mind wandered to where Jonathan was and whether he had met this American dude? Had he got the device yet? I was intrigued by Jonathan now: the idea of what he was and what he had been doing over the years, shadowing Max, waiting; well it sort of intrigued me. At one stage Max's new found friend got stuck on a clue. Max leaned forward, and tresses of hair slipped down over his face. He looked hot, his cheeks glowing slightly with sweat. I saw the man look up from the newspaper and stare at Max's forehead intently as Max read the clue again to himself. Something about the crow family. When Max sat up I was shocked to see that the dark mottling effect around his hairline was *very distinct* now and beginning to follow the line of his cheek bones. I disguised my shock well, and Max was still preoccupied helping: it did look, for the moment at least, like some weirdo neko style tattooing. I wondered what would happen if Max suddenly changed into an alien-hybrid in broad daylight? Was the process likely to be that sudden? Was there some sense in which he controlled it? The thought started me panicking again, my hands sweaty and hot.

When we changed at Birmingham for the Leicester train I told Max to fudge his hair up at the front, but the extent of the changes to his face were shocking. I had the distinct impression that everyone on the entire train would be able to identify him perfectly and in great detail. The Leicester train was some hideously small sprinter completely packed with commuters, all in passive cattle mode. Had I been on my own I simply wouldn't have got on it but Max pushed me gently forward and stood close to me, holding onto an overhead support, our bags around us as we swayed through some weird sounding stations – Water Orton being the weirdest. The ticket collector weaved his way past us after calling me a *duck*. Max shrugged.

'A local form of greeting, a generic term for a commuter?' he whispered, his mouth close to my ear. The press of people was useful in actually hiding Max, for once. He seemed self conscious now, his head often down, looking at the floor. The heat was appalling and there seemed to be no air. Max endured the discomfort in silence but I could see wide even patches of damp spreading under his arms into the fabric of the hoodie. We didn't speak much – a few mouthed questions, nods. At one stage, confronted with another uncomfortable surge of passengers, one yielding a bike, I fought off a serious panic attack. I felt Max's free hand touch mine.

'It's ok – you don't need your inhaler – you've never used it Jamie. It's a prop.' he said, in full third parent voice. The panic ebbed away. We got into Leicester just before 1 p.m. When we switched our phones on we both had several messages and missed calls from Zoë, one from Julian and one from my mother. Max texted back, lying about our destination again and I texted my mother saying we were still travelling. Before we left the platform we went into the station toilets and both changed. It seemed rather pointless, since we had probably been filmed going in and then coming out. Max scrunched his hair about, and washed his face. I saw him looking at his markings in the mirror with interest.

'They look sort of Buddhist or something?'

'How do you feel?'

He turned to look at me, his face dripping with water, his eyes intensely blue-green now, almost jewelled.

'I feel fine!'

We walked out into the main station forecourt and I got my first sight of Leicester – anonymous, a sort of high street that could have been anywhere, red brick Victorian, un-exotic. I thought we looked conspicuous, not enough luggage for tourists, too clean to be serious travellers, although Max might pass for an Italian. Despite the seemingly endless stop and starting of the trains we were early, with two long hours to kill. For a while we wandered about the taxi stands watching people coming and going and then we went slightly further, crossing the main road and eventually settling down outside what appeared to be a Museum. I kept looking at Max and asking him if he was alright in a way that clearly started to annoy him.

'Jamie, ease up. I'm fine – really – if not you'll be the first to know! We'll sit here until nearer the time,' he gestured towards a row of benches clustered around a disused and partly vandalised fountain. 'We're less exposed here, less obvious.'

I peeled my T shirt off and lay back in the heat.

'What do you know of this guy Lockwood, Max?'

He glanced at my torso, a look devoid of sentiment or interest other than the mechanics of my workout: I saw it in his face. It was the look of an engine enthusiast seeing a new car, checking it out, seeing it like one sees a spreadsheet.

'Not a lot. I was about six when he found me. Jonathan knows more about him, having met up with him last year in the wood. He's a dairy farmer, or was one, he must be in his late fifties, early sixties but I'm not sure. He saw the ship arrive that night – saw it and went out to look.'

He leaned forward, unzipped his bag and took out a bottle of water and then he asked. 'What are you doing for your shoulders?'

In the context of what was happening to Max the remark seemed almost comically sane yet one look at him showed that it was genuine. I confessed to doing chin ups at home. My dad had bought some contraption and had it downstairs over the kitchen doorframe. Margaret had protested because it had marked the plaster and now he had it up in the shed.

'Cool! They've come on really well,' said Max appreciatively. 'It's not fair really, having a gym Dad. Can you imagine Julian doing chin ups!'

I couldn't actually. I had a bizarre image of him doing them wearing his tweeds, with his brown brogues moving up and down like a pendulum.

'Not really. But can you imagine my father giving a lecture?'

Max snorted a sort of laugh and passed me the water bottle. He looked at my chest again, then up at the sun.

'You'll burn, man.'

The soft drone of traffic from the road was hypnotic, lazy. I felt incredibly and helplessly sleepy, thick now like an illness. My head kept falling forward in sudden exaggerated jerks. After defying Max's common sense for a few minutes I put my shirt back on and we changed benches, backing up into some shade. No one spoke. Max assumed a classic pose from his pre-alien days when all was well in my world: sitting back, head slightly raised, seemingly doing nothing, like a PC in rest mode. We must have sat like this for a twenty, thirty minutes. Eventually, driven on by boredom and hunger we found a *Subway* sandwich shop. Max's interest in the material world revived with the smell of food. He ordered so much stuff that I saw the guy behind the counter look outside to see if some coach party had mysteriously arrived, unannounced. We sat around a small metal table and I started to laugh.

'What?'

'Nothing – it's like we're on holiday – Jesus!'

Max smiled at me and I felt a suitable moment had arrived to apologise, to explain, even to say goodbye.

'Max I am so sorry about the Jonathan *thing*, and the tears and melodrama, and –'

'It's me who should be apologising to you, Jamie. Really. I never wanted to lie to you and sneak about. I mean there was enough sneaking about going on, what with Dad and Margaret plotting and stealing my hair!'

'Your hair?'

'Long story – and we all know I have enough to go about. But if it wasn't dad and Margaret, it was Sally and Louis, or the Americans, or for a time Jonathan! He was actually the most successful sneak of all!' he laughed to himself. 'You may be surprised to know that Jonathan suggested I told you everything, just after Christmas.'

'He did?'

'Yeah.' Max started demolishing a large slab of sandwich with remarkable ferocity. 'He watched you watching me in hospital and thought you were clearly cool and sufficiently –' he hesitated – 'Loyal.'

Max chewed contemplatively.

'How's your Seeth companion, Max, I mean, your *inner* alien?'

I frowned saying this. It was the first time we had spoken about aliens openly since the summit in the kitchen, and it felt odd, almost humorous, as if we were playing a game or something: Max the make believe half alien. Max laughed and spat lettuce onto the table.

'Sorry! Jamie don't choke me and end us both! She's fine – she's deep down and far away at the moment.'

'A she? And she's really pregnant?' I looked hard at the intricate patterns traced on Max's cheek bones. I still envisaged the Seeth like a parasite, something physical inside, waking up, taking over, something monstrous. I shivered. Max – clearly and distressingly attached to my mind like a limpet, shook his head despite the fact I had not spoken at all and said, after he had swallowed magnificently,

'It's not *like that*, Jamie. I am conscious of what the Seeth are doing to me, and the pregnancy is well, sort of metaphorical?'

'Max will you get out of my fucking head!'

We both laughed, a bit too loudly, nervously. I touched his arm, vaguely self conscious of doing so. Or was it a caress? Max took my hand in his, elbow to elbow as if we were going to arm wrestle.

'This *could* all end incredibly badly, Jamie,' he said simply.

It was the first piece of serious doubt that Max had expressed. It surprised me.

'Do you know that, Max? Is there something you should tell me, something you felt you couldn't tell me in front of your dad and my mother?'

'No, not at all, but getting the device back is obviously a gamble, and if it fails I will be lost forever.'

'Even if it works Max, you will be lost – I mean – how long will it take to return you – how far away do the Seeth live?'

We sat together in silence, both mulling over the risk of failure.

'I have no idea. It is all so vague, something unknown, *remembered*. I think they migrated somewhere close to *Tau Ceti*.'

The name meant nothing to me.

'A star?'

Max nodded. The conversation seemed quite usual.

'In the constellation of Cetus, the Whale. Look I am convinced it will work Jamie, and as for waiting – I want you to live your life, Jamie, find someone special, you know what I'm saying.' He sounded whimsical. I felt as if I had literally been knifed through the stomach. A woman on a nearby table looked at our hands together, and then down at our bags.

'*Max –*'

'And I want you to do something for me. I want you to promise me that if I don't come back soon you'll look after my father, that you will console him, and that you will care for Jonathan as much as you can.'

'*Please –*'

'Promise me, Jamie.'

I was too exhausted to crack up again. Strange as it seemed each wave of grief was less chilling than the last, the gloom more bearable as if I had never been happy, never free of the anxiety of losing Max. I wondered if this feeling would ever leave me now. I had the sensation perhaps of a man drowning, sinking slowly into great depths, away from the sun, dying gracefully, lazily rotating, down, down into a cold bleak space without hope or air.

'Of course I'll do that – but how can I console him? What am I to do?' Who would console me?

'And I want you to speak with Zoë; go through the letter with her,' Max said, ignoring my remark.

'Telling her everything? I mean – the full version?'

'Yeah.'

'Where's the letter?'

'It's in my bedroom next to my PC. Next to the one I wrote to you.'

He removed his hand from mine and resumed eating. I sat staring at him as if I was determined to recall him, every last detail and mannerism, before he left. Before he completed his change, before he became someone I didn't recognise.

'Did you have time to speak with your dad before we left, Max?' It was almost two thirty. My head hurt with the heat.

'I did. Did you speak with Margaret?'

'Yeah – she was ok.' I said evasively. 'She told me I needed to be ready for things as well, I mean for things ending badly. Ready for you to change and accept it, I guess, and for you to not come back. She mentioned that as well.'

Max looked at me knowingly. 'Your mother is smart Jamie, I mean really smart. I love her loads. Dad was *really* upset.' He sounded troubled, as if the memory of it upset him still. 'It took me some time to calm him down. He has some really heavy emotional shit bottled up inside him. He felt he had failed me, let me down; placed me needlessly in danger. He blamed himself about the device, about not following up earlier clues as to its existence and its purpose. It all came gushing out – a huge unsorted confession. There is so much guilt in his life, Jamie: it's amazing he can function at all! Guilt over Sally, over me, over Jonathan. I never realised what an emotional man he is!' Max frowned darkly. Then he added, softly, seriously, 'I never realised how much I loved him.'

'You told him, though?' I said, urgently.

'Of course I did. He wanted my forgiveness, for adopting me, for not adopting Jonathan, for waiting, for not being cleverer – it was *crazy*!' I wasn't used to Max talking like this. These kinds of conversations were new, the proximity, the sense of solidarity. The Max effect, the sense that there was a minute, unobservable, semi-permeable membrane between Max and the world had gone since last night and Max was shockingly, vividly revealed to me.

'How did you leave it with him?'

'Badly. Saying goodbye to him, to you, it's the hardest thing anyone can do Jamie in the entire world. It's a sort of death.'

We returned briefly to the benches and the broken, rubbish filled fountain. At one stage, borderline insane from waiting I walked across to the museum entrance but it was closed for refurbishment. It looked sad and abandoned like an old church, with its classical portico and pillars peeling in the heat. I stared through the glass doors into a wide dimly lit reception area and a deserted help desk. Behind it, grey with distance and distorted as if under water, I could see a large oil painting of a youth on a winged horse. It covered the entire wall and was mounted in a massive gilt frame. I could see that something dangled down by the animal's head, a bag or a sack, dripping with blood. The image distressed me. I walked back and sat next to Max, dozing in the heat. Finally, as three o'clock finally approached, we wandered back to the station. As we walked into the main forecourt I realised that neither Max nor I probably knew what Lockwood looked like. Perhaps Max would sense him? We hung about, anxious, feeling slightly illicit, watching people carefully.

I stood next to Max, suspicious that he was taller than I could remember. Sensing my growing anxiety Max reassured me that we would wait until dusk and then go to the wood ourselves. When I protested that we had no idea where it was he calmly produced a map from his bag and told me to relax. I scanned over the ordinance survey while Max basically lurked about in *ninja* mode. For the first time I wished I actually smoked, so I could fuss with something, play with my hands, look distracted. I stared at the wood. The location was relatively close, about nine miles to the north, marked out with a small band of green shading in an oddly empty landscape. I folded and refolded the map and began to entertain dark and worrying scenarios that Julian and my mother had been arrested and that Jonathan had been snatched off to the US. And how much longer would Max hold his current physical form? The banding was very visible now.

'Jamie stop worrying – he'll turn up.'

'Max the mind reading trick is really beginning to get on my nerves!'

'Sorry. It's becoming a habit.'

By 3:20, there was no sign of anyone who could reasonably be Lockwood; a man on a street cleaning device whirled by, a gaggle of youths, Sikhs in brilliant vivid turbans. Suddenly Max complained of feeling sick.

'Like unwell or as in about to throw?'

'As in about to throw,' he said quietly and then with unusual calm he left me with the bags and went into the toilets. Helplessly I watched him go and as I did I noticed two police cars pull up alongside the taxi rank. Several officers jumped out and walked urgently towards the ticket office and the platforms. I noticed, almost casually, that they were armed. I tensed up, looking down trying to merge into the wall. I was standing right in front of them. Max re-appeared looking pale, his face dipping with water. I walked over towards him, struggling with the bags. As he leaned down to help I caught a strong smell, something metallic, like the smell of rust.

'Max something's up –'

'Take your time, don't panic, look curious – look at them!'

There was the sound of another vehicle drawing up, a diesel engine rattling and then running ahead before cutting out. I glanced up to see a large man with a reddish white beard and sunglasses step out of a blue van and scan the station carefully.

'Daniel – thank fuck!' said Max under his breath, swinging up his bag instinctively. 'Don't run, Jamie.'

'How can you be sure –' but Max was already walking briskly towards him.

I glanced at the man again. He wore a green African

print shirt that was too young for him over faded blue jeans. He lifted up his shades and saw Max closing in on him. I saw the look of surprise on his face, as if he momentarily thought that Max was about to mug him but I realised it was the intuitive revelation of Max's identity. He seemed to stagger back slightly.

'Good God!' his voice carried.

'Not quite–'

To my surprise they embraced clumsily, Max towering over him. He looked at me as I approached and extended a large pink hand quickly and efficiently.

'Jamie? Good to meet you. Sorry about being *uber* cautious on the phone. Come on,' he took one of my bags. 'Sorry I'm late but there are police and army units everywhere. The traffic is chaotic!' he turned and briskly walked back to the van. Following, I climbed into the driver's seat, Max behind me, his head out of the window like a dog.

'Army?' I stammered, shocked, as if the concept was new to me. Max wiped his face with both hands and said calmly 'I'm not feeling so good, Daniel. Let's get away from here.' Daniel started the engine and drove slowly towards the exit. I could see that Max was sweating and I could smell him now. Daniel kept looking at Max out of the corner of his sunglasses. From behind us there came a sudden flash of blue lights and one of the police cars pulled around us quickly, wailing off into the traffic.

'Just relax,' said Max quietly, sitting back away from the windscreen. 'Just drive normally.'

I started rummaging in my bag looking for anti-nausea shots, my hands shaking slightly. There were no further police sirens and Daniel sighed with relief.

'Listen lads. I spoke with Julian briefly, on his mobile – he'd just come back from seeing DeMarr.' We had suddenly, rather inexplicably, turned off the main drag and were driving through rows of small red brick terraces.

'How was he?' Max asked, resting his face on the side of the door. We passed a mosque and several small playing fields. Daniel did another right hand turn. His face – large, fleshy, but not unfriendly, was tense.

'Ok, but he warned me that he was probably about to be arrested and that the police are going to issue some sort of fake virus story, announcing that you are highly infectious with the aim of detaining you quickly. Given the number of road blocks I've seen already it looks like they have already started!'

Max didn't react at first but leaned away from me with his eyes closed. 'Shit,' he said after a pause.

'A virus?' my voice sounded like I had swallowed helium. 'But I thought Davies wanted us to get to the wood?'

'Can you get back to the farm, Daniel?' Max asked, ignoring me, ignoring my tone.

'It depends. There is a possibility that they might evacuate several villages – we'll have to play it by ear.' Daniel looked anxiously at Max again. I knew immediately from the hesitant, troubled glance that Julian had told him everything about Max's final journey, the purpose of the experiment, the risk of some rapid shocking physical change. I imagined Julian speaking rapidly, a final urgent coda before his own detention. Max suddenly gripped my knee tightly and painfully.

'Daniel you'll have to pull over a minute.'

'Sure –'

He eased the van into a bus pull in and Max vomited violently but precisely through the half opened door down onto the pavement. I scrambled to get some water and Daniel managed to produce a box of battered, dusty tissues from under the dashboard. Max retched some more and then brought his head back, taking the tissues blindly out of Lockwood's hands. When Max turned to me I was holding a needle and he looked dutifully surprised.

'Where the fuck did you get that from?'

'My enterprising mother – it's an anti-nausea shot. Roll up your sleeve.'

'Guys be discreet.' Daniel was indicating to pull out into moving traffic again. God knows what this must have looked like to people in traffic. We have evidently pulled over for someone to be sick. Max had left a vivid liquid bloom on the curb stones.

'I can't inject him while you're moving.'

'Do you know how to use that?' said Max suspiciously.

'Yes.'

Daniel drove on for a bit until we came to a row of shops with metered parking spaces stacked at angles to the pavement. We pulled in but left the motor running. The phials were pre-measured thank God so all I had to do was break the seal and stab. I aimed at Max's vein in the crook of his arm with more skill than I had imagined. When I finished a red-black droplet of blood welled up like a tear. It no longer looked human at all, but thick, resinous, like oil. Again there came the strange heavy smell.

'Press this down and keep it there for a bit – ok Daniel – let's go!' It must have been adrenalin and terror but I seemed no longer scared at all; as if I injected Max all the time.

'Jamie you're awesome,' said Max 'but that really, really hurt!'

Daniel drove on and slowly the city thinned out as we moved into the suburbs. Max appeared to recover slightly and to doze, his head occasionally falling onto my shoulder and his hair in my neck and cheek. Daniel asked me a few random questions about school, small talk as he made good our escape, talk about my mother and weirdly about DeMarr. After a while expanses of dry dusty fields opened up between large prosperous houses and suddenly we were driving through open country.

'We haven't got far to go now.'

'And what do we do when we get to the farm? Wait?'

Max seemed asleep, his warmth draped on one side of me like a blanket.

'Yeah – the rest is up to Jonathan.' Daniel glanced at me cautiously, his attention distracted, and then we both heard the sound of sirens coming up from behind us. Max snapped to attention, his face glowing with sweat. A fleet of unmarked white cars, escorted by two police outriders, quickly overtook us.

'Don't accelerate, Daniel. Just keep driving,' Max said, his voice thick. He put a hand to his forehead and started to massage his temples.

'This looks really bad!' I muttered. We were approaching a cross roads littered with army jeeps and police. 'You ok, Max?'

Daniel started to indicate for a right turn and slowed down but as the cross roads loomed up, dense with soldiers, it was clear that the route had been closed. Two men in uniform waved us away with an air of boredom.

'Shit! They've sealed the Desford turn.' Daniel swore under his breath. He speeded up carefully, and continued straight on into open country.

'What now?' Max looked into the centre mirror.

'They might not have sealed off all the roads yet.'

'Yeah? You think?' I sounded both scared and appalled. Max was running a temperature. I could feel the heat radiating off him into my shoulder now, scalding hot.

'We'll soon be on my land Jamie, if that's of any comfort! We might have to make the rest of the trip on foot.'

The road snaked and rolled through wide open fields and eventually we turned right again, onto a minor road towards a place signed as Peckleton. There were no apparent diversions but my relief was extremely short lived.

'Guys I can't *see*,' said Max. His voice was tense, barely controlled.

I twisted around. 'What?'

Max was shielding his eyes with his hand as if he had lost something on the floor, his head down, searching,

'Jamie I'm blind!' the panic in his voice tore through me.

'Hold it, hold it, let me look – take your hand away!'

'Do you want me to stop again?' Daniel asked. He was close to panic now as well, trying to keep his eyes on the road, to see Max, to watch for signs of pursuit.

'No, no – keep going.' I peeled Max's hand away and angled his face so I could look at his eyes. They were now completely different, the irises elongated and narrowed. They were reptilian and shockingly blue, silvered as they turned and swivelled about by what appeared to be an additional eyelid rapidly closing and opening. The eyes were no longer Max's. They belonged to something else, the Seeth? Was it – *she* – looking at me? That thought really upset me. I almost lost it. I tried to feel calm, to radiate assurance.

'Can you see anything? Shapes? Light?'

'Nothing. It's complete blackness!'

Instinctively I brushed his face. 'Max it's ok, try and stay calm. The blindness is probably temporary or something.' I stroked his face again and rested my hand on his cheek. It was clammy and I could feel a trace of stubble against my palm, gritty like grains of sand.

Max nodded, breathing deeply and evenly. 'Ok, ok.'

I was aware that we had stopped and that Daniel was looking anxiously about him. To one side of us were a few houses and then a junction with another ROAD CLOSED sign stuck in the middle and weighted down with sandbags. Nonetheless the place seemed deserted. It must have been about 5 o'clock, the heat oppressive still but slowly moderating towards evening.

'Shit!' said Daniel, banging his palm on the hub of the steering wheel. 'Max can you walk?' He unfastened his seat belt and clambered down out of the van.

'I think so – where are we? What's wrong?'

'They've blocked the turn into Kirby Mallory. We're about two miles from my farm, between two small villages backing onto Newbold Verdon. We need to leave the van here. Two fields on, there is an abandoned cottage and barn – I use it to store stuff in. It's where Jonathan stayed when he came back last year. I'm going to take you both there and then try and find out what's going on.'

'Aren't we going to your farm now?' I sounded petulant, lost.

'It's too risky Jamie for now.' Daniel was standing by the side of the hedge. 'If they've sealed off Leicester Lane from the crossroads they will certainly have sealed off the approach to my farm – it virtually overlooks the wood.'

Daniel and I helped Max to his feet with some difficulty. He was hard to move; solid, long limbed and panicky, his blind face shockingly vulnerable. I left everything in the van except the medical supplies but then Daniel brought the holdall just in case the van was found and searched.

'Is it far, Daniel?' Max sounded tired, short of breath. I tried to recall my mother's guidelines about further injections, which colour coded drug did what, but I couldn't remember. By now I was literally drenched in sweat. We walked towards a sty that ran between thick hawthorn trees and then joined a path, rutted with heavy clay and baked hard as cement. The light was golden and heavy, angled low now through thick air fuzzed with high mowing grass. It felt completely surreal and yet as we walked I felt the sneaking recollection of my dream, running with Max, wolves behind us, closing in.

'What is it?' asked Max close to me. I was holding his

hand guiding him over the uneven ground.

'Nothing, just a weird sense of déjà vu.'

Daniel had drawn ahead of us and was looking about him as if he expected us to be arrested at any minute. He gestured us to move quickly up.

'Come on Max, mind the ground here –' the high grass swished and slashed about our jeans filling the air with pollen and dust. It was beautiful and yet scary, as if we were already dead. When I looked up Daniel was standing outside a low brick building, partly ruinous, with wide dark windows facing out from under a partially collapsed roof. The house was surrounded by a debris field of broken, mysterious looking machinery and stacks of blue bags like fertiliser. There was a strong smell of cow shit and damp, irreversible decay.

'Shit this is spooky.' I led Max into a sort of outhouse with a wide stone sink like a trough and lots of empty crates. Daniel laughed quietly. 'Yeah, it's a regular haunting! It was very Jonathan!'

'You own this?' I sat Max down. He was shivering now, hugging himself, rubbing his shoulders. It was hard to look at him, to control myself. I rubbed his shoulders hard as if we were in deep mid-winter. His teeth were chattering.

'Yes. It was once a tenant farmhouse but it's been empty for years.' Lockwood walked towards Max and took his hand. It was a surprisingly intimate gesture for a man who was almost a complete stranger, as if Daniel knew Max well. I saw Max smile.

'Daniel? What now?'

'I am going to double back another way into Peckleton and see if I can get some news. You two stay inside and keep down ok? If I don't return you can get to the wood yourselves, it's close now – about a mile and half to the north. You'll have to do the best you can.'

The implication that Daniel would not come back seriously scared me. Max seemed comatose, borderline delirious. He was muttering something to himself, almost in a different language.

'Ok young man.' Daniel patted my shoulder affectionately, a last attempt to reassure me. 'You can do this, Jamie. There's water in a mains tap in the next room but keep out of the house: the roof is unsafe and the floorboards liable to give way.' He stood up. 'Give me two hours. If I am not back by then something has happened and you're on your own.'

'Thanks Daniel,' Max said quietly at which Lockwood turned and walked to the back of the house and away into the surrounding fields. I watched him go and felt a sense of total despair. This time last night I was in my bedroom searching through Max's mother's homepage. A mere 24 hours later I was in a ruined house, Max ill and blind, his dad arrested and the surrounding countryside full of the police.

When I returned to Max he had pulled off his hoodie and was trying to take off his T-shirt, but it was covered in blood and reeking like oil.

'Shit, Max!' I scrambled over towards him, dragging the satchel with me and spilling some of the contents across the floor.

'It itches like mad, Jamie –' he paused as he felt the wet tacky blood. 'What's happening?'

'Don't pull at it like that!' I helped him peel off the T-shirt slowly, ripping it in places. His smell was thick and heavy, almost suffocating. I saw my hands were shaking and prayed to God he wouldn't feel them or mind sense my sheer terror. The light was still good outside but in the outhouse it was already becoming difficult to see.

'Hold it. Wait here. Don't move! There's rubble and crap all over the floor!' I picked up his hoodie and went through into the remains of what looked like a bathroom. I tried soaking the material in water to use as a sponge but in the end dropped it and, with difficulty, guided Max to the tap instead. He squatted down obediently, leaning against the wall like he'd been shot. Crouching next to him, I removed the final blooded shreds of material from his torso and then brushed his mane of hair away from his back. Immediately I could see the cause of the bleeding. The cartilage like intrusions along the shoulders and upper back had broken through the skin and were spreading out to form a crust of small diamond like plates scabby and oozing. The mottling effect was now dark and barred in broad zagging patterns down his back.

'Ok, ok – I see, I can see what's up.' I described it as best I could. I asked him if he was in pain and he said he couldn't breathe very well. I ran back to get the satchel but found I could no longer hold and read the labels because my hands were still shaking badly. 'Where the fuck is Daniel!'

'Jamie, try and look for some anti-inflammatory drugs?'

I moved towards the door where the light was stronger. Nothing made sense; the terms on the individual blister packs merged and bubbled and I realised I was crying soundlessly. I came across an anti-histamine spray.

'I can't find any Max!'

'Look for a pain killer, Ibuprofen will do.'

Even as he said the word, I saw it marked up on the back of a carton. I guided some into his hand and then fetched the bottle of water. He took the pills, rather a lot of them, choking them down but remained squatting. I tried to clean the blood off but the dabbing clearly hurt him and he pushed me away. When I persisted he suddenly and unpredictably grabbed me by the throat. He snarled and said something that made no sense, a noise; a sort of sharp brittle sound like glass breaking.

'Max, you're hurting me.' I tried to sound reasonable about this. Had it happened? Had Max gone?

He dropped me quickly and in shock and then suddenly said, 'Fuck Jamie what are you doing here? Thank fuck!'

I was gasping for air, holding my throat. He was clearly delirious now.

'I'm here – it's ok!'

Suddenly Max grabbed me but this time in a hard embrace. 'Where the fuck have you been! God I've missed you – how did you know to come here!'

I clung to him, lost, already grieving. His behaviour made no sense to me at all. Gradually his grip lessened and he seemed to calm down, to come to his senses. Then despite his best efforts, he began to doze. Eventually I guided him to where he could lie down, his back curled into an overturned table and his knees raised. We had no food, no real plan. He looked foetal like lying there, on the brink of his new birth.

'Can you see anything yet?' I asked eventually. I had assumed he was asleep but his eyes opened quickly.

'No, still nothing.'

I sat alongside him, my legs stretched out in front of me, stroking his hair away from his face. I felt like we'd survived some sudden and unprecedented disaster, a plane crash, the end of the world. When I removed my hand, he mumbled for me to continue. I snorted a laugh.

'What?'

'Nothing. Well, I was going to say I used to fantasize about this!'

To my relief Max laughed as well. He sounded almost normal, back to himself for a while at least. 'Yeah? Being in a ruined lean to with me blooded on the floor – God you're sick, Jamie!'

'No! You know what I mean. Running away with you, being with you. Living with you.' I felt myself hesitate but realised suddenly that this might be the last time I ever spoke to him.

'I *will* come back, Jamie,' he said softly, a mild rebuke.

'Max how? Light years, astronomical distance, even if you do come back Max – we might all be dead!'

'I know,' he said. The thought distressed him. 'But the Seeth came back, even in death! I'm sure there is a way here, some plan.'

I looked away, my anguish too real and intense to disguise. I realised that Max needed to believe he was coming back and so I tried to believe too. Sitting on the dirty floor of the outhouse, with the golden light fading into long fingers of cooling shade, I tried to imagine Max returning. He seemed to sleep again.

'I am so glad you're here,' said Max quietly, to himself, to the floor. I didn't say anything.

'How much longer do you think the transformation will take, Max?'

'Not long now.'

'Any word from Jonathan?'

Max shook his head. Outside a gaunt heavy silence lay over the fields. I checked the time on the mobile. Daniel was late. It was well past eight thirty now. There were no messages and although I was suddenly overwhelmed with a desire to text my mother, Julian, anyone, somehow I resisted. Max stirred himself, attentive, suddenly irritated, his head raised.

'What?'

'Listen?'

There was a heavy buzz of nothing. I frowned and then I heard a deep throbbing clatter briefly, louder and then dimming with distance.

'A helicopter!' I stood up, the sudden movement making me dizzy, and scrambled towards the front of the house. The noise of the helicopter came again, a lazy clap somewhere over the road. I walked outside, trying to keep inside the shadows of the house. The sky was a deep luminous blue, vast like an ocean.

'Jamie!'

Max's tone shocked me and I stumbled back towards

him. He was standing with his arms out but appeared to be looking at me intensely. His eyes were luminous and he looked frighteningly different.

'What is it?

'I can see! Oh shit, thank fuck, well I can see after a fashion!' I ignored the qualification and ran towards him.

'But the light,' Max added, 'the light is really painful!'

I looked about the dim interior bemused. I could hardly see now.

'Max there's a helicopter over the road where Daniel left the van. Perhaps they've found it?'

Max was looking at his hands and then looking about the room. 'Shit!'

'Max?'

'Jamie I can *see*! It's remarkable – it's like night vision or something – come here!'

I went over to him carefully. Stepping over boxes and rotten crates.

'Max we have to move!'

He took my hands and gently pulled me towards him. He looked at my face.

'God am I glad to see you! Every spot!' He towered over me, broad shouldered, naked from the waist up and with the plates on his body cleaner now and drier, hardened and decorated into brilliant black dots and dashes. He looked as if he was wearing armour. He was barely recognisable, still Max, but blurred and changing even as I looked.

'Night vision?'

Before Max could answer, the mobile buzzed. It made an extraordinarily loud noise and we both jumped. Max swung around to look at it on the floor next to the satchel and as he did so I saw his face and the top of his chest flush and glow with a sort of red tinge. I stepped back and the phone buzzed again loudly. We both looked at each other and then I bent down and snatched it up.

There was no caller ID.

'Hello?'

There was a whispery silence, remote and cold like the sound of water and then I could dimly make out Daniel's voice as if he was running through some sort of tunnel. The signal was poor.

'Jamie, Max is all over the news, photos, pictures of his dad, Oxford, the lot. It seems they initially thought you'd gone to London but you've already been identified by someone on the train –' his voice vanished and then wobbled back. 'I can't risk getting back to you and they'll trace the call. There are soldiers everywhere! You must go to the wood now!'

Chapter 17

I waited until Margaret and Jamie had left and then stood, tense and exhausted with my back to Max looking out of the window. I felt as if I was drowning, my chest and throat closed over with water. Only now in the final few hours did I see the entire, hopeless scenario. Even if the device was delivered to him in time I would still lose my son. I had none of his confidence in the Seeth and their ability to restore him. I also felt responsible for including Jamie, on a sort of whim, firstly by agreeing to see him at *Browns* and then propelling him into very real danger by suggesting he accompanied Max. It was obvious to me (and presumably Margaret) that he would go with Max to the bitter end. Whatever he felt for my son – and even given the fact that Max obviously had confided in him – it seemed reckless, if not rather callous of me. Margaret had been shocked. I had sensed it.

'Dad?'

I felt Max's gaze boring into the back of my neck. I stood for a while, trying to compose a face, an expression of calm before turning around to face him but I was paralysed both by the revelation of how much I loved my son and the fact he would be taken from me. When I looked at him he had to see hope; his own, the promise the Seeth had made to him.

'Julian?' He spoke slightly louder, more assertively.

I clenched my jaw and lifted my head slightly as if I was summoning the courage required to turn around and punch someone but before I could turn I felt Max's hands nudge carefully at each elbow and sneak around my waist, pulling me back into him, a beguiling, feminine gesture. Sally used to hold me like this, after an argument; it was her gesture of reconciliation, a sort of forgiveness. I looked down at two sunburned forearms.

'Say something. Anything.'

'What is there left to say? What a mess – placing you at risk – waiting for so long because part of me thought nothing was ever going to happen or that I had the answers! And now this – Jonathan at risk, Jamie –'

'They wanted to come!' he said. The timbre of his voice resonated through my shoulder like a struck cord, a deep bass. 'And there is nothing you could have done to stop them – even Jamie! Ok so you might have encouraged him! But he would have found out – he's been digging away at this for months! Come on, drop the doom and gloom, we both knew that this would happen one day.' He released me slowly. I turned and we embraced. I breathed in deeply, thinking of the wide open sky and the wet spring clays of that first journey, the white papery trees watchful, waiting, drawn out like a Greek chorus. I could feel the hard ridges of bone on Max's top shoulder against my cheek. The idea that he and the wood were one was absurd but for a moment very real.

'I have to tell you something.'

'Father?'

'When I adopted you – I did it because I was *angry*, I

was angry at DeMarr, angry at being excluded, *betrayed* by him. I was angry at Sally as well! I thought that if I had you close to me I could-' my voice faltered slightly, tears welling over my face. 'I could study you – and force Sally and the others to come to *me*.'

I lost my voice for a moment, I hid my face, wretched and self-hating. Max pressed his cheek against the top of my head.

'So you *did* adopt me as an instrument of your revenge!' He said, his voice odd, mischievous. I imagined him smiling, slowly at first, starting in his eyes. His tone of irony staunched my self-pity. I lifted my head away from him, appalled. Max's expression was iconic, indescribable. Had he known about *that*, as well, the conceit of my own fantasy? Professor Prospero?

'Come on!' he whispered, encouraging me like a child about to leave for their first day at school, to accept their first enormous responsibility, to step out into the world alone. 'Or should I call you the Duke of Milan?'

I groaned, shamed. 'Max!'

'I rather liked the Ariel metaphor!' and then he laughed, a soft bark. 'Look, being adopted by you was part of the plan, Dad. I'm not sure you had any agency at all. And why are you only telling me part of your story? The conceit, the anger? Tell me the other part? How you longed for a child, longed to feel you were not selfish and incapable of love, how you yearned to be whole and to feel. Tell me of the countless times you realised that adopting me was the most complete thing you ever did!'

'But I should have adopted Jonathan. I should have insisted, Max! Sally almost agreed – but then she hesitated I was so anxious to keep you I didn't push it – perhaps of all of us, he has suffered the most.'

'But he would still have suffered from the voices, and even if you had known about them, the end would have been the same. And Jonathan stays here – when this is over – you will have plenty of time to make it up to him.

He loves you, Julian, in his own angry way. You were the only person who cared for him! And you cared for me, and that is more important to him than life itself.'

'But what of the device? I first heard about that in 1993! Lockwood wrote to me at college Max, twelve years ago and I did nothing! I should have acted on the first rumour!'

'You did do something, you asked DeMarr, you asked Margaret – it's not your fault! For all their technological brilliance the experiment was random, for so advanced a race they were oddly impractical. And remember they destroyed themselves in the first place.' He spoke cryptically, like an oracle.

'You know that?'

'They tried to prolong their lives, to eradicate the telomeres in their genomes in order to live forever, to study the universe undisturbed by death but something went very wrong. And as for the device, you can hardly be blamed for ignoring it – so did Louis. It made no obvious sense. Brought to the wood after we had been taken into care? The experiment didn't even evolve the device until the second day after we had been found. Left in the mound, like a piece of rubbish, and poor Jonathan unable and unwilling to listen until he eventually got cleaned up from drugs and responded to the Seeth command! Whichever route we took, dad, the destination was always the same – as soon as the alien chromosomes took to my 22 and started their job!'

'Max without the device you are dead!'

'I've been dead already,' he said. 'Or as good as dead.'

'It doesn't give the Seeth the right –'

'They have every right,' Max interrupted quietly. 'Remember I would have been dead by my seventh birthday.'

I glanced at his face urgently. I saw the elegant banding in his hairline, beautifully drawn, like the mottling of a rare, ancient bird. I thought of the images in my dream, the youth with the dancing tattoos, a lizard language, brittle and dazzling.

'They don't own you, Max. Surely there was another way!'

Max looked up at the clock on the wall. It was past 7 a.m. 'Do you have a syringe in the house?'

I looked momentarily surprised but then realised he was referring to DeMarr.

'Yes, in my office.'

'Ok let me offer DeMarr some hope of salvation and then I am going to take a shower.'

I felt a shadow of a premonition fall between us, the stark and obvious realisation that I would never see him again.

'Max it will never work. He has not managed to isolate a cure in twelve years!'

Max moved his head quickly from side to side. 'You're such a rationalist – even now! Come on! Faith is about hope when there seems to be none! That's when faith matters – it's about believing when everything goes wrong!'

'Max I am a scientist, not a priest!'

Max smiled and flashed his eyes open, as if the two occupations were not so very different. The room was full of sunlight coming in from the hall and the front of the house. It was still, dazzling, like sunlight on water. Max walked silently and heavily up to my study and then, a grey plastic box in his hand, he returned quietly and offered me a broad muscled arm. I removed two phials of thick dark blood and left Max holding a small wad of cotton wool in the crook of his elbow.

'I hope he's worth it.'

I sat down at the kitchen table. I was so tired I literally closed my eyes and fell immediately into a light sleep; transparent about the edges, a shallow warm sea of unconsciousness in which I lay suspended face up towards the sun.

Typically it was Max who woke me. He crept into the kitchen and made his ubiquitous coffee with quiet efficiency. In my waking moments I was crass enough to think it was just another school day. He gently tweaked my ear and when I had managed to peel my eyelids back he stood in front of me, an indulgent look on his face as if I was in a nursing home and he was a surprise visitor.

'The time has come!' he said, in mock seriousness.

I breathed in deeply and then sighed. Stiffly I rose from the chair and saw at the foot of the stairs a holdall and a plastic bag.

'It's ok – really –' Max whispered, sensing my dread. 'And be nice to DeMarr. Remember that, even now, he wants to be your friend! And he wants your forgiveness.'

I walked with Max to the front door, trying to gather my thoughts, to dredge up all the important information he would need, dates, places, arrangements.

'Do you have the map?' I asked, looking at the bag.

'Yes.'

'Trust Daniel, Max. He will help you. I will try somehow to distract Davies for a while.'

I opened the front door and we walked out into a brilliant clear morning. For a moment we looked bashfully at each other. Max traced out something on my cheek with his right index finger, as if he was pulling away a hair, removing something. What was left in me to say? Max stooped down slightly and kissed my cheek, his raven black hair slanted over his eyes and then he turned with sudden decision, vanishing into the warm liquid light like the man in my dreams.

Once in my study, I looked about me like a captain preparing to abandon his ship. Most of the confidential material on Max had been destroyed. It had been in this very room, with Sally framed against the window, that we had made our pact to adopt him. It seemed light years away and yet, at the same time, bizarrely recent. I removed some personal items from the top drawer, a picture of Max, myself and Sally retrieved from Jonathan's secret stash, and finally Max's pebble. Taking a jacket from my bedroom I walked down the stairs and paused by Max's open door, the room still in soft darkness with the curtains un-drawn. Max had napped on top of the duvet. I could see his shape, the indentation in the pillow where his head had rested. The sight chilled me.

I walked down the Woodstock Road without seeing or feeling anything. It was a brilliant summer day, the air already warm and the sunlight glazing the house fronts and the full leafed trees that lined St Giles. I had been inattentive to the weather for so long, to the everyday life of the mundane and the usual. I walked past Magdalen church and towards Ship Street. I half expected to see Jonathan sauntering about, a magazine in his hand, looking defiantly into the face of fleeing pedestrians. Where was he now? Had the plan worked? As I approached the entrance to All Souls I recalled that my arrangements to meet Louis had been vague. I had been too cautious and then too shocked for precision. I stepped past the *College is Closed to the Public* sign, asked for Professor DeMarr and the porter, appearing to recognise me, looked up with the studied, immaculate indifference of his profession. DeMarr had not left. He had not ordered breakfast. I was advised, if not actually encouraged, to go and see if he was in his rooms.

I walked over worn steps and through chilled, mellow cloisters. On finding the right staircase, I knocked at DeMarr's door and waited, anxious. There was a stony, hollowed silence. I knocked again, more definitely but in a way that I hoped would not alarm him. There was a noise, a sort of shuffle and then Louis said in a sort of *whodunit* whisper;

'Yes?'

'It's me, Julian, I'm slightly early, sorry!' There was a pause, followed by a loud click and the door opened. To my surprise Louis was still in his dressing gown, a rather bizarre, floor length garment with golden rococo patterns on the collar and on the outside of large black cuffs. He looked stressed and unwell. He had evidently not had much sleep, either. The gown made him look like a priest or a Freemason.

'Thank the gods, Julian, come in, come in! I overslept. It's the pain killers, they knock me out. I was about to call the lodge and leave a message for you –' I walked in quickly, closing the door behind me. A suitcase, with some clothes half folded over the open lid, lay set out on the unmade bed.

'Did you speak with Max? Did he tell you anything?' DeMarr sounded breathless, rushed.

'He told me a great deal – but nothing which, in essence, we didn't know already.'

'And samples?' said DeMarr, his voice desperate but also filled with a sort of lust.

I brought out the phials from my jacket pocket. DeMarr took them carefully and went over to a small leather case.

'Good God, Julian. That's no way to treat something so precious!'

I sat on the end of DeMarr's bed. On a side table I could see a scattering of blister packs and pill bottles, the paraphernalia of a dying man. Despite the heat, the room felt chill.

'Max has gone,' I said and broke down without warning, a shocking and sudden rush of grief. My sobbing shook me and the bed.

DeMarr hobbled over to me, his hands clasped together in front of his chest, tutting to himself. He sat down next to me with difficulty, wincing from a pain in his abdomen. He put a hand on my shoulder, tentatively, as if he was unsure quite what to do.

'I am so sorry, Julian. Yet we both knew that this day would come. In our hearts we knew. Whatever wrong I have done you I am truly sorry for it. Have you spoken with Sally?'

I shook my head unable to speak, to move my mouth, to stop myself shaking.

He sighed wistfully and patted my knee. The irony of us being together at the end was not lost on either of us.

'We were right about the device, then?' he asked carefully and I nodded again. Eventually I took out a handkerchief and wiped my face like a patient with a fever.

'You look dreadful, Julian,' said Louis generously and turning to a cabinet produced a small hip flask. 'You need a drink.'

'Louis! It's not even 9 a.m.'

'Here! It's going to be a long day – brandy is such an effective beta blocker!' To my surprise I took a deep swig. 'Will you come to London with me?' Louis asked, gulping down the spirit and then screwing the cap back on the flask.

'No. I'll go to my office and wait there and...' I left the sentence unfinished. I presumed I would be detained or questioned sooner rather than later. Part of me was determined to simply drive to the midlands but it was futile. Max had gone.

'Very well, I suspect they will come for you first. If you'll forgive me I will pack my things and leave while it's still relatively quiet. As you know, neither James nor Samuel have much love for me. I tried calling Sally this morning myself, by the way, but couldn't raise her. I tried all her usual hideouts. She has been remote of late, angry with me, angry with Davies. She is up to something,' added Louis. He sounded troubled but his voice was full of admiration. I presumed Louis didn't know of her involvement with Jonathan, of his planned tryst with Davies. Louis sat for a while, twiddling his thumbs like a crafty school boy.

'I presume you know of the virus story? The plan to detain Max as a risk to the *vox populi*?'

'Yes. Sally told me last year, when she swapped the scan on Max's head. Do you think they'll really do it?'

Louis sighed at my obvious, irritating naivety. 'Of course, particularly if they're not sure where he is. I suspect Max has only just made it out in time.'

I stood up suddenly. 'You had better make a move Louis.' I paused, my eyes on the leather pouch containing Max's blood samples. 'What are you going to do with the blood sample? Retrace your earlier experiments?'

Louis stood up slowly and then tottered about, picking things up off the floor with difficulty. He seemed suddenly very old.

'I don't have time. I think I'll just inject myself with Max's serum and see what happens!'

'What! Are you mad! Max's blood is changing all the time. It's not even human any more judging by the colour and the consistency! You'll kill yourself!'

DeMarr laughed. 'That is rather the point, Julian! The proximity of death makes experiment ethics and safety rather moot!'

'It's madness, Louis!'

He tutted again, not unkindly. He shuffled into the bathroom and I heard random splashes of water and the sound of a faucet being turned. When he emerged he was wearing a crumpled linen suit the same colour as his face. 'Will you wait for him?' asked Louis, sitting down and hitching some socks on, grunting with the effort.

'I have no choice, Louis. How can I not wait? But what hope is there really?' I shrugged.

Louis looked up at me and said nothing. His face was

thoughtful and he appeared to ponder the question for some time. Once dressed and ready, I walked with him back to the Porter's Lodge and out onto the High where, to my surprise a car was waiting. At first I thought it was Davies but DeMarr smiled at the driver, a young man – perhaps in his mid-twenties – who climbed out and came gracefully to DeMarr's assistance.

'Good God, Louis – you have a chauffeur now?'

He grinned impishly at me. 'The term is rather anachronistic now, Julian. Anton is my PA. He is from Upper Silesia and speaks little or no English.'

Anton nodded to me as if his ignorance was a charade. I couldn't help smiling. My affection for Louis was suddenly sincere and heavy with sadness.

'Louis – take care. As for the treatment, just think about it. Is not conventional therapy a better bet?'

'Good God no. I may as well slit my own throat.' We shook hands and I saw that DeMarr was emotional too, his jaundiced face tight around the mouth and eyes.

'Max forgives you, incidentally. He told me to tell you.'

Louis sighed deeply and nodded. Anton assisted him into the back of the car and after a brief pause they drove off into the early morning traffic.

I walked back towards St Giles. I bought a newspaper and scanned it for my photo, a horror story of death and aliens, or a shot of Max in all his alien beauty but finding nothing I left it on a bench, crisp and un-read. I bought a croissant from a bakery at the top end of Little Clarendon Street although I was not particularly hungry. I sauntered down to Green College, my jacket over my shoulder. It was incredibly hot already. I felt entirely alone, abandoned, I hardly knew who I was any more. Somehow, instinctively, I reached my office where Lily Dear sat at my desk dealing with my emails and other administrative chores left to her ferocious competence.

'Professor, Mr Lockwood has been calling. He's called several times.' She peered over half-rimmed glasses at me questioningly. 'He says it's rather urgent.'

'Thank you, Lily. I can do this now – is there any post?'

She moved away from my computer, looking at me with some concern.

'Not yet. There's been some delay with the mail this morning.'

I walked to the wide high window and stood looking down over the quad. Not far from the entrance to the Observatory, I could see a small gaggle of men talking together. I recognised two – the College Warden and the senior porter. The other two looked official but strangely anonymous in their smart black suits and sharp clean cut faces, detectives, agents of some kind; possibly military personnel. I felt my pulse quicken. So soon? Lily Dear was asking me if I wanted anything doing, reminding me of an appointment later; the chairing of a committee on the use of college space.

'Thank you, Lily. That's fine – I have the agenda somewhere.'

'I retrieved it from the bin, Professor. You must have thrown it away by mistake.' She smiled secretively at me but I was distracted. She followed my gaze down and as she did, the Warden turned and looked up into the window, his face puzzled, anxious. Instinctively I stepped back.

'Is everything alright, Professor? Did you not sleep well?'

I had given no thought to my appearance.

'Not particularly. You know, the heat.'

She smiled distractedly and left through into her office. I placed my jacket over my desk and picked up the phone. I dialled Daniel's number but got the voice mail. I then tried his mobile which he answered immediately. I spoke quickly, telling him random bits of information, warning him of the virus cover story, assuring him Max was safe but also telling him who Max was. He seemed stunned and monosyllabic but to my immense relief ended by telling me he would do whatever he could for Max.

At 10:10 a.m. the warden telephoned me and asked me to come to see him. He sounded calm on the phone but when I arrived he was standing next to his desk with the two men I had spied out earlier. They greeted me affably and then courteously stepped outside into his secretary's office. The warden – a neurologist I had known for many years – offered me a seat.

'Julian, these people want you to go with them and discuss the 1993 committee.' His voice was heavy with questions. 'I thought all that business was over?'

'I think something has come up,' I said. I sounded almost whimsical.

'I see.' He looked at me quizzically. 'They say you have been involved in some sort of viral research? Is this true?'

'No. It isn't.'

'Good. I thought not. They're Americans,' he added with the soft intonation of someone who does not approve, 'are you in any trouble?'

'It depends, Warden. Not if I cooperate.'

'I see. Do you need a lawyer?' he asked with sudden gravity. The change of tone surprised me. He sounded almost afraid.

'I don't think a lawyer can do anything at this stage but thank you.'

The Warden looked up over my shoulder, a cloud of irritation darkened his face and I was aware that we were no longer alone in the room. The two men were standing behind me, one holding a small bag.

'We took the liberty Professor, of packing a small night bag for you,' one said rather defiantly. The young man spoke with a soft American accent, southern perhaps. I realised with a shock that the bag was indeed my own and that they must have been already to Farndon Road while I was with Louis.

'How very thoughtful.'

I have never been a conspiracy theorist, at least not in the conventional sense of the term. I had worked alongside people who were for instance convinced that the Americans never landed on the moon; that the US authorities faked the destruction of the World Trade Centre in 2001; or more generically (and appropriately) that governments had been working with aliens for decades. I never credited political institutions with the necessary skills to organise such things, the ability to keep them quiet or secret enough, or indeed marshal the institutional memory that requires them to sustain such lies. My life with Max had also convinced me that invariably, caught up in their own agendas, conspirators inevitably fell out and exposed each other anyway. As I was led away from the Warden's office I wondered vaguely if Louis too had been detained, whether Max had got to Leicester by now and whether Sally had succeeded in getting Jonathan to Davies. I crunched reassuringly across the gravel towards the main entrance of the College, my escort polite and oddly deferential. Outside on the pavement I was startled to see a gaggle of press already present and a great cannonade of cameras set off as if I were a celebrity or a notorious political prisoner. Vaguely nonplussed I gaped at several people as they all spoke at once, a cacophony of lies and misinformation: did I know where my son was hiding? How dangerous was the virus? Where had it originated from? Was there any truth to the story that someone had already died? I stepped forward blinking but one of my minders blocked me and with calm, quiet aggression pushed me towards a waiting car.

'You don't have to answer any of these questions now,' the man with my bag said. I was intrigued as to how he could be so polite and threatening at the same time. The press jeered and shouted, cameras held up high and fired off randomly.

'It's all lies!' I said loudly but my voice did not carry. 'There is no virus. No one is ill.' A hard neat shove to my lower back propelled me through the open car door. The two men climbed in as well, pushing me over to the offside window and we drove off smoothly towards the ring road.

We joined the M4 and headed towards the south east. No one spoke inside the car. We drove into central London and then crossed the Thames at Vauxhall. Eventually I was asked to wait in a sort of deserted warehouse not far from Battersea Dogs Home, an incongruous place filled with random furniture. I felt partly fear but also a dark sense of humour, as if I was in some sort of parody. I considered the possibility that they would just shoot me but thought, in my English way, that such things were impossible. The two Americans disappeared and then I was led into an isolation unit where I went through an elaborate, surprisingly polite, physical examination.

'This is preposterous and you all know it,' I said to two epidemiologists who took me down in a lift into a specially prepared, bizarrely expensive and very secret centre somewhere still on the Surrey side.

'Please co-operate with us, Professor Grey. This is a grave emergency,' said one with all the authenticity of someone who believes.

And yet all it took, of course, was one clever doubtful individual to text another, to speak to a journalist, to email someone, to check the evidence of a virus and to link it to the abductions, and the whole massive edifice of the LIE began to unravel. And of course Sally played a major part, and from a position within the government;

someone who was formidably respected if not even feared. In the two or three hours following my detention she more than paid me back for a decade of fornication and lies. She rang an independent news agency from the comfort of her own apartment, with a glass of wine in one hand, cell phone in the other. Then, slowly and deliberately, she called her friends and colleagues, serious experts who led solid and unadventurous lives but who knew what they were talking about, 'names' with authority throughout the scientific world. These quickly and efficiently spread the word that something was seriously amiss with the virus story, that something just didn't add up, that all of this linked to the children in 1993 and *aliens.* I found out the details later, of course, but it was a singular act of great courage. By 11 p.m. an American journalist (ironically perhaps) stated in a live interview that the British government were lying and that the lies went back to 1993, to the mysterious abduction of 24 children, to the John Radcliffe in Oxford and to my adoption of one Max Lennox Grey. There was also final and direct confirmation that a device of some kind had been found all along, hidden away and then sent over the Pond. By the time the government detained Sally – apologetically as it turned out and rather half heartedly – the hole in the lie was too big and too revealing, and it was peeling away the fabric of the government itself.

For a while, however, I was surrounded by people in plastic sheeting who clearly thought I was a monster. I was led into a quiet, dark room and left with a sort of airplane meal and a bottle of water. There was also a TV stuck to the wall, switched on but with no sound. I felt like Winston Smith in 1984. I worked hard on *not* thinking about Max, about where he was, whether he was even *Max* anymore, and where exactly Jonathan was as well. No one interrogated me or talked to me. I watched with a sort of morbid fascination images of my own life, of Max, of my home, of Sally, flash before the world and felt powerless to correct them. BBC 24 ran a banner saying 'GREY COOPERATES WITH W.H.O.' by which again I presumed they meant my wife. Several pictures of my son appeared and I toyed with a sort of folk fantasy of him at large, a beautiful bejewelled alien stranger hiding in woods and tapping on the windows of terrified villagers. It helped pass the time. Then, at about 1 a.m. there was a news flash that Louis DeMarr had been infected as well. I laughed to myself but felt his inclusion somehow sinister. Far from being the first victim of an alien virus, it was more likely that he had managed to give himself blood poisoning from his unorthodox use of Max's serum, or that the strain of the last few days had seriously affected his underlying condition. Then, at about 1.35 a.m., the TV went dead, judiciously switched off from outside or somehow disconnected. I should have taken that as a good omen but at the time it had a shocking finality about it as if everything was now over.

I sat for a while in the soft ambient light dozing and dreaming vividly of Daniel, of Max running across roofscapes like an MTV adaptation of *La Boheme*. I dreamed that Max was brought here, captured, his mission ruined, and jumped awake in horror to find DeSilva standing over me wearing one of his undertaker outfits. He did not wear protective clothing, not even a face mask. He smiled at me as if he was quite pleased to see me. He pulled up a chair and sat down, full of dark avuncular charm.

'Hello Julian.'

I was so tired – so stretched – so out of it – I laughed as if he had made a joke. DeSilva had the grace to smile slightly. I had not spoken to him in person since the day on which Max and Jonathan had been released. Between

1993 and 1999 we had corresponded as part of the committee's somewhat anonymous consultation process and although I had glimpsed him at the hospital in January, I had not looked at him closely. His hair was white now, and his face a pale, translucent walnut colour, worn black under his eyes into wide dark circles. He had always been thin but now he seemed positively skeletal. And yet he burned with a vitality that I could almost feel. I tried to stop smiling. I suspected it made me look senile.

'I am glad to see that you've retained your sense of humour,' he said eventually, puzzled by my reaction.

'Sorry, James. I appreciate it's entirely inappropriate but it's all I have left really. A sense of the absurd. I mean how much more absurd can this get!'

He scoffed slightly but remained silent.

'So what now? Have you detained Max? How many people have been infected by the virus?' My tone was suddenly bitter. With relief I realised from a brief flash of DeSilva's eyes that Max had not yet been found.

'All in good time, Julian. All in good time. We have Jonathan close by. We are about to unite him with his long lost communication device. As for Max we just have to wait in effect for him to come to us!' He smiled and I held his gaze defiantly. And then suddenly he changed his tone.

'Perhaps you will end all this nonsense and agree to get Max to co-operate with us, Julian, it is for his own good. We want to be able to control the circumstances in which the Seeth come and take him, to make contact, to advance our understanding – these are all virtuous goals, no? And you want Max to live, surely, and to stay with you?'

I frowned, unsure whether this was a statement or a question. How much exactly did DeSilva know?

'I will never co-operate with you, James. You have never co-operated with me. Why didn't you tell me you recognised the alien DNA the night the report arrived from Japan? Why didn't you cooperate with me, express your concerns, tell me about *Wild Fire* and what you had found, and ended the charade of me chairing a committee you sought to control?'

'Because you would not have co-operated Julian, you would not have seen the logic of our secrecy or the threat itself – even now you don't understand what Max's mission is for.'

I frowned again but tried to look confident.

'Besides,' DeSilva continued, 'I seriously under-estimated Louis. I erroneously thought that I simply had to wait for the information to fall into my lap.'

I leaned my head back. I recalled my meeting with DeSilva all those years ago, his anger, his fear. One thing still genuinely puzzled me.

'Why were you so obsessed with a retroviral agent, James, when there was no clinical or lab evidence at all?' I asked suddenly. The question seemed to surprise him.

'Yes. That was unfortunate. Prior to the abduction of the children, the aliens had manufactured viral intrusions to modify host genomes; that was their chosen technique. In the children however, the aliens very cleverly used their own cancers as an agent to modify the human chromosomes. The abduction of the children was quite new, Julian. Seeth activity on Earth had almost ceased by the late 1970s or so we thought. In 1993 we were shocked to find they had seriously upgraded and expanded their mission!'

'When, exactly, did you discover what the experiment was *for*?' I asked, taking a gamble: invasion or resurrection – did they really know? DeSilva looked at me cautiously as if he sensed a trap. He smiled rather unpleasantly.

'About five or six years ago. Davies is now pretty convinced that the Seeth are preparing for the re-colonisation of the planet.'

I tried not to show any surprise. The term re-colonise was odd but there was no immediate indication that they knew that the Seeth were dead.

'You think the children were part of some re-settlement program?'

'Yes.'

I felt a great sense of relief and for the first time since Max's departure, an overwhelming hope that Max – that the Seeth – would succeed.

'For God's sake, James. There is no real evidence that the Seeth want to return to live here – they might be looking for gene markers in the genome of an ancestor for some other purpose – as simple as that!'

James laughed. 'As simple? For what purpose? I am looking forward to meeting the Seeth and trading Max's genomes for their technology – so is Davies – it will revolutionise science! It already has in part of course. The equipment and the software we used on Max's 22 came in part from technology salvaged from a Seeth vessel.'

I felt myself go cold but forced myself to remain looking passively at DeSilva, his eyes mad and wide in the gloom.

'There are so many questions, Julian. Where on earth did they evolve? If they have destroyed their genome is it not unreasonable to assume that they might have destroyed their planet, their habitat? Now they wish to take back what they might reasonably claim is theirs!'

'God, you're relentless!'

'Well, soon – we should be able to get answers from the horse's mouth so to speak!' His reference to his Trojan horse metaphor was deliberate and irritating.

'What makes you think that the Seeth will trade?' I said weakly.

'Oh I think they will. Jonathan has agreed to use the communication device and to send them the terms. We already have the wood surrounded, and given what Max

Max contains, I am sure the Seeth will be willing to come to terms pretty quickly. They have been waiting to find Max for centuries, in a manner of speaking.'

'The Seeth might be slightly more advanced than you imagine, James, less easy to lie to than myself, or DeMarr? Remember they snatched the children from under our noses without anyone seeing them! And what if they don't come? What if they're already extinct?'

It was a dangerous bluff, thrown out close to the truth, but I was angry. James cracked his hands together, snapping the joints as if he was about to hit me. He stood up ignoring the comment and went off on a tangent.

'I never cared much for Louis DeMarr. I mean, I knew he was clever, and that people spoke of his potential but I never saw it. Or rather, I never saw it at the time! I knew about the device in the wood, but I couldn't get close to it until it was almost too late. I never imagined he would lie to me as he did to you, or your wife. As for the Seeth, you think you see everything Julian, you think you know the whole story: but you don't. They'll come, I am not sure they ever left, or went very far! But you know this of course.'

I tried to disguise another stab of doubt. Did he know about the ship?

'And besides, even if they don't come Julian, we will have Max. Davies and I have spent billions of dollars studying Max. We've found things about him that you can't possibly imagine!'

'Really? I can imagine quite a lot, James.'

'Did you know, for example, that your son's chromosomes – including his modified 22 – have a unique sequence of telomeres, a condition that in a normal human would undoubtedly lead to numerous replication errors in the genome and death? It implies that Max has the potential to live for a very long time. Did you also know that he contains selenium dioxide in his blood to a degree that should prove toxic, especially in solution? How it is that Max has not literally spontaneously exploded is just one of the many things we want to look into. And of course, as you've probably found out, his blood is now female?'

'I didn't know that,' I partly lied. It made sense. Max had referred to the Seeth as a she.

'Really? Well there you are then. Max is unique, he is as special as the Seeth in a way!' James turned to look at me with his dark intensity. 'You still think we're wrong about the experiment and the mission don't you? In that cold patronising English way of yours, you think you know because Max was your son, because he feigned to love you?'

The past tense shocked me.

'Really, Julian! What do you really think Max was doing, between 1993 and the early part of this year?' The question seemed random, as if DeSilva was improvising, but its tone worried me.

'Growing up perhaps? Trying to have a normal childhood?'

'What about all those strange nocturnal visits recently, and not always with Jonathan? And he picked two very eminent scientists as parents, isn't that odd? And hasn't Max surprised even you, on occasion, with his interests in physics, in literature, in your own work? Even you felt compelled on one occasion to follow him? Did you know that Max accessed the committee archives before the government moved them last year? Did you know that he removed large amounts of data and not just about himself. About the other children, and that he even traced some of them and made contact. Why would he do that?'

'This is ridiculous! And how do you know this, anyway?' Could Max have done any of this? I knew immediately that he could well have.

DeSilva was not to be deterred. 'And all the talk of monsters, of lizards and creatures of the dark, talk that so frightened his natural mother that she abandoned Max, do you give all this no credit at all. Given what you have seen yourself?'

'Evidently not as much as you do! If I didn't know you better, James I would even think that you were still afraid!'

Clearly James knew of the physical changes that were taking place in Max. Having talked ourselves to a standstill we glowered at each other in silence.

'Have you ever been bothered by visions of Max?' asked James with such sudden intense precision that I felt myself almost wince.

'No.'

He nodded slowly, and I was unclear whether he believed me or not.

There was some movement at the door, a sharp buzz and a security guard appeared. Irritated by the intrusion, James walked over and they conversed in sharp stage whispers. I caught the odd word. Suddenly James turned to me and said pleasantly

'I would like you to come and meet Jonathan. He has been asking for you, apparently.'

I felt myself stiffen with anticipation. I got up from the bed.

'Is Davies here?'

'God no. Davies is sitting in a wood in Leicestershire. As for Jonathan, I want you to be with him when he is reunited with his communication device.'

DeSilva watched me with a sort of sullen obstinacy.

'Is it wise, asking Jonathan to communicate to the Seeth before you have Max? What if they ask to see him? Wouldn't it be better to wait until you have my son in detention?' It seemed needless, even dangerous, to provoke DeSilva, but I couldn't actually resist it. He snorted, ignoring my remark and we walked out of the room into a long corridor which led off into a greenish-white twilight. There was a sort of bunker like feel to the place, or a prison, sinister but clean, modernist, something of the 1950s and the Civil Defence program about the place. I wanted to ask DeSilva where we were, what use this facility usually performed.

'Just think how many schools and hospitals we could have built instead of this?' I said, but the tone was wrong, weak, troubled and DeSilva laughed.

We came eventually to a pair of steel doors, looking ominously like a lift. DeSilva pressed a button and they slid open to reveal another corridor – slightly better lit – with half glass walls revealing what looked like offices and well equipped labs. We walked on for a while and then stopped to peer through a window. For a while I couldn't see anything and then I made out Jonathan sitting on the floor, his back to us. He was wearing a green operating gown, the back open. I could see his vertebrae sticking out rather painfully between his shoulder blades. His close cropped hair made his skull look grey.

'Good God, what have you been doing to him?'

'We haven't been doing anything to him – he was sedated slightly for the last scan.'

James knocked at the glass, as if Jonathan was some sort of pet monkey, caged, and then James punched an entry code into the wall alongside the window. The outlines of a door appeared and then slowly swung open into the room. Inside it was chilly, with odd black mat floors and metallic furniture. There was a TV on but without a picture. The screen was a slab of crackling white static emitting a strangely soothing sound like the sea. I walked over and squatted down, taking Jonathan's hand in mine. His pulse was weak, his eyes dilated. He was looking down at the floor.

'Jonathan – it's Julian. Jonathan – talk to me? Are you alright?' I looked at his arm and saw that he had been injected with something. There appeared to be some additional scaring on his arm and face.

'Was this part of the sedative as well?' Unexpectedly, and to my surprise as much as DeSilva's, I grabbed hold of James' collar and pulled him toward me. He looked bemused rather than alarmed.

'He was difficult – he bit one of the guards.' He looked at me with his hooded, racoon eyes, and they glinted with dark intelligence. I relaxed my grip. For a moment DeSilva had felt almost weightless.

'You have always sickened me, James.'

'If you don't mind?' he said, indicating my hands close to his throat. 'I suggest you put me down.'

There was the sound of footsteps approaching the room, a strange subterranean thud carried through the open door. I let go of DeSilva's jacket and returned to Jonathan. His eyes were open, unfocused, slightly bloodshot. Again, I said my name. Suddenly he seemed to recognise me.

'Julian. Where's Max?' I hesitated and before I could say anything, DeSilva said,

'Don't trouble yourself about Max. It is time for you to call home as it were, to make contact.'

The sound of feet had stopped at the door.

There was a curt knock, and without looking away from Jonathan, DeSilva said, 'Bring in the device. Put it over there.'

A marine in khaki uniform walked in carrying a metal case. He placed it on a nearby table. Two other soldiers, dramatically armed, stood with their weapons aimed on Jonathan. It seemed absurd, pathetic, but deeply distressing as if DeSilva had decided to escalate the stakes for no reason other than his own amusement.

'James what in God's name do you think you're trying to do!' My voice sounded unsteady.

'Shut up, Julian!'

DeSilva squatted down, close to Jonathan's face. He slapped it gently but unpleasantly.

'Jonathan. I want you to contact the Seeth and tell them that we have worked out their experiment, that we have Max and their genomes, and that we need to discuss terms with them. Tell them we are in the wood waiting with a reception committee. No one need get harmed.'

Jonathan looked at DeSilva, his gaunt face pallid and tired. I tried to catch the young man's eye, to reassure him, to give him strength. As I did so, something warm and soft, fuzzy, moved inside my head. For a moment I thought I was having some strange dizzy spell but the patterns formed words. They flared up like pictures.

'Julian, you must be touching me when I touch the device. Do you understand?' Had Jonathan spoken? I must have looked surprised, because the question – the sort of colour-voice – came again. *'Do you understand?'*

'Yes! Yes I do,' I said out loud. DeSilva, preoccupied with something, frowned and looked at me, irritated, and then he nodded to the Marine to open the case. Jonathan looked relieved. His eyes moved over DeSilva with barely disguised hatred and then up onto the table.

The case was open. It contained the device that had long deluded and mystified me. A long black cylinder, about four inches thick, by about ten inches long. Its sides were smooth except for a series of uneven grooves running down it in groups of three. The top and the bottom of the cylinder was rough and sharp as if the device had been broken from a larger piece of the same material. How and in what ways Max would be encased in it seemed suddenly irrelevant against the urgency of getting it to him before it was too late. DeSilva took the cylinder, like a baton, and held it quite close to Jonathan. Noticing it, Jonathan said softly.

'I will need some time. The Seeth might take time to

communicate with my tag.'

'Of course. But don't try anything or you will be shot, do you understand that? You are after all, and unlike Max, quite dispensable.'

There came the sound of more people moving towards us from outside, urgently, and judging by the distracted look on James' face, unexpectedly. There came the sound of a polite cough behind us. DeSilva, half turned, visibly angry. A gaggle of people – about four – were looking at him, at myself, and at Jonathan as if we were some sort of exhibit, a themed display. The soldiers were still pointing their guns at Jonathan on the floor. It must have looked quite shocking.

'Professor, the Prime Minister wants to speak with you. We will have to release the detainees.' A young woman spoke, suited and smart, looking visibly outraged by the spectacle in front of her. 'Someone has been shot,' she added, as if this would prompt a response.

DeSilva's eyes narrowed and his lips turned down, a mask of displeasure. And then I saw – or did I feel? – Jonathan coil back down onto the base of his spine. It was a soft, insidious move, predatory, instinctive. For a second Jonathan looked at me and then with absolute hatred, he stared at DeSilva. As Jonathan's eyes moved they flashed intensely, luminous about the irises, the pupils momentarily realigning as if focusing on their prey, narrow slits like a cat or a lizard, like Max's and before I had time to understand how this was possible, Jonathan launched at DeSilva with great speed and agility, knocking him forward with one massive movement. The top of Jonathan's head hit James in the face, sending a thread of blood out of DeSilva's nose. As he wheeled backwards in pain Jonathan snatched the device with one hand while grabbing my throat with the other. I had gone to scream, startled; I had heard a metallic clip, like a trigger pulled but in that instance the room was gone, dissolved, hurled away and we were suddenly in total darkness.

Chapter 18

Max took the phone off me and redialled Daniel's number but there was no signal. The sound of the helicopter rumbled out towards us from the direction of the road.

'Do you think they know we're here?' I asked, pointlessly.

'Yes, we have to go!' Max took my hand and pulled me quite literally towards the doorway. Evidently he could see now. His hand felt very large and cold in mine.

'We'll never get to the wood, Max! Perhaps they even know about the ship!'

'Jamie, come on!'

Outside, away from the gloomy ruinous interior of the derelict cottage, the evening was still surprisingly light and this seemed to cause Max some initial difficulties. He stooped down, shielding his eyes. 'Shit – wait a second.' His face – banded and narrowed by the tattoo-like tracings, contorted in obvious pain.

We stood in the abandoned courtyard with its strange

exhibits of machines and equipment, a sort of agricultural graveyard, while Max seemed to struggle with the pain in his head. Finally he stood up and squinted about him. I wondered vaguely why the Seeth needed to see in the darkness: a twilit world? A weaker sun than ours here, a nocturnal species?

'Ok, that's better. The wood is over here.' Max was looking over a series of hedges as if he had caught a scent or could see for miles. To our left, away in the middle of a mowed field heaped with bales, I saw people and dogs coming towards us.

'Come on!' and Max moved with such sudden astounding speed that for a moment I thought I was hallucinating. One minute he was next to me, watching the approaching soldiers, and then he was away near the hedge. 'Jamie!'

I ran after him, dropping the satchel away from me. It seemed redundant now, Max's point of danger over. Max climbed over a low fence topped with barbed wire, lifting it up for me to get through. It had cut his forearm and the side of his stomach.

'Max, you're bleeding!'

'Yeah, it's ok.' he deliberately lifted his arm and bled a sort of black tar-like substance that fizzled and popped as it touched the top of the fence like acid.

'What the fuck!'

'It will put the dogs off us.' There was a powerful, pungent smell and even Max moved his head back sharply. 'God! And probably everyone else as well!' He then ran off purposefully into the dim golden evening. Behind us came the sound of voices, loud in the stillness.

I tried to relax, to think of pleasant things, what I would do when this was over, how I would wait for Max, what he would look like when he came back. But all I felt was exhaustion, the flight through the baked summer fields, the standing crops of yellowing wheat and barley. Finally we reached the bottom of a long sloping hill, with a stand of ash trees shading a small brook, its outline smudged with reeds and vegetation. Max crossed the water and paused, waiting. For a moment I thought he might be lost.

'You ok?'

'Yeah – sure – hold it, it's Jonathan.'

He said it so casually that I actually turned around to look behind me, expecting to see the lanky thin shape of my former nemesis strolling towards us. Max laughed slightly and tapped his head. He then leaned down, his hands on his knees as if catching his breath, touching the ground. All down his back solid nodules of bone were hardening into scales. They followed the lines of his own muscles but stood out in sharp relief as if someone had carved a copy of Max and left unfinished clay sticking to his body. The bandings, too, were almost complete now, a weird compelling calligraphy, a warning, like the black bars on a wasp. Max was becoming something dangerous, I sensed it.

'Where is he?' I heard the helicopter again, still behind us, a lazy sound like summer thunder.

Max didn't reply. He appeared to be thinking hard.

'I think he's been drugged or something. He seems a bit confused. He's in London, but-' there was a sharp intake of breath and Max nodded his head mysteriously.

'They've taken the bait though! Davies is already here – in the wood.' His voice was heavy with relief. 'Thank fuck! And they still think the device is a sort of glorified phone!' he smiled at me and stood up abruptly sniffing the air. In the gathering darkness he looked powerful, tall, his posture quite different.

'Max this has to be a trap! We're walking into a trap!'

He nodded again, at me, or perhaps at some ongoing conversation with Jonathan. He suddenly started walking, following the line of trees hanging low over the water, oblivious to any obstacle. After about five or six minutes we found ourselves standing in a field of cut grass, the light clay soil ghostly white in the gathering dusk and bone hard under foot. The air was cooling now, almost chill. Max scanned about him, his hands to his forehead as if he was pretending to look through a pair of binoculars. Was he looking for the wood? For signs of Davies? Then suddenly, he ran furiously for about five, ten minutes, maybe less, sprinting hard. I tried to follow in Max's wake, using his eyes instead of mine, trusting him implicitly, but found it difficult to keep up. I was breathless and I had a strange sensation of moving through water. I realised as I beat the air with my elbows and forearms, propelling myself over the hard ground, that this was the dream again, the one I had glimpsed this morning. The light, the feel of the ground: *a premonition*, and behind us? We reached another hedge, thick with brambles, the ubiquitous barbed wire and another brook at the bottom of a steep ditch. Max guided me through it with amazing strength and we clambered down pausing in the middle – feet astride the water – catching our breath. I blew through my mouth, and put my hand to my throat; it was quite swollen and painful to the touch. Gradually our collective panting grew less. I could smell Max and feel his heat.

'I'm not sure I can keep this up Max, sorry. I'd thought our adventures would be evenly paced!' Max made a sort of laugh and lifted up his head.

'Yeah so did I.' I could dimly make him out because he was glowing, a dull luminous sheen like some intricate, ancient pelagic life form. It no longer seemed strange. He squatted down, his arm on his raised knee.

'Max? You ok?'

'Yeah – sort of.' He moved again, sitting down on the raised bank behind us and then he said quietly. 'I haven't got long, Jamie.'

'Max, you have to hold on – we haven't got the device!' I moved forward desperately. 'Where is Jonathan?'

Max took my hand and put it on the top of his right shoulder. He held it there, in case I was inclined to snatch it back. It touched *hard shell* – something smooth – but very dense.

'A human armadillo,' he said deadpan. 'Perhaps the Seeth were glorified dinosaurs?'

He let my hand go. I felt down the edges of the plate to where the muscles of his back seemed to resume, the bone plating sinking into flesh scaled and yet putty-like to the touch. I returned my hand to his shoulder, moving it down and towards his chest – the plating softened just below his throat, and then seemed to follow his sternum before sinking into the top of his abdominal muscles. I didn't say anything. It felt like nothing I had ever touched before. Max's smell remained on my hand, like oil, a heavy, feral musk.

I sat down, a root sticking in my back, thorns and twigs in my neck and head. I had started to cry again without thinking about it, without effort. It was all I seemed capable of doing now, the only emotion left.

'Jamie! Come on, look how special all this is! Come *here* –' he dropped his voice, coaxing me.

The inside of the hedge felt warm, den-like, oddly protective. I suddenly wanted to sit here forever, to sleep and to wake up and see Max *trying* to shave, trying to sneak a meeting with Jonathan, even sleeping with Zoë Craven, anything but this.

'I don't want you to leave me. Or be separated. Can't I come with you? Is that possible?'

'No, Jamie, it isn't! Be patient!' I could make out the shape of his head. He was holding it at a curious angle, as if he was listening for something, waiting for a sign.

'Max?'

I presumed it was Jonathan again. Max looked at me and said 'Did I grab you? Earlier, in the farmhouse?'

The shock of Max's sudden violence had almost been forgotten, lost in the tension of the race over the dark, hard fields; my relief over his recovery.

'Yeah, but it's nothing, really. You might need to watch that killer grip though!'

He moved his hand to my throat. We were very close to each other in the darkness.

'Max, its fine – don't fuss – you didn't recognise me. You thought I was someone else!' I felt his fingers against my windpipe, feeling about, almost a caress, tentative. I couldn't deal with this, not now.

'Leave it –' I said, without conviction.

'Is it sore?' To anyone else, the question would have been virtually inaudible. It was barely a whisper. Max's hair was across my face, in my nose. I shut my eyes tightly.

'It's fine Max, really, no damage done – you scared me, that's all! You were delirious.'

'Ok,' he left his long fingers on my throat, as if he was taking my pulse. He seemed to be thinking of something, or was he trying to remember? I looked at him. He was barely recognisable, *barely* Max. The bandings on his face had changed the shape of his forehead, making him look younger and older at the same time. Their odd glow made him look as if he was wearing a helmet of some kind, or a mask. The eyes were quizzical, unsure, looking at my throat and neck with a strange, intense, curiosity.

'I love you, Jamie. Do I need to say that?'

Max seemed to smell my neck, my hair, paused several times, and then strangely nuzzled my face, bird like, the neck slowly extending. It was a bizarre gesture that made no sense until I realised that the man next to me was not Max at all. It wasn't even human. I could sense it. It was something entirely different. Something I had never met. I sat quite still. The Seeth was still touching my throat. It was an ambiguous gesture, started but not finished by Max. Someone was in my head, quietly, almost gracefully looking at my thoughts like a stranger, trying to greet me. It was something that did not speak my language or know my kind. The sensation was intense but not necessarily frightening. I sat, looking at the creature in front of me trying to not recoil back or scream. The creature looked at me with glowing, brilliant eyes like stars. We stared blankly at each other, unable to read or translate the other's body language but then suddenly there came a gleam of recognition, as if in his final moments Max had succeeded in communicating my identity to the Seeth. The suddenness at which Max had winked away left me numb, without bearings, but the Seeth seemed to recognise me.

Max's physical appearance had not radically altered, his hair, his posture, his sheer size, the creature was still effectively humanoid. Despite Max having identified the Seeth as female there was no clear outward sign to me that any change in sex had taken place, although apart from the residual glow of my Seeth friend, the inside of the hedge was almost pitch black. Yet the difference was stark. Should I say something? Presumably, the Seeth could communicate with me? Or should I try to think, visualise a conversation? From somewhere above us there came a snap of wood. The Seeth's eyes flared up brilliantly and it whirled around at fantastic speed and crouched down low, as if it was going to spring up through the hedge into the next field. Then it made a sort of rattling noise, somewhere in its throat. That *really* scared me. It was an utterly inhuman sound, so completely strange to me that I realised – finally – that Max had really gone. I went to move forward, but the Seeth, started, jumpy with nerves, glowed deep red. It was not a good sign. I put my hands out, palm up, trying to think of some suitably submissive signal. Then I put my fingers to my lips. The red glow vanished, replaced by a dull sheen over taut, cut muscles and sinew, raw and unmade as if the Lizard creature had no real skin. I reached out and touched the Seeth's face, the curved ridge of cheek, a Max-like gesture, something it might recognise. The creature calmed down, letting me pet it while watching me intently with its strange luminous eyes. I started to move again, more successfully, squeezing out towards the top of the facing bank, the Seeth behind and below me still, squatting and evidently disorientated. I looked out over a dark haze of summer grass and saw straight away that we had been disturbed by cows. They had bunched up by the hedge, very near to us. I wiped by eyes with my sleeve.

'It's ok. They're –' but before I had finished the Seeth was actually *next* to me. The speed and silence of the movement was incredible.

'They're cows – they're animals – it's ok!'

The Seeth was looking at the field and was red again, glowing, steaming with heat and smell. It was evidently as afraid as I was.

'Hey. It's fine –' Did she understand? I tried to smile, to emanate calm. I ran my hand down the Seeth's arm like Max used to do to me. The creature seemed more bothered by the sky and the open field than the cows, who as soon as they caught the scent of this bizarre exotic creature, bolted in a thundering gallop down the length of the field. We sat for a while, close together but when I tried to go forward, the Seeth pulled me back. She almost took out my arm.

'We have to go now,' I whispered. 'The wood – *the ship* – the ship is over there,' I pointed straight ahead. The night was ominously silent. There was no sound of any helicopters or the army.

'We have to go – or do you want to stay here for a while? Stay?'

I felt desperate, utterly unprepared for some weird ambassadorial role but then to my surprise the Seeth said quite distinctly 'Stay.'

That word shocked me.

'Stay?'

'Stay.' It took my hand and pulled me back into the hedge where we resumed squatting, as if waiting for something. Soon my curiosity overcame both my grief and my fear.

'You can speak my language – I mean –'

'I think your language, Jamie Relph. It is easier for me. Jonathan Price is helping me. He is in my head.' Was the voice Max's? Was it slightly more feminine, or even deeper?

'Where's Max? Is he safe?' I said out loud.

'Max is here, with us. He is written into us. There is still time. Think, don't speak. The area in front of us is full of soldiers.'

'Shit!'

'This sense of space distresses me – and the light – even now,' thought the Seeth, the thought felt tentative, a sort of confession.

'We can run?' I whispered.

'Yes. The space is strange to me.'

'It's ok. Come on, Let's go!'

After some more coaxing, the Seeth shot out of the hedge and ran. I followed the dull smear of light in front of me. We pressed on in the general direction of what I assumed was the wood, but soon we hit a series of low fences like some sort of race course, then a series of sheds that pushed us away slightly in the wrong direction. Several times the Seeth stopped for me to catch up, listening, her body glossy with sweat.

'Do you have a name? Are you a woman, a female?'

The Seeth, distracted by my whispering, put a finger to its lips.

'A female?' It repeated, the question seeming to make no sense.

'Max said you were a female.'

'Yes.'

We skirted around some sort of pond and found

ourselves in another thigh high crop with the plough lines irritatingly crossing us at right angles. Shouldn't we have come up on the Kirby Lane by now, or seen Daniel's farm? I tried to recall the map. Then the Seeth stopped abruptly and stood upright, looking for something, scanning slowly, anxiously. Were we lost? I stared in the direction of its gaze and saw nothing, Apart from a blush of yellowish light in the distance – a large village? – there were just dark blooms of trees and pylons silhouetted against the opaque skyline, line after line, like some elaborate theatre set.

We waited for what seemed an age while Max-Seeth seemed to be holding some elaborate conference with Jonathan again. But it might have been only about ten minutes. It was hard to keep track of time. Above us the sky was a deep, translucent blue with a few summer stars high above us. There was still no sound of pursuit. Then, suddenly, the Seeth made a sort of growl. I jumped slightly, having nodded off effortlessly. A small pulse of light rippled over its torso. The Seeth stood and then staggered backwards as if it had been struck by something. For one horrible moment I actually thought it had been shot.

'What the fuck was that!' There was another pulse, an orange-red glow like a cigarette end, and then I saw a fine trace of light, a sort of green thread, momentarily streak out *away from us*, out into the darkness.

'The ship is coming,' thought the Seeth, holding its torso as if injured.

'Have you been hit?'

'No. The ship is coming.' Another pulse, another stab of light away from us – like tracer fire – off into the darkness, slightly to the left of our current direction. The Seeth was breathing hard as if in serious pain.

'What can I do?' my voice sounded desperate, pathetic. The Seeth seemed to be bracing itself for another stab of light. It seemed an absurd way to board a ship. The lines of light were clearly being drawn into the wood and they would be clearly visible to everybody. Another spasm, another streak of light.

'It will come,' thought the Seeth ominously.

The Seeth stood, and as it did so I saw that the markings down along the torso and waist were glowing a dull blue. I had not seen this colour before. And as I looked closer I saw with horror that the patterns – the waspish black lines – were *moving*, swirling and shifting, in dark whirls and eddies, as if something was hatching under its skin. There was something about the movement, small, blind, instinctive, that reminded me of embryos, half formed, twitching in their egg sacs. A form of spawn. The thought – the image – really shocked me, but before I could think anything, the Seeth was running like the wind into the darkness, parallel to the lines of light still sparking from its body. I staggered off after it.

We cleared two more fields. One seemed impossibly big and hedge less, its crop already harvested, the grass dried and the ground hard and flinty. The other was long but at an angle to us, so we crossed it relatively quickly. Once over a low wooden fence, I unexpectedly fell into another ditch and when I had clambered out, my face stung with nettles, I saw the Seeth standing in the middle of a minor road. It had shredded most of Max's jeans and was standing naked, its back to me.

'This must be the Kirby Lane, the one Max's dad walked down from Lockwood's farm back to his car all those years ago!' I thought to myself. To our left, back some way from the road, I could see a cluster of outhouses and a farm. A dog barked cautiously, loudly in the darkness. I guessed it must be Lockwood's farm. The *thinking* thing was very hard. The Seeth seemed perplexed – almost disappointed – to see the wood in front of it. Looking about me, I thought I could see a sort of tail snaking down from where the spine joined the pelvis, but it was too dark to see clearly. I walked forward, rubbing my eyes but standing alongside it, it was immediately obvious that the Seeth had a tail. I tried not to think about that, to imply anxiety or some new found prejudice. I tried not to look.

'We're nearly there,' I pointed to a gate slightly away from us. Next to it was a finger post visible against the sky. The Seeth's luminous threads were now spinning away from it without pain, and were beginning to mark out a sort of wake, a green glowing fog curving towards a dark wedge of trees. I looked carefully for a sign of a ship, something just above the trees, but apart from the dull glow there was nothing. Again, without warning, as if it had succeeded in gaining its bearings, the Seeth suddenly sprinted off. I followed, clambering over the gate, stumbling down and cutting my hands and as I cleared it there came the sound of helicopters again, very close by. They had clearly been in the next field, ready to take off at our approach. The Seeth flashed red. She half turned to me urgently.

'We're coming in at the opposite end to where the mound was. There are soldiers in the trees and in the wood itself – we must be careful!' The Seeth slowed and then walked forward slowly, attentively. I followed, aware as I did so that something was coming up behind us along the road.

'They are directing us into the wood! So many voices – they think the Seeth will come for Max.'

We kept low, darting forward, covering the ground as quickly as we could. We finally reached the last hedge before the trees. It was an eerie, ghostly sight. The Seeth was now radiating out great lines of light that were smoking up the area, filling the air with luminous dust. There was a powerful pungent smell everywhere and I found it difficult to breath. In the light, the trees in the spinney were now visible on the other side of the hedge. With a particular sense of familiarity, the Seeth brought me to a hole in the undergrowth that led down into the end of the spinney.

'We have to go through here – quickly – follow me.' We were now actually crouching in a sort of green mist. I realised that it was probably Jonathan directing the creature towards its home. He had been here recently.

The hole dropped down another steep bank into a stream. The Seeth splashed through and then climbed up into the trees moving in odd jerky movements. I hesitated, unable to judge the drop, disorientated by the luminous gloom, choking on the smell. The motes of dust were in fact steaming off the Seeth's body and up into the air like ash from a fire: the tattooed mottling was smoking away, shimmering and whirling about the tall alien. The sight was beautiful and shocking as if the creature was set on fire. Suddenly a brilliant, blinding beam of light came down from the tree tops and the Seeth seemed to literally explode! I screamed, falling back and the Seeth too was screaming – or chanting or singing – it was impossible to say – because the glare from the light was impossibly bright and loud, a rushing roaring sound, burning up with the white-blue intensity of phosphorous. For a brief moment I thought everything had failed, at the very end, but then the Seeth seemed to turn to me with a look of sheer ecstasy, screaming in its luminous pain, and above me, shimmering into solid form appeared a huge, silver ship, simple, elegant, shaped like the tip of an arrow, the widest part just above us. It literally materialised from thin air, setting up a great wind.

'Max!' I screamed his name pointlessly. There were shouts and noise all around me, behind, back from the road; the sound of gun fire. Where was Jonathan? Why wasn't he here? At what stage in this fiery rebirth would Max be irretrievably lost? Was it already too late? Again the thought took shape, a simple assertion – Max was gone. The Seeth no longer needed him. There was a silent rain of grit and dust across my face, razor sharp, drawing blood from my cheeks. From the corner of my eye, in slow motion, choreographed in a lazy arch from left to right, I saw bullets hitting the ground around my legs and close to the Seeth. For a moment I thought it was the Seeth ship, and then I realised that the firing was coming from behind. I went to drop down the bank into the water but someone shouted something and then I was punched hard in the side, a wet burning stab, followed by utter darkness.

Chapter 19

I thought Max was with me, at least initially. We were lying together reading a poem, something heavy, Eliot; possibly *Prufrock*. My head was on his lap, my face half turned and looking up at the spine of the book. It was definitely Eliot. Some *Collected Works* or other. It seemed real. I could smell the grass and feel Max's belt buckle near my ear, sharp, blood warm. Max had just whispered *'Till human voices wake us, and we drown'* and then poked a grass stalk playfully against my cheek. He'd whispered too softly, in fact, for human voices to hear at all. I had pushed the book away, catching his face, serene, sleepy. I wanted him to say *drown* again because his intonation resonated down his stomach through his groin and into my ear. A sleepover, a holiday, a day dream? A fantasy?

And then he was gone and I was alone in a great, vast blackness, unmade. Clearly I was dead. The idea that I would somehow know this and even contemplate it as a condition, seemed wrong however, inconsistent.

Perhaps I was half dead? *Maimed* – shit – and Max? I tried to move but couldn't. And as I tried I became aware that I was bitterly, intensely cold, as if I had plunged into deep water and been abandoned, left for dead? I started to panic, to claw and thrash about with limbs I could not feel, or scream with breath I did not have. Then someone called my name. It was very far away and very high, like an echo and then the darkness seemed to change texture somehow, it grew grey, less closed in, less claustrophobic. Again, my name, a shout so remote it seemed to come from inside my own head, like a memory. It sounded like Max, before he had become a Lizard thing, before he had died and been taken away. Another sound, and then a sort of redness emerged through the blackness, a blood-red tinge, growing purple and pink, bruising inside my head, like hot summer light seen through closed eyelids. And then someone definitely said, 'Jamie?'

The voice was very close to me now.

It was a voice I didn't recognise. I was wet and there was something on my face and neck. The light was intense now, painful, and when I chipped my eyes open, great shards of pain spiked my brain. I closed them tightly and then tried again. Slowly, with effort, I found that I was squinting through tall dewy grass; that I was laying on my side, bathed in brilliant low sunlight. Late evening, very early morning? I swivelled my eyes, afraid to move in case my head became detached from me. I could see a pair of knees close to my face and then a vista of trees, the knuckled black lesions of birches on white chalky bark.

'Jamie? Say something?'

I couldn't. I tried to visualise the words but they didn't make sense. I had another go at moving, and managed a half roll, like a beached whale. The knees belonged to Jonathan. He was wearing some weird hospital gown and without his baseball cap he looked quite handsome, fresh faced, *almost* healthy. It was sort of shocking seeing him like that, no longer the blasted Zombie.

'Jonathan?' I said, as if it was a game and I had to guess his name.

He seemed relieved to see me move.

'Hey he's ok. He seems ok!' I tried a further gesture of reassurance but moving my torso log-like was all I could manage for the moment. Someone approached me from behind Jonathan. It was Max's dad. I recognised the shoes immediately; brogues, and the faded cords; old man cords that swelled up and out towards the waist. The sort that men wore in 1950s movies, men who wore hats and smoked a pipe.

'Thank God for that! Jamie?' Julian squatted down, and touched my face. His voice seemed somehow too young, too raw to belong to him. I felt someone take my pulse. Julian came into view, close-up, magnified. He looked dreadful, his face ashen. I noticed he had been crying; that his eyes were red and sore, his face slightly swollen as if he had been punched. With effort, I tried to separate my tongue from my mouth and lips but they were all mashed together. Perhaps I no longer had a mouth. I tried to roll forward and sit up. Clearly my head really had fallen off. It had fallen off and been stapled or nailed back on. The pain in my neck was indescribable.

'Careful, Jamie. You were shot,' Max's dad said softly, indifferently, as if I had been careless. He sat down heavily, the tall wet grass pressed flat around his jacket, sweet smelling, the stalks broken down like spears. Julian looked defeated, as if he had no intention of ever getting up again. Jonathan, still kneeling, smiled at me encouragingly.

'Did you come in time?' I slurred at them both.

'Yes. We came in time,' but then Julian's face collapsed into a sob.

I tried to move, more successfully this time, swinging

around, using my hips and keeping my neck stiff and my shoulders set. Sensing my plan, Julian leaned forward and helped me raise my upper body, and then with effort, rest my head on a nearby tree trunk. We were far from where I had fallen, from where the arch of bullets had struck the soil. We seemed to be at the other end of the wood, right in the middle of the birches. I tried to get my bearings, to work out how I had been carried so far from the field, and as I looked, squinting in the sunshine, I saw *bodies* in the long grass, scattered beneath the trees; crumpled, flat, many face up, with things littered everywhere.

'What the fuck!'

Julian calmed me, as if I was a small boy. He rubbed my arm. 'It's ok, they're not dead. They're asleep.' I frowned, vaguely reassured.

'Asleep?'

'An enchantment!' said Jonathan, and then he stood up, in evident distress, and shouted 'Max!' very loudly, at the top of his voice. The sound scared me. Julian closed his eyes, slowly, painfully, and I saw tears reforming on his eyelashes.

'Jonathan, please don't do that anymore – it's of no use.' And I realised he had really gone. Max had gone. I looked away from his father back down an avenue of trees.

'The shooting started by accident, someone must have panicked when the Seeth started to oxidise and trigger the appearance of the ship. Davies and several other so-called First Contact experts were in the wood waiting. They had obviously not expected the process to be so spectacular or indeed so *automated*. The ship was here waiting, it had always been here, but Davies had never worked that out, or that the Seeth were dead.' Julian spoke slowly, as if the events were long ago, or badly jumbled up in his head. He was sitting oddly, how Max used to sit, arms embracing his legs, chin on his knee caps, head forward.

'Jonathan and I *arrived*, if that is quite the right word, as soon as Jonathan took the device from DeSilva. We had been in London, somewhere south of the river. Jonathan had been in contact with the Seeth female for some time, since the transformation.'

'The device? Did you get it to the Seeth in time to store Max?'

'Yes.'

I looked through the trees to where Jonathan was walking aimlessly, still calling for Max, his skinny arms waving about but calling quietly now, more to himself.

'We both materialised straight in front of you both – this side of the bank, in the trees. Max – I thought it was Max at first – was illuminated, burning like a flare. Jonathan pushed himself forward and gave the Seeth the device.'

'Did it work?'

'The light stopped slowly. And as it did so I saw the Seeth was standing in darkness, smoking with heat – it was a dreadful and yet beautiful sight. The device filled up with white light and then spun up into the ship. It was then that I saw you lying on the other side of the bank, near the hole in the hedge. You were clearly dead.'

I heard the word dead but ignored it, assuming that Julian was exaggerating or had meant to use another word instead.

'The Seeth said something, something strange, and then turned to pick you up.' Julian looked at me, his face ghostly now. 'You were dead, Jamie. Lifeless. Quite lifeless.'

Again, I ignored the absurdity of the statement.

'Max turned into a lizard thing, with a tail,' I said, almost carelessly.

'The Seeth lifted you up, Jamie. You were dead.'

Our two conversations stretched away, parallel, disconnected. It was a beautiful summer morning.

Around us the soldiers slept on, undisturbed. After a while I looked at Max's father and said, 'I don't understand.'

'She seemed to recognise you. She picked you up. She said your name.'

'Jamie?' I asked stupidly, as if I had another.

'Yes. And then the Seeth vanished with you. It was then that I became aware that there were people lying in the fields, bodies *everywhere*. As if there had been a massacre. It was Jonathan who found that they were unconscious, sleeping. We eventually found you at the far end of the wood, just after daybreak. It grew very foggy, and very cold. But you are alive now. You had been brought back.'

'How?'

Julian did not answer.

Bewildered, emptied by grief, I worked through the implication that I had been dead and somehow revived, that Max's companion had brought me back. By the time I had arrived at this deduction, Jonathan had wandered towards us.

'How are you feeling now?' he asked, shivering, rubbing his arms vigorously. He seemed friendly, all traces of anger gone.

'Ok. Better, thank you.' Tears streamed down my face unnoticed.

'I'm going to call you Lazarus from now on,' said Jonathan, playfully, touching my head. He looked at Julian and then sat down heavily between us. 'Now we wait.'

Epilogue

Like a roller coaster ride the road curves and bends through the dun coloured landscape. The world is unmade, still in its winter sleep. I pass few cars and once off the A-road there is an excess of sky that hurts my eyes. The secret is to come here and not think: to drive on and through and not remember, to not think of the dead years of waiting. Every time I come, I drive a different way, cutting towards Daniel's farm from another direction; avoiding, evading, looking neither to the right or the left. It has become a sort of test. Down from Market Bosworth, through Newbold, out again by Brascote village, and then towards Kirby Mallory: the name evokes images, memories, a slow action replay of some late teenage trauma. Usually the images are subliminal, drawn back but today they are close to the surface and for a moment, if I am not careful, I shall see Max. I shall see him both as he was before and after the changes, a blazing epiphany. I grip the steering wheel and narrow my eyes.

With evident relief, I catch sight of Daniel's farm set back in its pale, grey-green field. It looks bleak and monastic, safe: this is a place that he oddly never came to, never visited, never touched, although he had trailed past it on that final night, comet-like, careering into the sun. As I turn up the long drive, the low evening light catches the high gables of the house and the grey stone pointing. I smile as the car judders and shakes over the cattle grid: tired after the drive from London, relieved to be here. As I climb out, I do not look in the direction of the wood or the Kirby Lane. Rather I look intently at Daniel who is out in the yard walking towards me. He is wearing green Wellingtons and faded jeans and his ubiquitous blue fisherman's jumper as if he has been out hauling in nets. He has gained some more weight since I last saw him; he looks like Orson Wells, broad faced, bearded, an ancestor of some kind. He is glad to see me but anxious as well: I sense that. I walk over towards him, stepping over wide grey puddles that show off the sky. He kisses my cheek like a spinster and says I look very well. I feel I have not seen him for years: it is an odd, jarring sensation, as if time itself is not linear. It is cold outside, with the dusk metallic and hard. We go into the kitchen and I smell with joy that he has been cooking.

We talk about Julian Grey. I say I saw him a few days ago, blowing about London in spring sunshine, immaculately dressed, still elegant in his sorrow, still waiting, married to my mother and as happy as he can be in the circumstances. We had sat out in Old Compton Street surrounded by beautiful people, the weekend mild and spring-like. Daniel tells me he has heard a rumour that Julian is going to write a first hand account of the abductions and the disappearance of the Seeth for publication. I am politely sceptical. Julian has never mentioned Max to me once since he was taken. Daniel asks about Jonathan, pouring me some wine. Jonathan is fine. He has completed his studies and is a qualified nurse living in Nottingham. He has a girl friend of sorts. He still calls me Lazarus and we have grown strangely close; as if we shared the same lover long ago, he sends me strange, random gifts and I call him most evenings.

We sit up late until we are both vaguely drunk. We reminisce about things and I talk about my work and my research. He asks me if I have a partner and I say no and he shakes his head sadly as if this is regrettable or just understandable. He doesn't ask me why and I offer no explanations. The back room of the farmhouse is warm and there is a soft wind buffeting the bay windows from the direction of the wood. The curtains are un-drawn, a small act of defiance perhaps, or a weakness. Daniel is telling me about how he wants to move and live in a city before he dies, but suddenly I am distracted by the sensation that someone, somewhere, has *just* called my name. I discount the sensation, putting it down to drink; emotion. Daniel starts to ask about something but there is the sound again: the call of my name, in my head or just behind me and for one moment I think it is Max. Daniel senses my unease. Perhaps he thinks he is boring me? I feel panicky, suddenly unwell. I apologise. 'What is it?' Instinctively Daniel looks from me to the blind, dark window. It shows only a dim landscape of shadow, the inside of the room projected out onto spring darkness. He looks uneasy.

'I'm not sure –' and then the call again, clearer, if not more remote; and this time Daniel hears it. I see his face change, half fear, half hope, a look of shock. He stands up like a man who has been summoned and there is a muffled half bark from the kitchen. Daniel's red setter -

Sam – leaps up and the dog bounds in barking at us both. The sound is very loud. It stings my ears.

'Sam, get down!' Daniel's voice is anxious, different. 'What is it?'

Sam senses our fear and barks again for good measure. I am standing now, wide awake, very sober, looking through the bay window, through my own outline and up at the sky.

'Jamie?'

The dog is whining and running about the room, excited. There is clearly something outside, the dog senses it. The thought makes me almost visibly tremble.

'Jamie, it's probably some lads from the village or some alien hunters marking the anniversary – let's not –'

'I know, I know,' the sudden recognition that I have been waiting for Max for six years is almost overwhelming. I feel Daniel's hand touch the top of my shoulder. 'I'll go out and have a look – it's probably just the Roswell brigade!'

'I'll come with you. Just for a moment there!' I turn and half smile. Daniel, ashen coloured, nods in agreement. He walks into the kitchen cursing at the dog who is already sitting in the porch whining and scraping at the door. I pull on a coat and overshoes (a recent, *DeMarr*-like affectation) and outside we trip a security light. We are halfway down the drive when it finally cuts out, plunging us into sudden darkness. Sam bolts off diagonally across the field, a blur of movement, barking loudly. Daniel calls after him with no apparent effect. The night is grey as opposed to black. Low clouds furrowed above us reflect the yellow sodium street lighting from the nearby village. It is warmer now, the air wet, smelling strangely of the sea. When we reach the road, I am already emotionally shattered. If we go towards the wood now we shall join up with the route I took with the Seeth on that final evening. It is too much, too familiar, even now. There is no sound, the air still, expectant. To my horror, my grief is unimaginable.

'Daniel – let's go back. It's a wild goose chase, I'm hearing things,' my voice is flat. Daniel stops, hearing my bitterness. He points the beam of a torch up the road. It catches the mica in the tarmac, and the runes of bark on a nearby ash tree jump out in bold relief. A shadow appears suddenly and my heart leaps but it is Sam, emerging from the hedgerow, sniffing the road, his tail wagging. Daniel starts as well and then laughs nervously.

'Jesus! Look at us! We should both get out more!' he scolds the dog who ignores him again and then, above the distant line of the wood we see a dull glow, a rolling blush of light that washes in above the trees like a swell. I wait for a sound that will translate this into something normal: the throb of a helicopter, the intermittent grumble of a plane, thunder? There is nothing but heavy silence. Sam's enthusiastic bark comes to us from across the road now. He is in the field in front of the wood.

Daniel simply whispers 'Shit!'

The glow ebbs and flows and the low cloud obscures the source and scatters the light. There is an impression of movement as if something is coming towards us or descending slowly.

And suddenly I am running. I am running hard, measured, like a sprinter, using my toes and hands to propel myself forward. On my right I sense the fence where, years ago, I emerged onto the road to see Max with his lizard tail. I can hear Daniel struggling up behind me, shouting for me to wait. The glow is intense now, silver-white, it illuminates the top of the bare trees, throwing them forward like veins seen through a microscope. I am through the gate into the wide hedge-less field where I was shot. The ground is fallow now, thankfully unploughed, the scrub soft and tactile with spring rain. I slip and stumble forward, my lungs burning. Instinctively I find the hole in the hedge and the steep drop down to the stream just as I did that night. I draw to a halt as the brilliance is fading above me, beading away towards the village. As it rolls off I throw myself down into the ditch and clamber up the other side.

'Max!'

I am shocked at the sound of my own voice. It is a scream, something primordial, torn from me in great pain. I so rarely say his name that it seems odd, novel. I splash through water. It comes over the galoshes and soaks my feet, shockingly cold. After the brief, vivid illumination the darkness is now intense. I feel my way up the bank opposite and stand, gasping for breath. The trees are close and silent, surprised to see me. After the open field, the air is close and strange; as if I am on a film set. There is a movement, and I feel Sam brush through my legs and then bound off, barking again, heading through the wood. Slowly my eyes adjust to the night. Sam is suddenly quiet, dashing about, following a scent. I have a sudden, intense memory of Max taking me to this place in his head, the last evening we spent together at Farndon Road, and then waking here, that terrible morning after he had been taken, sitting with his father and Jonathan in the long summer grass. I walk forward now carefully, breathing quietly as if stalking something. It is very still. I want to shout Max's name, call him, but I hesitate, afraid of the silence that will follow, embarrassed, almost angry that I have allowed myself to be tricked. Then Sam barks softly, an odd sound of recognition. I feel the hairs rising on the back of my neck. I approach the far end of the wood. There are old signs of earthmovers, rutted marks in the clay, long grassed-over where the mound stood. All I can hear now is Sam growling playfully and water squelching in my shoes.

Ahead of me the trees thin out suddenly and the darkness is uneven, like ink pooled in water, and where the birches thin the sudden open spaces seem luminous. I stop. I can see someone standing, half turned possibly, with their back towards me. They are tall. Tears merge and blur the image. I walk forward very slowly now, afraid to wake myself, to disturb the illusion. The man is naked, he has shoulder-length hair string-like, corded, thrown to one side. He has heard my approach. There is a cautious, guarded look to the posture, the upright back, arms slightly bent at the elbows, the hands together. And then suddenly someone asks softly,

'Jamie?'